SHARON SHINN

D0038366

ARCHANGEL

THE AWARD-WINNING NOVEL

ACE

ALSO BY SHARON SHINN...

"A delightful world to escape into... Shinn has set out to create a sweet and beautiful story about love, magic, and honor and has proven that she can accomplish that task nobly, enjoyably, and well."—<u>Locus</u>

"Ms. Shinn takes a traditional romance and wraps it in a fantasy...rousing."
—<u>The Magazine of Fantasy and Science Fiction</u>

SHARON SHINN

"The most promising and original writer of fantasy to come along since Robin McKinley."
—Peter S. Beagle, author of *The Last Unicorn*

"The spellbinding Ms. Shinn writes with elegant imagination and a steely grace, bringing a remarkable freshness that will command a wide audience."
—*Romantic Times*

ARCHANGEL

And so it came to pass . . .
Through science, faith and force of will, the Harmonics carved out for themselves a society that they conceived of as perfect. Diverse peoples held together by respect for each other and the prospect of swift punishment if they disobeyed their laws. Fertile land that embraced a variety of climates and seasons. Angels to guard the mortals and mystics to guard the forbidden knowledge.
Jehovah to watch over them all . . .

Generations later, the armed starship *Jehovah* still looms over the planet of Samaria, programmed to unleash its arsenal if peace is not sustained. But an age of corruption has come to the land, threatening that peace and placing the Samarians in grave danger. Their only hope lies in the crowning of a new Archangel. The oracles have chosen for this honor the angel named Gabriel, and further decreed that he must first wed a mortal woman named Rachel.

It is his destiny and hers. And Gabriel is certain that she will greet the news of her betrothal with enthusiasm, and a devotion to duty equal to his own.

Rachel, however, has other ideas . . .

ARCHANGEL

SHARON SHINN

ACE BOOKS, NEW YORK

ARCHANGEL

An Ace Book / published by arrangement with
the author

PRINTING HISTORY
Ace trade edition / May 1996
Ace mass-market edition / April 1997

The Penguin Putnam Inc. World Wide Web site address is
http://www.penguinputnam.com

Check out the Ace Science Fiction/Fantasy newsletter,
and much more, at Club PPI!

ISBN: 0-441-00432-6

ACE®
Ace Books are published by The Berkley Publishing Group,
a division of Penguin Putnam Inc.,
375 Hudson Street, New York, New York 10014.
ACE and the "A" design are trademarks
belonging to Penguin Putnam Inc.

PRINTED IN THE UNITED STATES OF AMERICA

10 9 8 7 6 5

For my aunt, Mary Krewson

CAST OF CHARACTERS

In the Eyrie
Gabriel, leader of the host; an angel
Nathan, his brother; an angel
Hannah, a mortal woman; widow of the former leader
Judith, a young mortal woman
Obadiah, an angel
Matthew, an Edori

In Monteverde
Ariel, leader of the host; an angel
Magdalena, her sister; also an angel

In Windy Point
Raphael, leader of the host and Archangel of Samaria
Saul, his foremost follower; also an angel
Leah, Raphael's wife; the angelica

In Semorrah
Lord Jethro, a wealthy merchant
Daniel, his son
Lady Clara, Jethro's wife
Lady Mary, Daniel's bride
Anna, a bondwoman
Rachel, an Edori slave

Others
Elijah Harth, a wealthy Manadavvi landowner
Abel Vashir, another Manadavvi landowner
Malachi of Breven, a Jansai war leader
Peter, a former priest now residing in Velora

Naomi of the Chievens, an Edori woman
Luke, her husband

Josiah, oracle of Bethel
Ezekiel, oracle of Jordana
Jezebel, oracle of Gaza

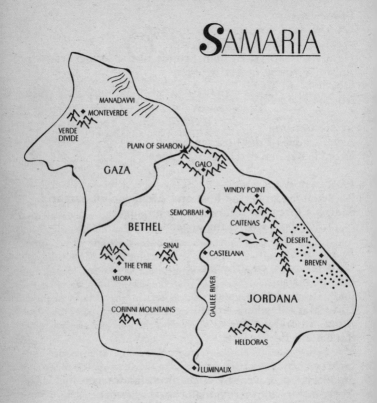

SAMARIA

MANADAVVI

MONTEVERDE

VERDE
DIVIDE

PLAIN OF SHARON

GAZA

GALO

WINDY POINT

SEMORRAH

CAITENAS

BETHEL

DESERT

SINAI

CASTELANA

THE EYRIE

BREVEN

VELORA

JORDANA

GALILEE RIVER

CORINNI MOUNTAINS

HELDORAS

LUMINAUX

CHAPTER ONE

The angel Gabriel went to the oracle on Mount Sinai, looking for a wife. He did not go gladly, even hopefully, as befitted a man eager to find his lifelong companion. In fact, he had put off this journey as long as he could, but his deadline was rapidly approaching. In six months, he would lead the annual Gloria to praise and gladden Jovah, and it was a task he would be unable to complete without his ordained partner at his side. Because he was next in line to be Archangel, and therefore Jovah had a special interest in him, Gabriel went to the Mount Sinai seer to learn who the god had chosen to be his bride.

Flying, Gabriel took less than three hours to cross the hundred and fifty miles from his home in the Eyrie to Josiah's rockbound retreat. It was easy flying, for the air was very thin in the valley between the two mountain ranges, with no treacherous currents such as one might encounter over the western Gaza mountains or the southern coast of Jordana. To a mortal, the frigid air this high above the ground would have been deadly, but angels carried heated blood in their veins, ideally equipping them for surviving the icy wind in the higher reaches of the stratosphere. Gabriel wore only a leather vest and leather pants, tucked into his boots, and he felt no cold.

When he arrived at Sinai, one of Josiah's acolytes led him to the oracle's room, moving soundlessly through the shadowy gray corridors of rock. They came at last to a small, well-lit chamber where the oracle could be seen leaning toward a glowing plate of glass and metal embedded in the slate-rock wall. The acolyte put a finger to his lips.

"Quietly," the boy said. "He is communing with the god."

Gabriel nodded, and gestured for the boy to return the way he had come. Clearly the acolyte would have preferred to stay, making sure Gabriel did not disturb Josiah at his prayers, but very few people would gainsay an angel, particularly this one. The boy left, and Gabriel leaned against the wall, waiting courteously. He was nothing if not respectful of the will of the god.

In a matter of moments, Josiah straightened, murmured an *amen*, and touched the face of the lighted screen. Instantly, the plate went blank. Gabriel stepped forward.

"Josiah," he said.

The oracle turned to him with a smile. He was a small, gray man, nearly lost in a voluminous blue robe. Unlike the angels, he suffered from the cold.

"Gabriel!" he exclaimed. "An unexpected pleasure."

The angel laughed, coming forward to take the seer's hand and bow over it. "Come, now," Gabriel said straightening. "You must have been expecting me anytime these past six months."

"These past three years, more like," Josiah retorted. "If by that you mean you have come at last to seek my advice about your bride."

"Jovah's advice," Gabriel corrected.

"You have not given yourself much time to woo and win," Josiah said.

Gabriel shrugged. The gesture caused his immense, immaculately white wings to flutter gracefully behind his shoulders. "These things are laid down by the law of Jovah," he said. "If I have no choice about it, then neither does she. I do not know that it will be a courtship in the traditional sense."

Josiah was watching him. "Nonetheless," he said, "she may need some time to accustom herself to the idea. She has not had fifteen years, as you have, to dream about becoming the angelica."

Gabriel smiled. He was a black-haired, blue-eyed man, with fair skin darkened to a perpetual tan from constant exposure to sun and wind. He was always striking, but never quite approachable until he smiled. "I thought all girls dreamt of becoming the angelica," he said.

Josiah snorted. "Those who have not met you, perhaps."

Gabriel looked faintly amused. "Well, at any rate, the girl handpicked by Jovah must be suited to me in all things, as I understand the theology," he said. "So she will be eager to be my bride."

Josiah regarded him, his small head turned a bit to one side. "She will complement you," he amended. "She will know things you do not, have skills you do not. If you were an angry man, she would make you calm. If you were a timid man, she would make you strong. As you are an arrogant man, I must assume she will make you humble."

"I am not arrogant," Gabriel said mildly. "Confident, perhaps."

Josiah smiled. "Well, then. We will let the god determine. Come sit with me while I ask him his will."

They pulled up two chairs before the screen where Josiah had been working when the angel arrived. Gabriel settled himself carefully, spreading his wings wide so that they unfolded lavishly across the cold stone floor. Even among angels, his wings were remarkable—entirely white, exceptionally broad in span, and taller than he was by more than a head.

Not waiting for Gabriel to grow still, Josiah leaned forward and touched the glass plate in the wall. Instantly it came alive with a soft bluish light. Strange hieroglyphics danced across the screen, changing as Josiah pressed the knobs and buttons on a small shelf lying before the interface. Gabriel watched, fascinated. As often as he had seen Josiah communing with Jovah, he never failed to be impressed. A man or a woman must be trained since birth to understand the rituals of the god; mere mortals, even angels, could not understand the words of the holy language.

At length, Josiah completed his dialogue with Jovah, murmured an *amen*, and closed down the window between humanity and divinity.

"Well?" Gabriel demanded.

"She was born in a small village in Jordana, not far from Windy Point," Josiah said. "Her parents are farmers, her family are farmers. She is twenty-five years old."

Gabriel stared at him in disbelief.

"It is unlikely," Josiah said, maintaining a serious expression, "that she has ever entertained thoughts of becoming angelica to the Archangel Gabriel."

Gabriel found his voice. "This is ridiculous," he said. "A

farmer's daughter? From the wilds of Jordana? What do we know of these people? Are they educated? Are they civilized? Can they sing, by the love of Jovah? For in six months, this girl will need to stand beside me on the Plain of Sharon and lead the Gloria. Can she do so? Can she sing a *note*? Can she be taught? Six months, Josiah—!"

"Perhaps you should not have waited so long to seek her out," Josiah responded.

Gabriel was on his feet. "No doubt! But I did not expect Jovah to have such a sense of humor! An untutored hill-farmer! I expected a girl from the gentry of the Manadavvi, or even a woman from one of the river cities—someone trained to take on the duties of a household such as mine—"

"You really have no one but yourself to blame," Josiah said unsympathetically. "As it is, you still have six months. A lot can be accomplished in that time frame. Search her out immediately."

"I will," Gabriel agreed somewhat grimly. "What is her name? Or did Jovah seek to make my task harder by withholding that information?"

"No, it was part of the registry," Josiah said. "She is called Rachel, daughter of Seth and Elizabeth. It is a small village in the shadow of the Caitana Mountains. There should not be many with that name and those parents."

Gabriel was still angry—fruitlessly so, because it was of no use to rail against the god, and he knew it. "And if she has changed her name? Or refuses to believe me?"

Josiah nodded at Gabriel, indicating the small amber stud embedded in the flesh of the angel's right arm. "There should be no mistake," he said quietly. "The Kiss will react. You will feel heat, and its light will flare—yours and hers. There is no denying the Kiss."

Automatically, Gabriel put his hand over the acorn-sized crystal in his arm. Like almost every child born on Samaria, he had been dedicated to the god when he was only a few days old—in fact, Josiah had been the one to perform the ceremony, although there were priests who did no work but this the whole year round. The Kiss of the God was embedded in Gabriel's flesh, grafted to the bone, to remain there until he died, and to be buried with him. It was through the Kiss that Jovah acknowledged the existence of all his children, tracked them through their lives, knew if they were ill or unhappy or dying. At times, when he had been most exhilarated or most afraid, Gabriel had felt the Kiss flicker against his skin, a slight sensation of warmth, a brief flash of light in the brandy-colored depths of the stone.

But. "I thought that was a myth," he said slowly.

"What? That the Kiss shoots sparks of light when true lovers meet for the first time? No myth. Have you never seen it occur?"

Gabriel shrugged impatiently. "Among some couples who have been married a long time and who feel great mutual affection—yes, I suppose I have seen a glimmer now and then," he said. "But—this business of recognizing your true lover the first time you meet—"

"Well, there should be some reaction," Josiah said. "As you are only seeking to confirm an identity—"

"And as I am not looking for true love—"

"Perhaps the reaction will be slight. Go to this village. She should not be hard to find."

Gabriel was still frowning. "I admit, it seems odd to me that she comes from a place so near to Raphael," he said. "For Leah came from Jordana as well."

"Jovah does not care about the angelica's origin," Josiah said. "He cares about her heart."

Gabriel made a slight gesture of disagreement, but continued to brood. Well, it was true. The Archangel Raphael, who ruled the host of angels quartered in the bleak mountain retreat of Windy Point, had twenty years ago chosen a bride from among his own people. Her name was Leah, and she was a pale, silent woman of whom very little had been seen outside of the annual Glorias held on the Plain of Sharon. If Jovah did indeed look to meld opposites when he selected consorts for his Archangels, he had come up with a definite contrast here. Raphael was suave, smooth-spoken and self-assured. Leah was tongue-tied, shy and docile. Or so she seemed. Gabriel had not troubled himself to converse more than politely with her for the past twenty years.

The fact was, he did not care much for either Raphael or his angelica, though he had done his best to work with the older man during Raphael's reign as Archangel. Harmony was, after all, the central tenet of their religion, and it was not for the Archangel-designate to cause dissension among the angels. But he had been shocked at some of the abuses that occurred during Raphael's tenure—the growth of power among the city merchants, the grad-

ual impoverishment of the lowland farmers, the increasing violence directed against the nomadic Edori tribes. These were circumstances that were within the Archangel's power to control,
and Raphael had not controlled them. To Gabriel, it seemed as
though the harmony of Samaria was out of tune—but Jovah had
still accepted their singing at the Glorias, and so to Jovah, perhaps, all still appeared well.

His dark meditation was interrupted by a woman's laughing
voice. "Let me guess," said the newcomer. "He is reviewing all
Raphael's misdeeds and vowing to do better during his term as
Archangel."

Smiling, Gabriel turned to meet the speaker. "Ariel," he said.
"Don't you have your own oracle to consult up near Monteverde?"

"I do," she retorted, crossing the stone floor to greet him.
She was a tall, slender woman with lush brown hair, just now
somewhat ruffled by the flight of her passage. Her wings—flecked
with patterns of beige and gold—were folded tightly to her back,
but the tips still trailed behind her on the floor. She led the host
of Monteverde and was generally popular with the angels from
all three realms. "I did not come for advice but for pleasure. You,
on the other hand, are looking so unpleasant that you must have
come for advice."

"Which has not agreed with me," he said.

"Advice seldom agrees with you," Josiah observed. "Ariel,
Gabriel, may I order refreshments for either of you?"

"Certainly," Ariel replied. "Whatever you have on hand."

"I'm not staying," Gabriel said.

"I hope you're not running away just because I've arrived,"
Ariel commented.

He smiled briefly. "You would hardly be enough to rout me.
No, I've got to attend to business—following Josiah's advice."

She gave a crow of laughter. "At last! You've come to seek
the name of your angelica! No wonder you look so cross. Has he
picked out someone you cannot bear?"

"Someone I've never met," Gabriel said. "I imagine no one's
met her. She lives secluded in Jordana, not far from Windy Point.
A farmer's daughter."

"A farmer's daughter! But how quaint!" Ariel exclaimed,
hugely delighted. "We'll have to hope she is not overwhelmed by
all the pomp and pageantry at the Eyrie—"

"Which is nothing to compare with the pomp and pageantry at Windy Point," Gabriel said dryly.

"If she's a hill-farmer's daughter, it's unlikely she's been there," Ariel pointed out.

"In any case, I do not have much time to waste. I'm off to find her, assuming she is where she is supposed to be."

"She should be easy enough to locate. Farmers generally do not stir ten miles from the place of their birth," Josiah said as he left to fetch refreshments. "Now, if she had been an Edori—"

"An Edori!" Ariel repeated. "Surely Jovah would not have chosen an Edori for the angelica. Why, most of them have not even been dedicated to the god! He has no idea that they exist."

"He knows they exist," Gabriel said evenly. "Jovah brought them to Samaria when he brought the angels and the mortals. Just because they do not all choose to receive the Kiss of the God does not make them any less his children."

"Oh, don't start again," she said warmly. "About the enslavement of the Edori—I can't bear it."

"Well, it is wrong, whatever Raphael thinks. Or you think."

"If Jovah objected, would he not have spoken by now?" Ariel demanded. "Gabriel, Jovah does not care about the Edori! At last year's Gloria, there were no Edori singers—none! not one!—and there was no thunderbolt from the god in disapproval."

"There was one Edori singer," Gabriel said. "In my pavilion. I did not wish to risk the god's wrath in such a stupid manner."

Ariel shrugged impatiently. "Well, then, your virtue has again saved us all. But don't you think—"

"I am not trying to parade my *virtue* before the whole of Samaria. I know you think I'm hopelessly self-righteous, but in the matter of the Edori—"

"My children, my angels," Josiah interrupted, reentering the room with a tray of refreshments in his hands. "If there is not harmony among angels, can there be harmony among men?"

"When angels sow discord among men, no, I doubt it," Gabriel said.

Ariel turned toward Josiah. "He's going on about the Edori again."

"His passion does him credit. We *are* all the children of Jovah," Josiah said gently. "But you should not discuss it if it makes you both so angry. Come, Ariel, sit with me and tell me of happy things."

Gabriel nodded to them both and turned to go, but Ariel, who had stepped away with Josiah, suddenly ran back to Gabriel before he could quit the chamber.

"Don't leave angry," she said, catching his arm. "I can't bear the dissonance you create when you're angry."

He smiled briefly and touched her hand where it lay on his arm. "All right. I'm not angry. It was good to see you, Ariel—it always is."

"Will I see you next month?" she wanted to know. "At the wedding in Semorrah?"

He raised his brows. "How could I miss it?" he replied sardonically. "Lord Jethro has practically made it a command appearance."

She smiled. "Will you be there and in a good temper?" she teased.

"I will be there. I cannot make promises about my mood," he said. "I bring Nathan with me."

"And your bride?"

"If I have found her by then. If she is fit to be seen in company."

Ariel choked back a laugh. "Gabriel, you're horrible."

He smiled. "Don't start another quarrel with me," he warned.

"I wouldn't think of it. Fast flight to you, and sweet dreaming."

Gabriel nodded again to the oracle. "Josiah," he said, and left the room.

It was with some circumspection that Gabriel entered the realm of Jordana. It was not that Raphael would have—could have—any objection to his presence there, but still. Gabriel was not eager to explain to the Archangel that he had come here seeking his own bride, who would stand with him when Gabriel took over the position Raphael had held for twenty years.

Nor did he feel like admitting that his angelica was a hill-farmer's daughter who had probably never heard his name.

Josiah had used a map of Jordana to show Gabriel the village where the girl had been born—*Rachel*, Gabriel reminded himself, *Rachel, daughter of Seth and Elizabeth*. It was half a day's flight from Windy Point, outside the protective bulk of the mountains, but some distance from the rich farmlands that characterized southern Jordana. They had probably eked out a spare existence for centuries, Rachel's family and their ancestors, knowing little more than the turn of the seasons, the capriciousness of the climate and the stinginess of their rocky soil. None of this knowledge would translate well to the girl's role as angelica.

Gabriel flew high for most of the journey, dropping to low reconnaissance altitude only as he arrived in the vicinity of the village. From the air, there had been little to see—no hearth smoke, no cultivated patches of green against the undomesticated brown and gold of the prairie grasses and weeds. Lower to the ground, he was surprised to find nothing yet—no outlying huts, no hard-won orchards, no sounds or smells or sights that spoke of human habitation. He flew in ever-widening circles, wondering if he could have missed a crucial landmark, or if Josiah had misread the information Jovah had supplied. There appeared to be no village here at all.

He had been quartering the same area for a good hour, looking for clues, when his attention was caught by a random scattering of boulders half a mile from a streambed. Not so random, if looked at just right—if a few of the boulders were rolled back into place, and a few more dug up from the loamy earth, they would form a series of rectangular shapes that once could have been small houses standing side by side.

Gabriel canted his wings and came down, landing with practiced ease on the balls of his feet. There was scarcely a hitch between the last wingbeat and the first footfall as he strode forward to inspect the boulders. Yes, definitely the remains of walls and foundations, three or four homes that had once housed near neighbors. But that had been some time ago, judging by the extent to which the wild grasses had reclaimed this section of land and the land for miles around it. Ten years, maybe more, since anyone had lived here.

Frowning heavily, Gabriel looked around him. What he had taken for underbrush and the large nests of prairie wolves now assumed a different aspect—of huts knocked down and fences pulled apart. He counted another half a dozen piles that might have once been houses, and it was safe to assume that he had overlooked a couple of solitary habitations a few miles away in each direction.

"But farmers don't abandon their homes," he muttered, kicking at a piece of moldering wood that might have formed the crosspiece of a roof. "They live in one place forever, and their children live there, and their children's children—"

Only plague, in his experience, could cause a whole village to uproot and relocate. Gabriel searched in vain for the ward signs against illness, the special flags hoisted to warn away travelers and call down the angels who would intercede with Jovah on behalf of the sufferers. He found nothing like that. Indeed, what he did find made him frown more blackly and puzzle more deeply: the charred remains of several buildings, scatterings of clothing and jewelry and other personal belongings—and here, on the very edge of the village, a collection of skeletons. The bones fanned out from the village proper, all facing away from the tumbled homes, as if the citizens had fled madly from a central menace and tried to escape in as many directions as possible. It did not look, from this morbid array, as if anyone had succeeded.

Gabriel walked to a high boulder some distance from the open graveyard and sat, thinking very hard. To all appearances, the village had been attacked and systematically destroyed, the inhabitants all murdered, or some—perhaps—carried off. It was hard to credit. True, Raphael had turned a blind eye to the ravaging of the Edori, but until this time, Gabriel had never heard that the Archangel had countenanced any violence against the simple hillfolk, who were notoriously devout. It was in Jordana that most of the outrages against the Edori had occurred—carried out, for the most part, by the warlike, wandering Jansai merchants—but these were not Edori. These were farmers, Jovah's true children, dedicated to the god and under the direct protection of Raphael. Who had attacked them, and how had it occurred without Raphael's knowledge? Why had Jovah not exacted a retribution?

And where was Rachel, daughter of Seth and Elizabeth? Had she died in the assault, Jovah would surely have known of it; he would not now have proposed her name to Gabriel as his bride. So she must be alive—somewhere, somehow—in Jordana, Semorrah, Bethel or Gaza, or even the fabled Edori homeland of Ysral.

Gabriel had six months to find her. And he did not know where to begin looking.

CHAPTER TWO

The instant she realized she was awake, Rachel shut her eyes tightly and made her mind a total blank. It was a trick she had learned five years ago, and these brief moments in the morning, before true consciousness, before *remembering*, had for that period of time been the best in her life. She did not let herself know who she was, where she was, what her situation might be; she just existed.

Today, that sheer existence lasted less than a minute. "Stupid girl!" she heard a moment before Anna swatted her across the back with a broom handle, and she leapt from bed, half-fearful and half-indignant. The chain rattled between her hands as her shackles resettled over her wrists; she shook her hair back from her face.

"What?" she said, with the sullen defiance they had been unable to beat or threaten out of her. "I'm awake."

Anna brandished the broom, but more to express her irritation than to offer harm. Though she was a bondwoman rather than a slave, and was considered invaluable by the head cook and the chatelaine, Anna's situation was little better than Rachel's, and there was a certain complicity between them.

"Well, and you should have been awake an hour ago. Guests arriving all day and the betrothal party tonight, and so much to do I don't know what to start first. And you sleeping like a baby, like a lord's daughter—"

"Oh, yes, I feel very much like a lord's daughter," Rachel

responded with heavy sarcasm. "Just tell me. What do you want me to do first?"

The list, it appeared, was endless, from cleaning out the guest bedrooms to helping in the kitchen to running errands across the length and breadth of Semorrah. This last Rachel did not mind so much; as always, she made the most of her brief, partial freedom. She dawdled a bit at the market, and stopped to rest on a park bench, where no one would see her and cuff her across the cheek for her slothfulness. It was a clear, warm day, and she turned her face to the sun, closing her eyes again, letting herself forget again who she was, where she was. . . .

But then she was stupid, as she was always stupid: After her errands were run, she went home by way of the River Walk. Semorrah was a huge, impossibly beautiful city constructed of milk-white stone—all its spires, domes, archways, towers and sanctuaries built of the same pale rock. Even more impossibly, it was built on a small island in the middle of the River Galilee, which divided Jordana from Bethel. There were only two approaches to the alabaster city—across the fabulous webbed bridge from Jordana, a delicate affair of ropes and steel that looked no more substantial than string; or by boat, through the water gates that faced the Bethel side of the river.

The city was so famous, and so wealthy, that it had long ago overrun the available surfaces of the rocky island that served as its base. Yet buildings continued to go up, one precariously balanced atop another; more and more people came to do business, or to visit, or to stay, so that the streets and bazaars and alleyways teemed with life. The whole world came to Semorrah. You could not walk through the market without seeing a lord's daughter reclining in her chair, carried by six slaves wearing her father's livery. You could not walk down the meanest street without encountering a Jansai merchant, a Monteverde angel, a Luminaux craftsman.

You could not stroll down the River Walk, your eyes turned longingly toward Jordana, without seeing another Jansai trading party coming in across the spidery bridge, driving their fresh catch of Edori slaves before them.

Which was why it was stupid to follow the River Walk home.

She could not help herself; she stood there and watched as the slaves were herded across the river. They looked dazed and exhausted, sore from the hard journey, hungry, afraid. Some of the wilder ones still continued to glance about them, judging distances, possible weapons, escape paths. The rest just plodded forward, lost already, hopeless. From a distance, it was hard to tell one from the other, for the Edori all bore a remarkable clan resemblance—high flat cheekbones, dark straight hair, bronze skin, brown eyes. Nonetheless, Rachel made herself look at each one carefully, straining her eyes, hoping she did not recognize in each sorry new arrival a familiar body, a beloved face. Once or twice she saw, or thought she saw, someone she remembered from a campfire at one of the Gatherings—a leader of some other tribe, a girl she had met in passing at a streambed, fetching water. But she never saw those of her own tribe, her adopted family, her friends—or Simon.

Even if they were alive, it was unlikely she would ever see them again. The whole camp had been dispersed or destroyed in the Jansai raid five years ago; everyone who had not been taken had died, she was sure of it. But Simon had not been among the slaves that had been walked to Semorrah five years ago, nor her cousins nor her uncle. That did not stop her from wondering. Every time she walked through the Semorrah streets, she watched the faces of the slaves. Every time she was sent with messages to another lord's household, and she found herself however briefly alone with another Edori, she asked after those she had lost. She never yet had found traces of them. And if they were not in Semorrah, they were probably dead.

But she still watched the incoming caravans, in case, in case.

Anna had lost no time in telling her how lucky she was. "The lady Clara, now, she's truly a devout woman," the bondservant had told Rachel on her very first night in Lord Jethro's household. "She doesn't hold for carryings-on. A man, even a guest, even her own son, found bothering the slave women—well! It just doesn't happen in Lord Jethro's house. You might be beaten, you might be starved—if you misbehave, that is—you might be sold, but while you're under this roof, you won't be molested. And that's a sight more than can be said about most roofs in Semorrah. You should fall on your knees and thank Jovah."

But that Rachel had been unable to do. She was more likely, as was her wont on most nights, to rail against Jovah, to bitterly question his wisdom and his kindness—or to importune him, as she did now, to unleash his powerful destructive wrath.

"O Yovah, if it be thy will," she prayed, her voice a whisper but fierce for all that, "call down thy curses on this thrice-damned city. Strike it with fire! With thunderbolts! Cover it with storm, and flood it with the raging river! Let everyone within its borders die, and let every stone be washed away to sea. And let me stand on the riverbank and watch." She took a deep breath, scowling at the now-empty bridge. "Amen," she added, very softly, and turned back toward Lord Jethro's house.

Late in the afternoon, Anna sent her to Lady Mary's room. "For her own woman's come down with some fever, and she can't seem to dress herself. No, nor style her own hair—"

Rachel stared at the bondwoman. "Well, *I* don't know how to style a lady's hair," she said.

"Well, you can do up the back of her dress and make a curl with the hot tongs, can't you?"

"I can do the buttons, I suppose, but I've never—curling tongs!"

Anna pushed her out of the kitchen, where they had both been helping the cook, and in the direction of the great stairs that led to the living quarters of the gentry. "Do what you can. Lady Clara says the little one's near hysterics."

Still protesting, Rachel allowed herself to be pushed from the room and wearily began climbing the three flights to the guest rooms. The lady Mary was to wed Lord Jethro's son, Daniel, on the following morning in a ceremony that bid fair to be the most lavish Semorrah would see this season. Already the palatial house was full to overflowing with visitors from all three realms—wealthy Jansai merchants from eastern Jordana, the Manadavvi landowners of Gaza, the craftmasters of Luminaux and angels from all three holds. Indeed, someone had said the Archangel had arrived the night before, although Rachel had not laid eyes on him. Not that it was a sight she pined for.

In the midst of all this confusion, the lady Mary looked like a lost soul. Her father had accompanied her when they arrived three days ago, and then promptly disappeared with his host to discuss politics, economics and fishing vessels. The young bride had no mother or sisters or friends, and the lord Daniel had not appeared interested in entertaining her, as the match was a financial one, not romantic. Rachel had actually found it in her heart to be sorry for the girl—small, mousy, hopeful and frail—and she was not a woman who generally wasted pity on any of the gentry.

Her impatient knock on Mary's door was answered by a quick "Come in!" uttered in a high, childlike voice. Rachel entered. The lady Mary indeed looked as if she might start crying at any moment. She was standing in her petticoats and chemise, shivering before a small fire, attempting with her hands crooked behind her back to wind her long, thin hair into some kind of knot. Nonetheless, she was trying desperately to hold onto her dignity.

"Can I help you?" the lady asked in a polite voice.

Rachel almost smiled. "I'm Rachel," she said, coming in and shutting the door. "I was sent to help *you*."

The lady dropped her hands. Her face was suddenly eager. "Oh, could you?" she exclaimed. "My poor girl is so sick, and she's the only one who ever does my hair, and helps me with my clothes, and she knows just how all the layers go, and I just don't think I can manage it myself—"

"I don't know about the layers," Rachel said, stepping forward. "And I've never done much with hair. But I'll do what I can."

"Thank you so much. Really, I just—thank you."

Rachel had dropped to her knees before the fire. "Let me stir this up a little. You look half frozen."

"A little chilly, maybe," the girl murmured. "I didn't know how to make it burn again—my girl usually does that."

Does this "girl" have a name? Rachel wanted to ask, but she refrained. Mary had identified Rachel's station with one quick glance, taking in the bare feet, the plain, ill-fitting gown, the wide chain hanging between the heavy shackles. She seemed so ingenuous that Rachel half-expected her to exclaim, "Oh, you're a slave!" but no; Mary had seen slaves before. She was not disconcerted by their presence.

In a matter of moments, Rachel had the fire burning merrily, bath water warming, and curling tongs heating in the heart of the blaze. The layers of undergarments were a simple enough matter to sort out if one applied a little common sense. Even the cosmetics arrayed on the washstand, which Mary dumbly pointed to, did not seem beyond Rachel's expertise. Indeed, she handled the rouge pot and the kohl stick with a certain bitter nostalgia.

"I think I remember how to use these," she said, speaking gently because she found herself unable to hate this helpless child. "Close your eyes and turn your face up. We'll do a little at a time and see how you like it."

The makeup was just fine; the hair was another matter entirely. Neither Mary nor Rachel could operate the curling tongs, and the wispy brown hair hung straight and girlish down the lady's back.

"There was a way the Edori women used to braid their hair, for festival nights," Rachel said. "With lace and ribbon twined in the braids, and all the braids gathered together in a knot. Do you think you would like that?"

"Oh, yes, please," Mary said gratefully. "It can't look any worse than it does now."

So Rachel picked through Mary's box of accessories and pulled out a strand of pearls, a long gold chain and a handful of ribbons, and began patiently interweaving them in the thin brown hair. "Now, if people compliment you on the style, don't say you got it from an Edori slave girl," she cautioned. "It will not give you prestige."

The lady Mary giggled. She was seated before an oval mirror, and Rachel stood behind her, working. "But you're not an Edori," Mary said.

Rachel briefly glanced at herself in the mirror. Her face was a long, pale oval; her hair, carelessly tied back with a length of boot lace, was waist-length, oak-gold and riotously curly. Not that she showed to advantage just now; neither face nor hair was particularly clean. "You don't think so?"

"Well, you don't look like one. And you've been dedicated." She nodded toward the mirror, in the direction of the Kiss high in Rachel's right arm. "The Edori don't dedicate their children."

"Some of them do. Not very many these days."

"Then you are an Edori?"

Rachel studied the movement of her hands. "I was adopted by an Edori tribe when I was seven," she said. "When my parents died."

"And how long have you been with Lord Jethro?" the girl asked.

Tactfully phrased, thought Rachel. "Five years."

"What was it like to be an Edori?" was the next question,

and Rachel was amazed to hear a certain envy in the sweet voice. "Was it wonderful?"

"It was—at that time I didn't remember much of my life before—so it was just my life," Rachel said, her voice low. "When I look back now, I think—yes, it was wonderful. We traveled every week. I have seen every part of Samaria from the seashores of eastern Jordana to the blue streets of Luminaux to the green valleys north of Monteverde. We camped when we were tired, ate when we were hungry, sang songs of thanksgiving when we were happy and dirges when someone died. There were Gatherings once a year, with the other tribes, and then the festivals would go on for days and days—food and song and storytelling and gossip. Deeds of valor would be recounted and births would be recorded, and those who had been lost would be mourned. It was—how can I describe it? The life was so much simpler than this one, so much better. Sometimes I think I imagined it or dreamt it. It doesn't matter. It's gone now."

"I've only been two places in my life," Mary offered. "Here, and home."

"Where's home?"

"Castelana," she said, naming one of the smaller cities a few miles down the Galilee River. Not so small that it did not boast a wealthy burgher population, and Mary's father was one of the wealthiest.

"And will you be glad to go back?"

There was a moment's silence. "I won't be going back," Mary said softly. "After the wedding, I mean. I'll be married, of course."

Of course. Stupid question. "Are you and Lord Daniel going to live with Lord Jethro, then?"

"For a while. For a year, Daniel says. His father is building a house for us near the River Walk. It's very expensive."

Rachel smiled. "I expect so."

"My mother says I will like having a house of my own, but I—well, the servants frighten me, some of them, and I don't know about things like candles and pigs."

"Candles and pigs?"

"You know. How many candles to order so you have enough in the house, and the right kind to get, because I heard Lady Clara telling her chatelaine that she'd gotten the wrong kind, and I didn't even know there were *kinds*."

"And pigs?"

"For the banquets," Mary explained. "Daniel says we will entertain, the way his father does. How many pigs do you need to feed a hundred people? Do you know? And it's not just pigs—there are the soups and the breads and the wines and the sweetmeats—"

"Maybe Lady Clara will teach you these things while you live here."

Mary sighed. "I hope so. I don't think she likes me very much, though."

"They say she is kind."

Mary was staring down at her hands. "I wanted to ask her—but then I didn't know how to ask her, so I—but I expect I'll find out after all."

Rachel decided she did not want to pursue that, so she made no comment. After a moment, Mary raised her eyes to meet Rachel's in the glass.

"Some people think it is very nice to be married," she said.

"So it is," the slave replied.

"Have you ever been?"

Rachel felt her heart contract. *Simon, Simon, Simon.* "The Edori do not marry the way the allali do—the cityfolk do," she amended hastily, for "allali" was not a complimentary term. "But I loved a man once. We shared a tent and a bed for more than a year. I believed I would share the rest of my life with him. But things change."

Mary turned suddenly on her chair, whipping her hair away from Rachel's grasp. "Then maybe you can tell me," she said eagerly.

"Tell you what?"

"What it means to—to love a man."

Great Yovah, guard my soul. Rachel stared down into the hopeful, pleading eyes and wondered how it was possible that her life had brought her to this point, explaining sexual mysteries to a frightened gentrywoman, and not hating her for her innocence. "Yes," she said slowly. "I suppose I can."

Mary at last was coiffed and dressed, and looked, Rachel thought somewhat smugly, quite pretty. The lady had begged the slave to return the next morning, to help her dress for her wedding day.

"Ask for me," Rachel said. "I cannot go where I choose, but if Lady Clara knows you were pleased with my services, I'm sure she'll let me come to you again."

"Oh, thank you so much! Thank you, thank you."

Returning to the lower quarters—and receiving a fearsome scolding from the chatelaine for dilatoriness—Rachel was instantly swept into the kitchen to help with final preparations for the meal. This was a task that kept nearly twenty people busy for the next three hours, cooking, arranging trays and serving. Rachel, of course, was not a server; that role was reserved for the highly paid servants who dressed and behaved with a hauteur sometimes exceeding that of their masters. Yet she did get a chance, with Anna's connivance, to glimpse the great dining hall where the titled and glittering guests were gathered.

They had been sent from the kitchen toward the ballroom, to ensure that the fires were laid there, the refreshments ready, nothing out of order. Anna led them a roundabout back way, to the corridor that ran behind the balcony that overlooked the hall. They crouched down to peer through chinks in the plaster.

"See?" Anna hissed, as if someone could hear them and look up. "Beside Lady Mary. That's the Archangel."

Raphael was an astonishingly handsome man, with strong, regular features, longish golden hair, broad shoulders and a well-developed body. Behind him, hooked over a chair specially built to accommodate them, his gold-tinged wings rose to the height of a man, then gracefully trailed to the floor. He was smiling, and everyone seated near him seemed to gaze at him with rapture and adoration.

"You've never seen him before, have you?" Anna asked. "He comes to Lord Jethro's, oh, every few months, but you're usually in the kitchens."

"I've seen him," Rachel said. "Who are the others?"

"There's the angel Ariel, across from Lord Daniel. She leads the host in Monteverde. That's her sister Magdalena, near her. Next to the lady Clara is the angel Nathan, brother to Gabriel, who leads the host at the Eyrie and who will be named Archangel at the Gloria this spring. Then, at the second table, where Lady Clara's brother is sitting, is the angel Saul, who always travels with the Archangel—"

Anna continued, naming lesser angels and politicians, but Rachel lost the thread. Her eyes had come to rest on the angel

Gabriel, and there her attention had fixed. He was dressed in formal black and silver, which gave an additional brilliance to the pure colors of his hair, his eyes and his wings. Even from this distance, she could catch the sapphire flash of bracelets around each of his wrists. Unlike Raphael, he was making no effort to entertain the people sitting around him, nor were his tablemates eyeing him with a high degree of enthusiasm.

"He looks ill-tempered," Rachel remarked.

Anna had far outdistanced her. "Who? Michael Cintra? Not that I ever heard."

"No," Rachel said absently. "The angel Gabriel."

"Him. He doesn't care much for Lord Jethro, or any of the noble lords, or Semorrah. Or so I hear. None of the merchants are happy that he'll be Archangel in a few months. Raphael is the businessman's angel. That's what I overheard Lord Jethro say to Lady Mary's father. They don't want to see Gabriel take his place."

"Can't they stop him?"

Anna looked scandalized. "Stop him? From becoming *Archangel*? He was chosen by Jovah!"

"I was just asking."

Anna had risen from her crouch on the floor. "Hurry, now," she said uneasily. "The dessert trays have been brought in. We don't have any time to waste."

They found the ballroom perfectly in order, but that did not end their duties for the night. After the guests left the dining hall that room had to be cleared and scrubbed, all the dishes and cauldrons and silver washed. That task was barely finished when the guest bedrooms had to be prepared for the night, and there was still the ballroom to be cleaned up when the dancing ended. But that, the chatelaine had said, could wait till morning. Rachel tumbled into bed a few hours past midnight and slept the instant her head touched the pallet.

Lady Clara had requested, through the chatelaine, through Anna, that Rachel continue to wait on the lady Mary, but there were other chores to be attended to before Rachel could turn her attention to the bride. It fell to her to build the fires in five of the guest chambers before the visitors awoke, so as dawn was giving way to true morning, she was trudging through the guest corridor with coal scuttle and tinder in hand.

Angels were light sleepers, Anna had warned, and many were early risers. She must be triply careful when she entered their rooms. So she had tiptoed into the chambers allotted Ariel, Magdalena and Nathan, but none of them had stirred. They too had gone to bed long past midnight.

Saul had appeared to be sleeping, but when she knelt before the fire, he addressed her softly from his bed. "So, Lord Jethro does provide entertainment," he said, in a slurred, sleepy voice that sounded unexpectedly sinister. "Come closer so I can get a good look at you."

She came to her feet, but stayed where she was. "Lord?" she said coldly, not sure how to address an angel, but certain that Saul did not deserve that title.

He sat up against his pillows and candidly surveyed her. He was, she saw in an instant, completely naked except for gold and ruby bracelets on either wrist. Like the Archangel, he was golden-toned, hair and skin, and his body was thickly muscled. "Most of the city merchants know that a man has needs, and they see to those needs," the angel drawled. "Lord Jethro, now, he never quite saw it that way, but if he's started sending beautiful slave girls to my room . . ."

Rachel backed toward the door. "I'm just here to build the fire," she said.

Saul swung his feet to the floor. "You can keep me warm," he said.

"I don't want to," she replied.

She had placed her hand against the door, when he suddenly jumped from the bed and crossed the room with impossible speed. But she was quick, too: She swung the iron poker between them, and he yelped as its hot point dug into his breastbone.

"Stay away from me," she said fiercely.

He laughed. "You aren't even afraid of me," he said incredulously. He reached out a hand to push the poker aside. "I just know you'd be a lot of fun—"

"Not for you," she said. She shoved the weapon again, hard, into his chest, dropped it, and whirled out the door. She was halfway down the hall before she realized he was not going to follow. She stopped, leaned against a wall to catch her breath. He was right: She hadn't been afraid of him. She'd been furious. The thought made her smile wryly. She had always been too stupid to know when she should be afraid.

And she did not have the luxury now to brood over her brushes with disaster. She willed her heart to slow its pace, shifted her grip on the coal scuttle and continued down the hall to the last room she was assigned.

The angel Gabriel, thanks be to gracious Yovah, was sleeping, as she saw with one quick glance. He slept facedown, covered from head to ankles by the snowy quilt of his folded wings. Rachel managed a grin, thinking that the angel would probably welcome a fire. Lord Jethro kept a cold house.

She built it quickly, with the expertise born of much practice, and warmed her hands for a moment before the blaze. Kneeling on the hearth, she could not resist one more quick look at the angel sleeping so silently on the bed, so different in coloring from the wide-awake angel she had just left. This one was taller than Simon, she thought; his hair, what little she could see of it, was even blacker than Simon's, though his skin was paler. Even from one story up last night, she had been able to see the blueness of his eyes.

A sudden pain seared her right arm, and she clapped her other hand over the burn, sure she had been stung by a spark spit from the fire. But her fingers touched only a glass coolness, and she quickly looked down to find the source of her distress. Through the fingers of her left hand she saw opal colors writhing in the Kiss of the God. She stared for a moment, too astonished to move, and wholly mystified by what the phenomenon might mean.

"Everybody loved my hair," was Mary's first greeting to Rachel. "Even Daniel noticed. Lady Clara told me I looked charming. So, thank you very much!"

"It will be easier today," Rachel said, smiling.

"But you'll help me anyway, won't you? You'll stay with me until it's time to go down?"

"If you like."

"Oh, yes. Please do."

So Rachel helped the lord's daughter bathe herself and wash her hair, and she combed out the thin tresses as Mary dried them before the fire. The fashion among the rich families was for the brides to appear as simply arrayed as possible, their hair undone down their backs and their bridal gowns severe and unadorned. Rachel had always thought this made the young girls look like children running away from home—but then, as she had told Mary, the Edori did not have bridal customs. Perhaps her opinion was worthless.

The very affluent had found ways to show off their wealth even under these restrictions. Mary's dress was made of the finest blue silk, covered with tiny flowers embroidered in matching thread. It had taken nearly a year to make. She had been allowed a single clip to hold her hair back from her face, and this was a silver and sapphire barrette made by the master craftsmen of Luminaux. She wore white gloves on her small hands, each glove encrusted with pearls from fingertip to palm, making it clear that this hand was made to do no labor even as strenuous as lifting a goblet to her mouth.

While she dressed the girl and made up her face, Rachel told her stories of Edori Gatherings to distract Mary from her growing nervousness. "At day's end, the clans would gather before the fire, and singers from every tribe would come forward to praise Yovah."

"Were there angels at these Gatherings, then?"

Rachel laughed. "No."

"But I thought you could only sing to Jovah at a Gloria, or when an angel came to lead you."

"That is what the angels tell you, perhaps, but the Edori have always felt their songs went straight to Yovah's heart, whether or not an angel was there to guide the notes. Do you want to hear the story or not?"

"Oh, yes, yes—I'm sorry, go on."

"Everyone was invited to sing—solos, duets, whatever. There was a woman from my clan, Naomi, who had gone to live with a man in another clan. We had been very close; we had sung together for years. At every Gathering we saw each other again, and she would teach me a new song she had written while we were traveling apart. And every time we sang together, the Edori cheered."

"Are you a singer, then?"

Rachel was silent a moment. "I used to be," she said. "I do not feel much like singing in Lord Jethro's house."

Mary's eyes lifted to Rachel's. Once again they were working before the mirror, Rachel brushing out Mary's long hair and preparing to confine a few tendrils in the clip. "I wish you were not a slave," the lady said.

Rachel almost laughed. "So do I wish it," she said.

"Because then, when my new house is completed, I could offer you a scandalous wage and you could come work for me instead of for Lord Jethro."

Rachel gave her a mocking curtsey. "And I would come."

"And together we could figure out everything about pigs and candles." Mary sighed. "And you could do my hair, and I would have one friend in the house."

"Well, you will be here another year. I can be your friend that long."

But something had occurred to Mary. She bounced in her chair, clapping her small hands together. "I had the best idea!" she exclaimed. "Daniel asked me just the other day, and I had no answer!"

"What?" Rachel said, amused.

"What I wanted from him for a wedding gift! I will request you!"

Rachel merely stared at her in the looking glass. Mary waved her hands impatiently.

"You. I will say I want him to buy you for me. And then you will be my slave, and I will set you free! And then you *can* come work for me when I have my own house, and I can pay you as much as I want."

Rachel found her hands were trembling. She carefully set down the hairbrush and the barrette. "But if I was your slave," she said, "I would come to your new house anyway, and you would not have to pay me anything."

Mary looked shocked. "But I don't want slaves," she said. "I would not want anyone in my house who hates me. All my father's slaves hate him, I know it. I would rather pay someone and know she was there of her own free will." She twisted around to face Rachel. "You would come, of your own free will, wouldn't you?" she asked wistfully. "I would pay you whatever you asked."

"You would not have to pay me very much," Rachel said, very low. "I would come gladly—if you would make me free."

The rest of Mary's wedding day passed, for Rachel, in something of a blur. Once she escorted the trembling girl down to the chapel, she had to hurry back to the kitchens, for there was so much to be done that additional workers had been borrowed from the homes of Jethro's powerful friends. Not for a moment did Rachel stop slicing, chopping, stirring, cleaning and running.

But whatever her task, her mind was far from it. She tried to crush down her rising excitement, but Mary's artless offer had given her a fierce hope such as she had not indulged in for five years. It was stupid—she knew it was stupid—to believe Mary had the power, or the will, to effect the sale merely because she wanted it; clearly, this was not a woman used to getting her own way. But if Lady Clara did not object—and why should she?—and if Daniel was agreeable—and why should he not be, new-married bridegroom that he was?—it was just possible that Rachel was about to step onto the long road to freedom. At last, at last.

But it was foolish to believe it really would happen.

But it could. It could.

Only once during that endless, harried day did Rachel break stride in her work or wrench her mind away from that delicious, terrifying vision. Shortly after the chapel bells tolled high noon, music washed over the house from above—multiharmonic vocal music so exquisite that Rachel felt her hands falter on the chopping block.

"What is that?" she whispered to Anna.

"The angels," the woman whispered back. "Singing to Jovah to ask him to bless young Lord Daniel and the lady Mary."

"Where are they?"

"Above the house. On the wing. Is it not the most beautiful sound you have ever heard?"

Indeed it was, and Rachel had heard fine singing before. The bright brilliance of the soprano line was warmed by the rich alto voice; the tenor notes wove through them like metallic thread, and the basses flowed beneath them all like a dark river. Rachel closed her eyes, remembering music. Her hands continued laboring of their own volition.

And then she stopped moving altogether. A single male voice broke through the choral murmuring and painted the air with color. The lyric line was one of happiness and hope, but Rachel felt her heart twist as if the man sang of tragedy; that was how elegant his voice was. When the chorus responded with its carefully measured intervals, she actually gasped. The soloist's voice disappeared into harmony and she felt her breath spiral away from her, felt her head grow light. For a split second, as his voice ceased, she felt her own pulse hammer to a halt.

"Jovah will certainly grant happiness to the young ones now," Anna leaned over to murmur. "How could he not, after such a concert?"

But Rachel scarcely heard her. Opening her eyes, she was shocked beyond measure to find herself in the cellar kitchen of a Semorrah house, dressed in rags, bound by a chain and working like a slave. She had, for a few moments, literally forgotten where she was.

Between the wedding, the luncheon banquet, the afternoon reception, the dinner and the grand dress ball, the guests did not have much of a respite either. An hour or so before midnight, when the chatelaine told Rachel that Lady Mary needed her services to undress for the night, the slave dried her hands, tied her hair back and ran up the three flights to the suite reserved for Daniel and his bride. She half-expected to find Mary sobbing and exhausted, for it had been a day to try the most robust woman, which Mary was not; but it was a calm and hopeful young bride who awaited Rachel in the large and dimly lit chamber.

"How did you fare today?" Rachel asked, coming in and closing the door.

Mary laughed and briefly shut her eyes. "I thought it would never end! But everyone was very nice to me, telling me how well I looked, and my father gave me this silver ring—see—and told me I was a good girl. So I thought it went very well."

"Come. Let's get you ready for bed."

Obediently, Mary let Rachel disrobe her, bathe her and rub her body with scented creams. She donned a white lawn night-dress (possibly as expensive as the wedding gown, Rachel thought cynically), and then the slave combed out the bride's long hair again.

"You look pretty," Rachel told her. "Do you remember everything I told you?"

"Yes. Oh yes, I think so. But Daniel was kind to me today, too—he kissed my hand and then he kissed me on the lips, and he smiled at me, so I think perhaps it will go well in any case," Mary said optimistically.

Rachel smiled. "I'm sure it will. Is this fire hot enough to suit you? Is there anything else you need?"

"Yes—no—I think— I'm ready, I suppose."

Rachel gave a small curtsey and stepped back toward the door. "It will be fine," she said. "I'll try to come by in the morning to help you dress. You can tell me about it then."

"Oh yes, that would be good. Tomorrow morning and then I can— Rachel, I forgot!"

Hand on the doorknob, Rachel turned back to face her. "What?"

The young face was glowing. "He said yes!"

"Who said yes?"

"Daniel. He said, yes, I could have you for my wedding gift. And his father agreed! Isn't that splendid?"

For a moment, Rachel was so dizzy that only her grip on the door kept her upright. "Splendid," she said faintly, shaking her head to clear it. "Lady Mary—I can't tell you how splendid," she stammered. "You can't know— You—this means so much—"

Mary laughed with childlike delight. "Well, good! It is the first time in my life I have been able to make someone else happy. Already I like being a married woman!"

"Thank you," Rachel whispered, then bowed again and went out.

Free, free, free. She returned to the kitchen and finished her chores, and the whole time her mind was chanting: *Free, free, free.* She lay on her pallet and let exultation drown her; she pressed her fingers to her mouth to keep from laughing out loud. *Free.* She was tired, but she did not want to sleep. She wanted to revel. That a useless young gentrywoman could give her the most precious gift struck her as highly ironical, but even that thought could not taint her elation. *Free.*

It was late before Rachel slept and early when she woke, but she was energized by a secret euphoria. The clank of the chain between her shackles sounded almost musical this morning; soon the iron bands would be sawed from her wrists, and she would be released. She took extra pains with her appearance this morning, knowing she would see Mary within a few hours, wanting to look her best for her new mistress so that Mary would not change her mind. She scrubbed her face three times, washed her thick curly hair and braided it back, still wet. She put on her best gown, clean and newly mended.

But there were things to do before she could tend to Mary. Again, she had to build fires in the guest rooms—although, of the angelic contingents, only those from Monteverde and the Eyrie were still in the house. As before, most of the guests slept through her visit, but the angel Gabriel was awake when she entered his room.

Standing in the dawnlight at the long, high window, he looked clean and sculpted as a marble statue. Rachel checked on the threshold, since she had not expected him to be awake, and he gave her one quick, blue, indifferent glance. Keeping her eyes down, she hurried across to the fireplace and quickly built the fire. Or tried to—some malice was in the coals that they did not want to light. Even the matches were troublesome, requiring two or three strikes to catch. She imagined the angel's lapis lazuli eyes fixed on her from across the room, and her hands became even clumsier.

At last the blaze was built and looked hearty enough to last. Rachel stumbled to her feet and edged toward the door—but he was there before her, blocking the exit, staring at her with those incredible jewel-colored eyes.

"Lord?" she asked hesitantly and bobbed a graceless curtsey.

He did not move out of her way. His eyes traveled over her face, her hair, the threadbare gown, the shackles and chain. "Unbelievable," he said, and even his speaking voice was melodic enough to make her absentminded. "Rachel, daughter of Seth and Elizabeth."

CHAPTER THREE

Gabriel had had an extraordinarily trying three weeks. He had spent a few days in the general vicinity of the ruined village, hoping to find information about the vanished community. He had no luck. The few hardy families he found on independent farms a few miles distant were either suspicious and misanthropic, or recent arrivals who could shed no light on events more than ten years past. He flew east to the Jansai trading city of Breven to see if he could find out what traveling bands went through that portion of Jordana, but the few who would talk to him at all unanimously disclaimed any knowledge. He had expected some wariness—after all, what Jansai would admit to an angel that he had participated in the destruction of a farm village?—but he was frustrated nonetheless.

"I am not trying to find a war band just to level accusations," he said to one nomad chieftain. "I am looking for someone who once lived there—"

The man had laughed in his face. He was big, deeply tanned, completely bald and draped with a fortune in gold. "And I am trying to tell you, there is nothing for the Jansai in the wretched farmlands of northern Jordana," he said. He counted on his fingers. "No gold—no commerce—nothing to trade for. Jansai only travel the routes of profit, my friend."

"Someone came through that village."

"Ask the Edori," the chieftain advised. "They travel all through Samaria, for curiosity's sake. Some Edori, at some time, has strayed into that village circle, I swear to you by Jovah's wrath."

"But which Edori? And why?"

The chieftain laughed again. He had very large teeth. "Who can tell one Edori from another?" he said. "And who knows why they do anything? Ask them and see what they will tell you."

So Gabriel had left Breven and begun an exhausting search through all of Samaria for an Edori tribesman who could tell him what happened in a nameless Jordana village ten years ago. Like most of the angels, Gabriel had little experience with the Edori, so he was awkward and unsure around them. The city merchants, the farmers, even the Jansai, felt respect and a certain fear for the angels; they believed that only the good will of the angels protected them from divine wrath. But the Edori were not so certain of this most basic principles of theology. When they cared to appeal to Jovah, they did so themselves, holding unstructured firelit Glorias at their Gatherings. They also sang to the god to celebrate a birth, a death or some other important event, and many of the Edori singers whom Gabriel had heard had exceptional voices.

But they did not believe that a baby had to be dedicated to Jovah at birth; they did not believe that only an angel's voice would find its way to Jovah's ear; and, most shocking of all, they did not believe that Jovah was the one true god, the only god, the source of all good and the potential source of total annihilation. Instead, they believed in a god more powerful than Jovah, who directed Jovah and to whom Jovah was answerable—or so Gabriel understood, though he could hardly credit it. It was contrary to the basic principles of his existence.

He flew, low and with no particular direction, a day and a half from Breven before he came to an Edori tribe camped at the far southeastern border of Jordana. He had always found the Edori willing to welcome strangers, and this time it was no different. The women greeted him with hot wine and offers of warm cloaks (for, as usual, he was wearing only his flying leathers, and to mortals these did not look warm), and the children ran around him in a frenzied circle, chanting out a verse. The men came forward more slowly, as befitted creatures of more dignity, and they nodded to the angel and waited for him to state his case.

"I am looking for information on the whereabouts of a young woman," Gabriel said, speaking slowly, looking from face to impassive face. "She once lived in a small village in Jordana, not far from Windy Point. The village is gone, she is gone. I thought perhaps Edori, who go everywhere, might know what happened to the people who lived there, and this girl in particular."

It was, as he had anticipated, a tortuous, tedious process. He was invited to stay for a meal while the most observant men and women of the tribe were called together to consider what he had to say. Could he describe exactly where the village had been? Did he know the names of any who had lived there? When had it been destroyed? What had destroyed it? His ignorance on most of these questions embarrassed Gabriel, but the Edori did not mock him or show irritation. Instead, with their help, he was able to sketch out a tolerably accurate map of the area—and, again with their prompting, he came up with clues that led to a more precise idea of when the destruction had taken place. For they asked him to name the grasses and the lichens he had seen on the boulders of the ruined houses: Was the mold brown with black spots or was it red with brown spots? Was the grass as high as his waist or only as high as his ankle and bearing seeds of a yellowish-green? With this information they deduced with certainty how long the site had been abandoned.

"Eighteen years," one of the middle-aged men had pronounced, and all the others in the group murmured agreement. "What tribe was traveling near the Caitana hills eighteen summers ago? Was it the Logollas?"

"No, they were in the Gaza foothills that summer," a woman said. "The Chievens, perhaps."

"They were with the Logollas."

"The Pancias?"

"Not the Pancias."

"The Manderras, then."

"The Manderras."

"Yes, the Manderras."

Gabriel felt a stirring of hope. "And where might I find the Manderras?" he asked.

The middle-aged man shook his head. He might have looked sad, but it was hard to tell; Gabriel found it impossible to read expression on any of the bronze faces. "The Manderras are gone," he said.

"Gone where?"

"Scattered. Dead."

Gabriel's eyes narrowed. "Attacked by Jansai?" he asked sharply.

Several of the Edori nodded. The others remained inscrutable.

"Are they all dead?" Gabriel persisted. "All of them?"

"Or enslaved," a woman said dryly. "And if you can find them after the Jansai have dispersed them, you will have no trouble finding one lost girl."

Gabriel uttered a small exclamation that encompassed many things—frustration on his own behalf, rage on behalf of the Edori. "So there is no one left who might know—"

"Naomi," someone said.

Gabriel swung around to identify the speaker. A young woman, in her early twenties perhaps, suckling a baby while she audited the conversation. "Who is Naomi?" he asked.

"She was born to the Manderra tribe, but she followed a man of the Chievens," the woman told him. "She was with the Manderras when they wandered through the Caitana foothills."

"Then she can tell me what happened to the village."

The young woman shrugged. "If the Manderras ever came upon the village. Who can say?"

Gabriel struggled with his irritation. "And where can I find Naomi?"

"With the Chievens."

"Yes, yes, I understand. Where can I find the Chievens?"

The middle-aged man who seemed to be as much of a leader as these people had spread his hands wide. "Who can say?" he said. "They may have gone to Gaza or to Bethel or to Luminaux. We will see them again at the Gathering."

"You mean, you have no idea where any of these people are at any time?"

"Not until the Gathering. Then we tell stories of where we have been and what we have seen."

"You can't even make a guess?"

"We could guess. We know where we would go at this time of year. But look, we are here and the Chievens are not. Where else would you like us to guess? One place is as likely as another."

Gabriel waited a moment, until his anger had passed. "And the next Gathering," he said. "When is it to be, and where?"

"In the fields west of Luminaux, five months from now."

"Five months! But I don't have five months to spare!"

The dark eyes stared at him from the circle of dark faces. None of the Edori had a comment to offer on that.

"I see," Gabriel said after a long silence. "You have no more help that you can give me."

"We have told you what we can."

"Yes, and more than I could have expected to learn from you," Gabriel said, rising to his feet. "It is not your fault I need to know more."

The middle-aged man rose too; the others remained seated. "Stay—eat the evening meal with us," the leader urged him. "You are tired and angry, and you should be refreshed with food and companionship."

"I am tired and angry, and I am in a desperate hurry," Gabriel said. "I thank you for your offer. And for all your assistance. But I must go now."

And he had left, knowing it was rude, knowing there was nothing he could learn during a night flight back to the Eyrie and that he should have stayed to show his appreciation. But he had spoken the truth: He was made restless by desperation, and he could not have stayed. Jovah guide him, where could she *be*?

During the next two weeks, Gabriel made an erratic search through the three provinces of Samaria, looking for bands of Edori who might through some fantastic stroke of luck be the Chievens. He did happen upon two more small tribes, but neither of them were the Chievens, and no one in either tribe knew where the Chievens could be found, nor did they know anything of a small farm village in the Caitana Mountains.

Once, when his route took him past Josiah's mountain retreat, he stopped to see if the oracle had any more aid to give him. Unfortunately he did not.

"All I can tell you is that she is still alive," Josiah said. "I cannot tell you where she is."

"Then how is it you could tell me where she once was?"

The old man gave him a faint smile. "Because when she was dedicated, a record was made of where the dedication took place, and where she was born, and who her parents were. I know she is still alive, because her Kiss is still animate—Jovah can still sense her existence. But as to where she is—" He spread his hands.

"Very well. She's alive. And she's lost. What happens if months go by and I still cannot find her? And the day of the Gloria arrives. What then?"

Josiah regarded him somberly. "That is a very serious question," he said.

"Will any woman do? Perhaps I can press Ariel or Magdalena into service—or, no, it must be a human woman—can I just find a mortal woman with a passable voice and have her sing the Gloria at my side? Will that satisfy Jovah? Or must it be this woman—this Rachel?"

Josiah was nodding thoughtfully. "The answer is—I don't know," he said slowly. "Because, in the past, there have been times when the angelica has been unable to perform. When Michael was Archangel, thirty-five years ago, there were three consecutive years when the angelica Ruth lay too ill to speak, and their daughter sang at his side. And there are stories from even longer ago, when the angelica or the Archangel was unable to perform, and substitutes were found, and Jovah accepted the new voices. At least, he has never unleashed destruction upon us after a Gloria.

"But the scriptures of the Librera are very strict," he went on, his voice troubled. "It is written there precisely who is to attend every Gloria and who is to participate. There must be the Archangel, who is chosen by Jovah, and the angelica, who is chosen by Jovah. There must be angels from the three hosts; there must be Jansai and Manadavvi and Edori and Luminauzi. Representatives must come from every part of Samaria to join in harmony together, to assure Jovah that there is peace on the planet and good will among all peoples. And if the smallest part of this decree is overlooked, then Jovah will be angry and cast down thunderbolts, and he will destroy first the mountain and then the river and then the world itself."

Gabriel stared at the oracle. Josiah's voice had been flat, almost matter-of-fact, but his words were chilling.

"Then if I cannot find her—" the angel began.

"Then, if you cannot find her, we may all be in grave danger. I don't know—it may be that Jovah will understand, and forgive, and listen to whatever voice sings beside you. He has forgiven these other lapses. But in each of those cases, the angelica was, in fact, the angelica. The Archangel had not capriciously chosen to install someone who had not been selected by the god himself."

Gabriel rubbed the heels of his hands into his closed eyes. He was very tired. "Then I must find her, that's all," he said.

So he continued his search, but he had no luck. Samaria was too big for one angel to cover thoroughly—and the Edori were constantly on the move. He could spend the rest of his life hunting one mobile tribe and never catch up with them. He would have to enlist the other angels from his host, have them quarter the three provinces and speak to every last Edori clansman.

After the wedding, of course.

Mentally cursing Lord Jethro of Semorrah, his misbegotten son and the girl who was fool enough to marry him, Gabriel returned to the Eyrie a few days before the event to collect his formal clothes and his brother Nathan. As always, he felt a sudden sense of deep peace envelop him as soon as his feet touched the smooth stone of the landing point. It was beautiful, the Eyrie—three terraces of interconnected chambers and corridors all carved from the warm, rosy-beige rock of the Velo Mountains—but it was not just the physical beauty that gave Gabriel the instant emotional lift. It was the singing.

Night and day, at least two voices were raised in constant sweet harmony, the notes resonating throughout the whole compound. For weeks in advance, the angels and mortals who resided at the Eyrie volunteered to sing duets in one-hour shifts, then took their places in the small chamber in the highest tier of the compound. Night and day, entering the Eyrie—or waking, restless, in the middle of the night—or eating, laughing or brooding—this music came to a man's ears and soothed him with the magic of harmony.

For a moment, Gabriel felt all his tension lift away. But even the sweet voices of Obadiah and Hannah could not make all his problems right this afternoon. Gabriel listened for a moment, then strode to the nearest tunnelway, and entered the Eyrie complex.

Candlelight and piped gaslight reflected back from the pale rock interior walls so that even at night and inside, the Eyrie glowed luminescent. Gabriel hurried through the tunnels toward the inner warrens, making his way through corridors that gradually widened into great halls and common rooms. Luck was with him; he made it safely to Nathan's chamber without encountering anyone he had to greet with more than a nod and a smile.

And he was still lucky; Nathan was there.

"Gabriel! I thought I would have to leave tomorrow without

you," his brother exclaimed, rising up from his seat at a narrow desk. Behind him, Gabriel spotted white scrolls covered with black notations. Nathan was writing music again. "And then I wondered if you remembered the wedding at all."

"I remembered," Gabriel assured him, stripping off his flight gloves and vest. Because more than half the inhabitants of the Eyrie were mortal, the entire complex was heated, and most of the angels found the temperature a bit too high. "And I considered forgoing the honor of singing at Lord Jethro's son's wedding, but I decided it would not be politically sound to offend the burghers even before I ascend to the position of Archangel."

"You're in a foul humor," Nathan observed, pouring wine for both of them without waiting to be asked. "I assume you have not found your angelica. Could Josiah not name her, then?"

"Oh, he named her. Rachel, daughter of Seth and Elizabeth. He even gave me the location of her dedication—some backwater farmland in the Jordana foothills."

Nathan raised his eyebrows. He looked a great deal like his brother, though his eyes were a deep brown and his appearance was not so striking; yet the resemblance was impossible to miss. "Jovah has a sense of humor, I see," he remarked.

"The theory, according to Josiah, is that my angelica will possess qualities I do not. Since, as Josiah so kindly told me, I am arrogant, she, apparently, will be humble. Whatever. I am sure Jovah had his reasons for picking her."

"But you cannot find this plot of land, this farm in Jordana, where she is supposed to be?"

"Oh, I found it. A little community. Homes, farms, a cluster of buildings. All—" Gabriel swept one hand before him. "All leveled to the ground some eighteen years ago."

"Leveled . . . By Jansai?"

"They say not. I went to Breven. Although why the Jansai should tell me the truth when a truth like that would cause me to call down Jovah's wrath upon them—"

"Then, what happened? Where is she?"

"I have not been able to answer either question in the past three weeks. The Jansai say the Edori may know. The Edori say, oh yes, perhaps a girl from a certain tribe may know, but we do not know where that tribe passes the winter months. And no one seems to have heard of this girl specifically. And I can't comb every cave and campsite in Samaria looking for Edori who may know something about some vanished farm girl—but may not know a thing!—and I have about five months now to find her. And instead of continuing my search, I have to go play tame angel in Semorrah to prove that I can deal reasonably with the merchants, who do not like me much anyway—"

"And they have reason not to like you, since you do not like them," Nathan said, smiling a little. "But back to the problem of this girl. If—"

"Rachel."

"What?"

"Rachel. That's her name. Josiah says she is twenty-five years old."

"If there are Edori who know where she is, can't we go to the next Gathering and ask all the Edori at once?"

"That's my last hope. But the next Gathering is only three or four weeks before the Gloria. And if I wait till then, and no one knows a thing about her, my situation is indeed desperate."

"How desperate?" Nathan asked, alarmed.

"Josiah says Jovah may not accept another woman's voice. In which case—the end of the world looms. But I cannot credit that. If I am unable to find her, then I will sing and someone will sing beside me, and if Jovah has any mercy in him at all, he will accept who I bring him. But I would prefer not to make the experiment. Because Josiah seemed so doubtful—"

"We'll go to the wedding," Nathan said decisively. "And then we'll organize a hunt. You and I and ten or so of our angels. And we'll search for the right Edori until the Gathering. And then we'll go to the Gathering. And until then we will not despair. And for now you need to rest, because we leave tomorrow for Semorrah and all the delights in store for us there."

"Amen," Gabriel said. "Let's leave at first light."

So it was not in the best of moods that Gabriel arrived at the magnificent home of Lord Jethro of Semorrah, and his temper was not improved by the opulence of the wedding itself. It was only in the past forty years—during Raphael's reign and the tenure of Michael before him—that the merchants had come to accumulate such wealth and prominence, so that the cities rivaled the holds of the angels as places of importance. Gabriel believed in a more literal translation of the Librera, which said, "Whereas each man differs from the other as the rose differs from the iris, yet is each one beautiful in his own way, and equal in Jovah's sight." Gabriel did not like to see one class of people gain dominance over another; he considered inequity a doubtful road to the harmony that Jovah required from his people. He had not troubled to hide his disapproval, which had made him unpopular with the merchants—and not a few of the angels.

Still, he was to be Archangel. Knowing his views, Jovah had selected him from all the angels of Samaria. And now Lord Jethro and the Jansai, and even the angels, were stuck with him for the next twenty years. So he had been invited to the wedding, and he had come.

He had even tried to be civil, although cordiality was beyond him. He found Jethro to be a shrewd, calculating, wholly untrustworthy sort of man, and the bride's father cut from the same cloth. Young Daniel bid fair to follow in his father's footsteps, and the lady Mary—sweet Jovah singing!—was small, shy, childlike and nervous, clearly a hapless sacrifice on the altar of intracity commerce.

Raphael, of course, had fawned over her, with that practiced grace that pleased the merchants so well. He had sat beside her at the dinner and smilingly complimented her on her looks and her hair. She appeared to be grateful for the attention, chattering to him easily after the first few moments, during which she had seemed overcome by the honor. Watching Raphael charm her, Gabriel had grimaced slightly, then glanced over at Nathan. Nathan was grinning.

So after dinner, Nathan had made his way to the lady's side and paid her pretty attentions, and this had seemed to please her as much as Raphael's conversation. Nathan was much more the diplomat and ladies' man than his brother, and Gabriel was not above deploying him in this role, for it was one he was no good at himself.

"Your brother seems to have won the lady Mary's heart," said a smooth voice behind him, and Gabriel turned to find himself face to face with the Archangel. As always, the first thing he noticed about Raphael was his sheer physical beauty. Hair, eyes, skin, even wings, had a tawny color to them; he was leonine, powerful and sleek. Yet aging for all that. Close up, Gabriel could see the fine lines around the eyes and down the cheeks. The beautiful hair was thinner than it had once been.

"You did not fare so ill yourself" was Gabriel's response.

Raphael smiled seraphically. "She is a sweet child with a gentle manner," he said. "It is a pleasure to converse with her."

"A pity to throw her into Jethro's den," Gabriel said, glancing around. The room was filled with landholders and bankers and petty burghers, most of them talking finance if Gabriel did not greatly miss his guess.

"She comes from just such a den, though I'm sure neither our host nor our guest of honor would thank you for describing it so," Raphael replied in a purring voice.

Gabriel laughed. "No, indeed. I'm sure Jethro and all the others will miss your charming manner when they are forced to contend with me instead."

"And the day fast approaches," Raphael responded. "Tell me. I was hoping to meet your angelica here. But I have heard no word about her at all. Is it possible you are keeping her a secret until the day of the Gloria itself?"

Raphael spoke with his usual melodiousness, but Gabriel thought he detected the faintest hint of malice in the tone. "I thought to bring her myself," he said. "It did not work out that way."

"But you have found her? Jovah has identified her?"

"Oh, yes. He's identified her."

Raphael was watching him with those golden eyes. The direct question would be impossible to evade, but Raphael did not ask it. He merely gave Gabriel that sleepy smile that so many mortals found endearing. "Well, I look forward to meeting her," he said. "Jovah's choices are always instructive."

Which comment did not improve Gabriel's mood either.

He endured the hours in the ballroom, successfully pleading ineptitude to avoid having to dance (Nathan was one of the few angels who had mastered the art and managed to hold his wings close enough to his body to prevent their being trod upon by everyone else on the floor). Gabriel made polite conversation with the merchants who were standing near him, dodged the angel Saul most of the evening, and went to bed exhausted by the effort of trying to conceal his true emotions for hours on end.

He woke in the morning conscious of two things—excessive heat and a dull ache in his right arm. The source of the heat was quickly identified—Jethro's admirable servants had slipped into the room while he was still sleeping and built a fire, an amenity that was completely unnecessary for an angel. For the pain in his arm he could find no immediate explanation. He rubbed the muscles along his biceps, wondering if he had slept oddly during the night. In a few minutes, the soreness evaporated, and he forgot about it.

It was a busy day. The wedding breakfast was elaborate, the marriage ceremony itself extraordinarily long and solemnly performed. The only part of the event that Gabriel actually enjoyed was the singing. But he always loved to sing.

It was when he, Nathan, Raphael, Saul, Magdalena and Ariel were aloft and in the middle of the Te Deum that he realized why his arm had hurt so much that morning. The angels had joined hands to form a circle, Nathan as always managing to get hold of Magdalena's fingers. Even as the swell of the music bathed him in a mild rapture, Gabriel watched them; he saw that Magdalena very properly had her face turned toward Jovah but Nathan's eyes were fixed on the Monteverde angel. Angels could not intermarry—it was one of their few prohibitions—and it was a law that had never been transgressed. But Nathan had been in love with Magdalena these past three years, and time did not seem to be diminishing his affection.

And indeed, when they were near each other, if you watched for it, you could see the faint flicker in the heart of each angel's Kiss, the divine reply of one to another. Jovah in all his wisdom had not foreseen that.

Gabriel tightened his grip on Nathan's hand, and his brother turned his face upward to the god. Again, Gabriel was half-drowned in the glory of the music. His tenor note held firm against Magdalena's descending alto line, and when Ariel's soprano rose ecstatically above both, he felt himself tremble all the way to the tips of his wings. Then his own voice took the lead, while the rest fell back in choral harmony, and he sang the words of invitation and celebration with delight.

And at that moment he felt the stabbing pain in his right arm again, and he suddenly knew what it was. A response to the music, a response to his voice, a response to him. The Kiss on his own arm was alive with muted sparks, and he felt that heat down to its anchor in his bone.

Against all probability, Rachel was in Semorrah, perhaps even in the hall below them, near enough to hear him and attuned enough to react to the sound of his voice.

* * *

It became a matter of importance, therefore, to speak to every woman in the house. It was a very different Gabriel who attended to his social duties this day. At the luncheon, the following reception, the dinner, the second ball, he moved with great determination through the throngs and engaged each of the women in courteous conversation. He complimented them on their gowns, their hair, their jewels, asked them if they had enjoyed the wedding, and whether they lived in Semorrah or had just come for a visit. He was not conscious of flattering anyone until Nathan drew him aside at the reception and laughed at him.

"So you've become a flirt, now and very abruptly," his brother said. "Are you planning to leave a trail of broken hearts among the merchants' wives since you cannot find your angelica anywhere?"

"I'm just talking to them."

"And a fine job you're making of it. I heard Lady Susan tell her daughter she was half in love with you."

"Don't be ridiculous."

"But Gabriel, what has sparked this sudden amiability? I could have sworn you were bored out of your mind yesterday. And what's more, so could everyone else."

"I think she's here."

"Who's here?"

"Rachel. I think—but I'm not sure."

Nathan glanced quickly around him. "In this house?"

"Maybe. I felt—while we were singing, my Kiss flared up. And this morning—I think she's in the house, or very near."

"The Kiss has been wrong before," Nathan said wryly.

"No, I don't think so in this case. Josiah told me— But I must talk to all the women of the house, you see that, and I feel very clumsy about it. Unfortunately, it's not a task you can help me with."

"And you've had no response since the Te Deum this morning?"

Gabriel was silent. Nathan exclaimed, "You have! Is the lady married? Is that the problem?"

"It was very faint," Gabriel said. "When I was speaking to the lady Mary—" Nathan laughed aloud, appalled. Gabriel grimaced. "I know. I complimented her on—her hair, I think it was— and she blushed, and I felt the slightest heat in my arm. But surely not enough—"

"That would truly be the greatest irony Jovah ever enacted," Nathan said, his voice solemn but his eyes alight. "To unite you with Lord Jethro's newly acquired daughter-in-law moments after you sing at her wedding—"

"But I think it can't be her. Perhaps someone else she spoke to, someone who commented on her hair. Someone she was thinking of when I spoke to her. And it's not as if I can ask her to list everyone she's spoken to today—"

"Stay calm. The case is not desperate. In fact, it's better than it was yesterday, don't you see? How long do you think we can stay in Jethro's house, searching? Can you make an excuse to remain another few days?"

"Raphael is leaving tonight, but Ariel and her sister will be here through morning. We can stay at least as long. After that— but it may do us no good to stay. She may be leaving with one of the other households. She may not belong here at all."

"A guest?" Nathan asked, watching his brother. "Or—a servant of one of the guests?"

"Let us hope it is a guest, the adopted daughter of some minor merchant. I would hate to think my angelica had been serving as a lady's maid any time these past eighteen years."

"If she has, she has," Nathan said philosophically. "Let's get on with the search while everyone is still here."

But Gabriel had no luck, though he managed to talk to virtually every female guest present—even those too young and those too old to be, by any stretch of diplomacy, twenty-five years old. The ball ended, the wedding was over, and everyone would be going home—and he was no closer to solving this most critical puzzle.

Very well, then. Gabriel did not like it, but it seemed she was among the serving class, most probably a visitor to the mansion, come in the train of some merchant's wife. He slept lightly for a few hours, then rose to prowl the lower corridors of the great house, stalking up and down the cramped hallways where the abigails and lady's maids were quartered. But the Kiss remained cool and dark against his arm. She was not there.

He returned to his room, to spend the last hours of the night brooding at his window. She was in Semorrah, she had to be. All right, she had heard him singing yesterday, but perhaps she had heard him from some vantage point other than this house. She had been in a passing cart, or listening at the window of one of the great houses a few blocks away. She was within the sound of his voice, that much at least he could cling to. Tomorrow—this morning—he could seek her again. He could take wing and hover over the city, singing the tender country ballads that women seemed to like so much. She would hear him, wherever she was. She would look up, and against her will, perhaps, stop whatever she was doing to listen to him, moved without knowing why by the timbre and cadence of his voice—

His meditations were abruptly interrupted by the opening of the door. He glanced impatiently over his shoulder to see one of Jethro's wretched slave girls entering with a coal scuttle and broom—no doubt the same one who had built the unwanted fire yesterday morning. He spared her only a glance before turning his attention once more to the empty cobblestoned streets just beginning to take shape in the dawn light.

He would sing, and she would hear him, and he would know she was near because his arm would burn as it was burning now, as if the slave girl had indeed lit the fire and held a live coal to his arm—as perhaps she had done the morning before—

He wheeled silently and stared at her. She was crouched over the hearth and did not look his way. Bare feet took him soundlessly to the doorway; not until she rose and made to leave did she realize he had moved. The Kiss on her own arm was alive with mutinous amber lights. She looked to be nothing but eyes and tatters and undomesticated golden hair.

"Unbelievable," he said, and then he spoke her name.

CHAPTER FOUR

Rachel stared up at the angel's face and felt a shiver of panic. Pride made her hide it behind a scowl. "Who are you?" she said, pretending ignorance.

He had clearly never been asked the question in his life, and was instantly affronted. "I am the angel Gabriel," he said stiffly. "I lead the host at the Eyrie."

"Oh," she said.

"And you?" he asked. "You are Rachel, daughter of Seth and Elizabeth?"

"I'm Rachel," she said cautiously.

"I've been looking for you for weeks."

She felt her panic grow, and her hostility with it. Both were unreasonable. "Why?" she asked in a most ungracious tone of voice.

He took a deep breath, seemed to consider somewhat hopelessly what to say, and expelled the breath. "Did you know," he said at last, speaking with great effort in a gentle voice, "that I am to become Archangel later this year?"

"You are?" she said.

He nodded. His blue eyes never stopped searching her face, as if he were seeking ways to slip behind the mask of her expression. She felt her scowl deepen in response. "Every twenty years, a new Archangel is chosen by Jovah, to lead all angels and all peoples of Samaria. This summer, I will lead the singing of the

Gloria for the first time." He hesitated. "You do know what the Gloria is, don't you?"

"Yes," she said sharply. "I'm not stupid."

He was still watching her. The jeweled color of his eyes was beginning to reverberate in her head. "Then you also know that one of the people singing beside the Archangel is the woman chosen by Jovah to be his bride—his angelica—a mortal woman joined to the angels in harmony."

This was getting deeper into dogma and ritual than the Edori had ever taken Rachel, but she nodded. "Certainly."

He took another long breath. "And the woman Jovah has chosen as my bride," he said, "is you."

She felt herself staring at him like a half-wit.

"That is," he murmured, "if you are Rachel, daughter of Seth and Elizabeth, born in a small Jordana farm town not far from the Caitana foothills."

"I was born near the Caitanas," she said, her voice almost a whisper. "But I have not been there . . . for years and years."

"I have been to that place," he said abruptly. "It appeared to have been destroyed. What happened to it?"

She shook her head. "I was very young. I have few memories of that time and place."

"Then what happened to you? How did you get from there— to here?"

"I was adopted by the Manderra clan of the Edori people," she said, her voice taking on a certain proud lilt; so the Edori always identified themselves to each other. "They found me when I was a child. I was with them until I was twenty."

"And then?"

Her expression became ironic. "And then what do you think? How do Edori women usually become allali slave girls?"

She deliberately used the contemptuous Edori word that once meant merely "city dweller" but had come to mean also money-grubber, cheat, slave trader, whoremonger and anyone engaged in unsavory commerce. She saw with satisfaction that he knew the word and did not like it.

But he managed to reply in an even voice. "I imagine, through the intervention of a Jansai war band," he said. "And that's what happened?"

"Yes."

"When?"

"Five years ago."

"Who was taken? Everyone from your clan? The other Edori I have spoken to said the Manderras were dispersed."

"Dispersed or dead," she said in a hard voice. "There were maybe ten Manderras in the slave train that brought me into Semorrah. There were also Edori from other clans, some that I knew, some I did not. What happened to the rest of the Manderras I do not know."

"I'm sorry," he said quietly. She did not reply. He spoke more briskly. "You can tell me more of your story once we are at the Eyrie."

She realized she was staring again. "At the Eyrie?"

"Yes. We will leave today—now—as soon as you are ready and I have told Lord Jethro that I am taking"—he paused, and eyed her somewhat unfavorably—"one of the members of his household with me."

"But I don't want to go with you," she said.

He stared at her as if she had spoken in tongues. "Don't want to? Are you mad? Don't want to come to the Eyrie with me—to be *angelica*? You'd rather—" His voice took on great sarcastic energy. "You'd rather stay here, in Semorrah, as a slave to Lord Jethro, when you could be a free woman in Bethel—a free woman, sweet Jovah, an angelica! What kind of choice is that? That isn't a choice!"

"I don't want to go with you," she repeated. "And I'm not a slave."

He swept her with one comprehensive glance. She felt her face flush. "I'm not," she said defiantly. "Or I won't be. Lady Mary has requested that I be given to her as a bride gift, and she has already promised to free me."

He was still incredulous. "To do what? Serve her the rest of your days? Braid her hair and fetch her drinks and listen to her inane chatter about her husband and her children and her pets?"

Rachel lifted her chin. "She's going to pay me."

"Trust me," he said grimly, "no salary would be high enough."

"I'd rather go work for her than be your angelica," she said.

"You don't even know what an angelica does," he said with some heat.

"No? I know what allali wives do, and a lot of it's worse than listening to inane chatter about husbands and dogs."

He was utterly furious, and he looked like a man who did not always successfully throttle his rage. She edged back just a little. "The angelica," he said, through tight lips, "holds the position of highest honor on Samaria. She sings beside the Archangel at the Gloria. She hears petitions that men and women fear to put before the Archangel himself. She can, if she chooses, be a great force for good among mortals, among angels. Many angelicas have had special relationships with Jovah, asking from him boons and favors which have been divinely granted. The angelica is one step from the god."

"The angelica, you said," she responded, "is wife to the Archangel."

She had not thought he could become angrier, but it seemed she was wrong. "If it is the thought of the physical relationship which repels you, you need not be concerned," he ground out. "They marry, but Archangels and their angelicas have often made their own arrangements."

She arched her eyebrows just a little. Stubborn unto death; Simon had told her that once. Stubborn just for the sake of stubbornness, and stubborn out of fear. Stubborn when there was no good reason for it except that she had never, not even in five years as a slave, learned to back down. "Edori," she said, "do not believe in marriage."

"You," he said, "are not an Edori."

"Nonetheless—"

"And you," he added, "have no choice. Don't you understand? The god has chosen you. Not I. Were I free to take a bride of my own choosing, believe me, I would not have gone to the Caitanas *or* the Edori *or* the kitchens of the great houses of Semorrah, looking for the woman of my dreams. You have been thrust upon me as this role has been thrust upon you. I suggest you accept it with as good a grace as possible."

She shook her head. "No. I will admit it is an honor, but I decline it. I will not go with you to the Eyrie."

He gave a small, bitter laugh and tossed his hands apart. For a second, she thought she'd won. But no. "You may say you are not going," he said. "You may resist. You may hate me, you may hate Jovah. But you are going. You cannot escape your fate. You cannot escape the dictates of your god."

"I have a right to choose my own life!" she cried suddenly, filled with an uprush of despair. "I have a right to refuse you!"

"Did the Jansai give you a choice? Did they allow you to refuse?" he said with an exasperated malice. "Understand this. Your life has been given over into other hands, and your will is insufficient. We leave in two hours' time," he added, turning away from her. "Tell who you will that you are leaving. I will see Lord Jethro myself."

And he opened the door and stalked out, leaving her staring after him in mingled rage, hatred, astonishment, shock and fear. Perhaps he had not meant it as cruelly as it sounded, but she felt very much as she had when the Jansai rode shrieking into her campground and forever altered her existence. It had been an unforgivable thing for the angel to say, and she vowed right then that she would never forgive him—not for saying it, and not for doing it. Once again someone was taking her life out of her hands, just when it seemed worth living.

It was hard to tell, Gabriel thought cynically, who was more embarrassed at the discovery that his angelica had been laboring as a slave girl in Lord Jethro's household for five years, but the Archangel-elect felt that he concealed his discomfiture better than his host. Jethro could not have been more apologetic or accommodating; in fact, his incoherent expressions of mortification palled quickly.

"All I ask is that you have her bonds removed as soon as possible," Gabriel said, interrupting. "Within the hour. And that you find her some decent clothing to wear so that I am not ashamed to bring her to the Eyrie."

"Certainly—oh, most willingly—but, angelo, let me assure you—in my house she met with nothing but kindness. There was no mistreatment, no importuning—"

"I'm sure of that."

"One thing more you can be sure of," Jethro continued earnestly, "I will tell no one—absolutely no one."

Gabriel shrugged, his expression wry. "This is not a secret it will be possible to keep," he said. "But I would appreciate it greatly if you did not facilitate the gossip."

He had made only one stop before heading straight to Lord Jethro's bedroom suite to demand instant admittance. The stop had been at his brother's room, to waken Nathan and tell him the mixed news. Even half-asleep, Nathan had been properly appalled and amused.

"Jovah guard us," Nathan had said, struggling to sit up and grind the sleep from his face. "Could it be worse?"

"It's worse," Gabriel replied. "She dislikes me."

Nathan choked back a yawn. "Already?"

"She does not want to go with us. She declined the honor awaiting her. I informed her she was not allowed to decline. I would not put it past her to make a run for it. I want you to get dressed and find her. Follow her. Keep her in your sight till I rejoin you."

Nathan shook his head to clear it, and came to his feet. "Gladly. Where is she? How will I know her?"

"Look for anyone racing from the house."

"Seriously."

Gabriel actually had to stop and consider. He had been so intent on the person behind the face that he had not consciously studied Rachel's physical appearance. "Shorter than me, but not by much," he said slowly. "Thin. Pale. Beautiful hair. Long and blond and very curly. Her eyes are brown. Her hands are chained together."

"She sounds most striking," Nathan said. "I will hardly be able to mistake her."

"I left her in my room, but I doubt she's still there. I have no idea where she would have hidden by now. I'm off to inform Jethro of the dishonor he's done me these past five years."

Nathan tried to force back another yawn. "And to think," he said, "you didn't want to come to the wedding."

Gabriel was tricked into a laugh as he strode out the door.

It was nearly an hour before he confronted his bride-to-be again, and in that time she had undergone a remarkable transformation. She had been thoroughly cleaned up, her hair ruthlessly combed, her ragged dress changed for a silken traveling gown of deep green. The chains that had bound her wrists were gone. But the expression on her face had not altered, and she looked at Gabriel with a mixture of defiance and dislike as he entered the salon where she and Nathan waited.

"She did not run" was Nathan's greeting.

"I'm glad of it," Gabriel said. He studied her. Now that he thought about it, she hadn't looked much like a slave girl this morning. Her attire, perhaps, had been wretched, but her demeanor had not for a moment been subservient. She certainly did not look like a slave girl now. Nor, with that hair, did she look like an Edori. Neither did she bear a resemblance to any of the weather-beaten, work-weary farm women he had ever seen. "And are you any more resigned to coming with me?"

"Well, I can't stay here," she said. "They would not have me now, even if I wanted to stay."

"Graciously spoken," Gabriel murmured. She gave him a killing look. He turned to his brother. "It will not be so easy to leave as I at first imagined," he said. "Jethro insists on dowering the girl with all sorts of treasures—clothing, jewels, gold, I don't know what. There's a wagonload being assembled in the court-yard even as we speak. I am trying to decide if courtesy demands that one of us travel alongside the wagon—"

"I will, if you want," Nathan said with a grin.

"I'll travel with the wagon," the girl said.

Gabriel turned back to her. "You will travel with me," he said. "I want to get you to the Eyrie as soon as possible."

She eyed him uncertainly. "What do you mean, travel with you?"

Nathan divided a glance between them and said, "Well, I'll just go check on some things," then left the room. Gabriel and Rachel remained facing each other warily.

"I will fly you back to the Eyrie," he said as pleasantly as possible. "The trip will take about six hours. By cart it would take maybe three or four days."

For the first time, she showed a certain apprehension. "I can't fly," she said.

"No, of course not. *I* will carry you—"

"No, I mean I'm afraid. Heights make me sick. I will faint or become ill, I really will—"

He frowned at her. Her distress seemed genuine. "Have you ever been in an angel's arms, above the earth?"

She shook her head. "No, but I have been on the bridge between Semorrah and Jordana, and I was sick halfway across. They had to blindfold me and carry me into the city."

"When you entered as a slave?" She nodded. "But you may have been ill from other causes."

"And in tall buildings—from the roof of this house!—when I look down, I become so dizzy, I have to sit. I have to crawl down the stairways on my hands and knees."

"But, Rachel—"

"Let me ride in the wagon," she pleaded. "I know you

think—you told your brother I would run away, but if you let me ride in the wagon, I swear I will arrive with it at the Eyrie. Please."

How could he refuse? She had been so rebellious before that this begging had the ring of truth to it. "Of course," he said. "I will send Nathan on ahead to prepare things, and I will accompany you and the cart. We are so far behind already that a few more days can hardly hurt us."

She gave him a quick smile of relief, and for a moment he thought, *Perhaps we will become friends after all.* "Behind?" she said.

"The Gloria is only five months away. There is a great deal you need to learn about—about everything. The music, the ceremony, the Eyrie, the way angels live. We do not have much time—and it took me so long to find you."

"Perhaps you should have started looking sooner, then," she said. "Five years ago, maybe?"

Her voice was pleasant, but she definitely intended the words maliciously. *Wrong again*, he thought, and made no answer. He merely bowed, and motioned her toward the door. The sooner they were quit of this house—the sooner they were at the Eyrie— the better off they would be.

As it happened, Jethro had prepared two vehicles to send with them on their journey. One was indeed a wagon, piled high with boxes and bundles. The other was a sturdy traveling carriage which would accommodate a mortal better than an angel. Each came with a driver and a team of horses.

"We are beginning to resemble a cavalcade," Gabriel observed. Rather than flying across the river from Semorrah to the Bethel shore, he had elected to stand beside Rachel on the crowded ferry. He had already informed her that he would make the overland journey by air, joining her whenever the vehicles halted for meals or overnight stays. She had not been disappointed to hear that he would not be in the carriage with her.

When the ferry docked, the two of them jostled off with the other passengers and watched as the long line of carts, carriages and coaches began the tedious process of disembarkation. Gabriel's stature—and hauteur—earned them some breathing space in the crowd; no one came too close. They stood side by side a moment, gazing across the water. In the lush late-morning sunlight, Semorrah looked like a fairy-tale city, all spiraling white stone and airy arches.

"I don't know when you'll see it again," Gabriel said to his companion, who had been silent for the whole thirty-minute boat ride. Hunched against the wind at the rear of the ferry, hands gripped around the railing, she watched the receding skyline with an unnerving intentness. "Say goodbye."

What she in fact said astonished him.

"O Yovah," she murmured, very soft and very fast, "call down thy curses on this place. Strike it with fire and thunderbolts—cover it with storm and flood. Bring down pestilence and plague—"

He grabbed her arm and shook her till the words stopped. "What are you doing? What are you saying?" he cried.

She wrenched her arm free. "It is the call to Yovah to beg for retribution," she said. Her voice was calm, but her eyes were fierce. "It is written in the Librera."

"I know what it is! You—no one has license to speak such a prayer!"

"It is in the Librera," she said again.

"And only angels have the authority to call down curses—and they never do! Not on Semorrah! Not anywhere on Samaria! Jovah most holy, do you know what you're asking for?"

"Yes. The destruction of this wretched city of the allali."

He stared at her. She was dead serious. "Do you hate it that much?" he asked, his voice quieter.

"It is a place where the wicked thrive and evil dances," she said. "And people I loved died so that those who live there could have servants and slaves—yes, and silk and jewels and spices and everything else that wealth buys. I hate it, and as long as I live I will ask Yovah to drive it into the sea. And if you were godly, as angels are supposed to be, you would stand beside me and make the same prayer."

She turned away from Gabriel and did not speak to him again. When the traveling coach was finally free of the ferry, she climbed inside and shut the door, not bothering to look in his direction. Gabriel took wing and spent the next few hours in lazy flight, sometimes over the carriages, sometimes ahead, sometimes ranging from side to side on the off chance that the scenery might offer him some entertainment. And although Rachel never peered through the windows, looking for him, his eyes were often turned earthward, following the progress of her coach, and he was more troubled by her words than he cared to admit.

They arrived at the Eyrie a little before sunset on the fourth day—or rather, they arrived at the base of the Velo Mountains, where the small city of Velora had sprung up in the past hundred years. Rachel's coach had stopped just outside the straggling city limits, and by the time Gabriel had circled in for a landing, she had climbed from the carriage and was gone. Gabriel directed the two drivers to the west edge of town, where there were systems in place for hauling heavy goods to the top of the mountain, and set off on foot through the city to find his bride.

If Semorrah was, as Rachel believed, a concentration of iniquity, Velora was a place of sun and symphony. Most of the houses, hotels and shops, bakeries, stables and schools had been built of the same rosy-beige stone that made the Eyrie a place of such warmth. Like the Semorrans, the Velorans were principally merchants, but since their whole aim was to enrich life for the angels and smooth the way for the petitioners who came looking for the angels, they dealt in items of ease and comfort. Because the angels were so near—and angels always wanted music—the city had become a place where music was revered. Large concert halls and tiny backroom taverns echoed continuously with the sounds of harps, flutes, reeds, viols, timpani and voices. Composers and singers renowned throughout Samaria made their homes in Velora, or journeyed there several times a year to meet their fellows. On every corner, street bands played lively melodies and young boys sang in heartbreaking soprano choirs. Blind old men plucked astonishing sounds from strings tied across broken wood boxes, and passersby whistled idly as they walked along.

Rachel had disappeared within the city in something less than five minutes, but Gabriel was not alarmed: Everyone who visited Velora went first to the central shopping district. He headed for the open-air bazaar and found her munching on a sweet pastry filled with cream and cherries.

"This is the Eyrie?" she asked him by way of greeting. "Why didn't you tell me it was so beautiful?"

"The Eyrie is beautiful, but this is not it," he replied. "This is the city that serves the Eyrie. The angels live above, in the mountains."

She glanced up with a flicker of apprehension, then continued eating her pastry. "This is like—it's a delightful place," she said. It was the first time he had seen her show enthusiasm. "It reminds me of Luminaux."

He was amused to hear her name the artisans' city. Situated on the southernmost edge of Bethel, Luminaux was considered the great intellectual and artistic mecca of Samaria; Velora could not even remotely compare with it. "And when were you in the Blue City?" he wanted to know.

"With the Edori. We passed through there almost every year to buy and sell—and look. Men of my clan used to love the silver flutes made by the Luminaux craftsmen. I have never heard any sound so sweet since I left the Edori."

"I have always wanted to learn the flute," Gabriel said.

"Can you play any instrument?" she asked.

He smiled. "I can sing," he said. He started strolling down the wide boulevard, and she fell in step beside him, dusting sugar from her hands.

"The Edori sing," she said. "I missed that sound when I came to Semorrah. There is no harmony at all in that city."

"Don't start on Semorrah again," he warned.

She smiled. "All right."

"And if you love singing—well, you will love the Eyrie, then. That is what angels do, you know."

She considered him. She seemed—at this moment, anyway—to be in a halfway friendly mood. He would have to remember to bring her to Velora often. "I have never had much traffic with angels," she said. "Every once in a while one would visit the Edori, but those times were rare. I lived in Semorrah before I realized that most people only pray to Yovah through the angels—or what angels were really here on Samaria *for*."

He could only stare at her blankly. To most citizens of Samaria, the angels were the highest court in the land, beings to be propitiated and approached with reverence. An angel's intervention could cause rain to fall on dry land, bring fire from the sky to wipe out a wicked man's house or a whole city, cause the heavens to drop down strange, wondrous seeds which took root quickly and could be harvested for the distillation of potent medicines. An angel could prepare Jovah for the advent of a dying soul, so that the god would have a place prepared for the one who crossed from this world to the next. An angel's word could cause the priests to cut a man's right arm off and so separate him from the Kiss of the God, so that Jovah would never, from that time forward, know that his child was still alive, and would not look for him, and would not welcome him when he crossed the broad river of death.

And she did not seem to have the faintest idea of why Jovah had brought angels to the earth.

"Have you heard angels singing?" he asked, more or less at random.

"Yes—once or twice—and the other day, at the wedding—" She stopped abruptly.

"Then you know how beautiful their music can be," he said smoothly. "I think you will like the Eyrie."

She glanced upward again, toward the tip of the mountain. "How do I get there?" she asked.

"I will carry you."

She put out her hands as if to ward him off. "No—I explained to you—"

"There is really no alternative," he said impatiently. "It is a flight of perhaps a minute. Close your eyes if you don't like it."

"I'll go up with the wagons," she said. "Surely you must have some way to take them up the mountain—"

"On an open platform, with a crane and a winch," he said brusquely. "I assure you, you would find that ride much more unpleasant."

"Then I'll climb up. There must be a path—"

"There is no path," he said. "Come. It will not be so bad."

They had reached the end of the avenue, virtually the edge of the city, and they were practically alone. Rachel glanced around quickly as if seeking shelter; her hands were still flung out before her.

"Gabriel—" she said.

He swung her into his arms and leapt into the air almost in the same motion. She shrieked, and for a moment twisted so violently that he had to tighten his hold considerably to keep her safe. But once they were well and truly off the ground, her resistance ceased; in fact, she grew so limp that he wondered if she had fainted. He glanced at her face and found it utterly colorless, her eyes shut tight, her lips moving in a soundless prayer. They were almost to the landing point of the Eyrie before he realized she was trembling uncontrollably.

He went to some trouble to come down smoothly, taking the shock of the landing on his flexed feet. She was motionless. He knelt, setting her carefully on the sun-warmed stone, supporting her head in his cupped hands.

"Rachel, we've arrived. Rachel, open your eyes—look at me. I'm sorry, but it's over, and you're here—you're fine."

She took a single ragged breath, then eased to her side, away from him. For a moment he thought she was going to vomit. Her shoulders shook and she covered her mouth with one hand. His sympathy was quickly turning to irritation; this seemed a little excessive even for someone with an irrational fear of heights. He stood.

"Let me know when you're feeling well enough to go inside and meet the rest of the angels," he said.

She rolled to her feet and launched herself at him. He was totally unprepared for her assault, and before he knew it, she was pummeling his chest and scratching savagely at his arms. "I hate you! You lied to me! I *told* you—oh, I hate you, I hate you, I *hate* you—"

The rest of her tirade was incoherent. Appalled, Gabriel snatched both her arms and forced her away from him. This only enraged her further; she kicked and screamed at him, writhing in his hold like a demon seeking to break an enchantment. He had never seen anyone in the grip of hysteria before, but instinct and anger supplied him with the antidote. Transferring both her wrists to one of his hands, he slapped her full across the face. Her screaming ceased; she turned to stone. Across the thicket of their interlaced arms, she stared at him, her eyes still wild.

"You hurt me," she whispered.

"I'm sorry," he said, though he knew his voice did not sound sorry. "You must calm down."

Her breath shuddered into her body. He thought she would speak again, renew her accusations. But words would not come to her. Staring at him, she shook her head helplessly and slowly began to cry, then collapsed to her knees, sobbing.

He dropped her hands and gazed down at her with dismay. He could not think of what to do or say. He had forgotten that help might be available from other quarters, so it was with great surprise that he heard a woman's voice address him from behind.

"Gabriel." Turning, he saw a tall, slim woman separate herself from the scarlet shadows thrown by the sunset against the Eyrie walls. Hannah, by Jovah's great mercy. "I thought you would arrive today," she said. "Is that Rachel?"

"As you see," he answered bleakly.

She stepped unhurriedly across the smooth stone and crouched beside the weeping girl, putting her arms around the shaking shoulders. "Rachel," she murmured in that voice which had soothed hundreds of distraught women and crying children. "Rachel, it's all right."

"Good. You deal with her," Gabriel said, turning on his heel and stalking toward the entryway. "Because I can't."

CHAPTER FIVE

So it had not been an auspicious beginning to her new life, Rachel thought the next morning. In fact, it could hardly have been worse. Not overjoyed to begin with at the thought of making her his angelica, Gabriel must now be wishing he could shatter the Kiss in her arm and tell Yovah to look around for a second choice. It was a prayer she planned to make herself as soon as she could pull herself together.

She had awakened early, keeping her eyes tightly shut as was her custom, briefly closing her mind against the sure knowledge that something awful had happened. But it was impossible to ignore the singing, the sweet voices rising and falling in perfect harmony. She imagined that in no other place in the world did one wake up to a sound like that.

She got out of bed to take a closer look at the room she'd been brought to the night before. Hannah had led her here and taken her directly to the bed.

"I think you need sleep," the woman had said in a quiet voice. "I will come back to you in the morning, and we'll sort everything out."

Rachel had clutched her arm. "What is that sound?"

"What sound?"

"The—those voices."

"Ah. Angels singing. At the Eyrie, there is always music. I believe, if you listen to it, it will soothe you and you will fall asleep. Sleep is what you need."

And she had slept immediately, lulled by those voices, or Hannah's voice, or so completely drained by her disgraceful emotional display that she had no energy left for curiosity. This morning was a different matter. She felt rested, ravenous and inquisitive.

The stone floor was icy beneath her bare feet; in fact, the whole room was chilly for a woman used to the humid river breezes of Semorrah. Rachel slipped her feet into the shoes she had worn the day before, wrapped herself in a blanket stripped from the bed, and strolled around the chamber.

Stone—everything was stone. Even in Semorrah there had been wood and iron and cast plaster inside the stone houses. Here, everything was rock—the walls, the floors, the ceilings. It was like being in a giant cave. Her Edori soul shuddered at the thought of being shut up inside a mountain, a maze of tunnels between her chamber and an exit. No doubt she was in one of the more desirable rooms, for it was fitted with a window to let in the sun— but she did not have the courage to go look at that view. She remembered all too well the flight up here last evening. Gazing out that window would bring on nausea and faintness.

Given that it was essentially a cave with a window, it was rather a pretty room. Across one long wall hung a gorgeous tapestry, into which tiny figures had been woven in patterns of gold and purple and green. Tales from the Librera, no doubt; among the embroidered mortal forms she spotted a number of angelic figures. In the middle of the room, a small table, a stool and cushions were grouped together as if inviting people to sit. Her own bundles—all her gifts from Jethro—were piled in a corner, awaiting disposal in various chests and trunks. There was no fireplace, but she felt heated air circulating in the room (not enough, in her opinion), and she suspected that it was somehow being forced through an ornamental grate at the foot of her bed.

And there was, faintly, the splash of water from not far away. Rachel followed the sound through a narrow archway and gave a low cry of admiration at what she saw. Steaming water fell from a pipe attached to the ceiling and into a marble pool. A small opening in the bottom of the pool drained the water away at the same rate at which it fell. Across the room, there was another arrangement of rivulet and drain, but this water fell more heavily and appeared to be cold. Hot water for bathing, cold water for drinking, all ceaselessly flowing, as constant as the angels' singing.

Even in Lord Jethro's house, where a viaduct ran from the city well, water had to be hauled upstairs by hand and laboriously heated. This room, as a slave girl well knew, was a luxury of the highest order.

She dropped her blanket, pulled off her clothes, and stepped into the hot stream of water. Luxury of luxuries; she would be a slave for ten years just for this experience. A cake of flaky soap had been placed at the side of the pool. Scented with herbs and honey, it left even her rough skin feeling smooth. She used half of it to wash her hair, but felt no need to hoard. A place that could offer a constant stream of heated water must be able to provide extra soap at any time a guest might wish it.

Rachel's eyes, which she had shut as she turned her face up into the falling water, opened in dismay. A guest. Hardly. She was a tenant now, a lifelong dweller. She was, or was soon to be, angelica, wife to the Archangel, and presumably the most important woman in this hold. The thought made her feel even more helpless.

She stepped from the water, wrapped herself in a towel and returned to the main chamber. Among the gifts from Jethro were numerous boxes of clothes. Surely something would fit.

She had barely finished dressing when a small chime sounded from the direction of the door. Rachel froze, her hands on the lacings of her shoes, and waited for something to happen. In a few moments, the chime rang again, and was quickly followed by a woman's voice.

"Rachel. It's Hannah. Are you awake?"

"Yes. Come in."

Hannah had brought food, and she waited in silence while Rachel devoured the meal. She had missed dinner the night before, and in any case, she was always hungry. Or always during the last five years. It had not been so before.

She looked up to find Hannah watching her inscrutably. "It's very good," Rachel said, setting down the last empty dish. "Thank you."

"Are you feeling better this morning? More rested?"

"Yes, I think so. Thank you."

"That's a very pretty dress you're wearing."

Rachel glanced down at it a little more critically. She had chosen this dress because it was of heavy wool and looked warm. But it *was* pretty, a deep-dyed blue with a narrow waist, full skirt and tapered sleeves. She tugged the cuffs down to cover her wrists. "A guilt gift from Lord Jethro," she said with some of her usual spirit.

Hannah smiled. "It is the irony of the century that Gabriel found you in Lord Jethro's house."

"Because I was a slave there, you mean?"

Hannah's delicate brows rose. "Because he did not want to go there. Because he does not like Jethro, or the city merchants. If he could have, he would have sent Nathan in his place. But Nathan would not have been able to find you. Therefore, it was the god's wish that Gabriel go."

"I am not sure that Yovah concerns himself so closely in mortals' lives," Rachel said dryly.

"He has in yours."

"So it seems."

Hannah smiled again. "Come. If you are done, it is time I took you around the Eyrie to show you how it is built, and to introduce you to some people."

Rachel came to her feet, prickling with apprehension. "How many people?"

"How many live here? About a hundred and fifty."

"A hundred and fifty angels?"

"No, there are only fifty angels. The others are mortals—husbands and wives of the angels, their children and those who work for the angels—cooks, launderers, repairmen, chatelaines—"

"And slaves?"

Hannah, who had started toward the door, turned back to stare at Rachel. "No slaves," she said quietly. "Why do you ask?"

"There are slaves at Windy Point," Rachel said. "Why should there not be slaves here?"

Hannah took a step closer. "What makes you think there are slaves at Windy Point?" she asked.

Rachel shrugged. "So I was always told. There are slaves everywhere else."

"Not at the Eyrie. Neither Gabriel's father nor Gabriel has ever sanctioned the institution of slavery—anywhere. Gabriel has been most outspoken against it, in fact."

"And yet, there are slaves. Every day Edori are taken prisoner—"

"And Raphael is the Archangel. Now. Perhaps when Gabriel

ascends to this rank at the Gloria, he will be able to change things."

Rachel moved slowly across the floor toward Hannah. "Gabriel," she said. "I know nothing about him at all."

Hannah leaned against the door. She was an older woman, in her mid-fifties, Rachel guessed; her black hair was streaked with white and pulled into a knot at the back of her head. She had thin, patrician features and would not have looked out of place sitting across from Lord Jethro at a Semorran banquet.

"Gabriel will be thirty years old this summer," Hannah said. "The youngest age at which an angel has ever ascended to the rank of Archangel. Jovah chose him when he was fifteen, so he has known for half his life what honor awaited him. It is an honor he takes very seriously—he takes most things seriously. He can be difficult. He can be very sure of himself, and so other people's opinions do not always matter to him. He thinks it is a very easy matter to separate right from wrong, good from bad, so subtleties often elude him. He is not patient. But he is—he is never less than committed to making things right. Everything he does is with the goal of bringing goodness to the world. I can't explain what I mean. There is no evil in him. That is a rare thing to say about anyone, even an angel."

"You sound as though you love him," Rachel said.

"I loved his father."

Rachel's eyes narrowed; surely she would not have spoken of Gabriel in those terms if he was her son. Hannah smiled, reading the question.

"Gabriel was born to the angel Jeremiah, who led the host here for forty years. I was Jeremiah's second wife."

"And Jeremiah?"

"Dead now for five years. Gabriel has led the host since then."

Five years ago. Yovah had certainly made life interesting at that time for both the Archangel-elect and his angelica. No wonder Gabriel had not rushed out looking for a bride.

"And when is it to happen?" Rachel asked, following her own thoughts.

"When is what to happen?"

"The ceremony. The—the wedding. Between Gabriel and myself."

"Soon, I would think. But there are preparations to be made. Angels from the other hosts must be invited, and the oracles, and some others. It is not a simple event. You and Gabriel must discuss it when he returns."

"When he *returns*?"

Hannah nodded. "He left this morning for Luminaux. A messenger had been awaiting him in Velora for more than a week. He will not be back for several days."

Rachel stared at Hannah, trying to conceal her reaction. Was it irrational to feel fury that she had been abandoned during her first day in a strange place by the one person she knew, and who had brought her here against her will? Considering that she did not even like the man who had carried her here and that he must, by now, have come to hate her? Still, fury was what she felt. One more item she was adding to the list of things for which she would never forgive the angel.

Not expecting to, Rachel fell in love with the Eyrie.

But it was such a lovely place, it would have been hard not to. Everywhere—rooms, corridors, great halls, small kitchens, floors, ceilings, walls—they were surrounded by that lustrous rosy rock, luminous as quartz in some areas, dense as granite elsewhere, but always faintly glowing, rich to the eye, sleek to the touch. Rachel had been born to farmers and raised among Edori; she had grown up among green things, sensitive to the demands and possibilities of the soil. She had hated white Semorrah, a cool alabaster prison—but the Eyrie, though it was also a place of stone, was beautiful to her.

Or perhaps it was the singing. She was never unaware of it as she and Hannah inspected rooms and climbed stairs and paused for introductions to the jumble of people who lived there. Rising and falling, the voices were always allied in perfect harmony, even as the voices changed; two women's voices held a double note on a high, ecstatic tritone, and two men sang the next words in descending thirds, and still the effect was the same. *Live in harmony.* There were many messages in the Librera, but that was the central one. *Live in harmony.* The Edori had taken that to mean "Live in harmony with the earth, with the growing things and the wild things and the men and women of your own people." The angels had settled on a more literal translation.

Having taken Rachel around the three separate levels of the

complex, Hannah now led her outside. After the muted illumination of the tunnels, Rachel was hampered for a moment by bright sunlight. When her eyes adjusted, she looked around with interest. They had stepped onto a wide, flat plateau, surrounded on all sides by the three terraces of the Eyrie.

"This is the place where we have games and celebrations," Hannah told her. "We hold informal sings here—nothing like the Gloria, but a way of practicing for the Gloria. We have meetings here, if there are things everyone should hear, for it is the only place all hundred and fifty can gather. Some angels choose to alight here, instead of at the landing rock above, merely because it is a quicker way to the kitchens."

"You have meetings here?" Rachel said. "Isn't it cold?" It was late autumn, and she was freezing.

Hannah smiled. "Not for angels. They are never cold. In the summertime, and even in the spring, it is a delightful place if the sun has warmed it all day."

"Well, it's nearly winter now," Rachel said, hugging herself for warmth.

"During winter there is generally a central fire, and perimeter fires all along the edges. See where the braziers are set up? I prefer the winter sings, actually, because I like to exist by firelight."

"You are a Manadavvi," Rachel said. "How did you come to be here?"

Hannah was silent a moment. She looked surprised and, unexpectedly, sad. "How did you know that?"

Rachel unwrapped one arm and raised it in a gesture of inevitability. "I was Edori. I traveled through Gaza and saw the great homes of the Manadavvi. One of your houses would have made the whole city of Semorrah look small."

Hannah turned away. "That was a long time ago."

But Rachel felt a certain kindred interest in the story of anyone else who had been brought, willy-nilly, to the high reaches of the Eyrie. "How did you come to be here?" she asked again.

"My father was a Manadavvi landowner of some importance," Hannah replied. "When I was a girl, my sister married; and angels from the three realms attended. One of them was Jeremiah."

"And he brought you back with him? Did you want to come?"

Hannah was recounting the tale slowly, as if she did not want to tell it at all. "I was nineteen. He was nearly thirty. He already had a wife, although she had not yet borne him children."

Rachel frowned. "Yes? And? He fell in love with you?"

"He—the Kiss on his arm leapt with light the first time he saw me. My own Kiss was like a live brand burning against my arm. I could not sleep for pain the whole time he was in the house. I had been told," she said a little more rapidly, "that this was how Jovah allows true lovers to know one another. Samaria is wide and filled with many people. Those who are meant to be together often do not find each other, or recognize each other when they come face to face, and so Jovah has devised this system for revelation. I did not really believe it," she added with a faint smile, "because it had never happened to anyone I knew. It is a fable young girls tell each other when they dream of the men they will marry. I did not believe it would ever happen to me."

Rachel felt heat rising in her cheeks as the mystery of her own experience was now explained to her. The Edori for the most part were not dedicated, so this had not been a story told among the tribes. "So you returned to the Eyrie with him."

Hannah shook her head. "He had a wife," she said. "I did not go."

"But—" Rachel frowned. "You go where your heart leads you," she said. "And the heart changes. There is no disgrace or dishonor in that."

Hannah gave her a quick, painful smile. "Is that the Edori way? I have heard you do not believe in marriage."

"The Edori do not believe in bindings of any kind," Rachel said. "The Edori know that the only permanence is Yovah. It is better to bow to the dictates of the wind than to try to chase or chain it."

"And the Manadavvi believe that a promise once given is sacred, and that to come between a man and his wife is a crime exceeded only by taking another man's life. I did not go with him."

"But—" Rachel said again. She was trying to remember something Gabriel had said, which she had been too angry to consider carefully at the time. "Among angels—what do the vows of marriage mean?"

"The angels tend to be more flexible," Hannah said, and her voice was a little dry. "Some do not marry at all, though they have lovers and they bear children. Some marry, and have lovers anyway. It is not encouraged, exactly, but it is not forbidden. After all, it is desirable that they have children. So if their hearts take them to more than one lover, Jovah is pleased."

Rachel was cold, and she wanted to go inside, but she also wanted to follow this conversation to its conclusion. She tightened her arms around her body and kept asking questions. "Why is it desirable for angels to have children?"

"So there will be more angels, of course. Only an angel can sire—or bear—another angel. And angels are only born from a mix of divine and mortal blood—two angels together produce monsters, demons, lucifers. And not every union of angel and mortal produces more angels, and there is no way to know until the child is born. And even if an angel and a mortal have one child who is angelic, the next child may be mortal. There is no way to know. And so angels love where they will, and Jovah permits it, even though to the Manadavvi such license appears to be a crime."

"And so Jeremiah wanted you to return with him, but you wouldn't. But then his wife died, and you came to the Eyrie. Is that how it went?"

"More or less."

"And you loved him."

"Oh yes, I loved him."

Rachel studied her. "But he did not make you happy."

Hannah started. "I miss him."

Rachel shook her head. "You were sad before he died."

Hannah gave a light laugh. "The Manadavvi are a stern people. It is just my habitual expression. You must be cold. Let's go back inside."

Unwillingly, Rachel followed her back into the labyrinth. Surely there was more to that story than she had been told—at a guess, Jeremiah's fickle attention had wandered again, and no doubt that was a tale Hannah would never relate to her. Still, Rachel had acquired some useful information, some of which she could turn to good account. Angels loved where they would and no one minded. She had not loved anyone for a long time. If she was not required to love the man she was required to marry, it might not be so bad after all.

Another thing had been made clear to her during this tour of the Eyrie. She was expected to sing—at Gabriel's side at the Gloria and any time she might be moved to beforehand. She felt the old defiant stubbornness rising, pouring through her bones like so much wax into a mold. And if she didn't care to sing—?

Before their interesting detour to the meeting plateau, they had come to a hallway buried deep in the lower level of the Eyrie. The top level, Hannah had explained, comprised the living quarters. The middle level was made up of kitchens, dining areas and common rooms. The bottom level was given over to storage, schoolrooms and music. Mostly music.

Perhaps twenty small rooms opened off either side of one central corridor. Each room was small, but high-ceilinged and exactly proportioned. Once the door was closed, the acoustics became perfect; even a whisper resonated from side to side with undiminished clarity.

"Recital chambers," Hannah told Rachel as they entered one of the rooms. "For anyone who wants to practice singing. They are completely private, and soundproof. Here the angels spend much of their time before the Gloria. Whenever one is available, you are welcome to use it."

Rachel crossed the room slowly and listened to the *shush-shush* of her gown echo to the ceiling and back. "And no one can hear you unless they're in the room with you?"

Hannah smiled. "No one. So your mistakes and your wrong notes are not witnessed by anyone."

"How long can you stay in one of these chambers?"

"As long as you like. Whoever arrives first has possession." Hannah crossed to a glass and metal plate built into the far wall. "Look. Some people think this is the best part of the recital chambers."

Rachel followed her, to be mystified by an arrangement of steel knobs and eerie, glowing lights. "What is this?"

"It is something no one truly understands," said Hannah. "It is music sung by the dead."

Rachel started back, unnerved, but Hannah motioned her forward again. "No, it is not the dead singing. It is— To teach us certain songs, hundreds of years ago, Jovah provided a way for us to forever capture the sounds of the first angels singing. But their voices can only be heard on these machines, in these chambers—and in chambers like them at Monteverde and Windy Point. There are hundreds and hundreds of pieces here, all the great works that we still sing at the Glorias today. Of course, there has been much beautiful music composed since then, and we can preserve it in written form, but we have no way of recording it the way these songs have been recorded. Would you like to hear one?"

"Yes," Rachel breathed.

Hannah touched an illuminated dial. "My favorite," she said. "It is called the 'Ave Jehovah.' "

"Yovah?"

"Jehovah," Hannah said again. "Perhaps a variation on the pronunciation? You yourself say the god's name differently than I do."

"The Edori call him Yovah," Rachel said. "So that is how I say it."

"Listen," Hannah said, and touched the dial again.

Instantly the chamber was filled with the liquid sounds of a coloratura soprano effortlessly caressing trills up and down the scale. Rachel threw her head back and closed her eyes. The music sifted into her brain, it wrapped itself around her head like a scarf bedecked with sequins. It crowded out thought and took the place of emotion. She had never heard such a beautiful voice in her life.

When it ended, she opened her eyes and looked at Hannah in wonder. The older woman was smiling. "You liked that," she said. Rachel could only nod. "That was Hagar, the first angelica. Hers was a voice that"—Hannah shrugged—"we will never hear the likes of again."

"Are there other—recordings? By Hagar?"

"Oh, yes. Maybe fifty. Maybe not quite so many. Most of them are part of choral arrangements, you know, and duets. Some of her pieces are truly impossible for anyone else to sing, but her recordings of the classics are probably the ones you should study the most."

"I should study the most? Why? I just want to listen to them."

Hannah regarded her with a somewhat troubled expression. "How much do you know about what the angelica does?" she asked.

Rachel felt the scowl rise, and tried to discipline it. "Almost nothing. I know I'm supposed to be there at the Gloria—"

"You're supposed to sing at the Gloria," Hannah corrected. "In fact, you lead the Gloria—that is, you are the first to sing. You choose the music. Do you know nothing about Gloria music?" Rachel shook her head. Hannah sighed.

"There are perhaps a hundred Gloria masses—and all the angels know all the masses by heart. Each one opens with a solo by the angelica—or the angelico, if the Archangel is a woman—and is immediately followed by a duet with the Archangel. Then come the small chorales, in which the angels sing. Then more solos, more duets; then large chorales sung by all the mortals who have been brought to the Plain of Sharon for the event."

"And do all the mortals know these hundred masses, too?" Rachel demanded. She was feeling sick with apprehension at the vision conjured up. How could she learn a hundred masses in five months? How could she learn one?

"The parts for the large choirs are all the same, from mass to mass," Hannah said, smiling. "It is easier that way for people who are not accustomed to singing."

"So which mass do I choose?"

"That is up to you. Traditionally, the angelica knows there is some trouble to be addressed in the realm—perhaps there has been famine, or plague, or violence against one people by another . . ." Hannah's voice trailed off as she saw an ironic expression cross Rachel's face. "There are masses that have different moods, that introduce different prayers. There are masses that are simply prayers to Jovah for kindness in the coming year, and masses that thank him for past months of bounty. It is clear to the angelica by the time of the Gloria which piece to choose."

"Then no one advises me at all?"

Hannah made an ambiguous gesture with her hands. "According to tradition, you do not even tell the Archangel which mass you will sing. He learns it as everyone else learns it, standing beside you on the Plain of Sharon. But that is a tradition often dispensed with these days, and in your case, I would think you and Gabriel might want to rehearse together as often as possible. Since you have never had a chance to hear each other sing."

Rachel was silent a moment. "I heard him sing," she said. "At the wedding. There were six voices, but—I knew which one was his."

"Some say, when he was young, Raphael's voice rivaled that of Uriel, the first Archangel," Hannah said. "And he does sing with great beauty. But Gabriel—he could melt the mountain with his voice. He could bring Jovah to earth, with his voice. What could he pray for, that Jovah would not grant? There is nothing."

Rachel gave her a quick, twisted smile. "He could pray for an angelica he did not dislike. Would that prayer be answered?"

Hannah frowned at her. "Don't talk that way. Jovah brought you to Gabriel for a purpose. It is right that you be together, though neither of you may recognize it now."

"And is Yovah never wrong?" Rachel asked, her voice sarcastic. Hannah remained serene.

"He has a purpose for everything," the older woman said, and opened the door and ushered Rachel out.

Only three of the people Rachel met during their tour of the Eyrie made an immediate impact on her, though she was sure she had made an unfavorable impression on most of the angels and mortals to whom she was introduced. Well, she couldn't help it. She could not feign a gladness and a graciousness she did not feel, so all these people who were eager to exclaim over the new angelica were treated to her cool stare, her short greeting and her brusque manner. She saw a few raised eyebrows on the human faces, some supercilious expressions on the angel faces, and she did not care.

"Jovah knew what he did that time," she heard one angel remark to another after she and Hannah could have been considered to be out of earshot. "She's as bad as Gabriel himself." Which was not a remark likely to improve Rachel's attitude.

The first person to whom she felt any reaction at all was a young woman about her own age, who was so beautiful that Rachel could not stop staring at her the whole time they talked. This despite the fact that she instantly and comprehensively disliked the young lady, introduced by Hannah as Judith.

"I'm so glad Gabriel has finally found you," Judith said, smiling up at Rachel. Small and dainty, Judith had doll-like features, a heart-shaped face, curly black hair, gray eyes, and a sweet smile. "I worried about him so much these past few months—he had so much on his mind already, and then he couldn't find you. I hope—I hope you realize how special Gabriel is. There's just nothing I wouldn't do for him."

"Judith was born here at the Eyrie," Hannah told Rachel in a colorless voice. "Her mother is an angel. Judith and Gabriel were brought up almost like brother and sister."

"Well, hardly that!" Judith said, laughing, but Rachel sensed she was not pleased. "We're close, but I never thought of him as a brother."

"Judith," Hannah said repressively. Judith gave her a pretty pout, then smiled again at Rachel.

"It's just that I'm not used to the idea of Gabriel being married."

"I certainly wouldn't want you to change your relationship with him because of me," Rachel said flatly. "Don't think of me at all."

A quick frown pulled down Judith's delicate brows and was instantly erased. She gave a soft laugh that did not, to Rachel, sound sincere. "Oh, don't be silly. I'm sure you'll be a wonderful wife. Jovah picked you, after all."

"Yes, Yovah picked me, not Gabriel," Rachel agreed. "Gabriel got stuck."

Now Hannah spoke Rachel's name in that reproving voice. Judith gave her another false smile.

"Well, I do hope you'll try to be friends with Gabriel—and friends with his friends," she said in a honeyed voice.

"Of course I'll try," Rachel said, accenting the last word very slightly. Hannah motioned her forward down the corridor.

"Come, now. There's more to see." And so they passed beyond the beautiful Judith before any more pleasantries could be exchanged. Rachel left her sarcastic comments unsaid. She did not think Hannah cared much for Judith, either.

The second person to whom Rachel spoke more than mere civilities was the head cook in the great kitchen. "You're the one who made my breakfast this morning?" she asked directly. "Where did you learn to cook Edori food so well?"

The cook, a middle-aged woman whose face was permanently red from the heat of the ovens, beamed in response to Rachel's compliment. "Ah, I spent a few summers in Luminaux when the Tigrera clan used to camp nearby, and I knew a boy and, well, his mother showed me some of her recipes." She had the pleasant lilting speech of the Bethel lowlander. "And I thought, after five years working like a dog in Semorrah, you'd probably be liking some of the good food again."

Hannah had stiffened at the oblique reference to servitude, but Rachel laughed. "But I'm sure I could teach you a dish or two to please a Semorran lord," she said. "I spent plenty of time in the kitchens, I can tell you. If you ever need an extra hand to peel or stir, let me know."

"That I will, angela, that I will."

It did not take Rachel long to figure out that there was a polite but definite caste system within the Eyrie, and that angels rose to the top while servants sank to the bottom. Natural perversity, therefore—and a certain fellow feeling—led her to be extremely friendly to all the cooks, launderers, seamstresses and cleaning maids they encountered, while she maintained her coolness to the angels and less workaday mortals. Hannah was wise enough not to criticize or even comment.

Only once did she venture an opinion to Rachel, even before she opened the door to a well-lit room in the middle level. "I think you'll like Matthew," Hannah said, a half-smile on her lips. "He is our leather worker. He makes most of the flying clothes for the angels—and bags and satchels and shoes and anything else we find a need for. He is a craftsman of a high order—and a tenor with a truly fine voice."

"Is he a Luminauzi?" Rachel asked.

"No," said Hannah, opening the door.

He was an Edori. He was bent over a low wooden bench, his back to the door, but there was no mistaking that silky black hair or the redwood color of his bare arms. The sound of voices at the door turned him around, a smile already on his face. Oh, how well Rachel knew that Edori welcome, given to everyone, proven friend or not. How had it come to be replaced with such bitterness in her own heart?

"Matthew. I've brought someone for you to meet," Hannah said.

But he had heard the Eyrie gossip; he knew who the new angelica was and where she had come from.

"*Raheli, sia a Manderra, ve a Edori,*" he said, holding his hands out to her. "*Gealamin, moschieaven.*" Rachel, daughter to the Manderra of the Edori people. Good welcome to you, rest from your travels. "So all the scattered are not dead. Yovah is good."

She answered him in the same tongue, asking after his clan affiliations. "But how does an Edori come to be in an angel's hold?" she demanded next, still speaking the nomads' language.

He released her hands to gesture with his own, and gave her

a smile. "You know the Edori are wanderers," he said. "I wandered too far into the Velo Mountains one day. And then I stayed."

"How long?"

"Going on fifteen years now."

"Fifteen years! Penned up in a cave miles above the plain!"

He laughed. "I leave from time to time. I have been to most of the Gatherings of the past fifteen years. Or—" He shrugged. "When I get the urge to roam, I leave. But I always come back. This is my home. I am getting old and it is a nice thing to be settled."

"And how do you leave?" Rachel wanted to know. "There is no way out."

"The angels are very obliging. They take me down to Velora and pick me up again when I want to return. It is an easy thing to come and go."

Rachel shook her head. "Not for me. I have—" It was a moment before she could recall the word from the expressive Edori tongue, but of course the Edori had a word for everything. "Height-sickness," she said at last. "I cannot be up and look down."

He nodded. "There was a woman from our clan who had the height-sickness. For that reason, we did not travel among the mountains until she died . . . But surely there must be a way to get you down from the mountain. If not in an angel's arms—"

"It hardly matters," Rachel said tightly. "I am here, and here is where Yovah wants me. Perhaps I will never leave this mountain again."

Matthew looked troubled. Hannah, who had politely forborne to look irritated when they began conversing in a language strange to her, laid her hand upon Rachel's arm. "You can return later to talk to Matthew," she said. "There is more of the Eyrie I would like you to see today."

So she bid farewell to the Edori and promised to return when she was able. It did not take any prescience to guess that Matthew's workshop would become a haven for her in the coming months, and all three of them knew it without the words being spoken.

CHAPTER SIX

Gabriel's trip to Luminaux had not proceeded exactly as he had foreseen.

To begin with, he did not go to Luminaux at all. True, the envoy awaiting him in Velora was from the Blue City, but he came, he explained, as an intermediary and not as a petitioner.

It was early in the morning after the disastrous arrival at the Eyrie with his furious angelica in tow, and Gabriel had not slept well. Consequently, he at first blamed his incomprehension on his exhaustion.

"Excuse me," he said to the small round man who had introduced himself as John. "Did you just say that you've come to ask me to make a weather intercession?"

"Pray for rain, yes," John said, nodding.

"For the farmers south of the Heldoras?"

"That's right."

"But that's in Jordana."

"True," John said, as if reluctantly conceding a point. "But they have had no rain for three months, and their plight becomes desperate."

"I don't quarrel with the situation. Clearly, they need an angel's attention. But shouldn't you—shouldn't *they*—be traveling to Windy Point to ask Raphael for intercession?"

John studied the level of the liquid in the glass of water he was sipping. "Ah," he said. "Well, perhaps."

Gabriel waited.

John stirred. His body was a shape rounder than the wooden seat was used to accommodating. "In fact, Raphael has been asked for assistance. In the past."

Gabriel felt his body narrow as his bones infinitesimally contracted. A whisper of premonition skittered past his ears. "What do you mean?" he asked slowly.

"Last year, same problem. Winter drought. The Archangel was asked for assistance. And the year before. And the year before that. Each time he said that the dry weather was Jovah's plan—that Jovah would send the rain when he chose. And each year," John went on, "the rain did come. But too late in the season to save the harvests. There have been enough crops to subsist on, but nothing left over to sell—and these farmers live on the produce they can barter. And the river has grown shallower every year. And some of the wells have dried up. If they do not get rain this year, it will be a catastrophe. They will have to give up their homes—their lives. They might as well emigrate to Breven and sell themselves as slaves."

Gabriel frowned at the reference to the Jansai, but he was so disturbed by the central problem that he didn't bother to speak a reprimand. "Has Raphael been there to view the danger for himself?"

"He has not."

"So he told you—"

"He did not tell *me*," John corrected. "He told the petitioners from the farm villages, who went three times to ask him for intercession."

"And how is it you have gotten involved in this problem?"

John smiled. "At Luminaux, we trade with everyone. My father and I have bought from these farmers for generations. Since some of the village elders knew me, they brought their problem to me—"

"And why did they not come to me directly?"

"They thought a man of Bethel should be the one to approach the angels of the Eyrie."

Gabriel nodded. That, at least, had been diplomatic. But the request itself—

"It is, as far as I know, unprecedented," he said, thinking aloud. "True, mortals may ask a favor of any angel who happens to be passing through their realm. But to seek out an angel from another hold . . ."

"Desperate times," John said mildly. "You are held to be an arbiter of great fairness. I thought you would at least give me a hearing."

"And if I refuse you, I suppose you will travel on to Monteverde?"

John looked grave. "I think, by the time I arrived in Monteverde, the situation would be beyond the power of the angel Ariel to repair. You are indeed the last hope my friends have."

Raphael would be furious—if, indeed, he ever found out. If John was speaking the truth, it seemed the Archangel spent little time overseeing his less glamorous and less wealthy constituents. Then again, Raphael *was* Archangel; perhaps the duties were far more onerous than Gabriel imagined, and it was impossible for him to attend to as many small details as he would like. Something Gabriel would find out soon enough for himself . . .

Raphael's wrath was not something he greatly feared—in fact, he was sure he could generate a little anger in return if the situation arose. How could the Archangel—any angel—allow his people to suffer so, when their plight was so easily remedied? It was beyond Gabriel's understanding.

"I'll go," he said. "But if I find that the situation has been misrepresented to me—"

"Not at all!"

"I will be greatly displeased. And I will remember it."

"You will find everything as I told you. I thank you. My friends will fall to their knees to bless you. I hope you will go as soon as possible—"

"I will leave now. Give me the map, and I will go from here."

It had taken a very long day to angle southeast across Bethel, cross the Galilee at its widest point and locate the dry plains spread out south of the Heldora Mountains. It was clear before Gabriel had even reached his destination that John had spoken only the truth. Even the uncultivated plains west of the Heldoras were brown with more than winter's habitual blight. Dry pools and unfed stream tracks pocked the terrain, clearly visible from flying height. In a year or two, if present weather patterns continued, the whole region could parch to dust and blow away.

He located the cluster of villages without difficulty, and spiraled in for a landing at the cobblestoned center of the largest one. At the appearance of the second-most famous living angel,

the townspeople seemed equally divided between awe and jubi-
lation. Some gaped at him from behind drawn curtains while others came rushing forward to personally and vehemently thank him
for coming.

Like all angels, Gabriel disliked being touched, particularly
by strangers and particularly on his sleek, sensitive wings. He took
a haughty stance to fend off the more enthusiastic greeters, since
physical force clearly would not do. The strategy worked, as it
usually did. His admirers kept their distance, still beaming at him.

"I was to ask for Levi Miller," Gabriel said, searching the
crowd for anyone who appeared to be a leader. "Is he here? Can
he be fetched?"

Levi was even then arriving on the run. Drought or no
drought, he had managed to eat well in the past three years, and
the sprint had made him breathless. "Good angelo," he wheezed,
arriving at Gabriel's side. "I cannot tell you how pleased I am
that you have come to us—"

"I think I understand the situation," Gabriel said, cutting him
off. "I will sing for you tomorrow morning, and you should have
rain by nightfall. Tell me please how the rain usually falls here,
from what direction the winds come, how many days it falls, what
months are wet and what months are dry . . ."

Levi turned to the crowd and shouted out two names; two
men detached themselves from the group and hurried forward.
"We must talk weather with the angelo," he said to them. "Back
to my house. My wife will cook for us."

So the men retired with the angel to Levi's kitchen to discuss
precipitation, cloud formation, the ideal annual ratio of sunshine
to rain. This far south, snow was almost unheard of, but winter
was traditionally the rainy season. Spring was damp, summer was
dry, the rains came intermittently again in autumn . . .

"Very well," Gabriel said when he had heard enough. "I
know what I must ask of Jovah tomorrow."

He accepted Levi's offer of a bed for the night, resigned in
advance to the usual discomfort of mortals' homes: excessive heat,
furniture that seemed specifically designed to entangle his folded
wings, the oppressive silence unbroken by harmonic background
singing. This night another unexpected, unwelcome distraction
kept him awake: the memory of stalking away from the sobbing
woman he had brought to the Eyrie to be his angelica.

True, Hannah had been there and Hannah was better qualified to calm her down than he was. But he should not have abandoned Rachel so abruptly. Bundle of hair and defiance that she was, she was still lost and alone in a strange place, and she was, after all, his responsibility. But to have attacked him that way—! Wilder than a marauding Jansai. How had she come through five years of slavery so unregenerate? And what was he supposed to do with her next?

The questions troubled him as he drifted off to sleep. No answers came to him in his dreams.

He rose early, ate the good breakfast prepared by Levi's wife, then went outside to take wing. He ascended effortlessly into the opalescent whiteness of the cloudless morning sky. Higher and higher, aiming straight for the zenith of the heavens, so high that even to his superheated blood the air seemed cool; so high that beyond the blank blueness of the sky he could sense an eternal, waiting night. Jovah could hear a prayer whispered upon the earth, but a prayer shouted from the heavens reached his ear faster. The angels had always believed that the nearer they were to their god, the better he would listen.

Aloft in the icy air, the Heldoras a flattened beige zigzag beneath him, Gabriel flung his arms wide and began to sing. He could hear every sound, this high up: the rhythmic stroking of his great wings, the brief catch and intake of his own breath, the faint sluicing of blood through the canals of his ears. But the sounds did not carry, had no resonance, left no echoes. The thin dark air was a vacuum. It sucked up even the sound of his own voice rising from his chest, carrying it in an almost discernible arc upward, a golden path of notes spinning from his mouth through the black layer of the firmament to Jovah's ear.

It was the song for winter rain coming from the west. There were songs for summer rain, and songs to stop rain, and songs for the rain that only comes at night. Gabriel knew them all, the pleas for winds from the south and thermal currents and moisture cooled to a precise degree. The words, prescribed in some archaic formula centuries ago and handed down from angel to angel, were nearly incomprehensible and did not matter anyway. It was the music, Gabriel knew, that moved Jovah and caused him to act.

He sang till his breath seemed to crystallize in his lungs, till his body was numb from the buffeting of the stratospheric winds. He had been aloft two hours or more. Already he could sense a shift in the air, a gathering of powerful meteorological forces. If he stayed up here much longer, he would be caught in a developing thunderstorm.

He descended through skies grown ominous with clouds, and coasted in on a damp, heavy breeze. What appeared to be the entire population of the town had turned out on the cobblestoned central square to watch the buildup of the storm. They cheered loudly when he touched down.

"You've done it!" Levi exclaimed, bounding over to shake Gabriel heartily by the hand. "So quickly!"

Gabriel disentangled his hand as soon as possible. "I'll stay the evening to be sure the weather really breaks. It should rain a good three or four days—this time—and then rain again off and on the rest of the season. If it dries up again, send someone to the Eyrie, and I'll come back and pray again."

"Thank you, angelo—"

"Many thanks, angelo! Jovah is gracious."

"Thank you—bless you—"

Gabriel heard the murmured, heartfelt outpouring of gratitude, and it filled him, as it always did, with a deep and almost fierce satisfaction. Thus, to be an angel. To be called to the scene of distress and disaster, and to bring healing and harmony. To succor and to save. To repair the damaged bridge that linked men to their god. He never felt the calling so strongly as he did at moments like this.

The rains swept in. Everyone ran for cover. Gabriel retreated to his room at Levi Miller's but waited in resignation for the inevitable summons; and it came. Levi knocked hesitantly on the closed door, then entered to find the angel standing motionless at the window, watching the liquid onslaught of the weather.

"My wife and I will be heading over to Jacob Carter's barn— bunch of people will be going there, I expect. Jake has a few barrels of wine he's made himself, good stuff, too. Folks will be wanting to celebrate, you know. If you'd care to come, I know everyone would like a chance to thank you."

"Everyone has thanked me enough, I assure you."

"Well, if you aren't feeling up to it—"

"No, I'll come for an hour or two."

So he went to the barn, and sampled the atrocious wine, and heard the townsfolk discuss in earnest detail the crops they intended to grow this year. He was no more successful at mingling with the farmers than with the rich merchants of Semorrah. Nathan had laughed at him once and remarked, "At least you're not a snob. You dislike everyone equally." He had felt moved to protest, but it was not far from the truth.

He stayed as short a time as seemed polite, then returned to Levi's house. Sleep was a little easier to come by this night, with the rhythmic dance of the rain to fill the excruciating silence. He was awake early, though the household was up before him, and he broke his fast with Levi's wife. Then he was back outside and once more on the wing, and glad to be gone.

It was wet flying till he broke through the clouds, and then he was dazzled by unfiltered sunlight. He flew steadily for most of the day, not following a straight line back to the Eyrie. He looped south over the prairie lands, and wove an erratic pattern in a northern direction, watching the land below him unroll. He had, from time to time, flying this way, spotted some anomaly that bore investigating, or a plague flag hoisted above a small town, or a flooding river that he could track to its source in a corner of the region where too much rain had fallen. It was the reason he was gone from the Eyrie so much—because he liked to watch over Bethel from above, like Jovah over Samaria.

"You love the land more than you love the people in it." Again, Nathan speaking. Again, quite possibly true. But they were the same to him, the land and the people, the same in an abstract way: things to be cared for the way some people cared for their crops or their livestock or their collections of glass and pewter. Though he maintained an emotional distance from his people, they were a part of him in ways he could not make anyone else understand. They defined him. They gave him a reason for being. If there were not people for angels to watch over, he, Gabriel, would not exist. And so he loved them because they told him who he was.

It was late afternoon before he arrived back at the Eyrie. Even before his feet touched the landing rock, he heard the voices raised in song—three voices, two women and a man. He felt trouble ease from him and the strain of a long flight fall away. He smiled, and gently laid his feet upon the stone.

The first person he encountered in the corridors was Judith. As usual, she looked delighted to see him. Her perfect face flowered into a smile and she held out her small hands to him. He took them briefly, then let them drop.

"Gabriel! You're back! It seems like you've been gone forever."

"I was here a few days ago."

She pouted, in the way that she so often did with him. "For one night! After you'd been gone for weeks and weeks. I never get to see you anymore."

He resumed walking, and she fell in step beside him. Long ago she had perfected the trick of walking close to his side but half a step ahead of him so that she did not accidentally brush his wings. She knew how he hated his feathers to be touched. She had done it once.

"I'm likely to have less free time as the Gloria approaches, not more," he said mildly. "And afterward—"

"You'll never have time for me anymore." She said it with exaggerated sadness, fluttering her lashes at him, acting as if it were a joke, which it was not. He shrugged.

"Things change and the world spins on," he said. "What have you been doing since I've been gone?"

"What I usually do. Teaching the children, mostly. Working on my gown for the Gloria. Going into Velora at night to hear the musicians."

"Who's been taking you into Velora?"

"Why? Are you jealous?" she asked quickly.

"Just curious."

"Obadiah, mostly. And Nathan took me once."

"Really? Nathan. Well, I hope you had fun."

"It would be more fun if you took me."

"It will be a few weeks, I'm afraid."

She caught his arm, careful still not to lean too close to his wings. "You'd take Rachel if she wanted to go," she said.

Aaahh. "Not likely," Gabriel said coolly. "She's afraid to fly. Heights unnerve her."

"Well, she wants to go to Velora. She's been asking Nathan and Matthew and everyone if there isn't some other way down."

Gabriel was silent, taking Judith's remark more seriously than she perhaps intended him to. He had not considered Rachel's predicament. Unable to bear the journey to or from the Eyrie in an angel's arms, Rachel was effectively immured here in a high prison. And she had been Edori, used to traveling where she would. How could she ever get down if she refused to let him carry her? How could she visit Josiah, which he would like her to do? Come to that, how would she get to the Gloria on the Plain of Sharon? He wanted to curse, but he would not give Judith an opening like that.

"Maybe we'll think of something," was all he said.

"She doesn't seem to like it here very much," Judith went on. Her tone was cautious; she was wondering just how he felt about his angelica, and hoped his response would give something away.

"She just got here," was his noncommittal reply. "How has she been amusing herself since I've been gone?"

Judith's small shoulders hunched in a shrug. "She spends a lot of time in her room. And a lot of time in the recital chambers."

"Really? She's been practicing?"

Again the shrug. "Who knows? No one's heard her sing. She hasn't volunteered for the harmonics."

He smiled. "Give her time! Maybe she doesn't know our music."

"I thought the Edori were such fabulous singers."

"Some of them are. I don't suppose they're all musicians."

Judith took his arm again and leaned inward, effectively stopping his progress. He looked down into the heart-shaped face, just now wearing a tragic expression. "Oh, Gabriel, I know it's not very nice of me, but I just can't *like* her. She's so unfriendly, so—so haughty, almost, and what she has to be haughty about when she was a slave for five years—"

He shook her off and frowned down at her. Uncannily, Judith seemed to have realized how much he hated Rachel's indentured past. She had brought it up before. "How can you blame her for that?" he said, making his voice stern. "Do you think she was a slave by choice? Do you think *you* should be blamed for it if you were suddenly taken prisoner and sold in the city markets? She has a right to a little pride now. The Edori are proud people—"

"Oh, the Edori!" Judith exclaimed. "You're always defending the Edori. They aren't even people of Jovah—"

He made an impatient gesture with both hands and began striding down the hallway again. She hurried to keep up with him. "All right, I'm sorry. I didn't mean to make you mad," she apologized, catching his arm again. "Gabriel, *please* don't run away from me. I've missed you so much."

Again she managed to stop him, this time by the wheedling tone in her voice. He gazed down at her and saw, not the pretty girl who very probably loved him, but a problem.

"Judith," he said slowly. "I am very nearly a married man. I am very nearly Archangel. My life is not my own. You should not be wasting your life with dreams of me."

He was not surprised when the wide gray eyes filled with tears. Judith had always been very good at emotional scenes. "I can't help it," she whispered. "I have always—"

He stopped her abruptly. "Don't," he said. "It doesn't get any better than this, Judith. Don't hope for more."

She might have persisted, but voices could be heard coming down the hallway and she had to prepare herself to face others. Minutes later, she was laughing with the angels Eva and Esau; no one would have known she had been on the verge of tears. Gabriel absently answered the questions tossed at him by the angels and covertly studied Judith. He had never entirely understood her, although it had always been clear to him what she wanted: him. It was her motives that eluded him. He had always had a hard time believing she was sincere, even when she seemed to love him. He did not know if this meant she was not sincere, or that she was so affected that even her sincerity seemed assumed—or that he generally distrusted everyone.

Quickly enough, he made his excuses and continued down the hall. He had just turned the corner toward his own suite when he encountered Nathan.

"Back from Luminaux already?" was his brother's greeting.

"Ha. Not quite," he responded. "Do you have a minute? This will take some telling."

They retired to Nathan's room, and Gabriel filled him in. Nathan's mild face took on a look of wrathful astonishment.

"Three years running Raphael refused them? And did not even investigate?"

"So they said."

"Were they telling the truth?"

"Based on the physical evidence, yes. Clearly the place had been in a drought for years. And surely if Raphael had seen it, he would have made an intercession. Therefore—"

"But it's incredible," Nathan said. "An angel's foremost duty—"

"I know. I keep thinking there must be reasons. He is Archangel, after all. Perhaps his time—"

"He would have time to send one of his own angels to the Heldoras!" Nathan exclaimed. "Any angel could have performed the intercession."

"Exactly." Gabriel brooded over it a moment in silence, then looked at his brother and shrugged. "In any case, it doesn't matter, or won't for much longer. In five months, I'll be Archangel—"

"Yes, but he'll still lead the host at Windy Point!"

"But I'll be able to order him to care for Jordana," Gabriel said. "And I'll fly patrols over the region to make sure he does it."

Nathan stared at him. "You're very dictatorial for a man who has not even ascended to his new position."

Gabriel smiled. "So anger makes me."

"Does it ever occur to you—" Nathan began, and abruptly stopped.

"Does what occur to me?"

"That this transition between Archangels will not go smoothly? I mean, you already know that the merchants don't like you. The Jansai don't like you. The Manadavvi are not your strongest allies—"

"Ah, but the Edori and the farmers love me."

"And Raphael seems reluctant to see his term come to an end."

Gabriel shrugged again. "It's occurred to me. I don't know what I can do to make the others love me. I don't know what I can do to make Raphael resign with good grace. Jovah chose me, and no one can change that. I must believe—we all must believe—he chose me for a reason. Everything has been laid down according to a plan."

Nathan spread his hands in humble acceptance. "As Jovah wills," he murmured. "Still, I don't think it will be easy."

They talked a few more minutes before Gabriel finally turned to go. Thus the day was almost completely spent before he was free to go to the place he had sought since he woke that morning: the chamber set aside for his angelica.

He paused for a moment before ringing her door chime, uncertain of the reception he would get and bracing himself for the worst. Well, he must speak to her sometime. He pressed the bell and heard her bid him enter.

She sat with her back to the door, leaning over a narrow loom which had been placed to catch the best of the sunlight from the single window. The first thing he noticed was her hair. The cascading knots of loops and curls made a physical impression on him; the texture was so dense, the gold color so rich, it was impossible not to want to touch it. He nonetheless resisted the temptation, and stayed near the door.

She turned to see who had entered. Her expression was habitually so guarded that he could not read any additional hostility in her face when she recognized him. He tried to take that for encouragement.

"Rachel," was his opening gambit.

"So you're back," was her terse reply.

It was going to be difficult, of course. There was no talking to this girl. He took refuge in formality. "I hope you've been made comfortable by Hannah and the others," he said.

"Quite comfortable."

"They have shown you—the dining hall and the recital rooms and the common areas?"

"Yes, thank you."

"Was there anything else you needed?"

She gave him a hard look, and it seemed she would hurl at him all the things she needed—freedom, an escape from this place, a way to refuse the honor of becoming his wife—but she surprised him by refraining. "No."

He stepped deeper into the room, gesturing at the cloth she had stretched across the narrow frame. "What are you working on?" he asked. "The colors are very beautiful."

The question seemed to startle her; she was confused enough to give a complete answer. "It's a weaving," she said. "I found the threads in one of the storerooms down by Matthew's workshop. I thought to make a gown or a cloak or something."

He came closer, touched the fabric with a delicate hand. Three different blues and a soft rose had been blended together in a complex pattern. Even though he did not understand the art, he could see she was adept. "Is it an Edori skill?" he asked. "I have seen cloth like this for sale in the markets, but I thought it was a Luminaux craft."

Unexpectedly, she smiled. "I learned it from an Edori who

learned it from a Luminauzi," she said. "Among the Manderras, mine was a much-prized talent. Everyone in my tribe wore something that I had woven."

"Nathan writes music," he heard himself say. "And my step-mother—Hannah—can draw portraits with a piece of charcoal that look identical to her subjects. But I have no skills whatsoever."

"You can sing," she said.

"So can they."

"I have not heard them," she said, "but I think you are better."

"You have never heard me."

"You sang at Lord Jethro's house in Semorrah. I heard you."

He was pleased beyond all reason by this admission, but he made a nonchalant gesture. "So I have one talent."

"And you can bring the rain," she pointed out. "So you have two."

He nodded. "Did someone tell you where I had gone?"

"Finally."

She was cool again. He gambled on the direct question. "And were you angry with me for leaving so soon after your arrival?"

She turned away from him to neaten the excess threads at the edge of her loom. "I should not have been, I know."

"Anger rarely answers to the dictates of should and should not."

She appeared absorbed in the task of unworking a tangle in the rose-colored threads. "Well, and I thought you were probably angry with me, too."

His face showed surprise, although she was not watching him to see it. "But why?"

"Because I—when you carried me up here—"

"I'm the one who should offer the apology," he interrupted. "I did not realize just how frightened you were. I admit, I didn't expect quite such a reaction, but I should have been a little more thoughtful."

Her shoulders relaxed; she seemed relieved. "When I was a child," she said, speaking with some difficulty, "there was a wise woman in our village. She mixed herbs and took care of fevers and made prophecies. She told me that I would one day fall to my death from a great rocky cliff. And ever since then, I have been afraid of high places." She turned to face him. "I know it's foolish, but I can't ever forget it. And I'm afraid of falling in general—down stairwells, on a piece of ice, whatever. I don't think I'll ever get over the fear."

"I'm sorry," he said. "I didn't understand."

"Anyway," she finished, "I apologize too."

He smiled at her, and she gave him a tentative smile in return. Perhaps this would not go so badly after all.

"So tell me," he said. "How have you occupied yourself the past three days?"

"I have spent a lot of time listening to music."

"Listening?"

"In the recital rooms. The recordings."

"Ah. And have you found much that you liked?"

"Hagar," she said simply. "Her voice. It's amazing. I play her disks over and over. I didn't know anything like this existed."

So she liked music—his voice and Hagar's, at least. That was promising. He still didn't know if she herself could sing. Among angels, it was considered impolite to ask mortals about their musical abilities. It was thought that the question might seem insulting, for all angels, by birthright, possessed sublime voices. Gabriel was sure the same reticence could not apply between an Archangel and his wife, but he still couldn't bring himself to ask.

"Hagar was the first angelica," he said, falling back on pedantry. "A very spirited woman. She had a special relationship with Jovah—and a difficult one with her husband, the Archangel Uriel."

"This sounds like very old gossip."

He smiled. "It is, rather. She left Uriel—oh, ten or twelve times during their marriage. She even had a place built in the Corinni Mountains, where—it's hard to describe—these giant stakes were driven into the earth all around the house and grounds, specifically so that angels could not land there without piercing their wings. Instead, she built this long, winding road up from the valley, a tortuous path, and anyone who wanted to visit her had to walk up it. Well, angels hate to walk. They will fly from one side of Velora to the other rather than cross the street. So she would go to this place for days at a time, weeks, and knew that Uriel would not come looking for her."

Rachel seemed to enjoy the story. "I think I would have liked Hagar," she said.

Gabriel laughed. "No doubt. She was, by all accounts, a

stubborn woman, but also very gifted. And Jovah loved her. There was nothing she prayed for that he did not grant. Especially when she prayed from the Corinnis."

Rachel tilted her head a little, considering. "Are certain places better than others for communicating with Yovah?"

Gabriel spread his hands. "Edori believe otherwise," he countered. "And angels say that Jovah will hear a whisper uttered anywhere on earth. But the fact is, there seem to be certain places on Samaria to which Jovah's ears are attuned. The Plain of Sharon, of course. Hagar's retreat in the Corinni Mountains. A valley in southeastern Jordana. It's as if songs sung in those places go directly to Jovah's heart. I don't know why this should be so."

"So who lives in this mountain retreat now?"

"No one. It always belongs to the angelica—to Leah, now, I suppose, and you later, if you choose. But I don't believe any angelica has set foot there for a hundred years or more. As I said, it is hard to get to and not adapted to angels."

"I have been through the Corinnis," Rachel remarked. "Or near them, anyway. They're not far from Luminaux."

"You must have seen every part of Samaria," he said. "Is there any place you haven't been?"

"Until four days ago, I was never in an angel's hold. And I have never been to Ysral."

The conversation had been proceeding so amicably that Gabriel had dropped his guard. So he was unprepared for the challenge implicit in the very word. "Ysral," he said sharply. "No one has been there."

"No angels, perhaps," Rachel said.

"No one. It does not exist."

She opened her eyes very wide. "I have talked to Edori who have talked to Edori who have been there and returned. They say it is a place beautiful beyond imagining. The rivers run with a water sweeter than wine. The apples fall to the ground in piles as tall as a man. Roses flower from season to season, and never fade, and never die. And while the forest is full of wildlife and the sky is alive with birds, the only men who live there are Edori, and so there is always peace among them."

"If this Ysral exists, why is it that only Edori have managed to find it? And only Edori believe it is there?"

"Because it's an ocean away—too far for an angel to fly, and too far for most men to travel. Even Jansai, who like to consider themselves nomads, will not venture some places where the Edori will eagerly go. Only the Edori have had curiosity enough to build boats, and courage enough to take them across the water."

"Ysral is a place the Edori have conjured up to comfort them for the persecution they have suffered here. It is a beautiful fable, but fable is what it is."

Now her eyes narrowed in consideration. "And does a thing have to be proved by an angel before it is true?" she asked softly. "You forget, I have seen Edori elders work the miracles you say only an angel can perform. I am not overawed by the pronouncements of the Archangel-elect."

He was instantly furious and struggled unsuccessfully not to show it. "You are among the angels now," he informed her coldly. "Tied to us—tied to me. It would be better for everyone if you chose to act like one of us instead of considering yourself till the end of your days an Edori outsider."

"I shall do as I wish."

"I don't have the smallest doubt of that," he retorted, and stalked from the room.

So perhaps it was not going to be better, after all.

CHAPTER SEVEN

"Mint sauce?" the cook asked dubiously.

Rachel nodded. "Just a touch," she said.

"I've put mint in a drink before, but never on meat," the cook said, even more doubtfully. "I don't think anyone will eat it."

"I will."

"Some other time," the cook decided. "When it's not such an important meal."

"Then let me make the sweetcakes."

"You," said the cook, "should not be here at all."

Rachel stiffened. "There's no reason I shouldn't."

"You've got more important things to be attending to."

Rachel preserved a tactical silence. In fact, she did have more important things to attend to, for a change. She should be dressing for dinner instead of making it. She should be, she supposed, supervising the table arrangements in the great hall, making sure the guest rooms were prepared, taking on the combined duties of chatelaine and great lady which her role as angelica (soon to be formalized) seemed to demand of her. But in the past month she had refused to take on any of the housekeeping responsibilities gently suggested to her by Hannah—and less gently by Gabriel—and let other people continue handling matters in the ways they must have perfected in the years before she arrived here.

She did not ask to be angelica; she did not want to be angelica; and she did not want to do any of the things angelicas were supposed to do. Let them change that if they could.

The question then quickly became, What would she do with herself? She had not realized how quickly idleness could pall. After five years of drudgery she had thought she would be content to just sit in a chair and doze her life away. This turned out not to be true. Nor was she fulfilled by the hours spent weaving; or the time spent learning leatherworking skills from Matthew; or the time spent in the recital rooms, listening to music.

She had figured out very quickly that Gabriel and the others wanted to hear her sing, although no one had said so directly. Hannah had alluded to the topic during Rachel's first day at the Eyrie, and others had asked her in even more roundabout ways. ("So, I understand there is a great deal of singing at these Edori Gatherings," Nathan had said to her casually. "Were you one of those who raised her voice at the campfire?") Since the angelica's role in the Gloria was of supreme importance, it obviously demanded the talents of a truly gifted singer—and none of them knew if she could sing a note.

Perversity kept her from ending their uncertainty. She had so few weapons to hand, she must use even the most unlikely. She met all artful inquiries with blank stares or uncommunicative responses. ("I preferred to listen to others sing," she had told Nathan.) She never volunteered to join other voices in the perpetual harmonics, and she never even hummed under her breath when anyone could hear her.

She did spend countless hours in the recital chambers, but no one knew how she passed her time there, since she always took in enough recordings to account for every minute she stayed. She listened to them, too. She was by now note-perfect on every mass and every solo Hagar had ever performed. She rarely bothered listening to the other sopranos' disks; clearly, no one could match the first angelica. But she never mentioned any attempts she might have made at learning to sing any of Hagar's pieces.

Confounding her new community gave her enormous satisfaction, but it only filled a few minutes of every day. For the most part, she was profoundly bored.

Boredom had driven her to the kitchen early on, where she and the red-faced cook had forged a quick friendship. True to her word, Rachel had taught the woman twenty or so of the finer dishes she had learned to prepare in Lord Jethro's household. This had been a way of passing the time, although she had been forced to strangle unhappy memories of slavery. In fact, she might have spent only one afternoon in the kitchen had not Gabriel made it imperative that she return as often as possible.

She had to admit that was not what he'd intended.

He had been back for one of his rare dinners at the Eyrie, and the cook had wanted to make him a special meal. Braised beef livers in wine-and-mushroom sauce; Rachel remembered the menu very clearly. The meal had proceeded well enough, if you discounted the fact that Judith had joined Gabriel, Rachel, Nathan and Hannah at the table in the dining hall reserved for the leader of the host. Nathan had even complimented Rachel on her gown.

"Is that one you made yourself, or part of Lord Jethro's dowry?" Gabriel had asked.

She disliked being reminded that she owed anything to Jethro's charity, but she managed not to scowl. "My own," she said.

"It's very pretty."

Nathan reached over to rub a fold of the material between his fingers. "Nice and heavy," he teased. "Warm as a blanket."

She smiled at him. She found Nathan much easier to like than his brother. "Not nearly warm enough," she retorted.

"Are you cold?" Gabriel asked.

"Most mortals are cold in the holds," Hannah murmured.

"How can you even ask?" Nathan demanded. "She always wears sleeves down to her fingertips and about five layers of clothing."

"But despite all that—you're still chilled?"

The concern disarmed her. "I'm fine," she said. She was relieved for the slight diversion when one of the cook's assistants came by to refill their water glasses. "Thank you," she said, smiling at the girl. The girl smiled back and departed.

"You don't have to thank them *every* time," Judith said.

Rachel's wary attention swung back to the beautiful dark-haired girl. "What?"

"When they bring you your water. When they bring you your dinner. When they take away your plates. Every time someone approaches the table, you thank them. It's a little excessive."

There was a moment's blank silence. It was so rude that Rachel could not even be offended. Hannah was the one to speak, in her well-bred, perfectly pitched voice. "Actually, Judith," said the Manadavvi woman, "you yourself could show the servants a little more appreciation without being considered guilty of any social indiscretion."

Judith pettishly hunched her shoulders. "They're doing their jobs," she said. "They don't need thanks—they're getting a good salary. It's not like they're slaves, after all."

"Judith!" This from Gabriel, of course.

"Oh, I *am* sorry," the girl said, turning ingenuous eyes on Rachel. "I didn't mean to say anything to bring up—you know, your other life . . ."

"You meant to be cruel, and you were cruel," Gabriel said. "I would have thought your upbringing and the smallest streak of courtesy would have prevented you from saying such things."

Rachel could not help it. She smiled warmly, if insincerely, at the angel for championing her. "*Thank* you," she said.

Judith jumped to her feet with a little huff. "I didn't *mean* it," she protested. "You're all just determined to think the worst of me."

"Now, Judith, don't get all upset over nothing," Nathan began, but she had whirled around and run from the table. Nathan watched her go and sighed. "There's trouble in a very pretty package," he said.

Rachel worked hard to keep her pleasure from showing. She couldn't stand the troublesome, pretty package herself, and it was hard to gauge exactly how Gabriel felt about this childhood friend. On the few occasions when Gabriel *was* at the Eyrie, Judith always seemed to be there too. This defection was almost a first.

"She's getting too old to keep trading on her childish ways," Hannah said. "Someone's going to have to take her in hand. We should be looking for a suitable husband for her."

There was an unexpected, wooden quality to the ensuing silence. Rachel looked up from her plate to find everyone else studying familiar hangings on the walls. "What?" she said. "What's so hard about finding her a husband?"

"The task of arranging marriages often falls to the angelica," Gabriel said expressionlessly.

Rachel stared at him. "You want *me* to look around for a husband for *Judith*?"

"Not any time soon," Gabriel said somewhat hastily.

"Judith can't stand me! And I am not even an advocate of marriage!"

"Unfortunate, since you will be married in a few weeks," was his dry response.

"You know what I meant! The Edori do not believe in marriage—"

"Neither, apparently, does Judith," Nathan said irrepressibly.

"Coming from an angel who does not hold to high moral standards himself, that remark is singularly unkind," Hannah said.

"Well, I'm not going to be responsible for her," Rachel said decisively. "She's your friend. You find her a husband."

"She's partial to angels. We could send her back with Raphael when he comes," Nathan suggested.

Gabriel bent a quelling look on his brother. "Is it your wish," he inquired, "that I send yet another person hurrying from the table in disgrace? If so, just continue making such ill-natured remarks."

"Well, *he's* in a poor humor," Nathan said to Rachel. "Don't cross him tonight of all nights."

"What put him in such a temper?" she asked.

Nathan shrugged. "Actually, this is pretty much what he's always like. It's better not to cross him at any time."

She risked a glance at Gabriel, to see how he was taking the banter, and found him busy with his food, ignoring them. "It's good, isn't it?" she asked.

He nodded, finishing up the last of his meat. "Our cooks must be practicing for the honor of serving the Archangel. I wonder where they got the recipes."

Rachel intercepted a warning glance from Hannah, but did not interpret it correctly. "Oh, I spent the day in the kitchen, teaching them," she said blithely. "If you think this is good—"

Gabriel dropped his fork. "*You* spent the day in the *kitchen*? *Cooking*?"

Rachel nodded. She saw that this wasn't going over well, but too late. "Of course. I know how to make anything you've seen on any table in Semorrah. Better food than the Edori ate—and probably better than what the angels usually eat. . . ."

"*You were cooking with the servants?*"

Now she became defiant. "And why shouldn't I? Is there something wrong with being in the kitchen? Is there something wrong with *food*? Is there—"

"You're angelica! You have—or will have—the highest ranking position of any woman in the three provinces! You have duties to the people in your hold, to petitioners, to Jovah—and you spend your time cutting up carrots in the kitchen!"

"If one of my *duties* is to see that people eat—"

"Your behavior gives rise to just the sort of unkind remark that Judith made five minutes ago! How can you expect people to treat you with respect when you yourself have no dignity? Do you *want* people to make references to your years of slavery in Semorrah? Do you plan to converse with them on the differences in rank between a bondwoman and a servant? Do you think they will be interested in your stories of carrying coals and cleaning out chamber pots and waiting on strangers? Or are there other, more sordid tales you wish to share with visitors, and, indeed, with us—"

Like Judith, she had had no choice. She had swept to her feet, nearly knocking over her chair in her haste to be gone. "You scolded Judith, but you're the one who's offended by my shameful background," she shot at him. "I can't change what happened to me and neither can you. But I can live with it. And I don't think you can. Any time you choose, just let me know, and I'll be gone from here. You can pick an angelica more to your liking the second time around. Make both of us happy for a change."

And she too had stormed from the room. After that, of course, only a meek woman would have eschewed the kitchen, and no one had ever called Rachel that. She had managed to spend part of nearly every day there, particularly those days when Gabriel was expected back at the Eyrie. Her only regret was that he never alluded to the fracas—or the infraction—again.

But the cook had been right. She had better things to do. Today was her wedding day.

She found Hannah awaiting her in her chamber, and gave the older woman a somewhat guilty smile. Rachel did not wish to be married, but neither did she wish to look ridiculous at the ceremony, so she had smothered her pride and asked Hannah's help in getting ready. Hannah had chosen the gown and agreed to help her dress. And Rachel was late.

"Sorry," was her brief apology.

"We don't have a great deal of time to waste," Hannah said. "Are you bathed? Is your hair washed?"

"I washed my hair this morning, but I think I should bathe again . . ."

They had perhaps an hour's worth of work to do. Rachel was reminded of the day, a little more than four weeks ago, that she had dressed the nervous Lady Mary and explained the wedding night mysteries to her. No need to worry about that part of this marriage, however; the other day Gabriel had pointed out to Rachel the door to his own quarters and told her to look for him there "if you ever need me and I'm ever home." It had been half an annoyance and half a relief to be so cavalierly dismissed.

Hannah worked swiftly to make up Rachel's face and arrange her hair. The angels did not affect quite as much simplicity in their wedding attire as the mortals did, but Hannah had not gone to elaborate lengths. She had caught up a knot of Rachel's hair in a gold clasp on top of her head, and coaxed some of the wild curls to spill down on either side of her face. The rest of the thick hair she allowed to hang free, tying tiny gold bows here and there in the dense tresses. The effect was at once windblown and elegant; Rachel liked it.

The gown, one of Jethro's gifts, was also gold, an exact match for the color of Rachel's hair. The rich silk was embroidered with gold thread in a pattern of doves, roses and deer, although the embroidery thread so closely matched the fabric that it was nearly impossible to make out the shapes. The cloth was stiff and heavy, encrusted with blond lace at the high neck and the tapered cuffs. It met Rachel's only two requirements: It was warm, and the sleeves covered her arms an inch or so past her wrists.

Hannah stepped back to admire her handiwork. "You look beautiful," she said. "Now if you can act somewhat regal—"

Rachel smiled. "I'll try," she said. "But it's not something I'm good at."

The door chimed. Nathan's voice called, "Are you almost ready? Everyone is assembled."

"Just a moment," Hannah called back. "Go tell Gabriel we're on the way."

A few more minutes and they were done. They hurried from the room, through the tunnels and down to the bottom level of the Eyrie. Music led them to the great open plateau, where the ceremony was to take place. Rachel stepped outside and her gown was instantly afire in the angled light of the late afternoon sun. She paused a moment to get her bearings.

As Hannah had promised, the plateau was warmed by a ring of braziers, all merry with fires. Several hundred people were crowded together in a space that seemed too small to accommodate them. Mortals were gathered on one side, angels on the other, with an aisle between them. Everyone was watching the doorway through which Rachel had entered. The muted, pervasive music was the sound of more than a hundred angels humming. She knew this mass; she had heard Hagar sing it. One written specifically for the ceremonies of joy.

Hannah had deserted her; what was she supposed to do? She stood there stupidly, lit by brilliant flame, unable to move. It was Gabriel who appeared suddenly at her side, a vision in black and silver and blue. He took her arm, and she clutched his in response. He slid his hand down until he reached her palm, and then he twined his fingers comfortingly with hers. He was smiling. The blueness of his eyes reflected the blueness of the sky. She felt some of her panic subside.

He walked her slowly forward, and the angels and the mortals closed ranks behind them. Soon they were in the center of the arena, and from all sides the audience pressed forward to watch them. Rachel felt her hand tighten on Gabriel's, but he did not protest. A small man detached himself from the anonymous crowd and came forward with his hands outstretched. He had a dignified authority and a sweet expression, and the smile he directed at Rachel calmed her almost at once.

"I am Josiah," he said to her in a low voice. "One of the oracles to the god. It is his wish that I speak the words that unite you in marriage to the angel Gabriel."

Later, she did not remember a single word that Josiah said, although the whole marriage rite was a new one to her. She did not remember being cold, although she knew she had been; she did not remember a single song the angels sang, although their quiet background music never ceased. But she remembered Gabriel's face, as she stood turned toward him, both of her hands now caught in his. He was so serious. His blue eyes, his striking features, the black hair falling in a frame around his cheeks—

each detail of his image was burned into her mind forever. She stared back at him and scarcely moved at all.

"Married in the sight of Jovah, the sight of angels, and the sight of men. Now and forever, till death dissolves the tie. Amen," Josiah said. And cheers went up from the hundreds of voices around them.

Gabriel smiled at Rachel and at last dropped her hands. "Amen," he said.

She smiled back, but she had no words.

That was the last moment of stillness she was to experience for the next few hours. From all sides, angels and mortals surged forward to offer congratulations and expressions of good will. The press of the crowd instantly separated them and Rachel felt herself tumble into the hands of strangers. "Thank you," she said over and over again, mechanically, not meaning the words but not having the energy to tell hundreds of strangers the truth: *I do not want to be married. He does not want to be married to me.*

There were only three faces she recognized among the hundreds who came before her. The first she thought for a moment she had conjured up from memory.

"Rachel! You look so beautiful. Don't you remember me, Rachel?"

She grabbed at the outstretched hands to have something to cling to. "Lady Mary! I didn't know you were here!"

Mary laughed like a delighted child. "Yes, Lord Jethro was invited, of course, and I begged and pleaded to be allowed to come. I wanted to see you for myself. Rachel, isn't this wonderful? Now we're both married. I'm so happy for you."

Rachel wanted to weep. Here was probably the one person in the world who was genuinely pleased for her, and she was practically a stranger. "And you? Since you've been married, how has it gone—?"

"Oh, splendid! I love being married." Mary was beaming. "And—it's a secret, of course, but I have to tell someone—I'm going to have a baby. Well, it will be months and months, but it's still wonderful. . . ."

"Wonderful—" Rachel echoed, but hands came between them, faces and bodies, and she was again hearing the congratulations of people she had never seen in her life. Mary completely disappeared.

The second face she knew belonged to the angel Saul, who greeted her with an insolent smile. Her hope that he might not recognize her died instantly. "You've come up in the world since I saw you last," was his greeting. "And Gabriel's gone down a bit."

"Is it worse to marry a slave than to try to assault one?" she said, very bluntly. "A man who gives honor receives it upon himself."

"You're mighty haughty for a slave," Saul sneered.

She smiled with great superciliousness. "For an angelica," she said and turned to go. It was the first time she had been glad to boast of her new title.

The third one she recognized before he recognized her, and then he only knew her by her distinctive gown. The Archangel took her hand before she could back away, and bent to kiss her fingers. When he straightened, he looked down at her and smiled without releasing her hand.

"So, Gabriel has found himself a bride after all," Raphael said. "One hardly knew what to expect when the rumors began flying around Samaria that you had been—ah—residing in Semorrah for so many years. But you are quite the prize, my dear. I congratulate Gabriel."

She didn't think she could stand his touch. She concentrated on breathing regularly, and stared back at him, saying nothing.

His smile widened. "Who would have thought," he continued. "A Jordana girl, and one not far from my own home. We might be related, you and I, for our coloring is so similar. You must know that my mother was a golden-haired girl who grew up not far from the Caitanas. It's a common type in that region."

Still she said nothing. His grip on her hand was quite painful, and obviously intended to be so. He was still smiling.

"She had a sweet voice, my mother. She sang me lullabies when I was a child. But her singing was not—how shall I say— of the caliber you would expect from an angel. Or an angelica. But you, I am sure, must have inherited a vast talent for Jovah to have picked you for the singular honor that awaits you in—I believe it is four months' time? I am sure you are prepared for it. Only the strongest voices carry across the Plain of Sharon."

She might have no voice at all; certainly not one she intended to use now.

He laughed, and dropped another kiss on her hand. "So you do remember me," he said, in a lower, silkier voice. "I thought you might. I never thought the day would come when I would be giving you congratulations on your wedding. But so it has. And I offer you my most sincere felicitations. Believe me, I can imagine what joy you will have with your new husband."

Still she did not answer; still he did not drop her hand. They might have stayed entwined that way forever if Gabriel had not suddenly materialized at her side.

"Rachel. They want to start the dinner. We need to lead everyone in."

Raphael bent his smile on Gabriel. "I was just telling your bride what a charming husband I thought you'd make."

Rachel turned her eyes in mute appeal to Gabriel. He misread the look; his own expression was rueful. "I'm sure she agreed with you wholeheartedly."

"She has been very quiet during our conversation. No doubt overawed by the honor of speaking to an Archangel."

"Rachel is seldom overawed by anything," Gabriel said. "Come, angela. We have crowds of hungry revelers to feed."

Raphael surrendered her hand to Gabriel and smiled at her again. Gabriel led her inside, and the murmuring crowd followed. Her husband glanced down at her after a moment.

"Or was I wrong?" he asked. "Has this ceremony actually cowed you? I thought nothing could."

"It's very unnerving," she managed to say. Her voice sounded faint to her ears. "I am not used to so many people in such a small space."

"Well, eat hearty, stoke your strength," he said. "The festivities are just beginning."

The meal itself seemed endless. There was no way the great dining hall could accommodate the hundred and fifty residents of the Eyrie and the hundred or so guests all at once, so they ate in shifts. The bridal couple remained at the table the whole time, nibbling on food and conversing with the parade of well-wishers who visited their table. Raphael and his contingent—Saul, Leah and a woman to whom Rachel had not been introduced—sat with them for the first half of the meal; the Gaza angels sat with them for the second half. Even in her disturbed state, Rachel noticed how Nathan managed to sit by the Monteverde angel Magdalena.

Their chairs were pulled so close together that their wings inter-laced. They spoke softly, their heads bent forward, and seemed oblivious of anyone else in the room.

Rachel looked over at her husband once to find him watching Nathan with a dark frown. "What's wrong?" she asked.

"I'm considering murdering my brother."

She glanced again at Nathan and Magdalena. "Hannah said angels were not allowed to love angels."

"That's why I'm thinking about killing him. Or her."

She toyed with her soup. "What a crime," she said softly.

Now she had his attention. "I agree. And although I have discussed this with him often—"

She shook her head. "No. What a crime that people who love each other should be forced apart. For any reason. By any law."

"I suppose Hannah told you why the unions are forbidden?"

"Because they bear monster children."

"Yes. Children who live briefly, die painfully and disturb everyone who looks upon them."

Rachel shrugged. "There are ways for a man and woman to love each other and not conceive a child."

He stared at her. "Angels don't believe in contraceptives."

Now she was the one astonished. "Don't believe in— So you engage in the act of love only to produce children?"

He looked quickly around, but no one was listening to them. Nathan and Magdalena were absorbed in each other, the lively Ariel was talking to a Bethel man, and for the moment everyone else was devoted to eating.

"It's more complicated than that," he replied stiffly. "Passion can be dissociated from the desire to bear children. But angel children are born so rarely. Any chance to produce more angels cannot be overlooked—it *is* a sin, a crime, to prevent conception, if there is a chance an angel might be sired."

"That's only if you believe there aren't already too many angels in the world," Rachel said sardonically.

His irritation showed, though he tried to hide it. "I suppose the Edori believe differently, as they seem to about everything."

"What the Edori believe," she said, "is that a bond to a child is the one tie that cannot be broken. So that to have a child is a decision to be taken only after a great deal of thought. And since an unwanted child is the greatest burden a woman can bear, women have ways to prevent such a thing from occurring."

He gazed down at her with such mixed emotions on his face that she struggled to guess at them all. Did she know how to take these shocking precautions? If she was never to be his wife in fact, did it matter what she knew? If Jovah had brought them together for a purpose, might it include childbearing? and if so, how were they to reconcile their many differences and produce angelic offspring?

"Don't worry about it," she said, with a touch of malice. "I also know ways to enhance fertility. Every Edori who has ever wanted a child has eventually had one."

Although briefly heartened by that little conversation, Rachel found herself increasingly exhausted as the interminable evening wore on. And, as Gabriel had warned her, there were more activities to face. Pleading a headache from the tight gold clasp on her head, she escaped to her room to loosen her hair and change clothes. She lingered there as long as she dared, but eventually made her way back down to the arena. Now clad in a sober dark gown, with a black shawl thrown over her head for warmth, she was much less visible than she had been in the gold wedding dress, and she slipped almost unnoticed through the celebrating throng.

What she had returned to, apparently, was an exhibition of angels. Six angels stood in a circle—Saul and Raphael, Ariel and Magdalena, and Nathan and a young angel named Eva. First one angel would improvise an impossibly complex line of music; then the one standing beside him would repeat it, note for note, and add his own difficult measures. The next angel would sing everything that had been sung before, add his or her variations, and turn laughingly to the next contestant. The impromptu song was nearly five minutes long before Ariel missed a note and was cut from the competition. The whole thing started again from the beginning. Eventually, Raphael was the victor. Everyone in the crowd cheered.

Another Eyrie angel—Obadiah, she thought his name was—stepped forward to sing a pretty melody; someone began harmonizing softly behind him. This, no doubt, could go on all night. Rachel glanced around to see what other entertainment was offered. The whole enclosure was lit by flame: Decorative wrought-

iron candelabra held blazing tapers a foot or so above the crowd;
braziers spaced around the edge of the plateau added a dim
orange glow. The combined effect was one of cheeriness and
warmth. The main activities seemed to be listening and—despite
the huge meal that had just been served—eating. Servants were
circulating with jellies and candies and chopped fruits, and nearly
everyone carried a glass of some bubbling beverage. Those who
were not entranced with the singing had fallen back toward the
edges of the arena and were engaged in quiet conversation.

As Obadiah was succeeded by another singer, Rachel began
to drift through the crowd, looking for the lady Mary. Without
her gold dress on, no one seemed to recognize her, and no one
spoke to her. She felt like a wraith, a shadow, a visitor at her
own wedding; she entertained the idea that this could all have
happened without her—which, in a sense, was true. What they
celebrated was not the marriage of Raheli sia a Manderra to Archangel-designate Gabriel, but the fulfillment of the decree of the
god, and the formalized ritual of change. She was a prop, necessary but not a differentiated individual. Yovah's wavering finger
had come to rest when it was pointing at her; and so here she
was in the Eyrie, hearing the angels sing.

Mary did not appear to be anywhere in the press of people.
Easier for the visiting pregnant woman to beg off this affair than
for Rachel, the nominal centerpiece, to do so. Although perhaps
if no one realized who she was, no one would notice when she
had gone. . . .

What kept her there was yet another change in singers. She
was too close to the perimeter to see who was taking center stage,
but she knew this singer just by the material he had chosen. Matthew, lifting a lilting tenor voice heavenward, crooned one of the
tender Edori love songs Rachel had not heard in five years. The
sound stopped her where she stood. She felt much as she had
when Gabriel had scooped her into his arms and soared up to the
Eyrie—dizzy, disoriented, despairing. Simon had sung this song
to her. . . .

"Here. Chairs have been set up by the wall here. Your hands
are cold, and no wonder. It's freezing. Let's take seats next to this
nice fire. There. Would you like some wine?"

She had been ushered to a chair and pushed into it before
she entirely realized that someone was speaking to her. He had

handed her a goblet of wine before she took the trouble to identify him.

"Josiah," she said slowly. "Isn't that right?"

He nodded. "Drink up. Come now. Drink it all. There now. Yes, I'm Josiah. I wish we had been properly introduced before this afternoon, but I did not arrive until very late, I'm afraid. You're Rachel, of course."

He was so very small and unalarming, so different from the angels and the rich gentry she had been surrounded with lately, that she found herself liking him almost on the instant.

"You're the priest," she said.

"Well, I'm one of the oracles, actually."

"Is that better?"

He laughed lightly. "More select. There are several hundred priests. There are only three oracles."

"There are?"

"Three oracles for the three provinces. The god finds power in the triumvirate. Oracle, angel and man. Gaza, Bethel, Jordana. If it comes to that, the three dooms that will be visited upon Samaria if the Gloria is not performed—the Plain of Sharon destroyed, the River Galilee destroyed, and the world itself destroyed."

"I don't know much about theology," Rachel said apologetically. "Forgive me if I seem stupid."

He considered her with great interest. "It is truly amazing to me," he said, "in a culture like ours which is so completely self-contained, that there could be anyone who does not know all the doctrine, all the trappings, inside and out."

"I wasn't taught—"

"Oh, I know. The Edori have their own mysticism. It is just that I so rarely come in contact with the Edori. Nearly everyone I deal with subscribes to identical philosophies and ideals, and knows his place in the order, and certainly knows mine. So to come across a spiritual innocent is a somewhat wondrous occurrence."

Half of what he said made no sense to her, but he was intriguing; she was willing to talk religion to please him.

"The Edori are believers," she said.

He smiled. "And what do the Edori believe?"

"That men should live in harmony with men and animals

and the earth itself. That Yovah will punish those who do not live in harmony and reward those who do." The soft Edori syllables crept back into her accent as she parroted the beliefs she had learned as a child.

"And how does Jovah know whom to punish and whom to reward?"

"Yovah sees everything and knows everything. He hears every prayer. He exalts the virtuous and wreaks vengeance on the wicked, although sometimes he does not act as quickly as men and women would wish."

"And who controls Jovah?"

"The nameless one," she answered readily.

He smiled again. "Yes, you see, that is where the Edori slide into blasphemy, I'm afraid. I'm willing to concede that the chain of mediators may be dispensed with—that is, the oracles and the angels. Perhaps they are not necessary, perhaps even ordinary men may speak directly to the god. But Jovah himself controls himself. His is the final arbitration. There is no other hand guiding Jovah."

She knew that her face registered astonishment. "But Yovah is the tool, and the nameless one created him just to watch over us. And for every star that we see in the sky at night, the nameless one has created another god specifically to watch over its people. And each god is just, but each god is the tool of the one who watches over all."

"This is very interesting to me," Josiah said. He did not seem at all offended by what he must consider her heresy. "The people of Samaria are, by and large, a very homogenous group. Barring some social distinctions of money and class, they have a remarkably similar world-view and theological base. All of them—Manadavvi, Jansai, angeli, Luminauzi—all of them believe in the same god and that god's principles. All except the Edori. Why do the Edori differ? Who taught them their precepts? When did the schism occur?"

She was totally baffled and showed it. He laughed.

"I am—all the oracles are—students of Samarian history," he said. "We have access to documents about the founding of the civilization that do not entirely make sense to others. That is— Well, what do the Edori believe about how men came to live on Samaria?"

This part she knew. "Yovah brought us here, hundreds of years ago, from a place of violence and dissonance. He brought us here to live in harmony with each other, and he stayed to guard us."

"Yes, that is true—although scholars still debate how Jovah managed this feat and where this other place might be. But men have only lived on Samaria for five hundred years. It seems we lived some other place centuries ago, and it is the miracle of our god that he brought us here to begin our lives completely anew. Those he brought here—can you conceive of the glory?—actually conversed with the god, actually experienced his warm hand on their bodies as he carried them here from—someplace else. They were all face to face with the god, you understand. And so they all settled down, and chose lives as farmers or merchants or miners, but they had all seen the god, and so they all shared the same beliefs. And they passed on their beliefs to their children, and so on through the generations.

"But the Edori . . . Who first whispered a different version of the story into their ears? The main tenets of worship are the same, that is plain enough. But somewhere, sometime, someone revised the philosophy. I cannot stop wondering who—and why—and what made this someone believe as he did."

She was beginning to get a headache. "All Edori believe as I do," she said in a helpful voice.

He smiled at her again. "Yes, and you have no idea what I am blathering about, do you? I do apologize. It is just that I so rarely talk to one of the Edori, and I thought I would take the chance to ask—"

He paused, and glanced thoughtfully at her long-sleeved black dress. "Although you were not born Edori, of course," he said.

"I was born in the Caitana foothills," she said. "I have been with the Edori almost since I can remember."

"Yes, the highland farmers are very devout. You must have been dedicated days after you were born. Otherwise I would never have been able to find you."

"You found me?"

"Jovah chose you, and he told me your name, and I told Gabriel where you could be found. Or so I thought—"

She glanced around. Matthew had long since stopped singing. Ariel was center stage now, her pure soprano ringing with an unearthly silver clarity. "So I have you to thank for this," she said.

He laughed. "Only secondarily. I interpreted the god's will. I take it this is not the life you would have chosen?"

She was silent a moment. "The life I would have chosen," she said slowly, "was taken away from me when I was twenty. I loved an Edori boy, and I wanted to spend my life with him. I never dreamt of anything like this. And Gabriel is no happier than I am. I think Yovah's wisdom failed him this time."

"Jovah is never wrong, though we sometimes misinterpret," Josiah said softly. "Gabriel tells me that his Kiss flared to life the first time you walked a few feet into his room. And the Kiss is never mistaken."

She laughed shortly. "I think it must be. If it only comes to life when you have found your true love—"

Josiah smiled. "Well, now. I think Jovah's motives don't always match human desires. I have always thought he brought a man and woman together for underlying purposes having more to do with generations and bloodlines and genetic mixes—"

"What?"

"Children," he explained. "If you chart the history of the great leaders of Samaria, you will often find that their parents were those who were united by Jovah—that is, those who were drawn together by the Kiss."

He laughed. "There is a story. You might know it, in fact, for it is an Edori tale. It has been cited to me as the reason most Edori choose not to be dedicated. The story goes that hundreds of years ago the Archangel-elect—also called Gabriel at that time—was looking for his bride. He sought her in every city and small village from Gaza to Luminaux, but she was nowhere to be found. One evening, he broke his flight to stay the night with a band of Edori.

"There at the camp, his Kiss came to life and guided him to the side of a young woman who had recently become consort to the chieftain of the clan, though she had not yet borne him any children. She loved her chieftain and had no interest in becoming angelica, and so she told the angel. However, this Gabriel believed the dictates of Jovah superseded human will, and he took her by force back to Windy Point. Where she lived the rest of her life, bearing him many children, all of them angels. Now from this story," Josiah concluded, "I deduce that Jovah cares less about the human heart than about the gene pool. But I can also understand why the Edori prefer not to be Kissed by the god."

Rachel smiled. "I have heard the tale of the angel who swept away Susannah," she said. "But it was told to me as a reason to be wary of angels."

Josiah laughed again. "It is Jovah who tracks you, not the angels."

She considered. "Can he track anyone who has been dedicated? Anyone at all? He knows where they are—if they are alive or dead—as long as they bear a Kiss?"

"He knows everything about everyone, even if they have not been dedicated," Josiah said. "But he can only communicate to the oracles about those who have."

"But if someone was dedicated—and was still alive—you would know?"

"Who are you looking for?" he asked.

"A man—a boy—an Edori I knew years ago," she said, stammering. "He was the only other person in my tribe who bore a Kiss. His mother had taken him to the priests the summer he was born, because his father had been a Luminauzi merchant and made her swear she would dedicate their child. We were curiosities even in our own tribe, which may have been what made us friends—" She stopped abruptly. Friends. Lovers. Alive or dead, Simon was beyond her reach now. Still, if there was some way to know . . .

"If you can tell me his name, his parents' names, the year he was dedicated and the place—yes, I can tell you if he is still alive. Do you think he is not?"

"I think all of the Manderras are dead except those who are slaves," she said baldly. "And I would rather he was dead."

He nodded gravely. "I will ask the god, once I get back. I cannot ask him from here."

"His mother was called Mariah. His father's name was also Simon. He was dedicated in Luminaux thirty years ago," Rachel said, staring straight ahead. Then she hesitated, and risked a look at the oracle directly. "Don't tell Gabriel."

"No. I won't."

Almost on the words, she heard someone call out her new husband's name. Soon other voices took up the cry, and there was a general laughing insistence until the angel finally came forward.

"It's my wedding day," he said, his words carrying back to the edge of the plateau where Rachel sat. "I have provided enough entertainment for you already." The crowd vociferously disagreed with this. Rachel heard Gabriel laugh.

The oracle smiled over at the new bride. "I believe your husband is going to sing," he said. "This should be a treat. Let's go closer."

She shook her head. "I'm so tired. I'll stay here. You go."

He rose to his feet, then paused to take her hand. "I enjoyed talking with you," he said. "You must come to me sometime so we can continue our theological debates."

"I'd like to," she said. "If I ever get off this mountain."

He bowed and left her. There was more good-natured raillery in the center of the plateau as Gabriel or his friends suggested and rejected works for the groom to sing. No one appeared to be paying any attention to Rachel at all. She slipped from her seat and made her way silently through the crowd, eyes down, shawl wrapped around her bright hair, utterly invisible.

Judith's throaty contralto sounded before Rachel had made it to the tunnel entrance, and she paused in surprise as she identified the song. The Lochevsky *Magnificat*. It was one of the Gloria masses—Rachel's favorite, in fact—which she had played over and over again for the sheer delight of hearing Hagar's voice master the full three and a half octaves required for the female solo. Rachel did not think Judith's voice had the requisite range, and indeed, as the music made its first spectacular leap upward, Ariel took over for the notes in the higher register. Her lovely soprano voice cascaded downward on a succession of massed arpeggios, and Magdalena smoothly broke in to carry the middle mezzo line. Rachel smiled to herself. It took three contemporary musicians to sing the mass that Hagar had performed with such virtuosity.

Once again she turned to go—and at that moment, Gabriel's voice lifted in close harmonic duet with Magdalena's. The female voice fell away, and Gabriel sang on in a luxurious, exultant tenor. He reached the top of his vocal range as the song exploded in a joyous trill. His voice was liquid fire, and each note burned against Rachel as it fell. She shut her eyes; her body tightened in a brief moment of transport as if the music physically yanked on the thin cord running up her spine. Then he eased downward on the scale in a series of fluid thirds alternating between major and minor intervals.

Divine Yovah, his voice, his voice. She had never heard anything so beautiful in her life.

She could not leave the arena while he was singing, but she was too stunned to stand upright. She sidled through the crowd, making once more for the perimeter, and backed herself against a supporting wall. The women were singing again, tossing the melodic line from throat to throat as if they had practiced this before, but she knew the tenor line would soon reappear. Impatiently, she waited through the second duet (shared by Ariel and Magdalena) for the second male solo, this one longer and more complex than the first. When his voice broke free of the high soprano line, she wanted to sink into the rock itself. She felt her palms flatten on the wall behind her and press so tightly that the smooth stone seemed grainy and rough against her skin. His voice divorced her from her body; it replaced her soul. While he sang, he owned her.

She had forgotten that every mass contained a choral response. When the mixed crowd of angels and humans came in on cue, at the end of Gabriel's solo, she was so startled that she jumped away from the wall. They sang the simple refrain softly, but in this semienclosed space the sound seemed immense, oceanic, a massive coming together of harmony and motion. The tidal pull of the music drew Rachel forward; she mouthed the words along with the singers. Not until the chorus fell silent in deference to the next soprano solo did she lean against the wall again.

But this was ridiculous. If she was overwhelmed by the informal recitations of a few hundred singers at a wedding banquet, how would she endure a Gloria mass of a thousand voices where she herself was to sing the lead?

She stayed at the wall till the mass was over, letting the music wash over her, soak into her, fill her up. When the final chorus ended, the audience broke into spontaneous applause; everyone congratulated the women on the smoothness of their transitions and Gabriel on the magnificence of his range. Rachel shook herself and ran lightly for the exit before anyone else could begin singing.

CHAPTER EIGHT

For the most part, Gabriel had not been displeased with his wedding day. He was never a happy man at a fête, but this one had gone smoothly enough. Although he was not comfortable in the role of host, it was something he would have to get used to, and these were some of the people he would have to regularly entertain. So he forced himself to talk to Lord Jethro and Lady Clara, their son and daughter-in-law, and others of the Semorran contingent. Also present were Jansai from Breven, Manadavvi from Gaza, artisans from Luminaux, and of course the requisite angelic representatives. It was a microcosm of Samarian society, a smaller version of the group that would be assembled in a few months for the Gloria.

Of the group, the only one he really enjoyed talking to was Ariel, who had cornered him after dinner, while the impromptu singing contest was going on.

"I'm always the first one to mess up the music," she remarked, taking his wineglass from his hand, sipping from it and handing it back. "I don't know why I even bother to play."

"You have other sterling qualities, I'm sure," he responded, making a great show of holding his glass up to the firelight to inspect it for any impurities she had left behind. "If you spit in this—"

"Don't be ridiculous. I'm more likely to have poisoned it than spit in it. Can we go somewhere and talk?"

The abrupt request made him raise his eyebrows, but he said,

"Certainly," and led the way indoors. They went into the first room they came to, which was one of the smaller recital chambers.

"Oh, put on some music," Ariel said, shutting the door behind them.

He was slightly amused. "Any preferences?"

"Well, something happy, seeing as this should be a happy day for you."

He cued up one of the celebrations, turned the volume low, and settled himself next to Ariel on the stone floor. "I'm married," he said, "so this is the wrong time to tell me you're hopelessly in love with me."

She sat with her back against the wall, legs straight out before her, wings curved forward protectively over her shoulders. Like most angels, Ariel preferred wearing leather flying gear, close-fitting and businesslike. For the wedding, however, she had arrayed herself in a flowing silk dress and silver sandals; she did not look like the quick, decisive, slightly reckless Ariel he knew.

"She's really quite beautiful, your Rachel," she said. "I haven't had much chance to talk to her, but she certainly looks the part. That hair—!"

"Her best feature," Gabriel said dryly.

"Well, she certainly doesn't look like she was ever a slave. I mean, she has a certain haughtiness of bearing."

"Indeed she does."

"Doesn't look much like an Edori, either. If anything, she looks like—well, like Raphael."

"Not surprising, since she came from the Caitanas. I heard him say something to her about being related."

"She doesn't like him," Ariel said abruptly.

"Who? Rachel doesn't like Raphael?"

"Did you see her looking at him? While he was holding her hand? She looked like she'd stuck her fingers in a pile of horse manure and maggots."

"Ariel!"

"Well, her expression was one of loathing."

"I can't imagine why she'd dislike him. As far as I know, she's never met him before. Then again," he added with some bitterness, "I know virtually nothing about her. And she is not eager to supply details."

Ariel smiled faintly. "What? This is not the romantic fairy-tale wedding it appears to be? In fact, it is a marriage of convenience?"

He returned her smile briefly. "I think she would say, convenient for me, not for her. Although she was not averse to being rescued from slavery, she has made no attempt to disguise the fact that her new life is just another kind of bondage."

"She'll get used to it soon enough," Ariel assured him. "Any girl would."

He kept his doubts to himself. "But surely you didn't drag me from my friends and beloved family just to discuss my new-found bride."

"Well," she said, "beloved family is really what I'm here to talk about."

He sighed, and drew up one knee to link his hands around it. "Nathan and Magdalena," he said. "What are we going to do?"

"I am incapable of wrestling with the long-term problem, because the immediate one is so frightening," Ariel said. "Old Abel Vashir has asked Nathan to come spend the month with him, teaching his house musicians some of his original music. Now, Nathan's a wonderful composer, and of course I'm glad to have him on good terms with any of the Manadavvi, but—"

"But Vashir's place is less than a three-hour flight from Mon teverde," Gabriel said.

"And Magdalena has friends in Vashir's compound—she's there all the time. And without you or me there to force them to observe a little decorum, well—"

"I'll tell Nathan he can't go."

"Oh, Gabriel."

"No, really. There's plenty he can do here to help me."

"Abel would be offended. Very offended. I don't think you have so many allies among the gentry that you can afford to sacrifice influential Manadavvi."

"Then send Magdalena away for the month."

"It had occurred to me, but where?"

"Here," he said.

Ariel looked doubtful but not entirely without hope. "For what reason?"

He shrugged. "Say Rachel wants to get to know angels from

all the holds. Or say Rachel's having a hard time fitting in here—
which is true enough, as Jovah will testify—and I thought she
might enjoy Magdalena's company."

Ariel half-closed her eyes. "That might work," she said.
"Magdalena is very tenderhearted."

Gabriel grinned. "Well, Rachel is very hardhearted, so you
must warn your sister that hers will not be an easy task."

"That's even better. If Rachel rebuffs her, Maga will begin
to believe us. Otherwise, I'm afraid she'll know it's just a strata-
gem to keep her from Nathan."

"She's not a child. She knows that she is the one who should
be keeping herself from Nathan, anyway."

"This will serve for now. But—Gabriel, they are truly in love.
I don't know how we can keep them separated forever."

"Marry them off to others," he said.

She made an impatient gesture. "That will hardly keep them
apart."

"We'll deal with them after the Gloria," Gabriel said, rising
to his feet. Ariel held a hand out to him and he hauled her upright.
"Right now, I must get back to my own party."

She took a little time readjusting the folds of her gown
around her hips. Her gold and emerald bracelets jingled musically
on her wrists. "I hate dresses, I hate them," she said. "Give me
leathers and a pair of boots any day."

"Yet you look charming," he said, giving her a little bow.

She laughed. "Why, Gabriel. How courtly."

"I'm brushing up on my romance," he said, leading the way
out. "After all, I have a wife to please now."

She laughed again and followed him out.

The part of his wedding that Gabriel enjoyed the most was,
of course, the singing. The *Magnificat* was by far his favorite piece
of music, rarely sung these days and never formally, because mod-
ern women did not have voices that encompassed the phenomenal
range. He was singing his first solo, experiencing the same euphoric burst he often felt upon surging into flight, when he felt
his arm burn with a sudden and painful fire. The black linen of
his wedding jacket kept the signal covered, but he knew what it
was without looking: the Kiss, flaming against his skin. Rachel,
though he had lost track of her in the crowd, was somewhere
listening to him sing. The thought gave him a peculiar narcissistic
pleasure. He lifted his voice again, driving it against the high notes

with all his power. The pain in his arm did not entirely fade until the song had been over for five minutes.

But when, yielding the floor to other musicians, he drifted through the crowd to look for Rachel, he could not find her anywhere. Others stopped him, cried out their congratulations on his marriage and their compliments on his singing, but Rachel had disappeared utterly. Not that he was surprised. She hadn't wanted to be here in the first place.

Nothing really went wrong until the following morning, and then it was a disaster. Hannah had persuaded him that he needed to hold a formal, intimate breakfast to honor the most consequential of his guests, to thank them for coming and speed them on their way. He had agreed to it. Therefore, the next morning he and his bride sat down to a meal with perhaps thirty influential outsiders, including the visiting angels, the high-ranking burghers and the Manadavvi elect.

He had not seen Rachel since their last meal together, at which she had calmly discussed blasphemies and he had found himself wondering what unlikely combination of events must occur before either of them would be willing to share the other's bed. Face to face with him, she always displayed utter indifference, unless he had made her furious; but he was beginning to have his doubts. Against her will perhaps, but incontrovertibly, she responded to him—if nothing else, responded to his voice. The fire in his *Kiss* had proved that.

"Good morning, Rachel. I trust you slept well," he said, seating himself beside her at the middle of the long table. She seemed almost childlike in one of the ornate high-back chairs reserved for mortals in this most formal of the hold's dining halls. His own chair was elaborately carved with a narrow slat to provide support for his back while leaving plenty of space for his wings to swing free.

"Thank you, I slept as well as I have since I arrived here," was the two-edged response.

"I'm glad to hear it," he said. He studied her. This morning she had chosen to dress in a gown of lilac brocade, long-sleeved (naturally), high-necked and completely unadorned. The color was wrong for her; it made her creamy skin look pale and bloodless. Nothing, of course, could diminish the glory of her hair.

He himself wore semiformal clothes—a full-sleeved white silk blouse under a black vest; black pants, black boots, and the silver and sapphire wristlets that he never removed. The other guests, filing in, had also dressed in their second-best for the occasion.

Raphael and Leah sat across from them; the other notables arranged themselves by rank and began talking quietly across the table.

"Good morning, Gabriel, Rachel," the Archangel said. He shook out the silver folds of a napkin and laid it across his wife's lap with a solicitousness that raised Gabriel's eyebrows. Then the Archangel looked back at his hostess. "We missed you last night, angela. You were gone from the throng so soon."

"I was tired," Rachel said briefly. Gabriel glanced at her.

Leah leaned across the table. Once again, as he always did, Gabriel gazed at her with a half-frown, trying to commit her features to memory. Twenty years he had known this woman and she always, in his mind, remained a blur. He could not get a fix on her; she made no impact. "You looked beautiful last night, Rachel," she said, in her soft, sweet voice.

"She looks beautiful now, my dear," her husband corrected her.

Leah definitely blushed. "Yes—I did not mean—I just wanted to say how exceptional you appeared last night."

To Gabriel's surprise, Rachel smiled at the Archangel's wife. "Thank you," she said. "I appreciate your kindness."

One of the servants stopped at Raphael's place to spoon baked apples onto his plate and Leah's. When the man had moved on, Raphael spoke to Rachel again. "I admit I was disappointed," he said. "I had hoped to hear you sing for us last night. A prelude to the concert at the Gloria."

Gabriel preserved his expression, but he could not tell if he was more shocked at Raphael's directness or eager to hear Rachel's nervous explanation. But he had underestimated his wife. "I was much more interested in listening than in performing," she said. "I have only heard the masses sung on the recordings. I wanted to hear them sung live. I learned a great deal."

Good answer, Gabriel thought. Leah, uncharacteristically, spoke again. "And which piece did you like best?"

"One that I was probably the only person to recognize. The Edori love song that Matthew sang."

Gabriel winced inwardly. "Matthew's voice is a treasure," he said gravely.

"Hardly to compare with an angel's," Raphael said.

"Or an angelica's," Rachel agreed. She nodded to Leah. "I was sorry you only sang once. Your voice is very fine."

Leah blushed again, this time at the compliment. "Thank you," she said. "My voice is my only asset."

"Your best one, maybe," Rachel said, again smiling at the shy angelica, "but surely not your only one."

Raphael sipped at his goblet of juice, then said, "Ah, so you are a connoisseur of singing. Tell me, which of the men's voices gave you the most pleasure?"

Again, the subtle dig. Again, Rachel seemed equal to the challenge of fencing with the Archangel. "They were all delightful," she said coolly. "My husband's was undoubtedly the best, but I found myself wishing I had heard you when you were younger, and your voice was at its best."

She made no attempt to pitch her voice so that it did not carry, and across the whole table there had fallen one of those intermittent lulls that allow a private conversation to be public. Every last person in the room heard the perfectly phrased words, the seeming compliment that was in fact the greatest possible insult to an angel. The silence became profound.

In the instant before she spoke, Gabriel caught Ariel's eyes upon him. "Oh, don't feed his vanity," the Monteverde angel called out. "Raphael likes to imagine that he's Uriel, with a voice that will carry down the ages. We have to listen very carefully to try to catch him in any wrong notes. The best day of my life was when he sang an F-sharp instead of an F-natural in the Helgeth *Cantata*."

Everyone laughed, swept with relief. Rachel nodded across the table at the Archangel. "Forgive me," she said. "It was not my intention to feed your vanity."

Nearly everyone else missed that remark, still laughing or dropping back into interrupted conversations, but Ariel's eyes flicked again to Gabriel's. He nodded imperceptibly. She was right, then. Rachel did hate Raphael. Her malice had been deliberate.

"Of course I forgive you," the Archangel returned lightly. "You have set me a challenge. I shall now have to try and win you over. Perhaps you will come to Windy Point sometime for a visit, and I can sing for you privately."

"I prefer to listen to the duets," was the quick response. "If your wife will sing with you, then I would be delighted to accept."

"Rachel doesn't have time for visiting just at the moment," Gabriel broke in, his words seeming brusque and clumsy after their edged repartee. "She has much to do and learn before the Gloria."

Now his wife's subtle malice was turned on him. "Yes, I am pretty much kept prisoner here on the mountain, studying my new duties," she said brightly. "The angels come and go daily, but I have so much to do that I don't have time to be flitting around."

Leah leaned forward again. "I understand how you feel," she said sympathetically. "I sometimes think if it were easier to leave the mountain now and then—" She stopped abruptly, glanced over at her smiling husband, and sat back in her chair.

Rachel was intrigued. "So Windy Point is like the Eyrie? High up?"

"Wholly inaccessible," Gabriel said shortly. "Higher than the Eyrie by at least a thousand feet. You cannot get to it unless an angel takes you."

"I am familiar with that inconvenience," Rachel said dryly.

"But it possesses a wild beauty all its own," Raphael said in his sugared voice. "You were born in the shadow of the Caitanas, angela. You know how rugged and romantic that range can be. Were you never at Windy Point?"

"I was a hill-farmer's daughter," she said evenly. "We were not often invited to visit the angels."

"And yet—surely—I have always made such an effort to interact with my people," Raphael said. "Did I never visit your village?"

There was a moment of silence even more tense than the one before, but at least this one was not witnessed by everyone else at the table. "If you had," Rachel said at last, "surely the event would have been so momentous that I would never have forgotten it."

To Gabriel's relief, the servants came through again with another course. Conversation, when it resumed, was a little more guarded but along much the same lines. Leah spoke little, watching her husband covertly during most of the meal. Gabriel spoke up whenever he got a chance. His wife and the Archangel continued to spar.

Gabriel was never so pleased to see a meal come to an end. He had not expected it to be such an ordeal. He could not imagine

why Rachel and Raphael had taken such a dislike to each other
that they were willing to show their feelings in public—although
Rachel, at least, seemed willing to do verbal battle with anyone
at any time. And then, even more inexplicably, she had seemed
to feel a certain fondness—no, that was not right—protectiveness
for the cowed and tentative angelica, to the extent of championing
her three or four more times before the breakfast ended. He had
never seen Rachel act nicely to anyone before, except the servants.

But it was over, Jovah be thanked, requiring just a last little
bit of theatrics before the whole affair concluded. Gabriel rose to
his feet, tapping his knife against his glass to draw everyone's
attention.

"Friends—angels—I want to take this chance to thank you
all for attending one of the most important events of my life," he
said. He hated speechmaking, but it had to be done; Nathan had
helped him with the words late last night. "The ceremony had
double meaning for me, because of your presence and your affection."

He glanced down at Rachel. She could school her features
into impassivity, but he read the suspicion in her eyes. He could
not help a faint smile. "I wish also to pay tribute to my beautiful
new wife, the woman who will be my angelica and stand beside
me on the Plain of Sharon for the next twenty years. It is a custom
among angels," he said, now speaking directly to her, "to give
gifts to their loved ones on auspicious occasions. It is also a custom among angels to wear a certain item—and for angelicas to
wear them as well. I thought our wedding would be the perfect
time for me to give you—these."

He handed her a white velvet bag secured with a gold draw-
string. Her hands shook very slightly when she took it from him;
now there was no mistaking the wariness on her face. He smiled
again.

"Open it," he said. "Put them on."

She loosened the bag and shook its contents onto the table-
cloth. An appreciative murmur went up all around the table as
angels and mortals craned forward to get a better look. Gabriel
had given his bride the traditional wedding gift of bracelets, but
these were more beautiful than most. He had commissioned them
last month in Luminaux, two bands made of braided gold, studded with sapphires arranged in floral clusters. They were delicate,

as befitted a lady's wrist, but the woven design had seemed to Gabriel to perfectly reflect both the sturdiness and the complexity of Rachel's character.

"When you wear these at the Gloria," Gabriel continued, now speaking to the top of her bent head, "Jovah will know who you are and who you represent. All angels from the Eyrie wear sapphires in their wristbands. Those of my family wear the sapphires arranged in just such a pattern. No matter where you go among angels, when you wear these bracelets it will be instantly known that you belong here, and to me."

There was light applause around the table at this pretty speech. Nathan had not helped him write that one; it had come to him extemporaneously as he gazed down at the unruly curls. She had not looked up. She had not even touched the plaited metal of the bands. He was seized with a sudden cold premonition of catastrophe.

"It would please me," he ended formally, "if you would wear them now."

"Put them on!" someone called out, and others took up the cry around the table. He heard other murmurs—"They're so beautiful!" "Where did he get those?" "Lucky girl"—but the predominant response of the crowd was one of urging. "Put the bracelets on, Rachel," Ariel said.

Abruptly, the new bride came to her feet, next to him. He had thought she was pale before, but now she was completely colorless. Across her face was the old defiance; her expression was absolutely stony.

"Thank you for the honor," she said in a tight, controlled voice. "I cannot wear these. Now or ever." And she strode from the perfectly silent room without another word.

It was nearly an hour before Gabriel could get to Rachel to demand an explanation, and he would forever mark that hour as one of the worst in his life. First, there was the excruciating fifteen-minute interval to endure at the breakfast table, as angels and powerful mortals sat and stared at him in stupefaction, disbelief and—he had to believe—secret glee at the sight of this most supercilious of angels humiliated in public. He had Nathan and Ariel to thank for filling the vacuum with a few exculpatory comments and brisk observations that all new couples had some problems to work out. The group broke up very quickly after that, people excusing themselves with remarks about getting their packing done and how they needed to be home right away.

Gabriel stood where Rachel had left him, nodding at those who made their farewells, accepting their good wishes, trying not to grimace at their good-natured jokes and assurances that all would be well. He didn't really hear anything that was said to him until a small, timid hand was laid upon his arm. He frowned down and tried to place the face; the woman was of the type he always immediately dismissed as negligible.

"Angelo," she said in a voice that matched her appearance, "be kind to her."

His frown deepened. "I assure you—"

"She—at heart, she is such a good person. I know she has made you angry, and a woman should not make her husband angry, I know—but do not scold her too cruelly."

Lady Mary of Semorrah. The name suddenly came back to him. Young Daniel's wife. "I am not in the habit of scolding anyone, nor am I in the habit of practicing cruelty," he said, although his freezing voice belied both assertions.

"She is Edori," the young lady said helpfully. "Perhaps they don't wear jewelry."

This shy young noblewoman seemed truly anxious to dissipate his rage. Her partisanship was so unexpected that, unconsciously, the edge of his fury was worn away. "Madame," he said, inclining his head to her slightly, "I will ask her. Your husband is awaiting you and I wish you would go to him. Have no fears for Rachel."

With this she had to be content; young Daniel indeed was watching her impatiently from a group that included his parents and her own. She lifted her skirts and skipped back to them. Gabriel found himself confronting the Archangel, who had come to his feet on the opposite side of the table. The rest of the room had suddenly emptied.

"A decided show of spirit," Raphael murmured. "I congratulate you on your choice of bride."

"Merely a misunderstanding," Gabriel said stiffly.

Raphael was still sipping from his juice goblet. He seemed prepared to stay and enjoy a tête-à-tête for the rest of the day. "But such a public one. Perhaps you should rehearse your appearances a bit more often with your angelica."

A double meaning to the word rehearse. Gabriel flinched,

knowing it was true. On both counts. "It was an unfortunate occurrence," he said. "Still, I prefer a woman who speaks her own mind to one who does not speak at all."

Raphael laid down his beverage and began nibbling on left-over fruit. "An unkind observation," he said mildly. "And my wife is used to thinking of you as such a courteous man."

Gabriel's face flamed; he had not meant to insult Leah, though it was true he would prefer Rachel any day to someone as vapid as the current angelica. "We all suit ourselves to the god's choices," he said.

"And yet," Raphael said, still in that smooth, ruminative voice, "one sometimes wonders about the god's choices. The differences between generations are so striking that one almost cannot see any parallels. And—actually—any continuity."

Suddenly, Gabriel felt alarm cycle through him, coldly allaying the anger that had consumed him for the past quarter hour. He regarded Raphael through narrowed eyes. "Things change," he said. "That is the way the world is set up."

"Gabriel," Raphael said sadly. He spread his hands, for this moment empty of either food or drink, as if words alone could not convey the depth of his emotion. "Gabriel. I lie awake at nights dreading the Gloria. Not for your sake—you have a powerful voice and we all know Jovah spreads his ears when you sing. But—Gabriel. This woman? As angelica? Even you, eager as you are to take the power from my hands, must see that she is not fit for the role. She will bring the wrath of Jovah down upon us if she sings on the Plain of Sharon."

Gabriel was so shocked, he could not answer.

Raphael began ticking off liabilities on his fingers. "A hill-farmer. When there has never yet been an angelica who was not bred among the gentry. An Edori. When the Edori do not even believe Jovah is the supreme power. A slave." His gesture conveyed just how impossible that was. "And—may I ask you?—can she sing? Has she a voice? What will we hear, what will Jovah hear, if she tries to lead the Gloria in a few months' time?"

Gabriel wanted to put his hands over his ears, to physically shut out the questions that eternally circled in his own mind. "All of what you say may be true—is true, is indisputable," he said, his voice very hard. "And yet the doubts of men are invalid. Jovah chose her. Jovah wishes to hear her voice—be it melodious or wretched, her voice is the one he asked for. Hers is the voice that must be heard on the Plain of Sharon this spring—or in truth there will be death and destruction, as you fear."

Raphael delicately toyed with the silver serving trays still on the table. "Not necessarily," he said. "There is still an angelica, proven and beloved, also chosen by Jovah. She could sing this spring. Your Rachel could be—given more time—trained more properly. In a year or so—"

"But for Leah to sing at the Gloria, you would have to sing beside her," Gabriel interrupted.

Raphael nodded. "Precisely. But in the interests of the realm, I am willing to do that. For you. For—well, for Rachel."

It was brilliantly clear to Gabriel, suddenly, frighteningly. "You don't want to give it up," he said, his voice disbelieving. "The Archangel's power—you don't want to cede it."

Raphael made a gesture of denial. "I am Jovah's servant, as you are," he said graciously. "I exist merely to worship him, and to bring to him the word of inarticulate mortals. As we all do. But those same mortals depend on us, to defend their lives, their homes—this entire planet. Gabriel! An untrained angelica lifting a cracked voice to Jovah while the fate of all Samaria hangs on her song? Can you risk that? The lives of every man and angel on this planet? While there is still an angelica available and an Archangel willing to sing at her side?"

"I have to risk it," Gabriel said, his words hurled like rocks at Raphael. "You have given your twenty years. Jovah never asks for—never *wants*—more than that from any angel. If you were to sing at the Gloria this summer, then indeed we would see the doom descend that you are so worried about."

"But I say—"

"*I* say that you are an ambitious man who has learned to love the taste of power so well that you cannot tear yourself from the banquet," Gabriel flung at him. "Is that true? Is that what you are in fact telling me? Do not come here pretending to be my savior when in fact you are plotting against me—and my bride. Tell me openly what you desire."

"I desire the well-being of the realm," Raphael snapped. "You are a fine one to talk of ambition. You close your eyes to the unsuitability of your own angelica because you are too power-mad to admit she will destroy us all."

"I am not power-mad," Gabriel replied grimly. "I am not the one seeking to overturn divine laws. But I thank you for your offer. You have now made it clear to me where you stand—and what I have to expect from you until I am Archangel."

"If you become Archangel," Raphael said in a low, silky voice.

Gabriel gave him the slightest of bows. "Oh, I will. Make no mistake about that. Your time is coming to an end, Raphael—and the sooner the better for all of us." He turned and strode for the door, pausing at the threshold for one parting shot. "Thank you so much for attending my wedding."

His intention was to go directly to Rachel's chamber—and, if she was not there, to track her down wherever she had hidden—but Ariel waylaid him when he was ten steps out the door.

"It couldn't be better!" she exclaimed in a low voice, clutching his arm and stopping him when he would have stalked right past her.

"How strange you are," he replied. "To me it seems things could not be worse."

She waved one hand, still gripping him with the other. "So it was an embarrassing moment for you. But Rachel has given us the perfect opening. In fact, I think it's almost arranged."

"Ariel, could we discuss this later—"

"No, listen to me! We were leaving and Maga said that Rachel looked so unhappy when she was running from the room, and I said I thought she *was* unhappy and that you'd told me she was having a hard time making friends, and that she was suspicious of all the Eyrie angels, and if only I had time to try to get to know her—"

Gabriel had started edging down the hall, perforce dragging Ariel along with him. "Well, it sounds like you know just how to convince her."

"Gabriel, she volunteered! She said that she felt so sorry for Rachel, and she had thought before how she'd like to make friends with her, and if I didn't think you'd mind, maybe she could stay on for a few weeks—Gabriel, are you *listening* to me?"

He stopped again, abruptly. "Ariel, do you think I'm power-mad?" he demanded.

She blinked at the change of subject. "Are you— Well, I've never given it any thought. No, I don't suppose you are."

"Good." And he began striding down the corridor again. She hurried to catch up.

"Well, for all the— Aren't you going to tell me who does think you're power-mad?" she asked.

But he was still unnerved by his run-in with Raphael, and couldn't repeat their conversation until he'd analyzed it in private. "Forget it. It's not important. Look, I'm glad she's staying. I'm delighted. Tell her for me—"

But Ariel did not have to convey any messages, for the next curve of the tunnel brought them face to face with a resolute Magdalena and an angry Nathan. By the way Nathan whirled around at the sound of their footsteps, Gabriel suspected his brother had been standing a little too close to the Monteverde angel.

"Gabriel, Ariel said she thought you would be pleased," was Magdalena's greeting. "I offered to stay a couple of weeks and try to make friends with Rachel—"

"Yes, wonderful," Gabriel said. Nathan cast him a glance of supreme irritation. He exerted himself to say a little more. "Although she is an extremely difficult woman. She may not take to you, either."

"Everybody likes Maga," Nathan muttered.

"Yes, that has been my observation," Gabriel agreed. "You would do me a great favor if you could charm some of your own sweetness into my wife." Magdalena giggled. "Now if you will excuse me—"

"I'd like a word with you, actually," Nathan said.

"Come. Let's go see what you need, and I can have things sent here to you from Monteverde," Ariel said, tugging on her sister's arm. In a moment, the brothers were left alone.

"Well?" Gabriel said.

"Maga may say it was her idea, but I saw you and Ariel plotting yesterday, and I know what this is all about," Nathan said with unwonted heat. "I know she told you that I was going up to Abel Vashir's place—"

"And that's another thing," Gabriel said, although he had mentioned no antecedents. "I would have preferred to learn of such a thing from you—"

"I've been busy—*you've* been busy—that's not the point," Nathan said impatiently. "The point is, you're afraid that if I'm so close to Monteverde, I would see Maga every day—"

"And wouldn't you?" Gabriel was goaded to say. "You can

stand there and tell me, with temptation three hours away, that you would keep to the schoolrooms of the Manadavvi and never think about Magdalena once? That you would not meet with her, scheme to be with her alone, away from my eyes or Ariel's or even Abel Vashir's—"

"It's none of your business!" Nathan cried.

"Oh, yes, it is entirely my business! It would be my business if I just led the host here—if you weren't my brother and if I wasn't to be Archangel. As it is, I have triple the responsibility for seeing that divine law is not transgressed. And I have the power to do it. I have tried to be fair. I have tried to be understanding. I have not forbidden you to see her, which I could have done—which Ariel could have done. Nathan, the laws were laid down by Jovah himself—"

"Then why did he break them?" Nathan asked fiercely. He ripped open the front of his silk dress shirt to show the amber Kiss still faintly illuminated, fading testimony to Magdalena's effect on him. "I was taught—we were all taught—that this is Jovah's signal, that it calls one lover to another. Jovah makes the Kiss light, not me! I cannot control it! Answer that for me, and then tell me I am contemplating a sin."

"I can't," Gabriel said, suddenly weary. His own Kiss had betrayed him; he did not have any moral superiorities to fall back on here. "I don't understand it. The ways of Jovah are not always clear to me. Take it up with Josiah. Perhaps he can answer you. But for now, let it go. Magdalena will be at the Eyrie for some time. If you choose to return here while she is visiting, do so. But—be very, very careful."

Once more Gabriel turned his steps toward the upper quarters; once more he made no headway. This time it was Hannah who stopped him, telling him that the merchants were leaving; he must make formal farewells. And so he lost more time in pointless, insincere rituals before he finally made good his escape and climbed the two stories to Rachel's chamber.

All the interruptions had served one good purpose: They had dissipated his anger and left behind a weary puzzlement. Clearly he would never understand his bride. But this time he would ask her to explain herself.

There was such a long pause between the ring of the door chime and the invitation to enter that he thought she had not, after all, taken refuge in her room. But she was there. He opened the door, stepped inside and shut the door behind him.

She stood across the room, as far away from him as possible, close to the wall, but not backed up against it; no cowering for this girl. On her face was the expression he had come to know best—a mixture of rebelliousness and stubbornness. She did not look sorry.

"I thought," he said in a voice much milder than he had thought, an hour ago, he would be able to manage, "that I would give you a chance to explain why you rejected my wedding gift so forcefully."

Some of the fight went out of her at this reasonable opening. Obviously she had expected fury and was braced for it. She hunched one shoulder. "I was not anticipating something like that," she said.

He came a few steps farther into the room. "A gift?" he said, almost pleasantly. "Or that particular type of gift?"

"Both. Either," she said. "I—you should have warned me."

"Warned you?" he repeated. "I thought it would give you pleasure."

"Well, it didn't!"

"That was plain to everyone in the room."

She was silent.

He strolled forward again. She held her ground, although he could tell she wanted to move away by as many steps as he advanced. "So tell me," he invited, "is this an Edori prohibition? No jewelry? No bracelets? Is it the gold you dislike, or the sapphire pattern—or the fact that it comes from me?" The last few words were spoken sharply. She winced very slightly.

"No, I— Thank you, I suppose, for the gift, the *idea* of the gift. I'm sure it was very thoughtful, but I—you see, I don't care for bracelets."

"Why not?"

"Because. If it's important that I wear something with this— crest on it, or what have you—then maybe a hair comb, or a necklace or something . . ."

Her speech had grown increasingly disjointed the closer he came, and now he stood just inches away. He had to give her credit; she didn't break and run for it, much as he knew she wanted to.

"Why not a bracelet?"

"Because I—"

"Why not a bracelet?"

"Gabriel, don't," she said, suddenly so serious that it pulled him up short. "Please. Let it go."

He took her hand, which surprised her. She fought to free it, which surprised him. He held on. "You have too many secrets," he said, his voice gentle. "How will I ever know what you like and what you don't like and why, if you won't tell me? Because it seems that a simple bracelet—"

"A simple bracelet!" Abruptly, again, she was roused to fury. With her free hand, she stripped the buttons from the other cuff of her blouse and jerked the sleeve up toward her elbow. "I wore simple bracelets every day of my life for five years, and I cannot bear the touch of anything on my wrists now—"

She would have wrenched away on the words, but he automatically tightened his hold. He felt sick to his stomach. The bare wrist bore a ring of thick and reddened scar tissue four or five inches wide, from the heel of the hand partway up the forearm. Over the knobby bones of her wrist, the tissue was ridged in places, thicker than the rest, rubbed more often by the heavy metal of the shackle. Her arm was so thin that the back of her hand was also scarred, although not as deeply, by the iron falling forward on her arm.

He held out his free hand. "Let me see the other one."

Again she tried to twist away. Her voice sounded unexpectedly shy. "It looks like this one. Gabriel, let me go."

Even under these circumstances, it gave him an odd pleasure to hear her speak his name, something she rarely did. He shook his head. "I want to see it."

She hesitated, then surrendered her hand. He undid the buttons and gently pulled the fabric away. Again, the deep band of scar tissue, mostly an ugly, shiny pink, broken in places by tough white lines. He turned it front to back to see it from all sides. This time, when she squirmed to get free, he released her.

Finally he raised his eyes to her face. His own expression, he knew, must be painfully somber. "I'm sorry," he said. "I had no idea."

She gave the ghost of a laugh and busied herself with rebuttoning the sleeves. "Why would you?"

"Why didn't you tell me?"

She glanced at him, started to speak, and looked away. She shrugged—not to signify that she didn't know, but that it was impossible to explain.

"What other scars do you bear?"

"None like those," she said.

"Tell me."

"Gabriel, what does it matter? You hate to be reminded that I was a slave—oh, don't bother denying it, you can't hide how much you hate it—well, I hate to think of it, too. I hate it. That part of my life is over. I don't want to talk about it now. I'm sorry about the bracelets. But I—I really can't wear them."

"No, of course not," he responded absently. She had taken the opportunity, in the exchange of hands and the refastening of her cuffs, to move away from him. She straightened her blouse and took another small step. He turned to mark her progress. "But this isn't about the bracelets anymore. I should have known before this. I should have known a lot of things about you that I don't know. There are too many secrets in your life."

"How can you say that? You know where I have spent every year of my existence." But she did not look at him when she spoke. She had stopped before a small gilt mirror on the wall, to make minute adjustments to her collar.

"I don't know what happened to your village when you were—what, seven? I don't know what destroyed it."

Now she inspected her reflection for signs of damage to her coiffure. "I was so young," she said. "I have very few memories of the time before I lived with the Edori."

"My mother died when I was five," he said slowly, "and I remember that very clearly. I think you recall what happened to your village."

She met his eyes in the mirror. Her own were very dark. "I remember—people shrieking. I remember fire. I remember noises, for things I couldn't even put a name to. Like rocks falling, trees falling. Now I think it must have been the houses themselves collapsing. Who knows what caused all that? Maybe I've chosen not to remember."

It was a partial answer, but he did not think she would tell him more. "And the Edori found you—how?"

She moved away from the glass, restless, circling the room slowly. "I was alone on a road. I don't remember where. Away from the village. I don't know how many days I had traveled. I don't remember what I ate or drank. I know I had been running. Crying. Having nightmares. The Edori found me one day when I was half-starved, half-dead, and they took me in. At first I was afraid of them. And then I grew to love them."

"And when the Jansai came?"

She took a quick, deep breath. "Why must I recount for you all the horrors of my life?" she demanded. "You can imagine that one for yourself. If you think these are secrets, you have a poor idea of what secrets are. These are just bad memories, and I do not wish to discuss them."

"All right," he said. "But I think this one does qualify as a secret. You hate Raphael. Tell me why."

He had surprised her, but like a hunted animal, she had protective coloration. In her case, it was disdain. "Hate him," she said. "I never spoke to him in my life until yesterday."

"Don't *lie* to me," he said sharply.

"If I chose to," she said icily, "I would lie to you every time I opened my mouth. As it happens, I have always told you the truth."

"Maybe," he admitted in an angry tone. "You are clever enough to word things into half-truths. So maybe it's true that you never *spoke* to Raphael until yesterday. But you hate him. I want to know why."

"I'm not particularly fond of any angel," she said. "And I suppose you can't figure that out on your own?"

He held onto his temper; she was being deliberately provoking. "You don't trust me," he said. "You think all angels believe the same, act the same. But—"

"But if I choose to dislike Raphael, that is my business," she interrupted. "I grew up in the Caitanas, and spent most of my life wandering through Jordana. None of this gave me a high opinion of the Archangel. You don't have to try and pry reasons out of me. You're none too crazy about him yourself, but I don't see you announcing that fact from the mountaintop."

As a defense, the sudden attack was very effective. He stiffened, remembering the conversation he'd just had with the leader of Windy Point. "You're right—I have had my share of differences with Raphael," he said. "Sometimes I think . . ." He let the words trail off.

"Think what?"

He shook his head. "That I should be more wary of him.

That he is—a dangerous man, maybe. I don't know. But that makes it all the more important," he added, suddenly rounding on her again, "that you should tell me anything you know to his discredit."

"He's cruel to his wife," she said.

"What makes you think that?"

She shrugged. "Because it's true."

"You were unexpectedly friendly to the angelica."

"I felt sorry for her. Someone who has had a worse life than I have."

He smiled faintly; few people would have come to that conclusion. "Why is it," he said, "you are always drawn to the powerless? You are positively kind to the servants and the downtrodden and to mistreated wives, although in general you are a fractious and contrary woman."

"I'm drawn to the powerless because I have an innate distaste for the powerful," was the immediate response. "Fellow feeling, I suppose."

Now he gave a soft laugh. "You," he said, "in your worst moment, were never powerless or downtrodden."

She dropped him a quick curtsey. "Thank you, angelo. I take that as a compliment."

"And so it was meant." He hesitated; he had not felt so in charity with his bride since the hour they met. "You lump me in with the hated ruling classes, I know," he said slowly, "but still, we could deal better together than we do. My fault, I know, for things that happened, at least at the beginning—"

"Actually, if it's any comfort to you, I think you're the best of the lot," she said. Her voice held its customary mocking edge, but he thought she might be sincere. "You don't abuse your power, at any rate. You actually seem to have some desire to do good in the world, though you'd rather do it from a distance, I think. And of course you have other faults—"

"Arrogance," he said with a faint smile.

"No, I don't think that's it," she said thoughtfully. "I think it's impatience. A sort of broad irritation that not everybody else thinks exactly the way you do—when your way is clearly right."

He was irrationally pleased—and, at the same time, unnerved—that someone who knew him so little could so perfectly describe him. In return he gave her a playful bow. "Thank you for the kind words," he said. "I am greatly moved."

She actually laughed. "Consider it your wedding gift," she said. "I didn't think to prepare anything else."

He felt the smile come back to his own face. "I have two more gifts for you," he said. "One of which you will like, and one which you might not."

She was instantly on guard. "What are they?" she asked.

"First the one you might dislike. Actually, it is not so much a gift to you as a problem for me." He glanced over at her; her face was completely impassive. "I know you disagree with the sentiment behind it, but *try* to understand. Nathan and Magdalena—"

"If you're expecting me to find a husband for Magdalena—"

"No, no. Nothing like that. It's just that Nathan has contracted to spend a month in a Manadavvi compound very close to Monteverde. Ariel wished to send Maga here to keep her away from Nathan. I agreed, and we presented the idea to Maga as a— well, as a chance to do me a favor, do you a favor, telling her that you hadn't made many friends among the angels here, and perhaps she could win you over. And in fact," he added, "I really do think you would like her. She's very sweet-tempered. Eager to please. Thoughtful, kind—all the things you admire."

"I'm surprised you didn't realize," Rachel said evenly, "that I'm much more likely to abet her in meeting Nathan secretly than to try to convince her that she should give him up."

"I realized it," he said. "But my options were limited."

She opened her mouth, hesitated, then spread her hands helplessly. "What is it you want me to do with her?"

"Just be nice to her. If it'll make it easier, consider her one of the poor unfortunates that you're so fond of. Teach her how to weave. Practice songs together." He couldn't believe he said it; hastily he added, "Visit Velora for fun."

"I can't get to Velora," she replied.

He had turned toward the door and, as she spoke, was halfway across the room. He stopped with his hand on the knob, and smiled at her. "Oh yes, you can," he said. "That's my last wedding present to you. A way off the mountain."

CHAPTER NINE

Two weeks later, Rachel sat with Magdalena in a sunny Velora pastry shop and thought that life was really very good.

True, it was nearly the heart of winter now, and even at sea level, the air was too chilly to travel without a cloak, but she had survived cold weather before. Everything else was marvelous. After a solid week of miserable, rainy weather, the sun had broken free of the clinging clouds and blazed down upon them with a sort of lunatic delight. Magdalena had proved to be the most agreeable person she'd met in the past five years, impossible to dislike, touched with a tentative charm that instantly breached Rachel's outer defenses. And she was off the mountain.

Gabriel's last wedding present had been, by far, his best. He had made her wait until every last guest had left the Eyrie, then taken her to Matthew's work chamber to collect the Edori leather worker. Together, the three of them had wound through the lower tunnels of the compound, toward the farthermost storage chambers, where nobody ever went.

"The first week you were here, I remembered this," Gabriel had said over his shoulder to Rachel. "Or remembered hearing about it. I don't think anybody's used it for a hundred years. Since Isaiah led the host here at the Eyrie, and his daughter had the same problem you have."

"Height-sickness," Matthew murmured.

"Whatever. So he had this built. Chipped out of the rock in

the most laborious fashion. It took more than a year, so the histories say. Personally, I find the whole thing a little creepy. I can't stand to be in places that are so closed in."

What Isaiah had built for his daughter was a small wooden cage that used a complex system of weights and pulleys to travel up and down a narrow shaft cut into the mountain itself. A door at the base of the mountain (long ago grown over with vines and shrubbery) allowed the descending passenger to exit; a similar door opened onto the bottom tier of the Eyrie tunnels. The shaft had been cunningly designed with ventilation holes to provide adequate fresh air. An emergency bell-cord had been installed in the car, attached to a chime at the upper level, in case the car became stuck in transit.

Many of the ropes and wires which had hoisted the car through its vertical tunnel had rotted or worn away in a century of disuse, but Matthew had painstakingly replaced or repaired them all. The leather craftsman, it seemed, had the usual Edori tinkering skills as well as a fascination with anything that moved. The angel and the Edori had repeatedly tested the resurrected lift before allowing Rachel to ride in it.

"These are the rules," Gabriel had said. "You always tell someone you're taking the cage down, and you always ring the bell before you get in the cage to come up. I cannot conceive of any more horrifying end than to be trapped in some little box deep in the heart of a mountain. If you *don't* observe these rules, I swear to you, I'll have Matthew cut the cords and never let you get in the cage again."

She would have liked to flout his rules, but the idea of freedom was too precious; besides, she had to admit that the prospect of being stuck for hours in the stone shaft was far from attractive. So she readily agreed to both conditions. They watched her make a trial run, and she was secretly relieved on two counts. The levered weights were easy enough for her to manage, and piped gaslight down the length of the shaft provided comforting illumination.

And then the door at the bottom of the mountain opened and she was on flat, solid ground, and she was *free*. The only reason she came back up so quickly was because she did not want to give Gabriel any reason to rescind this most wonderful of privileges. When she stepped from the car back in the Eyrie, she could have hugged her husband in gratitude. She refrained.

But she knew she was glowing, anyway, as incandescent as the gaslight throwing an eternal nimbus against the rosy mountain walls. "Thank you, thank you, thank you," she exclaimed, the words dancing out of her mouth, her feet dancing across the stone floor. "This is the best thing you could ever have done for me—"

And she had been surprised by the wistfulness that had momentarily crossed Gabriel's face. Was he sorry that he hadn't given her this gift sooner, or sad for her that her joys were so few? It scarcely mattered; she didn't care at all. She could get off the mountain. She was a prisoner no more.

Magdalena, the third wedding gift, had proved to be almost as wonderful. As Gabriel had said, it was impossible to dislike the Monteverde angel, although Rachel had been willing to try.

Magdalena had come to her late the day of the ill-fated breakfast, and even her manner of chiming the door had been unobtrusive. Rachel let her in but did not invite her to sit down.

"I think you've been kept here under false pretenses," Rachel said without preamble. "They told you I needed a friend, but they really wanted a way to keep you away from Nathan."

"I know," Magdalena said gently. "But I too was looking for a way to keep away from Nathan."

Rachel stared at her. "Don't you want to be with him?" she demanded. "When you're together, you look as if you're in love."

Magdalena gave her a sweet smile. "I am. We are. I scarcely remember a time I wasn't in love with Nathan."

Rachel made a broad gesture. "Then—"

"If I can't have him, it is easier not to be near him." The angel stepped slowly around the room and began to inspect it. When she spoke again, she had changed the subject. "It's so surprising," she said. "I've seen this room before, and it's always looked exactly like this. Same tapestry on the wall, same furniture. Haven't you brought in anything of your own?"

"I didn't have anything when I came here," Rachel said evenly. "I had nothing to bring except guilt gifts from Lord Jethro."

"We should go shopping, then. Down to the Velora bazaars. What kinds of things do you like? They have almost everything there."

Intrigued, Rachel thought about that. "I don't know . . . The

Edori traveled so much, we didn't have many *things*. Decorative things, that is. Everything we carried from place to place was useful in some way."

"How strange. My whole life I've been surrounded by beautiful, useless objects—gifts, mostly. People are always giving angels gifts. Ariel loves them. The more delicate and ornamental a thing is, the more she loves it. Which is also strange, because for the most part, she's an extraordinarily practical person."

"She must like Luminaux, then."

"Her favorite place in the world. All that glass and crystal."

"I like colors," Rachel decided. "Maybe all Edori do. Bright weavings, and embroidered head scarves, and blankets dyed red and blue and purple. Color is the only way to make practical things beautiful."

"We will have a wonderful time in Velora," Magdalena said solemnly.

Rachel laughed. "But what do I buy with?" she asked. "I have nothing to barter. In Semorrah, everything was bought and paid for with gold. But here—"

"Velora and the Eyrie have a credit agreement," Magdalena said. "Many of the cities have such arrangements with the angels. You just show your bracelets—" She stopped abruptly.

"Ah, yes, my bracelets," Rachel said dryly.

Magdalena did not ask questions. "Well, could you carry them with you if you don't feel you can wear them?" she asked. "Put one in your pocket or something?"

Rachel considered. "Well, I could . . . But how do I know how much I've spent if I'm not using gold or bartered goods? What if I spend too much?"

Magdalena laughed. "The Eyrie is rich beyond the dreams of Semorrah," she informed the angelica. "You could not possibly spend too much on a few dresses and a couple of items for your walls."

Unlimited wealth, a choice market and a companion who seemed to have no concept of economy. Despite her innate caution, Rachel felt a certain anticipation rising. "Let's go, then," she said recklessly. "Down to Velora. Tomorrow morning."

They spent the better part of the next three days in the small, elegant city at the foot of the Velo Mountains. Magdalena would not let Rachel buy anything the first day.

"You don't even know what you want yet," the angel said. She sounded serious, but Rachel suspected she was inwardly laughing; surely the act of purchasing could not be this complex. "You must look at everything first, and then go back to the things you thought you liked, and make sure you still like them. And then you must look at everything that you didn't like and make sure you didn't overlook any good qualities. And then you must make sure nothing new came in overnight that you might like better than everything else."

But the ritual was enjoyable nonetheless. The bazaar stalls were full of exotic items, from pottery to jewelry to gloves, and Rachel found herself savoring every last piece of merchandise, holding jewels up to her ears, trying scarves around her head, stepping into and out of pair after pair of hand-sewn shoes. Velora could not compare to Luminaux, of course, and even Semorrah had a greater range of wares available in its open-air markets, but it had been so long since Rachel had the chance to squander any money on herself that the experience seemed almost sinfully luxurious.

The second day they went back to buy. Magdalena had instructed Rachel on how to bargain with the petty merchants ("Because they overprice everything, particularly when they think they're selling to the angel holds."), and Rachel entered into the haggling process with zest. Three of the shopkeepers congratulated her, once the transaction was completed, on her tenacity and skill. She laughed, and gathered up her goods.

She did not bargain at all as she bought apricot silk at a small booth on the edge of town, run by a thin, nervous, teenaged girl. Magdalena scolded her once they were out of earshot, but Rachel shrugged.

"She looked hungry."

"But still! You could have brought that price down by half and she would have eaten well for three days—"

"I'm going back tomorrow to buy the blue silk as well."

When the spree was ended, Rachel had bought enough clothes and furnishings to transform herself and her room. Weeks ago she had noticed how the close-fitting leathers gave the angels much greater freedom of movement than the full-skirted gowns she had always worn, so she had bought—and commissioned— several woolen outfits that approximated the vests, shirts and trousers that even the women angels wore. That meant she also needed boots to tuck the trousers into, and shawls to dress up the plain patterns, and scarves with which to tie back her hair.

For her room she bought rugs, wall hangings, potted plants, an etched mirror in an ornate wooden frame, a small maple table with a checkerboard inlay of onyx and pearl, a silver hairbrush, and five embroidered pillows. Most of these items had been delivered to the hauling platform at the edge of the mountain which was used to hoist bulk goods up to the Eyrie. She did wonder from time to time how Gabriel would feel about her headlong plunge into pure hedonism, but she could not ask him. He was, of course, gone again. He was usually gone.

The shopping was curtailed by a spell of cold, wet weather, so Rachel and the angel stayed in for several days. These hours passed agreeably as well. Magdalena taught Rachel the intricate board games that she had seen some of the affluent Semorrans play (and lose huge amounts of money on, though she and Maga did not gamble). In return, Rachel taught her some of the rudimentary weaving skills that had earned her such fame among the Manderras.

And they each spent some time, separately, in the recital chambers—Magdalena, no doubt, to rehearse, and Rachel to listen to recordings. Magdalena also signed up for several one-hour harmonic shifts, and sang duets with three or four of the Eyrie angels during those rainy days. She had a pure, wistful alto; her voice was not as strong as her sister's, but sweet in tone and absolutely true. Rachel liked to listen to her. Or maybe she just liked Maga.

She was not the only one. The Monteverde angel was a universal favorite with the Eyrie residents, and while she was in Magdalena's company, Rachel could count on continuous brief visits from mortals and other angels. After the first day or two, she stopped glowering at the visitors and just ignored them while they talked to Maga. Most of them returned the favor.

The only person, as far as Rachel could tell, who did not like Magdalena was Hannah. This had become evident on the first day that Maga was there, when the older woman joined them for breakfast.

"I understand you're staying with us for a few weeks," Hannah had said in her usual measured tones.

"Yes—a month or so," Magdalena replied.

"You realize of course that we'll expect you to sing some of the harmonics while you're here."

"Certainly. I'm looking forward to it."

And Hannah had not said another word to the angel except to admonish her sharply not to dip her sleeve in the milk. Rachel had observed all this in surprise, since Hannah—although not especially warm—had always been kind to everyone Rachel had seen her with before.

It was late in the second week, during a rainstorm that had turned, messily, to snow, that Rachel asked Magdalena for an explanation. They had just returned from trying out Rachel's new boots in the snow that had fallen on the plateau, and Hannah had severely criticized them for tracking in water.

"I've never heard her speak to anyone the way she does to you," Rachel said, once they were ensconced in her room. "Doesn't she like you? I thought Hannah liked everyone. I thought everyone liked you."

Maga was toweling her thick, short hair. "She used to like me. But this whole business with Nathan—" She shrugged and folded up the towel. "She thinks it's all my fault, I suppose."

"But why does she care? More than anyone else, I mean."

"Because Nathan's her son."

Rachel stared. "Her *son*? But I thought he and Gabriel were brothers—"

"Half brothers. It's rare that you'll find full-blooded siblings among the angels."

"You and Ariel?"

Maga shook her head. "Oh, no. You don't know that story?"

"No one talks to me. I don't know any of the gossip."

"No one talks to you because you're extremely unfriendly," Maga retorted.

Rachel grinned. "I don't care much for angels, as a rule."

"You married one."

"Duress."

"And you seem to like me well enough."

"Everybody likes you. Tell me your story."

"Well, my father was an angel, and he was married to Ariel's mother, and she was born. Shortly after that, a young woman came through Monteverde and drew my father's attention. Well, she drew the attention of several of the men at the hold. She was one of the angel-seekers, and she'd been to Windy Point—"

"Wait a minute. Angel-seeker? What's that?"

"A woman who seduces angels in hopes of bearing an angel child and thus being accepted into the hold."

Rachel's eyes grew big. "You mean, that's her goal? Her purpose for loving a man? Are there many women like that?"

"Oh, yes. Haven't you noticed them in Velora? I'll point them out to you next time we go."

"So they seduce angels and—then what? If they have an angel child—"

"Then they can choose to raise the child in the hold, and live there as long as they like. Angel babies are rare and precious, you understand. A woman who bears one gains a certain status for life. It's a gamble, of course, because so few women do have cherub children."

"And what happens if her children are mortal?"

Maga shrugged. "It depends on the woman. Sometimes she raises them. Sometimes she abandons them. There are a lot of stray children in Monteverde. And Velora is overrun with them. Surely you've seen them in Velora. Some of them become almost feral—street children, with no one to care for them but each other. There are even more in Breven and the other Jansai cities. That's where a lot of the angel-seekers end up, because the Jansai cater to women with—certain moral standards."

Rachel was shocked to the core. "How can a mother abandon her child? Just leave the baby on a street corner somewhere—"

"Or in a field or a cave or a wagon by some roadway. It's gruesome, I know. To these women, children are a liability. Mortal children, anyway. When you're around angels long enough, you'll come to expect it—the sight of these lost children who would have had such different lives if they'd been born angelic."

Rachel felt physically ill. "I can't imagine— Among Edori, children are valued above everything," she said. "You would sell yourself into slavery before you would permit harm to come to your child. We don't believe in allowing ourselves to have children unless we are able and willing to care for them. To have one on a gamble, on a chance, for some other purpose than to love the child for itself—"

"You are appalled, I know, but to me the chance seems worth it," Maga said seriously. "You see, I know how few angels there are, and how worried the host leaders become when baby after baby is born mortal. There is such rejoicing when a new angel enters the world. They say even Jovah dances. I don't believe the mortal children should be abandoned, but I cannot blame anyone for trying to sire—or bear—an angel."

Rachel shook her head, still amazed and disturbed, but clearly she and Magdalena would never agree on this subject. "So—your mother," she said, her voice sounding a little strained. "She was one of these—angel-seekers . . ."

Maga nodded. "And she came to Monteverde. Ariel had just been born and my father was feeling proud of himself, confident that he could sire another angel. So when my mother approached him, he was eager enough to sleep with her, and within a few weeks it was clear that she was pregnant. He was delighted. She should have been delighted, too, but meanwhile she'd fallen in love with another man—a mortal man, I mean, a Jansai—and she wanted to leave Monteverde and go off with him. My father refused to let her go. So they left anyway, in the middle of the night."

Magdalena paused, resettling herself on the pillows next to Rachel. "And they were gone," she said simply. "No one could find them. My father searched for the next year. He went to Breven, he went to Luminaux; he had portraits of her sent to every hold and city. No one had seen her, no one knew what had happened to the baby. He finally stopped searching.

"Then, one day a few years later, he was on a routine search flight over Gaza and he saw a plague flag over a rocky area where he knew there were no villages. He came down and found a little camp—a tent, a hut, a few rabbits in a hutch. The Jansai man was dead. My mother was dying. I was lying in the hut, crying and hungry but not sick. Angels rarely succumb to plague, for some reason. My father brought me back to Monteverde, and that's where I've been ever since."

Rachel was fascinated. "Do you remember any of it?"

Maga shook her head. "Nothing. Ariel's mother once showed me one of my mother's portraits, but I didn't remember the face. I don't remember anything but Monteverde. I wonder about her, though."

"What do you wonder?"

"Why she did what she did. It's almost incredible. I mean— angel-seekers, that's what they live for, to bear an angel child. And she—first, she left without knowing what kind of child she would bear. And then, when she *had* me—when she could have taken me to any hold in Samaria and been welcomed for my sake—still she chose to hide me, to live as far from angels as possible, to be with the mortal she loved rather than with my father. I've never heard of anyone else who did such a thing."

"She loved him," Rachel said softly. "She dared everything for love."

"She could have given me up to my father and still lived with that Jansai man," Maga said. "She didn't have to hide the way she did."

"She loved you, too," Rachel said. "She couldn't give you up either."

"Maybe. I'd like to think so, but—"

"There's no other explanation."

"And then I've always wondered. The plague flag. Did they really hope an angel would come in time to save them? Or—"

Rachel shook her head. "She raised it for you. So an angel would come down and find you. She knew she was dying and she could not leave you alone. But she wouldn't give you up till the very last moment."

"Maybe," Maga said again, her sweet voice wistful. "I would like to believe she loved me that much—"

"You have to believe it."

"The funny thing is, I sometimes think my father loved her till he died. He didn't talk about her, and if I asked, he would curse her, but he kept a portrait of her in his room. I saw it there once when I was a little girl, and it was still there the day after he died. I know, because I was the one who cleared his room out and bundled up his clothes. And sometimes I think—I wonder if maybe they weren't true lovers—you know, intended by Jovah."

"Why?"

"Well, something he said made me think that when he met her, his Kiss flared. You know"—and here Maga's voice was edged with sarcasm—"the great sign from the god that lovers have met. Because he told me, a few days before he died, never to trust the Kiss, that it only led to sorrow. I had met Nathan by then, of course, but we were still young—friends—nothing had happened between us. The first time Nathan kissed my mouth—and the crystal on my arm came to life—I remembered what my father had said. And I realized he was right."

Rachel frowned. They were half-sitting, half-lying on the

floor amidst Rachel's new pillows, on top of her new rug, and it reminded her very much of sitting around an Edori campfire talking late into the night. She stretched out on her stomach, still frowning.

"At my wedding," she said slowly, "the oracle Josiah talked to me a little about this. The reason the Kiss lights in someone's arm. He said that Yovah is not so much interested in true love as—bloodlines. The children that two people might bear if they are brought together."

"Breeding," Maga said with a slight smile. "I've heard this argument before."

"So then if *your* parents were brought together by the Kiss—and *Nathan's* parents were brought together by the Kiss—"

"Were they? I didn't know that."

"Oh, yes. Hannah told me that the first day I was here. So that means Yovah united each of your parents specifically so you could be born. And if you and Nathan have been brought together by the Kiss—"

"I think, rather, the intensity of our love has caused the Kiss to light in each of our bodies," Maga said. "Because angels are forbidden to intermarry, and Jovah was the one to lay down that prohibition."

"Because of the monster children?"

"Right."

"Hannah called them lucifers."

Maga smiled a little. "That is the term for it among the Manadavvi—the term for anything dreadful and perverted. To them, even a rainstorm that goes on too long can be called a lucifer, because it is a good thing turned to evil purposes."

"Hunh. Among the Edori, the word 'lucifer' means a false light. Certain insects at night give off a glow that looks like candlelight—they are called lucifers. Some swamp woods can burn, if you use them to build a fire, but only for a few minutes. They are called lucifers as well. And the Jansai—they have learned to build tent fires near Edori camping grounds, knowing the Edori will come seeking fellowship—and those fires are called lucifers, too."

Maga smiled again. "The word really comes from the time of the founding of Samaria," she said. "After Jovah brought us here and settled us into the three provinces, and divided everyone up into men, angels and oracles, he withdrew into heaven to watch over us. And there was peace for a generation. But as the sons and daughters of the first settlers grew to adulthood, they began clamoring to see the face of Jovah for themselves.

"At that time, the Archangel was a man named Lucifer—he had succeeded Uriel, who was now dead. To quiet the people, Lucifer said he would fly to the heavens and visit Jovah, asking him to return to earth. And he took off from the Plain of Sharon and he was gone three days, and no one saw him return. But on the third day, he reappeared on the Plain, and beside him was a great figure of a man, wrapped head to toe in glowing white cloth edged with gold. There were crowds of people gathered on the Plain, and they shouted out glorias when they saw Lucifer return with the god. And they crowded forward to touch the god, and beg for his blessing and ask to be healed by his hand.

"Now this went on for days and days, with people from all over Samaria making pilgrimages to the Plain of Sharon to personally touch the foot of the god. And Lucifer began to grow jealous, because no one was honoring *him* anymore—all the attention was going to Jovah. Finally, he grew so enraged that he ripped the white cloths from Jovah's face—to reveal, not the god at all, but a poor giant half-wit that he himself had dressed up for the role. And so the word 'lucifer' has come, at least among angels, to mean anyone who betrays a sacred trust—who pretends to bring you love, for instance, and brings you dishonor instead."

"What happened to the Archangel?"

"He was banished. I don't know where. There is no mention of him anywhere else in the histories."

"And what happened to the half-wit?"

"Stormed by the crowd and bludgeoned to death."

"Maga!"

"Well, you asked."

"I don't think I'll ask you for any more stories," Rachel exclaimed. "Everything you tell me has a sorry end."

Magdalena was laughing. "I apologize. How can I make everything right again?"

Rachel sighed. "Bring back the sunshine. I hate this awful cold and snow."

Magdalena came to her feet. "All right. The snow will be gone by nightfall. Tomorrow we'll go into Velora again."

"What are you doing?"

"I'm going to go aloft and pray for a weather intercession. We'll have sun in the morning."

"Pray for— Can you really do that?"

Maga laughed again. "Of course I can. Weather is the easiest thing for an angel to control. Want to come with me?"

"*Flying*? I don't think so."

"All right. I'll only be gone an hour or so."

And she left the chamber. Sure enough, late that evening, the snow stopped falling; the clouds drifted apart; the stars appeared fiercely white against the absolute blackness of the night sky. When Hannah remarked at dinner that the air seemed much warmer than it had that morning, both Rachel and Magdalena thought it prudent not to explain why.

And the next day they were back in Velora again.

It was too cold to shop for long at the outdoor bazaars, so Rachel and Magdalena had taken refuge at a pastry shop, where they drank hot spiced wine and nibbled on cheese rolls. Rachel had seated herself by the window.

"Sunshine, sunshine, sunshine," she chanted. "I think I'll just sit here all day."

"Eating cake and getting fat and lazy," Maga agreed. "Sounds good to me."

"Sounds good to me, too," said a man's voice behind them. They both looked around quickly to see the slim, graceful form of the angel Obadiah thrown into high detail by the angle of the sun. He had entered the shop and come to their table without either of them noticing. "Can I sit with you and put on a few pounds?"

"Of course," Maga said. Rachel merely looked surly. Obadiah pulled up one of the metal chairs—like the Eyrie chairs, carefully designed to accommodate angels—and gracefully disposed his wings over the back. He gave them both a seraphic smile.

"Lovely weather, for a change," he said. "I compliment you on the efficacy of your prayers."

Maga choked back a laugh. "What makes you think—"

"I can scent an intercession unerringly, lovely. I was on the point of going aloft myself, when I noticed a distinct improvement in the temperature last night. And if, as I believe, it was the angelica's idea, I compliment her as well."

"Not my idea," Rachel said. "I didn't even know it could be done."

"Well, it's not supposed to be," Obadiah said thoughtfully. He raised a hand to signal to the shopkeeper for service. "Gabriel gets very testy when angels misuse power for personal comfort. But then, almost everything makes Gabriel testy. If we all conformed to his standards, we would sit mute and motionless inside the Eyrie, thinking only pure thoughts."

Rachel could not stifle a giggle. Obadiah slanted her a sideways look and then grinned at Magdalena. "So she does laugh," he said to the other angel. "I confess, I have never even seen her smile in the weeks she has been at the Eyrie. I was beginning to wonder if she hated us all."

"She likes me," Maga said serenely.

"Everybody does."

The shopkeeper brought wine and rolls to Obadiah, who flashed his bracelet in lieu of payment. The man nodded and left.

"You mustn't be misled by our forbidding, disdainful appearances," Obadiah continued, addressing Rachel this time. "You think angels live such fabulous lives, performing good deeds and communing with the god—lives to which poor, unworthy mortals could not even aspire—but I assure you it is not all rapture and glory."

"I never thought it was," Rachel said dryly.

"I, for instance, was called away three days ago when a traveler to Velora said he'd seen a plague flag hoisted over a homestead fifty miles from here. You recall the weather, of course—Magdalena had not yet charmed the snow clouds from our gloomy skies—so there I was, darting past the flakes and even beginning to feel a bit chilled as I flew west for an hour. I spotted the flag, found the homestead—and entered the house to find one robust woman, a healthy man and half a dozen farm children gamboling around the fireplace. Not a cough to be heard, not a sore or lesion in sight.

"So I introduced myself politely, inquired in the kindest of voices about the presence of the plague flag, and received nothing but blank stares from the lord and lady of the household. Ah, but young Ezra, who looked to be about ten years old, came running in from the barn saying, 'Is he here? Is the angel here?' I admit to feeling, at that precise moment, a surge of misgiving."

Maga was laughing openly. Even Rachel was amused by the

light, sardonic tone of Obadiah's voice. He was fair-haired, open-faced, slightly built. Though he told the tale as if it pained him, the laughter behind his eyes was easy to read.

"The lady of the house turned to young Ezra and exclaimed, 'What have you done? Surely you didn't call an angel down here to look for that fool animal,' and the lord of the house expressed his intention of giving the boy a good sound whipping. He strode off somewhere, presumably to find a nice sturdy piece of leather. Ezra, meanwhile, evaded his mother's hands and came running up to me, grabbed me by my belt and began sobbing into my chest. 'He's been gone for three days—I know he's going to freeze to death in all this snow. I can't find him and I've looked everywhere.' "

"Let me guess—a dog," said Maga.

"A *goat*, if you please, a white goat with white horns, who was no doubt destined to be slaughtered for dinner in a month's time, anyway."

"What did you do?"

"What could I do? I went out looking for the goat. I brought Ezra with me so I could have an extra pair of eyes—at least that's what I told him. Really I just wanted to postpone the whipping if I could. We were out for three hours."

"Did you find the goat?" Rachel asked.

"Oh, yes. Holed up under a fallen tree, all snug and comfortable. And if you don't think *that* was a pleasure," he added, "flying back four miles with a ten-year-old boy under one arm and a squirming goat under the other, well, then, you have no imagination."

Both women laughed aloud. Obadiah surveyed them benevolently. "So," he said to Rachel, "the next time you are overawed by your angelic counterparts, remember me and the goat, and it will all whittle down to the proper perspective."

"Thank you, I will."

"Well, you're very kind," Magdalena said. "I don't think Gabriel or Nathan would have gone searching for a pet."

"No, somehow it's always me who ends up with the bizarre or humiliating assignments," Obadiah agreed. "I remember, my second or third time out, responding to a pilgrim's petition—"

For the next hour, he entertained them with stories of his misadventures. Rachel could not remember ever laughing so hard. Magdalena contributed a few of her own stories, and even Rachel recounted a tale of an ill-fated Edori campsite which had not, at the time, been funny. It felt good to laugh, to remember, to share. It had been so long since she'd had friends.

It was Magdalena who brought the session to an end. "But we came down to buy thread and yarn for my weaving," she said. "Let's go look some more."

Obadiah accompanied them back to the bazaar, where they wandered between the booths and were occasionally separated for a few moments at a time. Rachel was by herself in front of a booth of glassware when she was approached by a frail, dark-haired girl who looked about seven years old.

"Please, lady," the girl said, tugging at Rachel's sleeve. "My brother's sick and he's awful hungry. Could you give me something—"

The pale, paunchy man who owned the booth took a menacing step forward. "Get out of here, you. Go on—get!"

Rachel laid a hand on the filthy, tangled hair. "I don't have any money with me," she said gently. "Where is your brother?"

The girl pointed. In an alley off the main boulevard sat a huddled bundle of ragged cotton topped with a tousled dark head. "He's been sick for two days and all he wants is some bread—"

"Let me go see him."

"Lady, do you want the glass?" the shopowner demanded.

"No," Rachel said over her shoulder, and followed the girl to her brother's side. His eyes were closed and his hands folded across his stomach, and he moaned in a small voice as he rocked from side to side. He seemed even more emaciated than his sister.

"Does he have a fever? When's the last time he ate anything?" Rachel asked. She dropped to her knees to get a closer look.

It was a tactical mistake. Someone shoved her hard from behind; as she toppled forward, the sick boy leapt to his feet, miraculously recovered. Hands yanked on the gold chain she had hung around her neck that morning; nimble fingers untied the silk scarf from her hair. Before she could regain her balance, they had stripped her few valuable items from her and gone skipping down the street. She heard cries of anger and outrage follow them as the brother and sister wove through the throng and disappeared.

She had not even tried to resist. The instant she'd recognized the scam, she had frozen, allowed them to take what they would.

Now, as running footsteps hurried up from behind, she steadied herself against the alley wall and pushed herself slowly to her feet.

"Rachel! Are you all right? What happened? Those children—!" Magdalena was the first to reach her, with Obadiah right behind. Strangers formed a crowd behind the angels as she turned to face them.

"I didn't even see them. What did they look like?" Obadiah demanded. "I might be able to catch them."

Rachel shook her head. "I'm fine. Don't worry about me. They just took a couple of things."

Maga had already noticed the thefts. "Oh, your pretty gold necklace! And your silk scarf. And—your belt with the gold disks—oh, Rachel, it took us three days to buy that belt!"

Rachel laughed shakily. It was no very pleasant thing to be attacked, even by children, and even though they left you quite unharmed. Seeing her whole and relatively calm, the gathered onlookers began to disperse. "The belt and the necklace hardly matter," she said. "I hope they can find some nice little shop to pawn them for a few gold pieces. They looked hungry."

"And you looked like easy prey, lovely," Obadiah said. "One of us should have been with you. I'm sorry."

"It's disgraceful," Maga said. "That an angelica can't walk safely through the streets of Velora—"

"It is disgraceful," Rachel interrupted. Her trembling had stopped; she was feeling, instead, the steadying power of righteous rage. "Disgraceful, that in a town less than a vertical mile from an angel hold there should be starving children on the street, reduced to begging and robbery to survive."

The angels both stared at her. Obadiah, predictably, began to laugh.

"But Rachel—aren't you angry?" Maga asked, puzzled.

"Of course I'm angry! How can such things be allowed to happen? Why aren't these children provided for? Why doesn't someone care for them? You yourself told me that at least some of them have been sired by angels, though they aren't fortunate enough to bear wings when they're born. Is that their fault? Among the Edori, you are responsible for your child no matter how he looks when he is born—no matter if he has hair of a color you dislike or a foot deformed in the womb or a mind that will never cease to function like a child's—"

Maga glanced around to see who might be listening. "Rachel, hush. This is not the time or place—"

"Angels who think it's so important to sire more *angel* children and then not caring what happens to the mortal babies that are brought into the world. Leaving them to starve or die or turn into street urchins who know no way but violence to survive—"

Unlike Gabriel, these two had not had an opportunity to see Rachel in full spate before. Maga was distraught, but Obadiah remained cool. He blocked Rachel's way as she began to pace, spreading his wings wide and backing her toward the building. When she lifted her hands as if to strike him, he caught her wrists and pushed her gently against the brick of the wall.

"You can't solve anything when you're crazy like this," he said, his light voice taking on hypnotic, soothing rhythms. "Calm down, discuss it—we can work it out."

"Solve it! Discuss it! What can be done? It's disgraceful—"

"It is, I agree, calm down. There are things to be done, things you can do, but you have to stop a minute, think, calm down—"

Quickly enough, the beautiful voice had its effect. She stopped resisting his grip, took several long breaths and stared fixedly down at the cobblestones until her vision returned to normal. When she looked up at her companions again, she was still angry but in control.

"I'm not sorry," she said defiantly. "You think I behaved badly, but such a thing should make you angry, too."

Obadiah released her. Maga rushed in to give her a quick hug. "But Rachel, you should not get so upset about things. You frightened me—"

"Well, I'm sorry for that, but Maga, this is terrible. How is it nothing is being done for these children?"

"Something is being done," Obadiah said. "I think there is someone here in Velora you should meet."

His name was Peter and he had been, he told her, a priest for forty years. Like other priests, his life's work had been to travel from city to city, village to village, homestead to homestead, dedicating newborns to the god and grafting a Kiss onto each small arm. Three winters ago, his life was changed.

"I suppose I had seen the urchins of Breven and Semorrah and Castelana before," he said reflectively, "but I had not really noticed them. I dealt with infants, not children. They were not my concern."

Rachel nodded, never withdrawing her eyes from his face. He was a tall, gaunt man with completely white hair, pale blue eyes and a mild, studious expression. He looked as if he had spent his life reading handwritten texts by inadequate lighting. Magdalena's sunshine poured in through the huge windows of the place they were in, a mostly unfurnished warehouse on the edge of the Velora shipping district. The old man and the angelica had taken the only two chairs in this corner of the room; the high, curved backs did not accommodate angel wings. Rachel's companions sat on the floor, also listening in silence.

"That night—it had been very cold for days, and I was glad to get back to my inn—I was very annoyed to hear knocking just as I sat down to my dinner. But I am a servant of the god, and so I rose from the table and answered the door and discovered, to my surprise, a very young girl standing on my doorstep offering me what looked like a loaf of bread. I was so surprised to see a child there that I didn't immediately take in the details—how thin she was, how raggedly dressed. I did manage to speak in a kindly voice when I asked her what she wanted.

" 'I found this baby,' she said. 'I've been watching him for a week now, but he won't eat bread and I don't have any beer, and I think he's dying.' Well, I—bread and beer!—I was astonished on so many counts I hardly knew what to say to her first. I told her to come in, to sit by my fire and explain to me what she was doing walking around with a baby in the middle of winter."

He paused. While he told the story, he seemed to be unaware of his visitors, although he had seemed sharply curious about them when Obadiah first guided them to his door. Now his eyes were fixed on a different scene, in a city far from here on a night three years ago.

"So she said she had found the baby in an alley a week before, and she'd taken it with her back to the drainage ditch where she had set up her own cozy little bed, and she'd tried to nurse the baby back to health. But all it did was cry and sleep, and it wouldn't chew bread, and she had no beer. And she said again, 'I think he's dying, but I heard a priest was in town, and I know that priests can send babies back to Jovah.'

"I was—the word 'shocked' doesn't cover it. Among other things, her theology was wrong, because priests don't send anyone

to Jovah—angels do that. But I could not get past the initial horror, the fact that this child, this feral child, had brought to me an
abandoned infant, a babe *she* had tried to care for with her limited skills—I mean, where were *her* parents? Where were this
baby's parents? Why were either of them on the street? And then
this baby—" He shook his head. "It could not have been more
than ten days old. So frail, so small—so close to death. And Jovah
did not even know he had been born.

"Because, among all the bigger shocks, I realized to my dismay that this baby had not been dedicated—would not, if I did
not work fast, ever be recorded in Jovah's great book of names,
would die without the god's knowledge that he had even been
born. And so, with my dinner cooling on the table and the street
girl looking on, I blessed that baby with the Kiss of Jovah, gave
him a name, offered him to the god and watched him die on my
hearth."

Maga took a quick, sympathetic breath. Peter glanced over
at her and his watery eyes were suddenly focused on the present
again. "You feel sadness for that wretched baby—but what about
that wretched girl?" he asked. "It only occurred to me, as I
wrapped the infant's head in a clean cloth from my own luggage,
to wonder if there might be other unfortunate children in the
world who had been left in back alleys and by riverbeds and on
street corners before their parents had a chance to give their
names to the god. And that one of them might be standing before
me even then. And I looked at her bare, thin arms, and I saw that
she was one of them, and that Jovah had no idea that she existed
on this world."

He shook his head. "It took some time," he said, "but I
convinced her that she should take the opportunity, then and
there, to be dedicated. She had got it into her head somehow that
the god only lays his Kiss upon those who are about to die—that
if she was dedicated then, she would die by morning. I had to
explain at length. I had to agree to let her spend the night in my
room, safe at my fire, promising that she would wake up alive
and whole the next morning. So she let me implant the Kiss in
her arm and speak her name to the god, and in the morning she
was fascinated to see how the sunlight caught the glass and turned
it to colors. And she went off quite cheerfully into the bitter cold."

"What happened to her?" Maga asked.

"I have no idea," Peter said somberly. "She who changed my

life so completely disappeared before it occurred to me to secure her. Her name was Josephine, I know, because so I recorded it in Jovah's book. And she lived in Breven. And she is still alive, for Jovah still registers her Kiss in the oracles' communications. But I have never seen her again. And I wonder every day how she fares."

"Changed your life," Maga repeated. "How? What has happened to you since?"

The day that Josephine left him in his inn, he told them, he effectively renounced the priesthood. He became obsessed with finding all the lost children of Samaria and dedicating them to the god. He stayed in Breven nearly a year before the Jansai elders came to him, complaining, and he was none too politely asked to leave the city.

"Complaining?" Maga asked. "Why?"

Rachel could answer that one. "Because it is much harder to sell a dedicated child into slavery," she said softly. "And that's what the Jansai elders did when they rounded up the street urchins."

Peter nodded at her. "Precisely. So I left Breven—protesting loudly, I might add—and drifted across Jordana. But there are too many Jansai there, and I could find no allies. My plan was to go to Luminaux, for I hear the child gangs are quite numerous there, surviving very well in the warmer climate and the more generous city, but I was detoured into Velora. And I have found so much here to occupy me that I have not left yet."

Rachel leaned forward. "What is this place? A home for the street orphans?"

"To a large degree. I had been here nearly a year, dedicating the children I could persuade to accept me, before I realized that merely giving their names to the god could not protect them in their daily lives. So I begged for money and goods and favors from the local merchants, and they gave me this place, and I have stocked it as best I can with beds and clothes and food. Not many of the children take advantage of it—more in the winter, of course—but even then, I don't know how to reach them all, how to make them want to come here, how to convince them that I could give them something better, safer, than their lairs in the streets and the alleys and the ditches."

Rachel was still intent. "It needs to be more than a shelter in the winter," she said. "It needs to be a school—a place where they can learn skills they can peddle now, crafts they can practice when they become adults—"

"Few of them live to be adults," Peter said.

"What happens to them?"

Obadiah stirred and spoke softly. "They freeze in the winter, tumble under carts, fall ill with lung disease, die of untreated wounds. Some are snatched up by Jansai passing through, looking for more fodder. A strong child fetches a higher price than a healthy adult."

"This can't be allowed," Rachel said rapidly. "We have to save them."

"I would love to save them," Peter said. "I am doing what I can. Anything you have to offer me I would gladly consider."

CHAPTER TEN

Gabriel spent the first three weeks of his married life traveling. It had not seemed like a bad idea originally, since as far as he could tell his bride would be just as happy if he were gone, but it proved to be wearisome all the same. As he neared the end of his third week, he found himself thinking more and more of the comforts of the Eyrie—its warm quartz walls, its soothing harmonic music, its fellowship, its peace. Although he did not list his wife among his familiar comforts, it was perfectly natural that his thoughts would turn to her, now and then, with speculation if not affection.

But he'd had little time for longing thoughts of home. It had been a grueling trip and he was not pleased with what he had found out.

His plan had been to make a circuit of the major cities of Samaria and speak to the civic leaders there, in general terms, about his upcoming tenure as Archangel, and to sound them out on any concerns or grievances they might have. Good will toward him was about as high as he could reasonably expect, since he would be making brief visits with many of the leaders who had just attended his wedding; they owed him some civility for his recent hospitality.

He had gone first to Gaza, flying back with Ariel and the angels of her host and spending a few nights at Monteverde. He had always liked Monteverde. Like the other two angel holds, it was situated on a relatively high mountain, but the Verde Divide was almost ridiculously easy to scale and thus there was constant, ready access to the hold. In fact, Monteverde seemed much more like a small, bustling city than a hold, for scattered among the angel dwellings were mortal residences, commercial shops, schools, inns and markets. Angels, humans and pilgrims lived together in happy community amid the green trees and lush shrubbery that gave Monteverde its name.

One morning he had left for Elijah Harth's compound, Elijah being the most powerful of the Manadavvi patriarchs who possessed the greatest wealth and power in Gaza—perhaps in all of Samaria. As always, Gabriel was amazed at the sheer size of the Manadavvi holding, a walled fortress complex at least as big as Monteverde. Maybe five hundred souls lived inside the Harthhold gates; a few thousand more were tenants on the rich, black land whose bounty was the base of much of the Manadavvi wealth.

Elijah Harth would be pleased to meet with the angel Gabriel. Would the angel Gabriel kindly wait while the Manadavvi lord finished up other business?

So Gabriel stationed himself at a huge window in a faultlessly furnished drawing room, and looked out at the gardens below. What he at first took to be a scattered crowd of visitors strolling through the hedge mazes and rose beds was in fact an extraordinary number of gardeners laboring to keep the gardens trimmed. Gabriel was not an especially ascetic man, but he was disturbed by the corollary implications of such extravagance. How many servants kept the rooms clean, the water heated, the food cooked, the patriarch and his family dressed? Were there not better uses to which both the labor and the time could be put?

Elijah himself interrupted these musings. Like most of the Manadavvi, Elijah was thin, very well-kept and sophisticated; his intelligence could be quickly read on his bony, high-cheeked face and in his hooded, watchful eyes. He was dressed in a pale blue robe which fell sheer from his shoulders to the floor; every hem and seam was stitched with intricate silver. The robe was closed at the throat with a Kiss-sized sapphire which, sold on the open market, could feed a family for a year.

"Gabriel," Elijah greeted him in his smooth voice. "How good to see you again so soon."

"Elijah." They shook hands, and Elijah motioned the visitor to sit. Angels came often enough to this house; there were plenty of chairs carved to accommodate the great sweeping wings. Gabriel sat.

"As you know," the angel said, "in a few months I will become Archangel. I have always respected and admired you as a leader among Manadavvi, and I know the power you wield among the clans. I wanted to discuss policies with you before they are implemented, to get some of your ideas a few months in advance."

Elijah inclined his head. "I appreciate that. May I say at the very beginning that you could do no worse than to follow Raphael's example in every particular?"

Gabriel kept his countenance, but he was surprised. He had not expected the Manadavvi to be such loyal supporters of the Windy Point Archangel; Jansai, yes, but not Manadavvi . . . "Unfortunately that might not be possible in every instance," he replied coolly. "But perhaps if you told me what specifically you are reluctant to see changed—"

Elijah made an elegant gesture with his well-manicured hands. "For instance, the tax structure," he said. "I am old enough to remember that in Michael's day, there was a higher percentage levied on the commercial farmers, such as we Manadavvi, when they brought their goods to market. Raphael agreed with us when we pointed out that since we fed and supported so many dependents within our compounds, we should not be unfairly taxed in addition."

Aaaah. Special privileges for the rich. Gabriel had not known about that deal before. Still, as the angels' holds, which profited from the taxes, were not in any sense deprived, there seemed no reason to restructure the agreement. At least presently. "I understand the reasoning," Gabriel said gravely.

"I like, too, the unrestricted commerce between regions," Elijah pursued. "Again, in Michael's day, to ferry produce across the Galilee River was to pay an excise fee, and thus many farmers did not do their marketing in Jordana. Jordana, and particularly Breven, suffered more from this situation than did the Manadavvi. Raphael, who after all could not help considering Jordana interests, was quick to strike down the fee."

Gabriel spent a moment wondering how much of all this Ariel knew, since Raphael's arrangements with the Manadavvi essentially kept money out of the Monteverde coffers—and since the Archangel Michael had been her grandfather. But again, he nodded. He was saving his arguments for matters he cared about more deeply.

"In fact," Elijah was saying, "I am sure that we—and Malachi of Breven—and other leading merchants such as Jethro of Semorrah—are far more conversant with appropriate measures for taxation and intraregion trade than you are. We would, I am sure, be glad to form an advisory committee—"

"I appreciate the offer," Gabriel interrupted, smiling faintly. "No doubt at the moment you understand the intricacies of the situation better than I do. But I am willing to learn—and I have many advisors already. Any inequities that come to my attention in the next few years will certainly be addressed."

"I am pleased to hear you say it."

"One inequity which I intend to stop immediately," Gabriel went on pleasantly, "is the enslavement of Edori and their sale to whoever is rich enough to buy them. I am aware that the practice is prevalent mostly throughout Jordana and the river cities, although Gaza is not entirely free of the taint of slavery. Yet I feel certain that you, as an enlightened, educated man—"

"Deplore the institution of slavery. You are quite right," Elijah said, interrupting in turn. "But I am afraid it is not all as simple as you would like it to be. Moral right and wrong often fall victim to economic imperatives."

Gabriel frowned. "Surely you have enough tenants and vassals to farm your lands without resorting to slave labor. And—since you have just told me yourself that your taxes have been adjusted to reflect the drain on your resources—you cannot sit here and tell me that you cannot afford to pay your workers."

"My finances are sound," Elijah said a little coldly. "But for many of those I deal with, slavery is an economic necessity."

Gabriel's eyes narrowed. "Perhaps you could explain."

"In Breven, for instance. The slave trade accounts for a good portion of the city's wealth. I deal heavily with Breven merchants. If they can't sell their human goods, they cannot buy my produce, and I have a glutted market. And prices fall, and income falls, and I am unable to pay my workers what I would wish, and some of them begin to go hungry—"

"Are you seriously telling me," Gabriel said, "that you support the murdering and enslavement of hundreds of souls a year solely to keep your grain prices from slipping?"

"You oversimplify. A vast number of factors are affected in the complex network of trade."

"Still, you are valuing human life below the price of corn."

"The price of corn, as you put it, translates into the wages I can afford to pay, and directly affects the lives of my bondsmen. What if they were to starve because of a ban on the slave trade? Would those deaths weigh less heavily on your conscience?"

"Whoever starves in all of Samaria, it should not be anyone within a hundred miles of Manadavvi land," Gabriel said bluntly. "You could feed the whole world three times over."

Elijah gave him a faint smile. "We are not just talking food, Gabriel. We are talking the economic structure of an entire continent."

Gabriel came to his feet. "Then I must urge you to consider ways to amend that structure," he said. "For, whether it comes slowly or all at once, whether it bankrupts you or enriches you or turns the whole Manadavvi region into a wasteland, slavery has come to an end in Samaria." And on that distinctly undiplomatic pronouncement, Gabriel stalked from the lovely chamber and left behind what he was fairly sure was an enemy.

He had had highest hopes of the Manadavvi; therefore, he was not surprised when the rest of his visits went along the same lines, or even less well. Lord Jethro of Semorrah, Lord Samuel of Castelana, and various other river-city merchants gave him Elijah's exact argument, though phrased less nimbly; Malachi of Breven merely laughed at him.

"If we can sell slaves, we'll get slaves," said the oily, balding old gypsy. "What the market desires, the Jansai provide."

"I would not wish," Gabriel said shortly, "to be forced to use violence to reverse your opinion."

Malachi stared at him incredulously. When he laughed, all the dangling gold at his throat and wrists jingled musically. "Call down the wrath of Jovah on us, do you mean?" he demanded. "On the whole city? On *Breven*? Fry us all with one thunderbolt from the god?"

"I would not like to do it," the angel said ominously.

"You won't," the trader said with certainty. "The city's only half Jansai, after all—and you aren't the man to slaughter thousands of innocents just to prove a point."

"I think I could ask Jovah to be a little more selective," Gabriel said. Inwardly he was wondering how he had come, this early in the game, to be threatening with his direst weapon. "Certainly I could make sure that any lightning strikes precisely where you are standing—"

Malachi laughed again. "Gabe," he said, "I don't believe you."

"You don't *believe*—?"

"When is the last time an angel called down a thunderbolt from the god? In Raphael's time—in Michael's—in the time of Ariel before that? Do you really think it can be *done*? Oh, yes, there are the weather intercessions and I have seen angels pray now and then for seed and it has fallen—but no one believes Jovah will strike us dead. No one believes the angels have that kind of power. Or, human nature being what it is, we'd all have been burnt up by now by somebody with a very edgy temper."

Gabriel had thought that Rachel had taught him to be impervious to shock, but Malachi's words left him utterly dumbfounded. That anyone on the planet should doubt the ability of the god to mete out punishment, and the ability of the angels to call it down, had never occurred to him before. It was as if someone were to tell him he no longer needed to breathe, that he would exist just as well underwater or buried beneath the earth. It was inconceivable.

"You are right to assume that I would be reluctant to invoke the righteous fury of Jovah," he said slowly, "but I cannot believe you are sincere when you say you doubt Jovah's power to strike you down. That is the foundation of our life upon Samaria—that is the tenet around which all other beliefs, all other actions, all other truths, cohere."

"Prove it to me," the Jansai invited. "We'll go a ways out to the desert, and you can ask the god for a little demonstration. Ask him to burn up a tree or strike a rock with lightning. If I see it, I'll believe it. And then we'll discuss this Edori business."

Gabriel shook his head slowly from side to side. "It is an awesome power to invoke for such a petty reason," he said.

Malachi gave a great booming laugh. "You see? You've never done it either! You don't believe it can be done! Because, frankly, I don't think this is such a petty reason if it has you soaring all over Samaria to try your plan before the merchants." He laughed again, apparently amused at the continued look of blank astonishment on Gabriel's face. "Don't feel so bad," he said kindly.

"A few years ago, I was a true believer, too. Might have gone to my grave fearing the whiplash of the god if Raphael hadn't set me straight. And if *he* says—"

Gabriel's eyes had lifted quickly to the gypsy's broad face. "Raphael told you—that the god had no power to strike you down?" he asked quickly.

"Swore it for a solid day and then took me to the desert to prove it. I read along with the words in the Librera while he spoke the curse aloud. No lightning. No thunder." Malachi shrugged. "No god. Life has been a little easier for me ever since."

Shock after shock; and behind the waves of disbelief, a rising tide of unanswerable questions. Did Raphael actually believe what he had told Malachi, or had he merely tricked the Jansai into believing something which was somehow convenient for the Archangel? Gabriel thought he himself could put on a pretty convincing show of seeming to call out to the god without really engaging in prayer; but why would an angel *want* to convince someone that there was no god?

Was that what Raphael believed? If so, why? Was the Archangel, in fact, incapable of enlisting Jovah's aid—in punishing the wicked, in helping the hungry, in changing the weather? Was that why he had failed to bring rain to the Heldoras? Was that why he had allowed the merchants to gather so much power in the past two decades?

And if Raphael indeed had lost all ability to summon Jovah, who had guarded them for the past twenty years? Why were any of them still alive?

And even if the god no longer heeded Raphael, surely the god was still there—?

A few days later, Gabriel and his questions arrived at Sinai to pay Josiah an unannounced visit. The oracle, as always, was delighted to see the angel. He listened attentively to Gabriel's account of the meeting with Malachi, but did not seem as sobered or alarmed as Gabriel expected. Gabriel said so.

"Why aren't you appalled by this? Surely this is catastrophic news."

Josiah gave him a quick half-smile. "Catastrophic, perhaps, but not exactly news. Perhaps not even catastrophic. For some time now, I have been—oh, uncertain about Raphael's faith. Certainly he has been a bad Archangel. He—"

"Wait," Gabriel interrupted. "You never said to me—never indicated in any way—"

"What could I have said? What good could it have done? You have disliked Raphael sufficiently on your own without dark hints from me. But he has hardly been the spiritual leader the country needed. An imperfect choice, and Jovah must have realized it from the beginning. That is why he selected you so early in your life—to prepare you more fully, and to let Raphael know, before he was very many years into his tenure, that his position was only temporary."

"But—" Gabriel spread his arms. The implications were so vast that he found it hard to reduce them to comprehensible size. "If he does not believe in the god—and he has convinced others that there is no god—and he has been our advisor, led us in the Gloria, answered prayers, judged petitions—if he has done all these things for all these years, and we have believed him, and the god did not strike him down—then—the question must inevitably arise—"

"Not the question you fear most," Josiah said imperturbably. "Not whether there is in fact a god, but why the god chose not to act."

"I think," said Gabriel, "both questions must be asked."

Josiah regarded him with compassion, and not the fearful wrath Gabriel had half expected. "The great scholar Solomon taught that gods are created by our belief in them," the oracle said. "That is, a man who believes in a god, creates a god. A culture which worships a god always in fact has a god to worship. Most people are not comfortable with this philosophy because the omnipotence of the god is the single greatest allure the divine can have. The one real reason to believe is to put your faith in something greater than yourself, and if you have yourself created a god it cannot be any greater than you. Still, you see, that without faith there can be no god at all."

"Josiah."

"I know, forgive me. It's just that I rarely get a chance to debate theological principle . . . Failing faith, we have miracles to rely upon to prove that our god exists, and failing miracles, we have the small daily reminders. The seasons change, the sun rises and sets, babies are born and beauty lies all around us. These things must be the work of Jovah.

"You yourself have experienced repeated and personal demonstrations of divinity. When is the last time you called down a rainstorm or diverted a river? When is the last time you dropped to a small village overrun with fever, and prayed to the god, and had in answer seeds fall to the earth that were ground into powder and fed to the ill and resulted in cures? When you sing to the god, how do you feel? Elated, ecstatic, like a conduit of power? Or indifferent, uncertain, full of doubts? I know the answer to that one. Who but Jovah fills you with such deep emotion?

"As for myself, I have constant proofs of the god's existence—I can touch the fingertip which he still lays upon the heart of Samaria. I can ask him a direct question and receive a direct answer. I can say, 'Are you there?' and he will respond, 'Now and always.' It is not possible for me to doubt him. He speaks to me."

The gentle, persuasive words had an effect on Gabriel like music; they soothed him, they made him whole again. Yes, it was true; there were too many proofs, too many instances in which the god's presence was incontrovertible. But then—

"Why does he allow Raphael to deny him? Why does he allow Raphael to represent him—for *twenty years*—acting as our Archangel, pretending piety, and slowly perverting the minds of those who should be devout believers?"

"In the life of Jovah, twenty years is a very small period," Josiah said. "I expect that Jovah looks down, sees an unworthy Archangel and weighs his options. Is Samaria being harmed? Not really. Is the Gloria still being observed? Yes, every year. Are all peoples in harmony—"

"No," Gabriel interrupted.

"No, but harmony can be restored quickly enough," Josiah said serenely. "Jovah has read your heart and sees it is absolutely without malice, and he says, 'I can wait a few more years till this one is ready.' And he bides his time. And the time is almost over."

"It could be. It may be as you say," Gabriel said. An uprush of relief was flooding him, but he was still not entirely reassured. "And yet I now have on my hands Malachi and perhaps Elijah and Jethro and Samuel as well, who doubt the god's power—and my ability to intercede with Jovah. If they refuse to abide by my decrees, and if they do not believe I can punish them for wrongdoing, what then? I confess that Malachi read me right. I am not a man to destroy a whole city merely to prove a point."

"You do not have to loose the thunderbolts," Josiah said,

watching him closely, smiling almost. "There are other ways to convince them you are in earnest. You have already determined how to do so."

Reluctantly, Gabriel smiled back at him. "I have given it some thought," he admitted. "I have always been best with the elemental prayers—storm, sunshine, wind. I can turn Breven itself into a desert and raise the waters till they flood Semorrah."

"It will not come to that," Josiah promised. "A few weeks of rain, a few days of high winds, will convince them. They will see you have the ear of the god."

It was true; it was almost easy. There was heavy going ahead, but it was not out of his scope. Gabriel felt as relieved as a boy reprieved from a beating. "You are indeed a wise man, Josiah," he said.

The small man laughed. "And you are my favorite among angels," he said. "Jovah did well when he chose you."

"Jovah will not be so pleased with me when he ponders my doubting nature."

"It is good for a man to doubt. It makes him think up proofs. It strengthens his beliefs. Jovah will not think ill of you for doubting."

"Then he is gracious indeed."

Josiah laughed again, and led him away for a meal. The unobtrusive acolytes served them, and the meal went at such a leisurely pace that it was quite late before it ended. Gabriel accepted the invitation to spend the night.

"Although I had planned to return to the Eyrie tonight," he added. "It has been weeks since I was there."

"How does your bride fare?"

"I don't know. That is one reason I must return as soon as I can."

"I liked her."

"Did you? You are one of the few. When did you have a chance to speak with her?"

"After the wedding feast, while the singing was at its height. She asked me a question, for which I did not have an answer at the time. But I have it now. You must let me give you a letter for her before you go."

"What was the question?"

"If she had thought you would have the answer," Josiah said equably, "I'm sure she would have asked you."

Gabriel raised his eyebrows at the rebuke. "You have taken her part very quickly, I see."

"I liked her," the oracle repeated. "Hers is a fierce spirit. Not one you can easily control."

Gabriel laughed with very little mirth. "No, indeed. I have considered that. Someone like Leah—a very biddable angelica. I could have controlled her with no trouble. Someone like Judith—easy to understand, easy to strike a bargain with if you're willing to give her what she wants. Ariel, Magdalena—all the other angels, all the other women of my acquaintance—they might have a certain independence of mind, strong wills, a great deal of character, but I could handle them. I could persuade them, I could convince them that I was right. But not Rachel. I have her cooperation only if she chooses to give it. I have no influence over her at all. I'm not sure she would ever be willing to strike a bargain. She won't even tell me the truth all the time. It is like bringing a live fire into your home and asking it not to burn."

Josiah chuckled. "Well, Jovah picked her carefully and just for you. Perhaps he wanted to see your confidence shaken."

"He has set me a wide range of trials, it seems," Gabriel said with a certain grimness. "Between Raphael and Rachel, I have no peace left at all."

"Only the strongest are put through the fire," Josiah said. "And the forge creates things of great strength and beauty."

"Then I shall be truly glorious by the time my tenure ends."

CHAPTER ELEVEN

It was early afternoon the next day by the time Gabriel finally made it back to the Eyrie. As was his habit, he attempted to identify the harmonic voices before his feet even touched the landing stone. One voice was definitely Matthew's. The other, he thought, belonged to Esau. He listened a moment, his wings folded around him, coming for a brief time absolutely to rest. Then he shook off his abstraction and headed down into the residential tunnels.

Nathan, usually his first contact when he returned after a long flight, was still at Abel Vashir's—or should be. Elijah's anger with Gabriel could have spread to the other Manadavvi households, resulting in Nathan's ejection. Gabriel hoped it wasn't so. For one thing, he needed Abel's good wishes. For another, Magdalena was still at the Eyrie—or should be. Gabriel sighed. Yet another one of the trials with which Jovah had chosen to beset him.

"Truly the forge for me has been stoked very high," he murmured, and headed directly to his own chamber.

A thorough cleansing in his water room restored his mood somewhat, and he changed into fresh leathers with his body still damp and his hair still wet. He supposed he should seek out Rachel, or Magdalena, or at the very least Hannah, and discover what had happened in his absence. A soft melody played on his door chimes made that unnecessary—someone had already come to him.

He was not best pleased, upon opening the door, to find himself face to face with the smiling Judith. She, on the other hand, seemed overjoyed.

"Oh, you *are* back! I thought it was you, but I wasn't sure— Gabriel, you've been gone so very long! I missed you!"

Without being invited, she stepped inside his room and sank to the floor on a plush red rug spread before his favorite chair. It did not seem worth it to be either cruel or rude, so he stayed, seating himself before her and allowing her to take his hand.

"Tell me everything," she said. "Where you've been. Who you've seen. You must have flown all over Samaria to be gone three weeks."

"Pretty much," he said. "From Gaza to Breven and from Sinai to here."

"And why?"

"I am to become Archangel in a few weeks. It seemed like a good idea to talk to some of the leaders with whom I will be dealing."

"Was it pleasant?"

Sweet Jovah singing. *Pleasant.* "We talked serious business," he said. "It was not designed to be entertaining."

"Did you go to Luminaux?"

"I didn't have time. I wanted to get back here."

"You missed us," she said happily.

"It is tiring to eat with strangers every day and sleep on their ill-designed beds," he said.

"Did you go to Windy Point?"

He frowned down at her. "Why would I?"

"Well, you said you were in Jordana."

"I have seen quite enough of Raphael in the past few months, thank you."

She laughed softly. "I don't understand why you don't like him very much," she said. "He's so handsome."

He smiled. "That's a reason that would appeal to a woman more than to a man. And good looks are not essential for an Archangel, anyway."

Now she sighed. "I almost wish he would be Archangel forever," she said.

His voice hardened. "Why do you say that?"

She appeared surprised. "Because once you become Archangel, you will never be here at all. I will never see you. But if you were just plain Gabriel forever—"

"I will be plain Gabriel," he said. "I just will be plain busy Gabriel."

He wished she would release his hand, but he did not like to draw it away from her. He walked a tricky line with Judith and he was never sure he walked it right. She was not the sweet-tempered ingénue she acted, yet her devotion to him had been unswerving since they were children, surviving every romance either one of them had had. Often he was tempted just to ask of her, "What do you *want?*" though the answer seemed so clear; she wanted him. Or perhaps she had wanted to be angelica. It was hard to know.

"So what transpired here while I was gone?" he asked, to head off any more questions about his own miserable journey.

"Martha had her baby—a mortal girl," she said, answering the question before he could ask it. "Obadiah had an adventure rescuing some little boy's goat in a snowstorm. It's a very funny story—you should ask him about it. Magdalena and Rachel have gone into Velora practically every day and haven't invited anyone else to go with them—except Obadiah, of course. He and Rachel even go down together when Maga stays here to sing."

"Rachel and Obadiah? They're becoming friends?" he asked doubtfully.

She was watching him closely, pretending not to. "Oh, yes!" she said, with deliberate emphasis. "They're together all the time. I don't believe Obadiah's gone on any missions since that snowstorm thing. When they're not in Velora together, they're eating meals together or playing games. She taught him some Edori game that no one else would learn, and now he can even beat Matthew at it—"

"Well, Obadiah's very clever," Gabriel responded.

"Hannah thinks it's not very nice of them to spend so much time together while you're gone," Judith said, her voice artless but her eyes keen. "I heard her say so to Rachel one day—"

Fatal mistake, Gabriel thought. No doubt that had just made the angelica and the angel inseparable. "Hannah has a very stern sense of propriety," he murmured. "Runs in the Manadavvi blood. But enough about Obadiah. What have you been doing while I've been gone?"

Perforce she had to change the subject, so she gave him a detailed account of her own activities for the past three weeks, which he listened to distractedly. Silly to be disturbed by her malicious words, and yet—

Judith was still describing some piece of jewelry she had admired in a peddler's caravan when the door chime sounded again. "Come in," Gabriel called with some relief. He had not thought to free his hand from Judith's before the door opened and his wife stepped inside.

"Gabriel, how can I get money if I want it?" she asked, coming across the threshold with a bounce. He had never seen her so animated—nor so exotic. He only had a moment to take in the effect of her costume—close-fitting woolens, bright scarves, a glitter of gold—before the soft blur that was continuous existence resolved itself into the cold, hard crystal of a single bad moment.

Rachel had stopped halfway across the room and eyed the warm tableau of angel and supplicant. "Oh," she said, in a much altered voice. "I see you're busy."

"Not at all." Calmly, so as not to make it appear that he was snatching his hand away, he freed his fingers from Judith's and came to his feet. Judith—surely on purpose—gave a soft embarrassed laugh and brought her hands to her cheeks.

"Oh, I'm blushing!" she exclaimed. "Rachel—truly—this is nothing but two old friends talking after a long separation—"

"Three weeks," Rachel said. "Hardly any time at all."

Which nettled Gabriel. "I was coming to see you," he said to his wife.

"Obviously," was the dry reply.

Judith stood gracefully, though she needed to catch at Gabriel's arm for a moment when she almost lost her balance. "Rachel, really, don't be hurt," she said in her sweetest voice. "I just burst in on Gabriel and didn't give him a chance to leave the room."

"It doesn't matter to me who sits with my husband and clutches his hand," the angelica said distinctly. "*I'm* the one who's embarrassed. I didn't mean to intrude."

And she turned and stalked out of the room as only she could.

Judith turned a guilty smile on Gabriel. "Well, now I've gotten you in trouble," she said. "But she's so prickly, Rachel."

"And now I'd best go see what she wants." He ushered Judith toward the door.

She went, sighing again. "I suppose this means you're going to tell me I can't come to your room anymore," she said. "Or eat with you, or talk with you—"

He would have told her that, if Rachel hadn't made that last remark—should still tell her that, except that he was now approximately as angry as his wife. "Don't be silly," he said somewhat sharply, because he was not entirely pleased with Judith either. "Nothing has changed for any of us. But I must go see what she wants."

And finally getting both of them out of the room, he strode down the hall in the direction of his wife's chamber.

Rachel had obligingly left the door half-open, so he did not bother to ring the chime. She was standing with her back to him, however, and did not turn around even when she heard him enter.

"Rachel, this is childish," were his first words. "You cannot be angry because I was talking to Judith—"

"I try to quickly leave any room that *she* is in," she replied instantly. "The fact that you were there had nothing to do with my walking out."

He shut the door. "You could at least not lie about it," he said with some heat. "If you're angry with me—"

"I'm not angry," she shot back. "I'm surprised that you don't have better taste in women. Perhaps the choices aren't all that plentiful at the Eyrie, but you could do better for yourself than Judith."

"Why shouldn't I like Judith?" he said. "At least she is pleased to see me when I arrive, which some *others* are not."

"But I have become so accustomed to your absences," she replied. "Is it any wonder I don't realize when you're back?"

Well, she had a point there; two, really, because there was no good reason he should have been sitting there hand-in-hand with Judith. Still. "Since you don't seem to have missed me while I was gone," he said rashly, "what did it matter if I hurried back?"

Now she swung round to face him, her dark eyes narrowed and her face full of warning. "And what's that supposed to mean?"

"I understand you didn't lack for company while I was gone, young Obadiah providing escort to Velora when you needed it—"

"But I thought," she said in a dulcet voice, "that you wished me to make friends among the other angels."

"And so I do," he said. "But not to become so friendly that it causes talk."

She actually laughed. "Perhaps I have misunderstood all along," she said. "I thought that fidelity was not a requirement among the angels. In fact, Hannah and Maga and half a dozen others have as good as told me that the whole race of angels desires nothing more than to reproduce, with the result being that angels love where they will, with whichever mortal agrees to it—"

He was so furious that it frightened him. He wanted to slap her, or maybe strangle her. Instead, he turned away from her and crossed the room. He found himself face to face with an unfamiliar wall hanging, an abstract pattern of green and burgundy. The room, like Rachel, had become transformed. He stared at it until he was calm enough to speak.

"You did not misunderstand," he said icily, still with his back to her. "In general, angels have very—lax—moral standards. And you know the reason, though you choose to treat it with contempt. You have made it plain that the Edori do not recognize the sanctity of marriage, and so I cannot be surprised if, these factors taken together, you see no reason to hesitate in—enjoying someone else's company."

Now he wheeled around to face her. His anger was receding, leaving a great black coldness in its wake. "But in case you are indulging yourself with Obadiah because of how you perceive my relationship to Judith, let me tell you that she is not, has never been and will not be, my lover. Despite what she may have told you and despite what she may hope for herself."

She was watching him again with narrowed eyes, but she looked a little more convinced, as if some of what he said was getting through. Hard to believe that someone like Rachel could be jealous of someone like Judith; the thought unexpectedly found room in his mind.

"She certainly seems to enjoy your favor," Rachel said, her voice still antagonistic.

"She seeks me out. Would you have me be cruel to her?"

"It's not like you don't know how to repulse someone."

He was surprised into a smile. "You're no amateur yourself," he said.

She looked a little self-conscious. The last of her animosity seemed to have faded away. "There is something about you," she admitted, "that makes me want to behave badly."

"Jovah's little joke," he remarked. The sudden evaporation of such intense anger had left him feeling slightly shaken, a little giddy. It was a strange sensation. He experimented with a smile. "So tell me," he invited, "how you have passed these three weeks that did not seem very long to you."

Her answering smile was utterly charming. "Well, I was very busy," she said. "That makes the time go faster."

"And how did you occupy yourself?"

"Mostly in Velora."

"Buying, I see. I like your new clothes, let me say. They seem to suit you."

She was pleased. "Thank you. But I did more than buy. I— How much do you know about the children's home founded by a man named Peter?"

Later he reflected that if he'd had any sense at all, he would have sent her to Peter to begin with. Everything he knew about her pointed to the fact that she would be a powerful champion of Peter's abandoned waifs. She had always shown a special protectiveness for the disenfranchised and a fierce sense of responsibility toward children. He heard her out attentively. It was a relief to be able to encourage Rachel in some passion, to pronounce approval of some of her deeds.

What was wanted, apparently, was funding.

"Peter's got the place and it could easily sleep a hundred," she said. Gabriel had seated himself in one of the plush new chairs, while she paced before him excitedly. "But there are two problems—three problems. And they all must be solved with money."

"Tell me."

"Well, first, he needs more than space and beds. He needs to be able to buy clothes, food, supplies. That all takes cash. And the building needs to be more than a place to sleep—it needs to be a school. He must hire teachers from every part of Velora—musicians, cooks, scribes, weavers, horse trainers—to come in •
and instruct the children in the various trades. We could even

develop an apprentice system with some of the Velora merchants, I think, though that might be a few years down the road—"

"And it will take money to pay the teachers. I see that. What's the third problem?"

"The children," she said. "Street urchins who've fended for themselves for eight or ten years are not going to want to stay indoors learning their letters when they could be out stealing. It just won't happen."

"Then how—"

"Pay them, too," she said. "It was Peter's idea, but such a good one! Pay them for every class they take, or every examination they pass, or every night they spend in the dormitory—we can work out some system. I think enough of them would stay long enough to be reclaimed. It will take time, of course. Maybe a year or so before the school becomes a place where the children want to come—something they see as a refuge or a home. But it will work, I think. Peter thinks so. Obadiah thinks so." She smiled again. "Maga is not so sure, but then, she thinks I've taken leave of my senses."

"You must like her, if you call her Maga."

"Oh, she's marvelous. Your best gift, after the tunnel car."

"But she is skeptical of your plan?"

"She's not really comfortable outside the holds and the places of grandeur," Rachel said, defending the angel. "She's trying, but it's hard for her to understand poverty in any real sense."

"That's probably true."

"But *you're* the one who has to understand," Rachel went on, a trifle anxiously. "Because you must support it for this to work. You do realize that? If the Veloran merchants see that you're behind the plan, they will cooperate, I think. If it's just me and Peter— And also there's the money thing. I don't understand how it works, but I know that if you don't like it—"

"But I do like it," he interrupted. "I think it's wonderful. And the hold is rich. You can have as much money as you like."

He said it on impulse, but the reward was beyond his expectations. She smiled at him so radiantly that everything else fell away from him: Elijah, Malachi, Raphael, Josiah, Judith—the names and conversations of his recent past slipped from his mind. His consciousness was filled solely with this laughing face. Her hair flamed behind her in a golden aureole; she seemed lit from behind, from within, from the light reflected off his own wings.

He suddenly saw Rachel as she should be, and all other pictures of her disappeared. Perhaps Jovah had been right after all.

It was actually two days before he remembered Josiah's letter for her. In those two days he spent more time with his bride than he had in the past two months. It was certainly the most amicable time they had spent together, and he thought she was as encouraged by this fact as he was.

Most of these agreeable hours were passed in Velora, though not all of them at Peter's school. The white-haired old priest graciously accepted Gabriel's fresh interest in his project and did not make any comments about how the angel could have helped him out months before this. They walked through the building and discussed improvements. True, money would help, but Peter needed more than money. He needed civic support.

So Gabriel and Rachel toured the city, discussing the school with the merchants, the traders and the moneylenders, the artists and the craft guilds. In Velora, if nowhere else, Gabriel was liked; he had always been on excellent terms with the city leaders, who were anxious for good relations with the hold. And the problem of the street children was one which had vexed many of the honest business owners for some time, he found. Nearly everyone they spoke with was willing to make donations of materials or contract to train an apprentice under the aegis of the school.

Rachel, whom he had heretofore seen mostly at her worst, showed to advantage in these talks as well. First, she was so distinctive. Dressed as she was these days—in trousers and jacket that looked so much like an angel's flying gear, wearing Veloran scarves and jewelry, with her wild hair tumbling any old golden way down her back—she could not help but draw attention. Second, she was so passionate. She believed so strongly in this cause, and she spoke out so plainly, that her listeners found it hard to resist her. The Velorans might be a little awed by their angelica, but she impressed them favorably. Gabriel saw that and was immoderately pleased.

Obadiah accompanied them on some of these rounds, and Gabriel was not quite as pleased to see the easy, bantering affection that lay between the two. Well, it was impossible to dislike Obadiah, but Rachel was so wary. How had he charmed her so quickly?

Magdalena joined them once or twice, though she was clearly

not as comfortable with the whole concept of the orphanage as the others were. Rachel was right; Maga was not used to poverty. She could not think how to combat it. But she was trying.

The second evening, after a full day spent in consultation with the merchants, the three angels and the angelica rewarded themselves with a festive evening at one of the smaller music halls liberally scattered throughout the city. The proprietor ushered them to the best table in the small, dark room, overlooking the sunken stage. Angels came here often; nearly half the chairs in the place were carved to accommodate the great wings. Rachel squirmed awkwardly in hers when they first sat down.

"This is poking me," she said. "I can't imagine how you sit in something like this."

"Well, here," Obadiah said, rising to drag over another chair from a nearby table and, with elaborate care, reseating her. "Is that better, lovely?"

She smiled up at him. "Thank you, angelo. A great improvement."

Gabriel was conferring with the proprietor and so was able to overlook this exchange. "Anything in particular anyone wants to eat?" he inquired.

"Anything," Magdalena said.

"Isn't this the place where we got those wonderful cheese rolls?" Rachel asked Obadiah. "Let's get some of those."

Gabriel nodded at the waiter, who withdrew instantly. "So you've been here?" he asked his wife.

"Once. There was a Luminaux orchestra playing. Unbelievable music."

"Who's performing tonight?" Maga asked.

"Various itinerants," Obadiah said. "I think it's anyone who wants to."

"Well, that should be interesting."

"In Velora, it always is."

Indeed, it was a night of rich variety sprinkled with moments of sheer magic. Gabriel had never cared much for the percussion bands, though there was a very fine troupe from Breven playing this night and he did somewhat enjoy their interlaced staccato rhythms. The women seemed to prefer the singers, especially a trio of young girls who sang such close harmonics that it was hard to believe they were not one voice split with a musical prism into separate strands. Obadiah liked the stringed instruments. Gabriel was most impressed by the reeds and pipes, and leaned forward in his chair so as not to miss a note of the flute player from Luminaux.

He was surprised to catch Rachel watching him when he sat back at the end of the flautist's performance. "That's what you always wanted to play," she said.

It was true, but he could not remember ever having said that to her. "Did I look with so much longing at the stage?" he asked with a smile.

"You said so once. When we first came to Velora."

"The music is so pure," he explained. "With drums, strings—even voices, filled with words—I am always conscious of how the musicians are creating music. But the pipes don't seem to be making music so much as funneling it from somewhere else. Like a conduit carrying water from a river."

"Like an angel focusing the power of Jovah," Maga murmured.

"Yes, rather like that," he said, smiling at her.

"You could learn to play one. You're not too old to go to school yourself," Obadiah said.

"Thank you," Gabriel said somewhat dryly. "Although I rather expect I will be too old before I have the time to sit down and learn."

"Look, they're calling for volunteers," Maga said, pointing down at the stage. "Go sing, Gabriel. It's been weeks since I've heard you."

"I don't like to monopolize the Velora stages," he said. "Who would be fearless enough to tell me he didn't like the sound of my voice?"

"Well, you have your faults," Obadiah said, "but I've never yet heard anyone say you couldn't sing."

Rachel laughed. Obadiah cut his bright eyes over in her direction. "And I've never yet heard *you* sing," he continued. "Why don't you take the stage and delight us all with your debut performance?"

Gabriel caught his breath, amazed at the question but deeply interested in the reply. Rachel, predictably, refused.

"I don't want to sing."

"You never do want to sing. Aren't we ever going to get a chance to hear you?"

"At the Gloria. I assume you'll be there?"

"Well, I had planned to skip it this year, but since you'll finally be satisfying my curiosity, perhaps I will show up after all."

Maga was shocked. "You can't skip a Gloria!"

"He was teasing," Rachel said.

"You're the one who's teasing," Obadiah said. "*Why* won't you sing for us? I don't mean now, I mean ever."

"Perversity," Gabriel said before he could stop himself. But his wife laughed at him.

"Mostly," she agreed. "Because it makes you all so nervous."

"Gabriel most of all, I'll bet," Obadiah commented.

Gabriel was smiling back at his wife. "No," he said. "I believe she can sing as well as Jovah wants. He chose her to please himself. Therefore she no doubt sings—like an angel."

They all laughed. The owner of the hall approached their table with some diffidence.

"I don't wish to interrupt, but several of the patrons have recognized you, angelo, and asked if you would be willing to sing for us tonight? It has been some time since those of us in Velora were privileged to hear what the inhabitants of the Eyrie are lucky enough to hear on a daily basis—"

"I would be pleased to sing if you genuinely wish it," the angel said.

The proprietor was all smiles. "Oh, delighted! Nothing would please me more! Do you want accompaniment? Should I ask one of the harpists to stay?"

Gabriel shook his head and rose to his feet, following the owner. "No, no, I don't need anything, thank you—"

He was led to the back of the room and through a narrow tunnel almost too low to accommodate his wings; it was a relief to step into the comparative open space of the stage. He swept his gaze across the small room to find virtually every eye upon him, then glanced up at the table where his friends and his wife sat waiting. Until this moment he had not determined what to sing. It was that look at Rachel's face that decided him.

He bowed briefly to the audience, laced his hands before him and began to sing. Although it was not in his usual classical style, Gabriel had practiced this particular piece in his rare spare moments in the past few weeks, and he was pleased with his first public performance of it. He felt the low burning on his arm and saw from the corner of his eye his Kiss flicker with color. So his wife was pleased with his performance as well.

It was the love song Matthew had sung at their wedding, a simple ballad which required little more than good diction and the ability to sustain an occasional high note; but it was a beautiful piece for all that. Gabriel half-closed his eyes, working his way with physical pleasure up the slow scale at the refrain. He was so used to singing in Jovah's honor that it was a strange, almost sensuous experience to be singing for someone else's gratification—but he was, and he knew it, and Rachel would be a fool not to know it as well.

When he repeated the chorus at the end, this time switching to Edori, he felt the heat in the Kiss flame suddenly higher. Ah, that had surprised her; she had not thought he knew the nomad tongue. He held the last three notes a little longer than necessary, showing off perhaps, but the crowd did not find that a cause for censure. Indeed, the applause was as enthusiastic as any he had ever received. He smiled, bowed again and shook his head when there were calls for an encore. Some insistent fellow in the back row had begun chanting "Angels! Angels!" in a rhythmic voice which was taken up by the louder patrons in the hall. Gabriel saw the proprietor hurrying over to his table again, and Obadiah and Magdalena were on their feet. He made sure that he was out of the connecting tunnel before the other two entered.

"It'll be hard for anyone else to please this crowd after your performance," Obadiah said gloomily as they passed each other outside the narrow hallway. "I would much rather precede you than follow you."

Gabriel smiled, and rejoined his wife at their table. She looked over at him in—could it be?—approval.

"That was really beautiful," she said. "Thank you."

"I thought you might like it."

"I didn't know you could speak Edori."

"I can't. A few words. For the most part, I learned that piece phonetically. I couldn't translate it for you if I didn't already know the chorus."

"Ah, then you couldn't translate it at all, because the Edori chorus is different than the popular translation."

"Really? What was I singing?"

She shook her head. "Better that you don't know."

Now he was both amused and alarmed. "Tell me!"

She shook her head again, putting a finger to her lips. "Hush. They're singing."

Obadiah and Magdalena were a little more generous, singing three duets for the appreciative audience before they too yielded the stage. The applause that followed their performance was thunderous, and continued long after the three angels and the angelica had risen to their feet, waved farewell and left the hall.

There was a great deal of talk and laughter among the four of them as the angels accompanied Rachel to the tunnel car at the foot of the mountain.

"Come to my room when you've arrived," Gabriel told her when they stopped at the inset door. "I have something I forgot to give you before."

She was stepping inside and closing the grille. The thread of light inside the shaft threw the faintest illumination across her face, set the tangled hair to glowing. "What is it?"

"Something from Josiah. A letter."

She raised her eyebrows, but did not reply. Though Gabriel was standing right there, she reached over to pull the bell-cord, to alert those above that she was in the cage and would be coming up. He nodded.

"Very wise," he said.

"I never fail to observe this rule," she said. Then she lowered the activating lever and the car rose slowly into the mountainside and disappeared.

"I hate that thing," Maga murmured.

"She requires it," Gabriel replied.

Obadiah tugged on the Monteverde angel's wingtips. She twitched them away. "Don't get personal," she said.

He was laughing. "Race you to the top," he said. The two of them took off, great wings making a whuffling sound like banners whipping in the breeze. Gabriel followed at a more leisurely pace, landed, and headed directly for his room. In a few minutes, Rachel was at his open door.

"A letter from Josiah?" she said. "About what?"

He handed it to her, shutting the door behind her. "He wouldn't say and I can't read Edori," he said pleasantly. "You'll have to tell me if it's something I should know."

It only took her a few moments to open the letter and read the two paragraphs on the single page, but in those moments she changed utterly. One moment she was smiling and ironic; the next she was sick, stunned, clenched into a knot of pain. He crossed the room in two strides.

"Rachel! What is it—what did he say?"

She looked at him blindly, shaking her head. He thought that she had no idea, for a moment at least, where she was or who was addressing her. He took hold of her shoulders and pushed her gently toward a chair.

"Sit down. Here— All right, then, on the floor. Rachel, tell me what he said to you."

She had sunk to her knees on the thick red carpet, and he knelt beside her. He was still gripping her arms; he thought she would topple over if he released her. He shook her very slightly.

"Rachel, talk to me. What's in the letter? Is it— Did someone die?"

It was a guess, but a good one, and it shocked a response from her. "Simon," she choked.

Simon? "What happened to him? How does Josiah know?"

Her reply did not quite make sense to him. "He—we were the only ones who bore the Kiss, so the oracle said he could find out—and now he tells me that Simon is dead, has been dead two years—*two years*!" she wailed, suddenly coming to life. She twisted in his hold, but not to escape. She pounded both fists on the red rug, tossed her head from side to side in fierce denial. These were the signs of storm he was becoming familiar with. Gabriel kept his hold on her.

"I'm sorry your friend is dead, and you did not know it for so long—"

"He should have been dead much longer!" she raged. "Simon—a slave for three years! It took him that long to die, fighting the whole time, hating them, hating himself, wretched and beaten—Simon . . ."

The rest of her words were incomprehensible to Gabriel; Edori no doubt, words of imprecation or grieving, he could not tell. But now she was crying—huge, tearing sobs that were as fierce as her fury. He thought she would rend herself in two with weeping.

"Here—here—" he murmured, drawing her into his arms, holding her tightly against his chest either to comfort her or restrain her or muffle the tears, he hardly knew. All three, maybe. She resisted briefly and then gave in, grinding her face against his leather vest, clenching and unclenching her fingers against his bare forearms. He felt her nails rake against his skin hard enough to leave a trail.

It took her a long time to quiet down, and even then it was only by contrast. She still wept bitterly, though less passionately, and he still held her. She had come to rest with her back against his chest, both his arms wrapped around her, his head bent over hers. "Shh," he whispered again and again, rocking her a little, trying to convey some of his pity and distress. He felt so sorry for her. Whoever this Simon was, she had clearly loved him, and now he was dead. Yet another thing lost to her forever.

When she started speaking again, he thought at first the words were in Edori, and then he thought they were not meant for him. A farewell to this Simon, perhaps, a prayer to the god to receive the migrant soul. Yet the cadence of the prayer sounded familiar. He leaned closer to hear, till his ear rested on the wild golden hair.

What he heard stopped his heart.

"Yovah, if it be thy will, call down thy curses on the city of Semorrah. Strike it with fire, with thunderbolts. Cover it with storm and flood it with raging river. Bring pestilence and plague, and let everyone within its borders die. . . ."

In a weak, exhausted whisper she was calling down Jovah's curse as Gabriel had heard her do once before. He clapped his hand across her mouth and stared down at her in horror. He felt her lips move against his palm as she continued the invocation silently. She stared back up at him, remorseless and defiant, and he thought that this was perhaps one mortal whom the god would heed. And he pressed his hand more tightly against her mouth to stop her, and felt a sort of dread travel through him from his fingers to his heart.

CHAPTER TWELVE

Although she had been glad when Gabriel first returned, Rachel now spent some energy wishing he would go away again. There were many reasons, not the least one being the fact that she *had* been so pleased to see him again. And he had seemed pleased with her, and the whole world seemed unexpectedly harmonious.

And then the dreadful news had come, and she had gone a little mad, and now Gabriel hated her again; and so she wished he would go away.

He had not said he hated her. He had in fact been extraordinarily kind, but she had seen the look on his face when she whispered the curse on Semorrah, and she had been too stubborn to recant. Well, she had not felt like recanting. In fact, if she had the power today, she would go stand on the Plain of Sharon and call out the curse in her loudest voice, and watch with satisfaction as Semorrah tumbled into the foam-laced waters of the Galilee River.

To his credit, Gabriel had tried to understand. The morning after that dreadful scene he had come to her door, sober and solemn as always, to ask after her state of mind. He had stepped inside the room and stood squarely, though quite unconsciously, in the white plane of sunlight billowing in through the open window and all she could do was stare at him. He was so beautiful—all blue and silver and black—so beautiful and so serious, and here she was, once again, having played the lunatic at their very last meeting. So she had greeted him with an icy reserve, too proud to show embarrassment, far too willing to show him first that she hated him before he had a chance to make his feelings plain to her.

His own expression was remote, his gorgeous voice chilly. "I wanted to see if you were feeling any better today," he said in the formal way she had almost forgotten.

"Yes," she said flatly. "I'm fine."

He had hesitated, and then asked a carefully worded question. "Would you want to tell me who Simon was?"   •

"My lover," she shot at him instantly, hoping to shock him or at least unnerve him. "Five years ago."

But he merely nodded. No doubt he had worked it out for himself. "I'm sorry that he is dead," he said, which he had said last night. "Why do you think he died in Semorrah?"

"Because he did not die on the Heldora Plains, where the rest of the Manderras died," she said. "He lived three years longer. And the Jansai leave no survivors—only dead men and slaves."

"He may not have died a slave. He could have escaped. He may not even have died in Semorrah."

"Semorrah, Castelana, Breven—it is all one," she said, her voice still hard. "I would see them all crushed by the falling mountain and drowned under the rising sea."

And seeing her unrepentant, he had bowed and gone away. And he had avoided her ever since, and so he hated her.

Well, perhaps it was just as fair to say she had avoided him. In any case, they had not spoken much these past two weeks, and might never speak again, and Judith walked around smiling smugly, and Rachel did not care.

She did care that Magdalena had returned to Monteverde, though Rachel had begged her to stay another month, another week, at least.

"I can't—I have duties of my own back home," the angel had said gently. "People I have neglected quite shamefully. And—you know . . ."

"Now that Nathan is back, Gabriel is pressuring you to go."

"Not quite pressuring. Gabriel is too courteous to treat me unkindly."

Rachel had let a small sniff express her opinion of Gabriel's courtesy. Magdalena had smiled.

"But it is time for me to go. I miss my sister and my friends.

I have a class of girls I am supposed to be teaching for the Gloria, and that is only a couple of months away now. I'll see you again, then. It won't seem so long."

But it already seemed long, and the angel had only been gone two weeks. Rachel missed her all the more because—now that Gabriel hated her—she had only two friends left at the Eyrie. One was Matthew, who was fine; and the other was Obadiah, who could be trouble.

True to her nature, Rachel spent most of her time seeking trouble.

It was Obadiah himself who pointed that out to her, although she had not thought he noticed. And she denied it when he said it. But she knew it was true.

They had spent most of that second week together in Velora, working at the school. Peter's efforts had brought in about thirty street children who were more or less willing to attempt living in the experimental school cum residence, though they were highly skeptical and all looked ready to bolt at a moment's notice. Nonetheless, the lure of cash, as Peter had foreseen, was a powerful one, and they had attached a payment to everything. Each class taken, each night spent in the dorm, each project completed—everything was rewarded. Those who had learned mathematics were beginning to grasp what the sum total of such largesse might be, and they were the ones who seemed most interested in staying.

Rachel had set herself up as an instructor in a class on weaving, and was pleased when four girls and one teenaged boy elected to study with her. Obadiah had undertaken to set up a musical curriculum, staffed by several local luminaries and featuring in addition a revolving roster of visiting musicians. Basic theory was taught in these classes, as well as specific applications in voice, harp, flute and percussion. Obadiah, who could not promise to be on hand for daily lessons, had nevertheless assigned himself a full week as tutor, and that week had just now come to an end.

The angel and the angelica-to-be had agreed to have an elegant dinner at one of Velora's more gracious restaurants, as a treat after seven days of relatively intensive labor. The room was mostly dark; the accommodating host had seated these grandest of patrons in a semi-secluded private alcove. Over the food and wine, they talked first about the school.

"There's this one boy—James—do you know him?" Obadiah asked her.

"I think so. Very small. Very blond. Very difficult."

"That's him. Mostly I just want to slap him. I swear if I had been his father, I would have abandoned him, too."

"Obadiah!"

"But have you heard him sing?"

"I don't think so. Is he good?"

"Not yet. But he will be. I heard him for the first time—oh, three days ago. You could have pulled every feather from my wings and I wouldn't have moved a muscle. I was in shock. He has a voice."

"Probably an angel's son," Rachel said cynically. "Maybe even yours. Maybe you did abandon him, after all."

He smiled at her lazily. "I don't think so, lovely. I have always avoided the angel-seekers for precisely that reason."

She eyed him speculatively. "Then you've been very discreet about your romances," she said. "There doesn't seem to have been much gossip about you."

"And who were you asking?"

"Maga, mostly. Who else could I ask?"

"Well, Maga hasn't been around the Eyrie all that much. She wouldn't know."

"So, who? Tell me."

He laughed, seemingly delighted rather than embarrassed. "I cannot believe you would be so tactless as to ask me!" he exclaimed. "Let me assure you I have far more discretion than to tell you."

"I hope it wasn't Judith."

"No, she's far too scheming for my taste."

"Then—"

"Stop asking, dearest. I'm not the man to gossip about love."

"Then tell me something else," she said.

"I can hardly wait to hear the question."

"Why don't angels like their wings to be touched?"

He laughed again. "Before I answer, let me say that you're the first mortal I've ever met who learned that fact through observation rather than experience."

"What do you mean?"

"Oh, most mortals carelessly walk up to an angel and run their hands down his feathers as if they're petting a cat—and practically get their fingers broken for it. Not you. You'd as soon think of touching an angel's wings uninvited as you would—well—kissing him on the mouth."

"Well, that's almost what it seems like," she remarked. "I mean, it seems like a very intimate thing."

"It is. Actually, kissing isn't a bad analogy to how intimate it is."

"Does it feel bad?"

"Does kissing feel bad?"

"No, I mean—"

"To have your wings touched? No, on the contrary. But they're very sensitive. Very—I don't know—personal. To have your wings touched is like being embraced—or touched on the tongue—or stroked on the breast. Something like that. Not something you want a stranger to do."

She was thoroughly intrigued. She leaned closer. "What do they feel like?" she asked. "They look like feathers."

"They are feathers. The outer ones are much smoother and harder. The inner ones soft, fuzzier. See." And he unfurled one of his ivory-lace wings, there in the dark room, and let her examine it by candlelight. She studied the intricate interlocking of quill and branch over the translucent webbed membrane. The resulting mesh looked softer than washed silk, stronger than braided leather. She looked up at Obadiah wordlessly, a question in her eyes.

He laughed lightly. "Yes," he said. "But very, very gently."

So she reached out with one tentative finger and traced a line from right under his armpit to the very edge of his wingspan, noting how the texture toughened and thickened as she moved from the smallest feathers to the greatest. He had caught his breath the minute she touched him and did not exhale until her hand reluctantly dropped away.

"What? Did I hurt you?" she asked.

"You tickled."

"I'm sorry." A small smile grew in her eyes. "Did it feel good, though?"

"Yes."

"Shall I do it again?"

He slowly refolded his wing, regarding her somewhat thoughtfully as he did. "I think not," he said slowly.

She should have been abashed, but he was not trying to reprove her. She put her head to one side and returned his steady gaze. "Why not?" she asked.

He smiled very slightly. "You are the angelica, lovely, and wedded to a man I greatly respect. I have no wish to add to your already considerable marital woes, at least not so early in your life together."

She flushed, but answered defensively. "I did not mean—"

"Oh yes, you did. Perhaps you are not cold-bloodedly planning to seduce me, but you know that my being here with you troubles your husband, and that is one of the reasons you like to be with me. And let us not rule out seduction altogether. We are not children, and both of us are experienced. And you do not, by my observation at least, have much of a marriage with your husband at present."

Her chin went up. "I have no wish to discuss my husband."

He laughed. "Nor do I, but he is there, nonetheless, and he is a difficult man to ignore. And I—to my praise or my blame, I cannot really decide—find you also difficult to overlook. I shall not encourage you to toy with me, because I have no wish to break my heart over you. I imagine it is something I could do."

If this was rejection, it was phrased as beautifully as she had ever heard it. She scanned his face, trying to read behind the rueful smile. "Are you angry with me?" she asked directly.

"Not at all. Flattered, a little. Sorry, a little. Not angry."

"Because I really cannot bear to lose all my friends, one after another."

He stretched his hand out to her across the table, and she took it, though she did briefly wonder if this could be construed as encouragement. "Friends for life, lovely. And if—ah, but that's a foolish thing to say."

"Well, say it, though."

"Give Gabriel a year," he said. "Give yourselves a year, before you start looking around for consolation. By that time you will know if Jovah chose wisely or ill. I will still be at the Eyrie in a year's time. Who knows what will have changed by then?"

She could not help squeezing his hand tightly before she drew hers away. "Now you're toying with me," she said, but she was smiling.

He laughed and sipped from his wine. He looked very much at ease, but she sensed he was just a little ruffled under his charming exterior. Which pleased her. "We are all toys in the game between men and women, lovely," he said. "But sometimes the game is a little more enjoyable than others."

The time with Matthew, of course, was safer, and Matthew too was an instructor at Peter's school. Leather-working had become one of the more well-attended classes; so had a sort of undefined "mechanicals" course in which Matthew took objects apart and put them back together again to show his students how things worked. Actually, there was very little Matthew didn't know (at least in Rachel's opinion)—from weather forecasting to animal husbandry to voice training—so that he could have taught half the scheduled classes and done right by the children. He was far more favored by the students than Peter or the merchants or any of the angels. He seemed baffled by his popularity, but Rachel was proud.

Matthew frequently went with her when she canvased the streets of Velora, looking for new recruits. By now, most of the children of the city had heard about the school, whether or not they decided to attend; but new children arrived in town every few days with their itinerant parents, or slinking in from the uncivilized rough country, or in the trains of traveling peddlers. Or in Jansai caravans.

Rachel knew she should not look for students among the Jansai. Even if her own common sense had not told her she could not deal rationally with the mercenary nomads, Peter had told her bluntly that they were to be avoided. "They camp on the outskirts and trade, and Gabriel tolerates it, but they are not encouraged to linger," the ex-priest had said. "They have a few goods that the merchants want, but they are not well-liked in Velora. They're dirty, and they cheat, and they eye the women in a way that no one appreciates."

"But if they have slave children in their wagons—"

"Not in Bethel," Peter said firmly. "The Jansai don't go slaving in this realm. Any children in the caravan are freeborn—they might be urchins, overworked little wretches maybe, but not slaves. Not in Bethel."

But "overworked little wretch" sounded almost as unendurable to Rachel as "slave," and so she kept an eye out for the Jansai visitors. And when, a few weeks after the school expanded, a Jansai cortege made camp outside the city, she and Matthew strolled down to the wagons to see what they could find.

"Although you shouldn't be going with me," she told him, when they were close enough to make out the faces. "You know how fond the Jansai are of Edori."

"Well, and you're an Edori yourself, angela."

"Yes, but I don't look like one. You, now—"

He displayed his right forearm for her. Like the angels, he wore a sleeveless vest and no jacket, despite the freezing weather. "And haven't I been dedicated like a good son of Yovah?" he demanded. "Isn't that the Kiss you see there on my arm? They'll make no slave of me."

"A Kiss won't stop them," she said with some bitterness.

"Ah, Raheli, we're safe in Bethel."

They slipped unnoticed into the camp, which was disorganized and overrun with people. It was midday, and most of the Jansai men were in the city drumming up business, although buyers and sellers could be spotted concluding transactions before campfires and just inside the low tents. The white winter sunlight glanced off the gold jewelry and bald heads of the men, but could not penetrate the dark cloaks and cowled faces of the Jansai women. Glimpses were all that visitors got of the women, who ducked inside their tents whenever they felt alien eyes upon them. Matthew glanced over at Rachel.

"Aye, and there's the people you should be liberating next, once you've saved all the children of Samaria," he commented.

She could not help grinning, though she felt a little grim. "I think—by the horses?" she said, heading toward the far edge of the camp. "Surely that's a task that would fall to children."

And she was right. Three incredibly grubby boys were squatting on the ground outside a makeshift corral, fascinated by some drama unfolding at their feet and occasionally loosing shouts of triumphant laughter.

"There's a pack up to no good," Matthew remarked.

"Probably torturing small animals," Rachel replied.

Indeed, when Matthew hailed them in his burred voice, the three whirled guiltily around to face the newcomers, and a small furry shape instantly sped away in the opposite direction.

"I can see you've been having a pleasant afternoon, now," Matthew said conversationally.

The three miscreants instantly recovered their poise. "And what's it to you?" the biggest one asked in a sneering voice. "Look, fellas, it's one of them Edoris. Slave-bait."

Rachel was instantly affronted, but Matthew merely grinned. He shook back his long black hair. "Slave-bait, is it," he said. "I'm not the one who's been set out to guard the horses here on such a fine afternoon."

The big one scowled. "I like to watch the horses," he said defiantly. "A horse is a Jansai's life. Better than a woman. A horse will get you everything you need." His comrades supported this speech with a couple of heartfelt "yeahs" and some emphatic nods.

Matthew nodded. "Sure, now. A horse is a good thing. Take you across the mountain, take you across the desert. Of course, if you're always too poor to own your own horses, won't do you much good to love them."

"Who says I'm too poor?"

"Well, you're sitting here watching another man's beasts, now, aren't you?"

"Now I am, maybe. But I get paid for it. Paid plenty. I'll buy my own horse any day now, and then I'll pay some kid to look after him."

"Is that right, now? And how much do you think a horse costs, *mikele*?" Matthew asked, using the Edori term for young boy.

The mikele scowled even more darkly. "I don't know. Not so much."

"A hundred gold pieces, I'm thinking. Maybe more. How many gold pieces do you have saved up? Is it five? Is it one? Are your kind masters paying you in gold, after all, or is it perhaps silver? Maybe they're paying you in food and gear—"

Rachel had just begun to relax into the familiar, persuasive cadence of Matthew's argument for education when rough voices behind them abruptly interrupted.

"Hey, what's that damned Edori doing here? Chit, Brido, get away from the filthy Edori—"

The boys scrambled back toward the corral as Rachel and Matthew whirled around to see who had spoken. Two good-sized Jansai males were approaching them on the run, snarls on their faces and sharp-edged weapons coming to life in their hands. Involuntarily, Rachel stiffened at the sight of those long-handled knives threaded through with sinuous leather straps. She remembered those well enough—

But she would not give in to fear or panic. She made herself step ahead of Matthew, and haughtily stared down the half-naked Jansai. "We've come from the Eyrie to inspect conditions at your camp, and we'd appreciate a little civility," she said in an icy voice. "You are only here on sufferance, after all."

The tone surprised them; so did the clothes, the face, the whole package. Not the troublesome merchant's wife they had expected. They came to a halt a few yards away and inspected her, some of the menace dying away from their lean faces and bunched muscles.

"Pardon, mistress," said one, suddenly flashing her that wide white smile that she also very clearly remembered. "We don't like strangers meddling in our campgrounds."

"We weren't meddling," she said very coldly.

The second Jansai jerked his knife-hand at Matthew. "Who's he? Edori stay out of our camps."

"He's with me. For protection."

This second man was less easily cowed by a tone of voice. He stared back at her insolently. "And who are you?"

"I am Rachel, wife to Gabriel," she said with heavy emphasis. "I assume you will allow that I have the right to be anywhere in Velora I choose?"

She had expected the name to mean something to them—she had learned, in Velora, it always did—but she hadn't expected the sudden interest that leapt to both Jansai faces. Inexplicably, she felt she had made a mistake. The second man gave a small laugh; the first one kissed his fist to her, the only gesture of respect known to the Jansai, but the expression on his face was mocking.

"Two Edori, after all," the first Jansai said, smiling that white smile again. "So you still remember our camps with fondness."

Instinct warned her against explaining her real motive. "Just curious," she said, still in that frigid voice. "I see they haven't improved any."

"Maybe they have," the second man said. "You're welcome to stay and look around. I'll be glad to show you where I pitch my tent."

"Thank you, no. I believe I've seen enough to remind me just what an unpleasant place the camp can be."

And she nodded regally and stepped forward, brushing past them with an odd sense of unease. Matthew was close on her other side, close enough for her to feel the heat of his bare arm against her woolen sleeve, but that did not make her feel any safer. There had been more Edori than Jansai in camp that night on the Heldora plains, and it had not been Edori who prevailed. . . .

But the two mercenaries drew aside to let them pass. "Angela," one of them murmured as she drew away, but she did not look back to acknowledge the word. Only willpower kept her from breaking into a run when they were a few yards away. She kept walking in a fast but measured pace, and within minutes they were safely back inside the city limits, and unharmed.

"So I guess the Jansai mikele survive without us," Matthew said finally, when the camp was far enough behind she couldn't even imagine that she still smelled it. The words surprised a laugh out of her; she clutched his arm and kept laughing, knowing she was a touch hysterical. He laughed, too, and patted her arm in a comforting way, and that was all they said about the adventure.

It was the next day before she realized that there might be repercussions. She was back in Velora, this time alone, walking through one of the sunless alleys that connected the bazaar to the business district. Having just purchased a sackful of blue yarn, and calculating how long it would last and which of her students would be asking for a different color, she was paying very little attention to the noises around her. Not that there was much noise. She heard a footfall—the small clink of knife against metal sheath—and then she was enveloped in darkness.

For a split second, she was too astonished to be afraid or even to understand what had happened. But when darkness was followed by sudden violent motion, she knew, and she started to scream and fight. Her voice was muffled by the heavy blanket over her head, and her hands were trapped inside it as well, but terror lent her amazing strength. She writhed and shrieked, kicking out ferociously at invisible shapes around her, clawing at her prison from the inside. She heard low voices swearing, and someone struck her a mighty blow on the head. Other hands grabbed her around her shoulders and flung her back against a wall. There were at least two of them.

One of them clouted her again; her skull cracked against the brick so hard she was dizzied. She kicked out frenziedly and an answering boot crashed into her thigh so brutally that she felt her flesh tear and her bones buckle. Unable to stop herself from falling, she pitched headlong onto the cobblestones, rolled, and slammed again into the wall. There was a laugh, a flurry of Jansai words, and another foot catching her unexpectedly in the stomach. She tried to scrabble up, but rough hands pushed her back down. She felt a length of rope pass around her neck and shoulders, and tighten as if a noose were abruptly shortened.

Her cry of despair was swallowed up by unexpected sounds—high yipping calls and a rattle of stones and bottles ricocheting off the alley walls. Her captors swore again, shoved her facedown into the street and took off running. Rachel lay where they left her, tangled and bruised, too stunned to even pull off the blanket and see who had rescued her.

In a matter of seconds, someone else performed this task for her. She found herself struggling for air and staring up into a most unexpected trio of faces. Three of her students—Katie, Nate and Sal—were crouched beside her, surveying Rachel with worried expressions.

"Angela—you all right?" asked Katie, the oldest and largest of the group. "Was they grabbing you?"

Rachel pushed herself slowly to a more vertical position, though she was incapable of standing just yet. "I think so," she said shakily. "Was it the Jansai?"

Nate nodded solemnly. He was the youngest student in the school, affectionate and intelligent; Peter had high hopes for him. "Two of 'em. We saw another one coming this way, but he run off when he saw us."

Rachel gingerly put a hand to her right leg, where the kick had gone home with some force. It was bleeding but not, apparently, broken. "How did you know it was me?" she asked.

"Seen your hair," Nate said.

"Katie said, 'They've got angela! We've gotta help her!' " Sal related. "And I was scared, but Katie got her a handful of rocks and we started coming at them real fast, and they run off."

"Well, you were very brave. All of you. I think you saved me."

"They was grabbing you?" Katie asked a second time. "Did they want you for their slave again?"

No secrets among the students, it seemed. "I don't know. Maybe. I think they were mad at me because I was in their camp yesterday."

"But everybody goes to the Jansai camp," Nate said, frowning.

"Yes, but I was trying to talk some of their children into coming to the school. I guess they didn't like that."

"Not their school," Katie said with a scowl.

Rachel regarded her. She was feeling a little lightheaded, but slightly euphoric as well. Saved by her schoolchildren. Something about that appealed to her. Surely three children couldn't have frightened off grown Jansai warriors; it must have been that they couldn't afford to draw attention here in the streets of Velora. "So you don't think the Jansai children would fit in? You think it would be a bad idea to invite them to live there?"

Katie nodded emphatically. The two boys, watching her, copied the motion. Rachel said, "But what if the Jansai are mean to them? Beat them—starve them? Shouldn't they have someplace safe to go, like you do?"

"Get their own school," Katie said distinctly.

Rachel gave a weak laugh. "Well, maybe you're right. In any case, I don't feel strong enough to go back to the camp to try again. Maybe in a year or two, when we're a little more established—"

"You're bleeding," Nate observed.

Rachel glanced down at her leg. "Yes, I know. I probably need to get that taken care of."

"Can't you stand up?" Kate wanted to know.

"I can. I'm sure I can."

"I'll go get Peter," Sal offered.

"No," Rachel said, quickly, without thinking. The three children regarded her with interest. "No," she said a little more slowly. "I don't want Peter—or Matthew—or anyone else knowing about this. You see, some people aren't so sure the school is a good idea. They might tell me it's dangerous if they hear about this. I don't want them to tell me to shut it down."

"No," Nate said positively.

Katie said, "Maybe they'll just tell you not to go to the Jansai camp."

Rachel laughed. "Well, they'll certainly tell me that. And they're right, and believe me, I'm not going to try it again. But I don't want anyone being even a little bit worried. So I don't want anyone to know about this. Will you promise me not to tell? All of you—will you promise me?"

Nate agreed promptly. Katie had to think it over, but when she gave her word, Sal followed suit. "Good," Rachel said. "Now, somebody please help me up."

They hauled her to her feet and insisted on walking her to the tunnel car when she said she didn't want to go back to the school for first aid. Katie even helped her tie her scarf around her hips so that it concealed most of the bloody tear in her trousers. Rachel handed the girl the bag of new yarn to carry to the school.

"But you'll be back tomorrow, won't you?" Nate asked anxiously.

"Oh, I'm sure I will. All I need is a bandage and I'll be fine."

"Okay, then," he said. They all watched her board the car and shut the gate, waving goodbye as she pulled the lever and rose out of their sight. Hoping to return unnoticed to her room, this once she deliberately neglected to ring the Eyrie chimes that would alert Matthew or Gabriel or Hannah to her arrival.

And she was successful, managing to slip down the cool hallways without attracting more than a casual glance from anyone she passed. Safe in her room, she swung the door shut and collapsed suddenly against it, sliding to the floor. Now, half an hour later, reaction was setting in. She trembled alarmingly; tears started coursing down her face and she could not stop them. Still pressing her back against the door, she made herself as small as she could, drawing her knees up to her cheeks and wrapping her arms tightly around her ankles. She wept so long that the room grew dark before she finally stirred and imposed some semblance of calm on herself. Painfully, she forced herself to stand and limped over to the water room, where she spent an hour bathing all traces of the dreaded Jansai touch from her body.

She was sore for two days, and the gash on her leg was ugly, but there did not appear to be other ill effects. Well, she was a little subdued, perhaps, but very few people here knew her well enough to notice that. Obadiah was out on a three-day mission, Maga of course was in Monteverde, and she hadn't seen her husband in more than a week. Matthew did inquire, late that third day as they left Velora, how she was feeling.

"Because you've seemed a bit jumbled lately, like you've things on your mind or a headache," he said. "It's not such an easy thing you've taken on, this school—"

She smiled at him as they headed back toward the mountain at a rather sedate pace. She had told him, the day before, that she had twisted her ankle falling in the water room, to explain away the slowness with which she was walking. "Peter does all the hard work," she scoffed. "And you. You're surrounded by the mikele day in and day out. I just sit around weaving, which I'd be doing anyway. It's not so difficult."

"Well, I was just asking. Because it occurred to me there might be something else clamoring in your brain that you haven't had the sense to ask someone about."

His phrasing made her laugh. "And what would that be?" she said, but she knew before he answered that he had scanned her mind.

"You can read a calendar," he said. "You know what happens this time of year. You wouldn't be thinking of attending the Gathering, now would you?"

She came to a halt, facing him in the middle of the road. She put a hand on his arm, half to steady herself, half to hold him in place. "You know I am," she said quietly. "It's been five years, Matthew. I can't tell you—you can't guess—"

"I can guess," he said. "It's to be held outside of Luminaux this year, did you know that?"

"Yes."

"A long trip. Have you thought how you would make it?"

She began to feel a rising stubbornness. She had not expected Matthew, of all people, to offer opposition. "You can hire horses in Velora, I suppose. I know how to pack a saddlebag and where to find water—"

But he was smiling at her. He had been teasing all along. "Edori should not travel alone," he said. "Seventeen years I've made that journey by myself, to wherever the Gathering was held. Sure I was thinking it would be a fine thing to make that trip with one of the people at my side."

She laughed, and gave him a quick, hard hug. They resumed their slow progress toward the mountain. "Yes," she said, "please come with me to the Gathering. I am so excited, and so afraid, I don't know if I can make it on my own."

They discussed the journey for the rest of the walk. Matthew even agreed to ride up in the tunnel car with her (though he didn't much like the cramped quarters), seeing as there were no angels in sight. Rachel tugged on the bell-cord and Matthew set the cage in motion. She was still bubbling over with plans. Matthew continued to listen in amusement.

Some of her enthusiasm faded when, arriving on the upper level, she stepped out of the cage to find Gabriel awaiting her in the hallway. In the half-light of the back tunnel, he looked almost phosphorescent, his pale skin distinct against the darkness, his huge white wings aglow behind him. The expression on his face was unfriendly.

"Rachel," he said, and his voice matched his face. "I've been wanting to talk with you. Could you come to my room immediately?"

She glanced at Matthew and nodded goodbye, then silently preceded her husband down the hallway. She was very aware of him following closely at her heels, and she was a little sorry when Matthew turned down the corridor leading to his own quarters. Gabriel said nothing until he had ushered her inside his room and offered her a seat.

"Let's see what you have to say first, and then I'll decide if I need to sit," she said sharply. Not a very amiable opening remark, but he did not make her feel amiable; in fact, it was clear she was in trouble for something. She was on the defensive.

Gabriel was too agitated to take a seat himself. Indeed, he was so disturbed that it seemed he didn't know how to begin. He circled the room once, taking great strides and careless of how his wings brushed against the furniture, before coming to a sudden halt before her.

"What happened to you?" he demanded. "Hannah came to me and said she found clothes of yours in the laundry—covered with blood."

It was totally unexpected; Rachel felt an entirely inappropriate blush coming to her cheeks. He went on in a hard voice. "Naturally, she came to me, concerned, wondering if you needed help—and I had no idea how you might have been wounded. As I never have any idea of what has happened in your life. It was not just a little blood, she said. It covered the whole leg of one pair of your new trousers."

She dropped her eyes, uncharacteristically contrite. "It was nothing—a scrape," she murmured. "I'm sorry to worry her— you—"

He stalked away from her to stare out his own small window

into the gathering blackness. "I knew you would say that," he flung at her over his shoulder. "I knew you wouldn't tell me, even if it was something simple and harmless like the fact you had fallen and hurt yourself. So I ask myself. What can it be? Some bizarre Edori rite, self-mutilation? Would Matthew tell me—should I demean myself by going to him and asking? Maybe it's something else—your tunnel car broke and crashed into the rocks, and you're afraid that if you tell me, I'll forbid you to use it. That would make sense, but the car seems to be in perfect working order. Then what? One of your schoolchildren beat you? Wild dogs in the streets of Velora attacked you?"

He whirled around to face her, but came no closer. "And then I ask myself—why? Why am I asking *myself* these questions? Because my wife doesn't trust me enough to tell me anything—good things, bad things, anything—and even if I ask her, she will not give me the truth."

Usually just a glimpse of his anger was enough to ignite her own, but now, inexplicably, she felt moved and apologetic. She took a few steps toward him, half-extended her hand before letting it fall.

"Gabriel—I'm sorry," she said, the unaccustomed words coming haltingly. "I'll tell you—but it will make you furious—which is why I didn't tell you before. And it was my fault, and I know better now, so don't tell me I can't have the school anymore."

He was staring at her with a heavy frown, but at the same time he looked slightly hopeful. "Don't be silly, I favor the school," he said a little more calmly. "Tell me, then. Something happened at Peter's?"

"No, I— Well. A few days ago, Matthew and I went to the Jansai camp. I thought there might be children there who would want to come live at the school. It was a stupid idea, I know," she hurried on, as his frown grew blacker, "but at the time I thought it was worth a try."

"You and Matthew in a Jansai camp," he said. "It makes my blood run cold."

"Well, and it won't happen again," she said candidly. "We found a few boys, and Matthew had just started talking to them, when a couple of Jansai men came running over to get rid of us. They said a few insulting things and then I—I told them who I was, and they looked like they wanted to eat me for breakfast.

So we got out of the camp as fast as we could, and I thought everything was fine. Then—two days ago—I was in the market and somebody threw a blanket over my head—" She gestured comprehensively to convey the horror of that. It was becoming difficult to keep her voice steady. "But before anything could happen, three of my students ran up, throwing rocks and yelling, and the Jansai ran off, leaving me behind. The camp's broken up and moved on now, so I can't see that I'm in any danger—"

As she had spoken, he had moved closer. He was now just inches away and his face was a study in alarm. "But Rachel, why didn't you tell me? Or why didn't Peter tell me—Matthew, Obadiah—someone?"

She was a little embarrassed. "Because I told the children to tell no one. I told no one. I thought—it seemed to me—you might tell me the school had become dangerous for me, or that Velora was dangerous, and I couldn't go there anymore, and Gabriel—I *can't* not go there, it's too important to me, not just Velora, but the school, the children, everything—"

He reached out a hand, as if he couldn't help himself, and touched a stray curl of her hair. "I know it's important to you," he said in a gentle voice. "I would never tell you to give it up. But Rachel—to confront the Jansai like that—even in Velora, where generally anyone is safe—swear to me by the love of Jovah you'll never do anything like that again."

"I swear," she said. "I was afraid, as soon as I saw those two. I hadn't thought I would be afraid, but suddenly all those memories— So I won't do it again."

"And when there are Jansai in Velora, it might be best if you have someone with you all the time—Matthew or Obadiah or me," he said. She was so surprised that he included himself as a bodyguard that she could only nod dumbly. "Although—it almost doesn't make sense to me—slaving is illegal in Bethel, and no one contravenes that law," he added. "So why would they want to take you? To what end?"

"Maybe they weren't going to take me," she said. "Maybe they were just angry that I'd come to the camp and they wanted to—make me sorry."

"So, the blood," he said abruptly. "What happened? How badly were you hurt?"

"One of them kicked my leg and it started bleeding," she

said, making the words offhand. "It's still bruised, but it's healed over. Nothing to be concerned about."

"Has someone dressed it for you?"

"No," she said. She was trying to be conciliatory. "If you're worried, I can ask Hannah to look at it. I think it's fine now, though. I really do."

"As you choose, then." He hesitated, glanced away and decided to speak. "I'm not—I know you have considered the Eyrie a prison of sorts, and me some kind of jailor, but—you have more freedom than that," he said, carefully picking his words. "This is supposed to be your home, and your life is what you make of it. I would not want you to think that your rights, your freedoms, your choices, are subject to my approval and that I would—deprive you—or interfere with any of them. Please don't be afraid to tell me—anything—that happens in the future because you are afraid of what privilege I will take away from you."

His diffidence made her, for the first time, truly repentant. "Gabriel, I'm sorry," she said yet again. She smiled tentatively. "The next time someone tries to abduct me, I'll come running to you—"

"Well, I wish you would," he said, smiling back. "But it is not just the abductions and assaults you can report to me, but anything that occurs in your day. I would like to hear how you're getting on. Really, I would."

"Then join me for dinner tonight," she said. "And I'll catch you up on everything that's been happening."

CHAPTER THIRTEEN

Such accord could not be expected to last forever, although for two weeks relations were harmonious between the angel and his bride. The break, when it came, was so sudden that Rachel was caught totally unprepared; and consequently it left her even angrier than she might otherwise have been.

Her wound was completely healed by this time, due mostly to Hannah's ministrations. The older woman had, without comment, examined the cut and bound it up after spreading a white salve over it.

"What is that?" Rachel had asked.

"Ointment made from manna root," Hannah had replied.

Rachel put her finger in the jar and touched the cream gingerly. "This looks so familiar," she said. "I think my mother used some once when my father was badly burned. She said she'd been saving it—for years? Could that be right?"

Hannah nodded. "It's very rare now. Almost all the roots are gone, and I haven't seen any new crops for, oh, a decade or more."

"What did you call it?"

"Manna root."

"Why is it so rare?"

"It comes from a flower that doesn't grow here anymore. All the seeds are gone, ground up by foolish girls. No more seeds—

no more flowers—no more roots. No more ointment. It's a pity, because I have never found another salve as useful as this one."

Sometimes she found it as difficult to get information from Hannah as Gabriel must find it to get information from his wife. "Why do young girls grind up the seeds?" Rachel asked patiently.

Hannah glanced up at her in surprise. "You don't know about manna? Perhaps the Edori never used it. They say it's an aphrodisiac—a love potion. Well, the seeds are, if they're ground up and slipped into food or drink. So the stories say. And only men are affected by the potion, so only women harvest the seeds and make the mixture."

Hannah glanced at her again, but the look on Rachel's face was clearly one of fascination, so she went on. "According to legend, Hagar is the one who discovered the potency of the manna, and she struck some deal with Jovah, as she was wont to do. She would go to her mountain retreat and sing to him, and he would send the manna falling down from heaven—clouds of seeds, a rainstorm of them, falling all over Samaria. Some would take root and grow, and other seeds would be harvested by girls looking to find husbands.

"Hagar and Uriel argued once about manna, the stories say. They argued about everything, but this fight went on for days. Uriel felt that the use of manna was unfair to men, that there was no defense against it, and that a woman could use it to ensnare a man who would never consider her without the aid of potions. Hagar said it was a woman's business to find a man, make him love her, and bear as many children as possible for the glory of the god. Hagar liked the idea that there were wiles against which a man was helpless."

"Who won the argument?"

Hannah was smiling faintly. "Hagar, of course. He had told her he would not speak to her till she apologized, and so they did not speak. Then one day she went to him, saying she was very sorry, that she was wrong. She took him to her room, and bathed him, and combed his hair, and fed him grapes and wine—but she had laced the wine with manna seed, and so he fell in love with her all over again. They say this was the last fight they had to the end of their days, but I don't believe it. I think they fought till they died, and loved each other anyway."

Rachel was considering. "And there have been no manna

blossoms since Hagar's time? These roots must be extremely old, then."

"Oh, there were flowers for hundreds of years after that—but fewer and fewer every year, since young girls would harvest them before the seed could fall. I remember manna blooming when I was a little girl, but I haven't seen any for years."

"So why don't the angels pray to Jovah and ask for more?"

"Some have tried. I think Ariel did, one summer, but no manna fell. Perhaps they did not know the right prayers. Perhaps there is no more."

"Too bad," Rachel said. "I like the stories."

At dinner a few nights later, she taxed Gabriel with the tale. "And Hannah said no manna fell for Ariel," she finished up. "Did you ask Jovah for it? Perhaps he would answer your prayers."

Gabriel had listened, smiling, but he shook his head. "I think that's a prayer only a woman can make to Jovah."

"But why?"

"Well, women are the ones who use the manna seeds, after all."

"Men benefit from it," Nathan said with a laugh. "At least some men would consider it a benefit."

Gabriel grinned. "Men may enjoy the consummation of desire, but women are calculating beyond that physical moment," he said. "Women seduce with a purpose in mind, more often than not. They're thinking about marriage and children and the next generation. Men usually don't think that far ahead."

"What about angel-seekers?" Hannah wanted to know. "The women who pursue angels in all the towns and villages."

"They more than anyone have a purpose in mind," Gabriel said seriously. "They know that to have an angel child will change their lives completely."

"Well, there are men who are angel-seekers, too—Ariel and Maga could tell you stories," Nathan said.

"Certainly. And they may be interested in siring angel babies, though I think glamour is more their aim. But that's a side issue! We're talking about the manna seed. When Hagar first prayed to Jovah for the manna to fall to earth, Samaria had only been settled a short time. There had been great hardships—famine, plague, flood—and hundreds of people had died in each separate disaster. She knew that if the settlement was not quickly repopulated, the whole race could die out, mortals and angels alike. And she prayed to Jovah for help, and manna is what he gave her. It was god and angelica working in concert to produce a whole new generation as quickly as possible. Uriel doesn't seem to have grasped the urgency quite as quickly as his wife. And that's why I say manna is a woman's prayer. Because women think most deeply about the next generation—and that is almost all that Jovah thinks about."

"You strip the romance from everything," Nathan complained.

"Well, I am not much of a romantic," Gabriel replied.

Nathan glanced sideways at Rachel, who was thinking over Gabriel's words with an air of complete absorption. "Give you time," Nathan said softly. "Give you time."

That kind of discussion had not been uncommon in the past two weeks—there had been disagreements, of course, but nothing acrimonious—but then, they were both trying hard to get along. Which was why the next serious argument caught them both by surprise.

Gabriel had stopped by Rachel's room late one afternoon, something he rarely did. She invited him in with an unaccountable sense of shyness, but he was not in the least loverlike. He seemed somewhat abstracted, wrestling with some problem. He had been gone for the past few days, and she was not even sure when he had returned.

"I need your advice," he said abruptly, after sitting silently for a good three minutes on her newest floor cushion. "More than that. I need your help."

She sank to the rug before him. "Well, of course. What is it?"

"Lord Jethro of Semorrah. What is he afraid of?"

She raised her eyebrows. "You mean, like spiders and rats?"

"No—much bigger. Is he afraid of losing his only son? Afraid his wife will leave him? Is money all he thinks of? Is he afraid he will lose his fortune and his standing among the other merchants?"

Why did he want to know? Rachel put the question aside and spoke thoughtfully. "Well, all the merchants are afraid of that. They're very jealous of each other. Lord Jethro used to sit with his son for hours and speculate on how much money some of the other Semorrah families had, calculating rent sums and tariffs and income from all their little businesses. He's obsessed by money, but they all are, I think."

"So—if I could find a believable way to threaten to take his money away, I could get his attention."

"Well, but you'd also make him hate you."

"He already hates me."

"What are you trying to prove to him?"

He sighed and ran a hand over his face. He looked very tired. "I have spent some time in the past couple of months trying to convince the merchants and the Manadavvi and the Jansai that the inequities of our current system must be righted. I have been spectacularly unsuccessful so far. I'd like to find a way to make them take notice—of me, and of the god as well."

"I know one thing Jethro is really afraid of," Rachel commented. "And that's water."

"Water?"

"He's terrified of drowning. He owns a pleasure craft, but he never uses it—Daniel does, sometimes, but Jethro never. He hates to take the ferry into Bethel, which is one of the reasons he trades with Jordana so much—because he can use the bridge to get to land. It's strange that a man who is so afraid of drowning lives in the middle of a river."

Gabriel frowned at her, brooding. "Well, that's something to think about. Perhaps I could cause the river to rise. On his way over here—or maybe he would be more impressed if it happened on his way back. Because I think, if I could sway one of them—"

"He's coming here?" Rachel interrupted. "When? And why?"

"In a couple of weeks. They all are—Jethro, Samuel, Elijah Harth, Abel Vashir, half a dozen of the Jansai leaders. I thought, if I saw them all together, I could get a better sense of who was allied with whom—and maybe make a few of my own points, though I'm beginning to think those points are going to have to be made in a drastic fashion, and not in my own hold—"

"Then maybe you should flood the river before he gets here so he's a little shaken up. Better yet, flood all of Semorrah. That will get his attention."

He gave her an absent smile. "I know you don't like him," he said, "but maybe you could spend some time convincing him that I'm capable of doing it. Fill his mind with fears. So that when he goes back on the ferry, even if the river is smooth as glass, he'll spend his whole time looking over the sides uneasily."

"I would," she said, "but I won't be here."

He stared at her blankly. "Won't be here? Surely you can miss a day or two of teaching—"

She shook her head. "No, I'll be in Luminaux by then. Or actually, outside of Luminaux a few miles."

"What are you *talking* about?" he demanded in an impatient voice.

"The Gathering. I'm going with Matthew."

"But you can't," he said. "I need you here. I just told you—all my enemies will be arriving at the same time."

"I'm sorry," she said. "But it will take us a week or more to travel there—longer, actually, because I'm going to stop at Mount Sinai for a day or two—and I'll be gone days before your guests arrive."

He was starting to get seriously angry. "Rachel, you can't leave," he said. "You must see how important this meeting is—*all* the merchants, half the Jansai, half the Manadavvi—it's as much a matter of social entertaining as it is a political maneuver, and I need you with me."

"Well, I'm sorry, Gabriel, but you didn't tell me you were planning it."

"Well, you didn't mention that you were leaving for—what is it, a month?—to go to this Gathering—which, among other things, falls too close to the Gloria for you to go."

"You said I didn't need your permission to do things. You said I had my own privileges."

"And so you do, but the joint responsibilities come first! I can understand that you wish to attend the Gathering—"

"I'm *going* to attend it. It's been five years since I've been to one, five years since I've seen any of my people."

"They aren't your people! They were kind to you, but—"

"They *are* my people! My family! I have no one but the Edori."

"You have the angels," he said stiffly. "You have me."

"You! You can't even understand why this is so important to me!"

"And you are making no attempt to understand what is important to *me*! Rachel, don't you see what I am trying to do here? Among other things, I'm fighting for the survival of the Edori. I am trying to force three powerful, wealthy factions to overhaul their lucrative trading agreements, to restructure the very basis of their wealth—and they don't like it, they don't want to do it, and I need every weapon I have in hand to fight them."

"Some other time, then! Change the day of your great meeting. Make it after the Gloria. I will be here then."

"Too many people are involved for me to do that. If you would just be reasonable—"

"Be *reasonable*—"

"Yes! How can you expect to prepare for the Gloria if you are gone for weeks and weeks beforehand? When will you practice? What will you sing? You have no idea how exhausting the performance will be—if you trek all the way to Luminaux and back—"

"What is it you are really afraid of, Gabriel? That if I go to the Edori, I will be so happy there that I won't come back?"

"Well, it wouldn't surprise me all that greatly," he said. "Since you have made it abundantly clear that you prefer your life with them to your life among the angels."

"If the angels were more agreeable," she said softly, "perhaps I could learn to love them."

He sprang to his feet and began pacing around the room. She stood too, unwilling to sit tamely while he strode about. "Yes! I can see why you would say the angels have given you no care at all! It was only angels who rescued you from slavery—angels who brought you to a position of power and honor—angels who have tried to befriend you: Magdalena, Obadiah, myself. But what do you give back to any of us? Me you delight in deceiving—you will not tell me your troubles, you will not tell me your plans—and now when, for the first time, I ask something of you, you refuse, and you are not even sorry that you cannot oblige me!"

"And that's exactly the difference between the angels and the Edori!" she retorted furiously. "The Edori took me in and asked nothing of me at all. Nothing! Except that I be happy among them, and I was. But the angels—! From the beginning, it was expected that I look a certain way, behave a certain way. I did not ask for the role you have tried to thrust on me. I did not ask to be brought here. I did not ask to be your bride. I have done as well as I can among people who are strange to me, people who do not like me, but Gabriel, I would gladly leave at any time and not come back again."

"You can't do that," he said flatly. "I won't let you."

"You won't *let* me? You won't *let* me leave here? How can you stop me?"

"Who gave you the means to leave this place, anyway, if it wasn't me? When you were afraid to be taken down the mountain in an angel's arms, who gave you the way out? Who said, 'You are not a prisoner here'? Well, I did—and I can just as easily revoke that. I can take away your escape route—"

"You can take away from me any privilege you wish," she said coldly. "And you can lose any hold on me you ever had."

"And what's that supposed to mean?"

"How do you think you can *make* me sing? In your precious Gloria. Can you slap me? Beat me? Chain me up? You may take me to your stupid Plain, you may have all your angels and all your friends gathered around, but if I don't want to open my mouth, no power on this whole world can make me sing. And you know it. Take away from me whatever you want. I can take away more from you."

They glared at each other for a full minute, both of them too angry to speak. Rachel's hands were balled so hard at her sides that her whole body was cramped to sustain the pressure. Gabriel, before her, looked like the incarnation of divine vengeance. His pale face was all angular, angry bone; his great wings quivered and hummed with tension. His eyes were so blue that they colored the air; they scorched her with a lapis lazuli fire.

"I cannot believe you mean that," he said finally, in a voice so tightly controlled that it trembled, though just a little.

"Well, I do," was her instant response.

He shook his head. "What was Jovah thinking of," he said, almost whispering, "when he chose you for this part? You will destroy me—you will destroy all of us."

And without giving her a chance to say another word, he spun around on his heel and strode out. The feather edge of his wing brushed her as he swept by, but she stood unmoving, her hands still clenched, waiting a moment to breathe so that the heat of his passage would have cooled and the air would be safe to take into her lungs. And then she flung herself on her bed and cried again, and hated him with all her heart.

*   *   *

They did not speak again for the next week, and studiously avoided each other, which was not hard. The Eyrie was big enough for a careful man and woman to keep out of each other's way.

She had informed her students that she would be gone for a few weeks, and left them detailed projects to complete in her absence. Peter told her he could foresee no problems arising that he would not be able to deal with.

"And if I do have any questions, I'll send Obadiah to Gabriel," he added.

"Yes, I'm sure Gabriel can solve any crisis that comes up," she replied coolly.

The students were sorrier to see Matthew leave than they were to see Rachel go, but he promised to bring them back treats from Luminaux, so they were resigned to it. "We'll only have a day or two at Josiah's, now," Matthew warned her. "That is, if you're still planning to shop in Luminaux before the Gathering. We could go afterward, of course."

"That's cutting it very close," she said. "We have to be here at least a few days before the Gloria."

"Well, then, it's tomorrow we should be leaving."

"Yes. I'm ready."

She was used to taking her evening meal at the school with Peter and the children, but for this last day, Obadiah invited her out to dinner. He took her to a small cafe she had not been to before, and ordered from the exotic menu.

"You may hate this food," he remarked. "It's very strange."

She smiled. "Then why did you bring me here?"

"Scheming. Hoping you'll get so violently ill you can't leave in the morning."

"Why, Obadiah. I didn't know you would miss me that much."

"I don't think I'm going to be happy with you gone," he said lightly. "I'll probably mope around the Eyrie, languishing, until you return."

"You could come with me."

"An angel at the Gathering? I don't think so."

"There are often non-Edori there, though I don't remember ever seeing an angel before, I have to admit."

"You should bring Gabriel, if you're going to bring any angel."

She was surprised, and kept silent.

"You're wrong, you know," he said, very gently. "To leave him this way."

"You don't know anything about it."

"I know that you fought, and that you haven't spoken since, and that you will be gone three weeks or more. I don't know what was said, but—"

"Unforgivable things," she interrupted.

"You really should be here for his meeting," Obadiah persisted. "I understand how much you want to go to this Gathering, but what Gabriel is trying to do is so important—"

"Oh, so now you're on Gabriel's side, are you?"

"I've always admired Gabriel," the angel said seriously. "I may jest about him, and laugh at him to his face, but I'm really very much in awe of him. He's a good man, Rachel. And he's trying to do good things. Sometimes I don't think you give him enough credit."

She was flustered and upset, but it was impossible to be angry at Obadiah. "Yes—no, I do, but—Obadiah, he doesn't make way for anyone else. He doesn't accept anyone else's reasons, he's so sure he's right."

"Well, many times he is."

"And even if he is right, I'm not staying," she finished up mutinously. "You think I'm being selfish, I know, but I can't—I have had nothing for so long. I have had everything taken away from me, and what the angels have given back to me is not what I want. I want—I need—to be among people I love again. I want—how can I explain this? I have never been as devout as Gabriel, as most of the angels," she said, her voice changing, calming, as she tried to make him understand. "And while I lived in Semorrah, there were times I hated Yovah, hated what he had done to me, and to the Edori, and to people I loved. But while I lived with the Edori . . . They are very religious people, you know. They pray directly to the god, much as the angels do. And while I lived with the Edori, I felt close to Yovah. I heard him whisper in my ear. I believed—I *knew*—that my words went directly to his heart.

"And if—" she said, her voice slowing still more, "if I am to go to the Plain of Sharon and sing to Yovah, ask his blessing on all peoples of Samaria, I must feel close to him again. And I think I must go to the Gathering, and listen to the Edori singing, to understand again how a simple woman can call directly on the god. I must be renewed myself before I can give what the angels want me to give. Do you understand that? Perhaps I am being selfish, but not completely."

"You could still go to the Gathering," he said persuasively. "Stay here for the first day of Gabriel's meeting, then let me fly you to Luminaux."

She jerked backward from him as if he had struck her. "No."

"You are afraid of heights, I know—"

"No. I can't. No."

He gave her a cajoling smile. "Do you think I would drop you? I have never dropped anyone, you know."

"Obadiah, I can't," she said, a trace of panic in her voice. "I won't—don't ask me. I'm sorry. I can't."

He raised his hands in a gesture of surrender. "All right," he said. "But it would solve so many things."

Their food came, and they ate for a few moments in silence. Rachel looked up to find him watching her expectantly. "What?" she said.

"Do you like it?"

"Actually, I do," she said, smiling a little. "Is it grilled horse manure or something?"

"No. Perfectly respectable food. But no one else will eat here with me."

Her smile broadened. "This shall become our special place, then. We'll come here again when I return."

"Agreed," he said instantly. "I'll reserve a table now."

The rest of the meal passed companionably, and Obadiah did not again bring up painful topics. When they had finished eating, they walked slowly back to the mountain, and the angel escorted the angelica to the tunnel car. It was full dark by this time, and the air was chilly, but it was clear that spring was on the way. The wind which had been so wicked all during the winter seemed merely playful now; the hard ground gave just a little beneath their feet.

"When do you leave?" Obadiah asked as she opened the cage door and stepped inside.

"Tomorrow. First light."

"Matthew has hired horses?" She nodded. "You know how to ride, of course."

She laughed. "Of course. It's been five years—almost six—since I have ridden, but I'm sure I haven't forgotten."

"I was on a horse once. I'd gotten extremely ill, oh, a day's flight outside of Luminaux. They tied me to a horse and escorted me back to the Eyrie. It was awful. He was afraid of my wings and kept leaping forward every time a feather would brush him. I was sore from my ankles to my—well, sore all the way up. I'd rather have died of fever, I think."

"I like to ride," she said. She had fastened the grille, but reached out a hand to him between the bars. "Don't be so sad. I'll be back in a few weeks."

His hand closed on hers. "I thought I was covering it up so well," he said. "I really wish you weren't going." He put her hand against his heart and held it there. "I'll sing for you each night," he said softly. "Jovah keep you safe."

She kissed the fingers of her free hand, then laid them against his lips. "And you also," she said.

He took her hand from his lips and clasped it against his chest beside the other one. "Now I've got you and you can't get free," he said. "Trapped in a little cage inside the mountain."

"With an angel holding me down," she finished. "Yes, that is how I feel much of the time."

Instantly he released her. "Truly, Rachel, take care," he said.

She rang the bell and activated the lever. "I will," she said. "Dinner again in a few weeks, my friend. The time will go very fast."

The car began its slow, lumbering ascent. "I don't think so," she thought he said, but the noise of the car made it hard to catch his words. She wrapped her arms tightly around herself and wondered why the night air suddenly seemed so cold.

She half-expected Gabriel to be waiting for her on the landing—or at the door to her room; and when he was at neither place, she half-expected him to come to her sometime later to wish her a formal farewell. So strong was this belief that she tarried over her packing, and waited till very late before taking her bath. Even after she had undressed and gone to bed, she lay awake a long time, listening to the harmonic voices and thinking he would come to the door. But he did not.

She slept badly and woke early, heavy-eyed. But there was little she needed to do to prepare; she had done most of it the night before. She closed up her bags, glanced once around her room and stepped outside.

Gabriel was nowhere in sight. She felt her whole body grow smaller, leaden, in a single sweeping rush of disappointment; she felt the way she sometimes did when the tunnel car dropped too fast. But that was ridiculous. She did not want to see him any more than he wanted to see her.

She stepped briskly down the corridors to Matthew's chambers, and found him awake and ready for her. His dark face was alight with excitement and he gave her a quick absentminded hug.

"To the Gathering we go, my girl," he said. "Ah, but I can hardly wait to be among the people again."

He rode down the mountain with her, and they hiked into Velora to pick up their horses. Matthew had, of course, chosen well, hiring a compact blond palomino for her and a sturdy black gelding for himself. Like most Edori, they used only bridles and the barest of saddles. Matthew strapped their luggage across the horses' backs, and swung up easily. Rachel stood and watched him, glancing from time to time back at the mountain. But no great white angel wings glided down from the Eyrie. No husband appeared to wish her a cold goodbye. She mounted, urged the horse forward, and did not look back again.

CHAPTER FOURTEEN

"I'm glad you came to me," Josiah said. "I've thought of you often."

Matthew had allowed himself to be introduced to the oracle, but excused himself from the dinner and the talk that came afterward. "I'm an old man, and travel tires me," he had said with his sweet smile, but Rachel knew that he was just tactfully giving her time to visit with Josiah alone. She had enjoyed the meal, served by soundless acolytes in one of the smaller interior rooms. Now they sat before the fire and sipped the most marvelous liqueur Rachel had ever tasted.

"I wanted to thank you for writing to me," she said. "Although the news was not welcome, it was better to know."

"I was sorry to have to tell you he is dead."

"I am glad of it," she said. "He hated life those last years. I know him. He is happier with Yovah."

"Peace on his soul," the sage murmured. "Will you pray for him at your Gathering?"

She leaned all the way back in her chair. "I have not done much praying to Yovah lately," she said softly. "Except to call down curses, which he has not answered. I don't know that he would listen to me—at the Gathering or at the Gloria."

"Ah," said Josiah. "Now I know why you are here."

She smiled faintly. "And why I am going to the Gathering. To remember what it is like to love the god."

"That is a very interesting concept," Josiah said. " 'Loving' Jovah. I am not sure that I love him myself."

That brought her straight up on the edge of the big chair to stare at him. "But—of all people—"

"He is not an easy god to love," Josiah said calmly. "He is not very warm. He is a just god, that I do believe. He has a great deal of passion, and a great deal of power. But does he love us? I have never been sure of that. He guards us well. He guides us. And he lets us make our own way until we err. Perhaps that is a kind of love, but it is not very affectionate."

She could not help laughing. "And I thought *I* spoke heresy—!"

"A learned man cannot help but consider the boundaries of his world, both physical and spiritual," Josiah said. "The oracles, you will find, believe most fervently in the god—more than the angels do, more than the farmers and the merchants and the Manadavvi. We know he is there. But who is he? What shape does he take? Has he ever come down among men? What is his interest in us, if it comes to that? Sometimes I think we—the whole race of humans, on this planet and elsewhere—were created as some vast, divine experiment, that he sets up a group of us on each world and gives us different environments and watches us to see which of us adapts the best. Other times I think he has given us— all of us—a puzzle, which we are somehow to solve, and he waits from generation to generation, giving us a few more clues with each new birth, to see how long it will take us to unravel it. And other times I think I do not understand any of it, and it is all as it was taught to me, and that is an end to it."

"I am beginning to feel less badly about my own isolation from the god," she said.

Josiah smiled. "Oh, I am not the greatest of all doubters, as you must be thinking," he said. "There is the story of the oracle David, who lived some hundred and fifty years ago. He had been a questioner his whole life—he was obsessed by the interfaces, the screens we oracles use to communicate with the god. He said he had discovered a way that a man could go directly to the god, see him face to face, and that the secret was contained in the interfaces. So he brought an acolyte in, and positioned himself just so—I can show you the place on the floor, because this all transpired on Sinai—and he told the acolyte to press a certain button. And, so the story goes, a great golden haze rose all about him, and the acolyte looked away in fear. When the boy looked for David again, he was gone."

"Where did he go?"

"To see the god, so he says. There is an account of it in his memoirs, although the language is very hallucinogenic and hysterical."

"And what did the god look like?"

"Actually, he never laid eyes on Jovah, just the place where he lives. It was wondrous and strange—as one might expect—filled with odd lights, and surfaces and textures that were wholly alien. The interface screens were there, so he was able to communicate with the god—until the day he learned that the god could speak to him, aloud, in a deep resonant voice that was, he says, wholly dispassionate. It was the voice more than anything which seems to have driven him mad."

"He was mad, then?"

Josiah smiled again. "Well, when he returned, bathed in the same golden glow, he fell to the floor and began sobbing, and he did not speak a coherent sentence for weeks. And then the things he had to say were so bizarre that no one would believe him. So he took to writing down his adventures, but his words were so revolutionary that the other oracles locked him away and had him tended until he died. They wouldn't even let him use the interfaces anymore, though he begged to be allowed to go back to the screen just once. So he died, raving and unhappy. And the oracles put his writings under lock and key, and let no one but their successors read about him."

"But what did he say that was so revolutionary?"

"Well, that's something the oracles only discuss among themselves," he said pleasantly. "Let us say he just cast doubts upon the omnipotence of the god. And while I may seem to you to be a heretic, I do not for a moment doubt that Jovah is capable of saving all of us or destroying all of us, if he chooses. And that whatever he chooses is right, because he is all-knowing and we are the ones who are faulty and in error."

Rachel sighed and sank back in her chair. She was not much interested in esoteric speculations on the nature of theology, anyway. "And I am among the most faulty," she said gloomily. "I have quarreled with my husband—again. I have left him without a word, though he knows where I am. I have made advances to another man. I have refused to give him the help he asked for. I have really done everything I could think of to spite him."

"Well, of course you have," Josiah said gently. "You love him."

She jerked her head in his direction. "*Love* him? Love *Gabriel*?"

"And you are trying to get his attention. It is hard to get Gabriel's attention—I know from bitter experience."

"I don't love him," she said positively.

"Also, you don't want him to swallow you up, which is very wise," Josiah said in an approving voice. "Gabriel has a very strong will. It is hard to stand against him, and a compliant woman would be totally absorbed into his personality. That is why Jovah chose for him a woman who is not at all compliant."

"Anyway, he doesn't love me."

"He is not whole without you," Josiah said. "And you are not whole without him. Neither of you has been willing to realize this yet. Which is why I am glad you are going to the Gathering. It will do you both good to know what it feels like when you are not at the Eyrie."

"I will feel fine when I am not at the Eyrie," Rachel said sharply. "In fact, I'm very glad to be gone from it now."

"Yes, I'm sure you are," the sage said, smiling again. "I wish you the merriest of times at the Gathering among your Edori friends. I hope you return to Velora rested and serene and sure of yourself. But I think you will miss your husband while you are gone, and he will miss you. If it is so, I hope you will act upon it. Jovah brought you together for certain reasons. Only one of those reasons was your happiness—but it is not the least of them. It is time you were happy, Rachel. I do wish you joy."

With these words ringing in her ears, it was hard for Rachel not to be thoughtful during the next four days of the trip. Matthew, a seasoned traveler, and a respecter of moods in any case, forbore to make conversation. The horses had been well-chosen; they were easy-gaited and strong-winded, well up to the journey. The two Edori traveled south at a good pace, and made it into Luminaux on the evening of a beautiful spring night.

"*Azulato*," Matthew murmured as they rode through the high marble gates. "The Blue City."

Nowhere in the world was there a place as beautiful as Luminaux, city of craftsmen, artists and intellectuals. It was indeed, as Matthew said, all blue. Its major buildings were all constructed from the same polished blue marble, richly veined with white and rose quartz. The cobblestones—laid in circular or fountained or mosaicked patterns—had been chipped from a grainy violet granite. Obelisks and monolithic statues appeared at irregular intervals at the street corners or in scattered parks, and all of them had been carved of lapis lazuli or turquoise. Hyacinths, violets, dahlias and lilacs bloomed in gardens and window boxes in front of every house; and even the darkening sky was an unmarred indigo.

"Truly," said Matthew, gazing around from the place where they had both, involuntarily, come to a complete halt, "this is a sight that refreshes the eyes."

They rode forward slowly, aiming for the stables on the edge of town. The buildings in this complex were made of wood, but they had been painted a serviceable navy color. The travelers knew before they pulled up before the wide doorway that the groom who would take charge of their horses would be a knowledgeable man who loved animals, for in Luminaux no tasks were considered menial; every man went to the job he loved, and was respected for mastering its complexities.

"Ah, good beasts, both of these," said the smiling ostler who came out to take the black and the palomino. "You did not push them too hard on the ride down, but I can see you've covered some distance."

"We came from Velora in easy stages," Matthew confirmed.

The ostler was stroking the gelding's soft nose. "And arrived in Luminaux to look for merchandise? Or to commission an artist? Or—" he glanced speculatively at Matthew's face. "Or to travel westward to the plains to join the Edori in their rituals?"

"We're here for the Gathering." Matthew nodded. "But we came a few days early to see the sights of the Azulato."

The groom gave them directions to a moderately priced inn, and they found it with no trouble, a sturdy two-story building not far from the central markets. It was built of inexpensive white stone but every one of its twenty wide windows was fitted with stained glass panels, cerulean and cobalt and aquamarine, and wisteria climbed over the painted lintel.

They were Edori and used to sharing quarters, so they took one room and sat before the fire till midnight, talking. Not of the trip down or Josiah's last words or even of life at the Eyrie—no, nor of life in Semorrah, which Rachel never wished to speak of— but of the nomadic life, the quiet freedom of the Edori, in harmony with the land and the wild creatures and Yovah. They told anecdotes about clan members they both knew, or had heard of; they remembered Gatherings when Hepzibah had sung, or the incomparable Ruth.

"And will you be singing at the Gathering, is what I've been wondering?" Matthew asked her. "For it's a fine voice you have, though it has been five years since you've raised it in song."

Rachel laughed softly. She was stretched out on a woven rug before the fire, feeling more comfortable and happy than she had in nearly six years. "And what makes you think my voice is so fine?"

"We never met to speak to each other before you came to the Eyrie," he said. "But we had been at Gatherings before, you and I, and you lifted your voice in songs I am not likely to forget. You and that Naomi lass, who is now with the Chievens. You used to sing together, and everyone came close to listen."

"Naomi has a beautiful voice," Rachel said lazily.

"Aye, that she does. And you also, or you did. But five years in the cursed city without a place to practice your songs—how you must have missed it."

"I used to go," she said dreamily, "down to the wine cellars. They were huge—caves built under the river, all damp and echoey and dark. I would stay there as long as I dared—hours sometimes—and sing. And sing. All the Edori songs I knew. And some of the new ones I had learned when Lord Jethro had minstrels in to entertain. I don't care for many of the allali songs, but there were a few I heard that I liked well enough to memorize. I can't tell you the number of times I got punished for disappearing, but I didn't care. There is something about singing—for me, anyway. It cleanses my heart. It makes me whole again. I would sing, and I would become stronger.

"Sometimes when I was singing," she continued, rolling over onto her stomach to stare more intently into the fire, "I would take my chains and shake them like tambourines. Make a joyful noise to Yovah. And on those days I wouldn't even hate my chains, because they had been part of the music. And if I had not had the music," she said, her voice dropping, and her head coming down to rest on her arm, "I would have died there, before my first year was gone."

"I understand why you will not sing for the angels," Matthew said, "but will you sing for us? For your people?"

"I may," she said. "But I am not sure."

They went to bed late, slept late, and rose still in the content, calm mood that had possessed them since they entered the Blue City. Matthew wanted to stroll through the bazaars and look for bargains, but Rachel had a more definite errand to run. They agreed to meet again at the inn for supper, and separated.

It took Rachel nearly an hour to get to her destination, since she didn't know where the craft hall was and, anyway, it was too fine a day to move forward with deliberate purpose. So she asked strangers for directions, and then paused to admire a view, or wander through a public garden, or buy a fruit drink from a streetside vendor and sip it where she stood. At noon the famous silver bells of Luminaux tolled out an Edori medley, in honor of all the nomads passing through the city, and of course she had to stay utterly still until she heard every last liquid note drift down.

But she did eventually make it to the place she sought, a long, low marble building with verdigris shingles on its arched roof and blue ceramic tiles leading up to its wide door. The air around the building hummed softly with each passing breeze, and she glanced around to track the source of the sound. Tall weathervanes planted in the ground, and layered mobiles hanging from nearby trees, were fitted with small pipes and flutes that caught each shift of air current and turned it into music. Rachel smiled, and knocked firmly on the painted door.

It was answered very quickly by a young girl wearing the unadorned white robe of the apprentice. "Yes, patron?" the girl asked, bowing very low.

"I want to purchase a flute," Rachel said. "A gift for my husband. Who here can help me?"

She was taken to a small, perfectly constructed chamber with slanted panels affixed to the ceiling—a rehearsal room, she instantly realized—and told the wait would be just a moment. Indeed, very soon she was joined by an older woman dressed in the deep blue of the master flautist, who was followed by three apprentices carrying leather cases.

"I am Giselle, one of the elders here," the flautist greeted her. "I am told you wish to make a purchase?"

"Rachel," the angelica said, naming herself and returning the elder's bow. "Yes. For my husband."

Giselle nodded at the apprentices, who unfolded small wire tables and opened their cases on top. "And is he interested in playing the instrument or merely collecting it for its beauty? If he wishes to play, is he a novice or an adept? What is his musical ability?"

Rachel approached the cases and began to study the merchandise. She had not realized there would be quite so much variety. There were wooden reeds and brass pipes, silver flutes, recorders, piccolos; some had complex fretted stops and some merely had intricately cut holes to be closed by the player's fingers.

"He is a singer," Rachel said at last. "He has a spectacular voice. He has never played an instrument, but he knows music. I thought—something simple to play but pure in tone. It is the quality of the sound that interests me most."

Giselle came to stand beside Rachel. "Well, for beginners I usually recommend one of the wooden pipes—"

"No," Rachel said instantly. "It must be of the finest material."

Giselle smiled slightly. "But, I was going to add, the silver pipes offer the sweetest sound." She touched first one, then another of the long slim instruments lying in their blue velvet cases. "Of these, the recorder is the easiest to play and yet most truly conveys the ability of the musician," she said. "The sound can be a bit unearthly, as if the music were created by the god himself, without any human intervention."

Rachel glanced at her sharply, for in almost those same words Gabriel had described the appeal of the wind instruments. "Let me hear what one sounds like," she said.

Giselle inspected her choices and then extracted a plain instrument with perhaps eight holes down its barrel. "Listen," she said, and put the pipe to her lips. The song she played was simple, a country ballad, and Rachel liked the pure tumble of notes. But—

"Is there another one that is more beautiful?" she asked. "I liked the sound very well, but the pipe itself is so plain . . ."

Giselle smiled again. "Few of our artisans bother to spend much time creating recorders that are works of art," she said. "As they are—comparatively—so simple to play, they are most often used by novices. But one of our oldest craftsmen has always loved the recorder best, and he has created some fine pieces. Very expensive pieces, of course, but if you want the best—"

"I do. Let me see them."

An apprentice was sent off. While they waited, Giselle demonstrated a learning pipe to Rachel, a curious little wooden instrument consisting of eight very small reeds bound together in ascending size from the smallest to the largest. The largest was no longer than the middle finger on Rachel's hand.

"We often sell these to children who think they want to learn to play the pipes," the flautist said. "They are also good for novices to begin on, because they do not require such great lung strength and yet they accustom the mouth and the throat to the exercises the flute requires. Perhaps you would like to give one of these to your husband as well."

The learning pipe made a tinny, happy melody that did not remind Rachel of Gabriel at all, but the logic seemed so sound that she agreed to buy one. The apprentice returned just as Giselle was handing the reeds to Rachel.

"The master's apologies, but there's only one recorder he's willing to sell," said the girl, speaking very rapidly and softly. "The others he wants to keep for himself, but he thinks the lady will not be disappointed in the quality of this one."

"Ah," said Giselle, taking the instrument from the girl's hand. "This may in fact be exactly what you're seeking."

She placed her palms on either tip of the recorder and held it up for Rachel to see. It was shaped much as the other one had been, but this was a thing of sheer physical beauty. The mouthpiece was accented with mother-of-pearl inlays; the brushed silver of the barrel was patterned with diamond-cut designs of vines and sparrows. A silver ring was soldered to its back about one-third of the way down its length, and a silver filigree chain was slipped through the circle.

"So you can wear it around your neck and not fear losing it," Giselle explained, slipping the necklace over her head. "Listen," she said, and played again the simple tune she had played before. Rachel closed her eyes. The music swirled around her head, making her briefly dizzy. Music Gabriel would admire indeed.

"That's what I want," she said. "I will take it with me."

*   *   *

Rachel and Matthew spent two more days in Luminaux, hedonistic tourists. They shopped at the bazaars to buy beautiful useless things they had no way to easily ship back to Velora; they ate at different restaurants for every meal; they went to concerts or lectures each night. They paid in cash for everything, since Rachel had refused to bring the wristbands which would have served as currency even here. Everything was expensive, and everything seemed worth the price.

On the morning of the third day, they awkwardly repacked their bundles and turned their horses westward for the three-hour ride to the plain outside of Luminaux. Rachel was more excited and nervous than she had thought possible. To be among the people again . . . The Manderras were scattered, or dead, but there were many here who had known the Manderras. There were many here who knew her name, knew her face by sight, remembered Simon, remembered her adopted family. Or had these friends too been taken by the voracious malice of the Jansai? Who was still left, who alive, who reaped by Yovah in the intervening years?

Still a few miles out, they spotted the massed tents and intermittent campfires of the Edori wanderers. Haze from the immense double ring at the heart of the camp was immediately visible; soon they could also see the white smoke from smaller fires built before individual tents. A buried pulse seemed to shake the earth as they rode closer, a steady, accented rhythm that at first seemed no more than their own heartbeats, curiously magnified; but as they drew nearer, the sound grew louder, more insistent, and resolved itself into an unbroken percussive beat coming from a hundred tandem sources.

"The drums have started," Matthew said, urging his black forward at a faster pace. "We're almost late."

They arrived at a scene of happy chaos. Everywhere were bodies, faces, children, campfires, knots of men in close argument, women laughing over embarrassing secrets, rows of tents raised so closely together that one set of anchoring stakes could be used for two. The fine cooking sent a tempting aroma through the camp. The drumbeats were overlaid with voices raised in the general welcoming chant. Snatches of conversation, song and laughter wove through the air with an actual texture.

Rachel brought her palomino to a halt and thought she would be unable to breathe.

"Ah, Raheli, it is good to be here," Matthew said, his voice sounding faraway and strange. He spoke in the Edori tongue, which up to now he had not used, even back at the inn when they talked till midnight. "Now is not the time to lose heart and grow faint."

She smiled, but before she could answer him, three small dark boys came running up to them shouting out questions. "What are your names? Which is your clan? How far have you ridden?"

Matthew answered them with mock seriousness. "Where are the clan elders who should be welcoming us?" he asked. "Where are your manners? You should be offering to take our horses and bring us refreshment before you begin asking us such personal questions."

The children giggled and reached for their bridles. "But we cannot take your horses until we know your clans," the oldest boy said reasonably. "I myself will carry your bundles to your clan leader, but how can I take them if I do not know where you belong?"

Before Matthew could reply to that, a gaunt, middle-aged woman hurried up. Her fine black hair had escaped its braid and her robe was splattered with gravy, but she smiled warmly at the new arrivals. "Welcome! I did not see you ride in. I thought we were all here, but Yovah be praised, there are more of us! Have you a clan campfire to go to, or would you like to share the meal with mine? I am Elspeth of the Barcerras."

Matthew dismounted and helped Rachel from the saddle; she was still feeling shaky and terribly tense. "I am Matthew of the Cashitas," he told her. "And this one is—"

"A guest," Rachel broke in before Matthew could identify her. Her gold hair set her apart instantly; no one would think she belonged here by birthright. "I have no clan here, but I am looking for the Chievens."

"The Chievens!" Elspeth said sharply, fixing her eyes on Rachel's face. Rachel felt her blood chill through each separate vein.

"They are not here?" she asked in a choked voice. "They—have been prevented from coming?"

Elspeth quickly laid a compassionate hand on the newcomer's arm. "No, no, they are here, all of them, and very safe," she said reassuringly. "But they did not tell me they were expecting a visitor. Indeed, I did not know the Chievens had any adopted children, and I am Barcerra—we are cousins to the Chievens."

"I used to ride with the Manderras," Rachel said, her voice very low. Elspeth caught her breath. "But all those people are gone. A woman from that clan followed a man who belonged to the Chievens—"

"Raheli," Elspeth whispered. "You are Raheli. I have heard Naomi speak of you. She does not know you are coming?"

Rachel's eyes lifted quickly. "She *is* here, then?"

Elspeth nodded. Her seamed brown face still showed wonderment; clearly she knew every wretched word of Rachel's history. "We are honored to have you among us, angelica," she said, with a formality foreign to the Edori.

"Oh, please," Rachel begged. "Do not call me that. I have traveled so far—I have been gone so long—I want nothing more than to be a Manderra among my people again."

Elspeth put her hands to both of Rachel's cheeks. Her face was sorrowful and beautiful, the look of the Edori elder who has seen much grief and much joy. "Child, you have been gone too long from our campfires," she said softly. "Welcome home. I myself will take you to the clan of your sister's family."

Rachel made her brief goodbyes to Matthew, who set off under the guidance of the three boys. Then she followed Elspeth blindly through the camp. Edori voices called out general welcomes to her, knowing she was a new arrival by her packed horse and her weary step. She kept her eyes on the ground before her but she was aware of the achingly familiar scents, sights and sounds of the Edori camp all around her. The incessant drums drove her own heartbeat; when she was able to breathe, it was Edori camp smoke that filled her lungs. She did not attempt to speak again.

"The Chievens," Elspeth said, drawing to a halt outside a loosely organized campsite. Rachel quickly counted ten tents, representing between thirty and fifty souls. The Chievens had grown in the past five years. "I believe Naomi's tent is there, the fourth one down—"

"I can't—" Rachel began, in a choked voice; but she did not have to. The tent flap swung back and a woman stepped out to check the stewpot over her fire. She was small but well-formed, and she moved with a brisk, efficient grace. She stirred her stewpot, then lifted her head, as if sensing some disturbance either in the tent behind her or the camp around her. She glanced first over one shoulder, then the other, and then her eyes came straight to the edge of the camp where Rachel and Elspeth stood waiting.

Rachel's lips formed the word "Naomi" but no sound came from her mouth.

Naomi dropped her long-handled spoon and flung her arms wide. A great smile transformed her rather solemn face into a portrait of delight. "Raheli!" she cried, her voice carrying easily across the twenty yards that separated them. "I knew you would come! And so I told Luke just yesterday afternoon! What took you so long?"

The words made Rachel laugh, and the smile broke through the fear that had kept her in place. She stretched out her own arms and ran forward to take Naomi in a fierce embrace. Not until that moment did she really believe that she was with the Edori again.

"I was always sure you were not dead," Naomi told her. "Luke told me it was foolish to hope—and cruel, too, because if you were living, your life was miserable—but I knew you were not dead. I used to want to go to Semorrah. Dress up like a merchant, or a southern Jordana farmer, and come to the city and look for you. What I would have done if I'd found you, chained in some lord's household, I had no idea."

"Simon *is* dead," Rachel said abruptly.

"You know? You saw him fall?"

Rachel shook her head. "No, he—I went to the oracle at Mount Sinai, who can track the life of any man or woman who has been dedicated to Yovah. And this man told me that Simon had died. Three years ago." Naomi gave a soft exclamation of horror. "I know. I had rather he had died in the fight."

"I don't wish to hear how dreadful it was," Naomi said hesitantly, "that life, that awful life in Semorrah—but if it will ease you to talk about it, you may tell me, and I will listen."

Rachel shook her head, smiling a little. "It eases me to not be there," she said. "I never think of it. Now and then I dream about it, a little. It could have been worse, I suppose. But it was bad enough."

Naomi shivered a little and drew closer to the fire. They were outside, seated on small woven mats before the fire; it was at least two hours past midnight, and they had not nearly had their fill of talking. Inside the tent, Luke and the children slept—two girls, three years apart, with faces as solemn as their mother's and hearts just as merry. Luke had been smiling and quiet, affectionate with his wife and clearly besotted with his daughters. He had folded them into their blankets when Naomi and the visitor retired outside to continue their conversation.

"And are you happy now?" the Edori woman asked. "With the angels? When the story went round among the people, that the angel Gabriel had chosen an Edori slave girl for his wife, no one could believe the news."

"Yes, they were equally shocked in the angel holds," Rachel said. "Gabriel still has not gotten over the mortification, I believe."

Naomi watched her with sharp attentiveness. It was not the first time Rachel had made a sarcastic reference to her husband. "Tell me about Gabriel," she said.

"What do you wish to know?"

"Well, is he handsome?"

Rachel considered. "Very. He has dark hair, but finer than an Edori's. And his skin is paler, though a little dark from weathering. And his eyes—Yovah guard me from his eyes."

Naomi's own eyes had widened at this. "Color?"

"Blue. Bluer than dawn breaking over Luminaux."

Naomi's face remained serious, but the laughter began to edge her voice. "And his body? I have not seen many angels, but I have studied their bodies before this—they wear very little clothing, I've noticed. Their arms are particularly attractive, very strong—"

"His body is much as any angel's body is," Rachel said repressively.

"And his kissing? His lovemaking abilities? Very important attributes in a husband, though I cannot believe an Edori woman would stoop so low as to participate in a marriage—"

"I have not sampled them," Rachel said.

"What haven't you sampled? His *kisses*?"

"Any of his—physical attractions."

"No! You're jesting!"

"It is a marriage of policy merely."

Naomi hitched her mat closer. "No, but Rachel—you've been his wife how long now? Four months? If I were married for four months to any man as desirable as the one you just described to me—"

"Well, you're not married to him," Rachel said irritably. "We have no—contact. That way."

Naomi stared, fascinated. "And in what way do you have contact?"

Rachel laughed shortly. "Mostly we argue. In fact, we always argue."

"About what?"

"Oh, everything. Edori beliefs. The existence of Ysral. My behavior. His behavior. Judith. Obadiah. This trip. We agree on practically nothing. He hates me, actually."

"He *hates* you? He has said so?"

"No. Well, he might not hate me. Well, I wouldn't blame him for hating me. What I said to him—but then, what he said to me was worse—and anyway, it's all horrible."

The mischief had completely left Naomi's eyes. "But Rachel," she said very gently, "tell me about it. Tell me everything."

Waking, Rachel shut her eyes tightly and tried not to think or move. Pushing conscious thought to the back of her mind, she was aware of two curiously opposing but distinct sensations: one of extreme spiritual well-being, and the other of cramped physical discomfort. She squeezed her eyelids together, willing the sensations to remain inchoate, unresolved, avoiding for another minute or two whatever realities she would be faced with upon gaining full consciousness.

"Rachel, you lazy allali half-wit," came a cheerful voice from right above her ear. "I swear I'll dump a pot of spring water on your head if you don't get up. It's past *noon*, girl, and you're still sleeping."

Slowly, wonderingly, she opened her eyes to find Naomi's laughing face inches above her own. Indeed, the Edori woman held a stewpot directly over her head and she looked ready to tip the entire contents onto the slothful guest. The smell of wood smoke and cooked pheasant drifted in through the open tent flap. The ceaseless throb of the drums ran under the earth where her ear was pressed against the ground.

She was in the Edori campsite. It had not been a dream after all.

"This ground is hard as iron," she complained, stirring slightly to indicate her discomfort. "And there are rocks under my back."

"My, my, the luxury of the angel holds has certainly made us unfit for the plain life among good, simple people," Naomi said. "I ought to douse you anyway just for saying that."

Rachel smiled up at her. "Don't. I swear I'll scream to set the whole camp howling."

"And you've got the voice for it," Naomi said, settling in next to Rachel on the thin mat that formed the tent's only floor. "Which reminds me. I forgot to ask yesterday. Will you sing with me tomorrow night? I have a new song. You have time to learn it."

Rachel curled up on one side. "Oh, Naomi, it's been so long since I've performed . . ."

"Yes, but no one will expect you to sound as you once did. Everyone knows who you are and what has happened to you— but that just makes it more important, don't you see? If you sing at the Gathering, all that sorrow will be wiped away from your heart. You will be as you once were. You will heal yourself."

Be as you once were. Rachel spared a moment to consider that. As she once was, twenty years old, happy, beloved, a wild young girl who had known, really, only one brief season of terror and that so long ago, she had nearly forgotten it . . . She would never be that girl again. Her life had taken too many dark turns.

"Well, let me try to learn the song, anyway," she said, sitting up and stretching her sore muscles. "Yovah's tears! This is a hard winter ground."

"Get used to it," Naomi said unfeelingly. "The river is also very cold. But it's good for the soul to bathe in it. Here are drying rags. Now go."

They spent the day as women at the Gatherings always spent their days, alternating between cooking huge pots of food over their own campfires and making visits to the women at other fires also preparing food for tomorrow's feast. Naomi, it seemed, knew everyone.

"That's Jerusha, see, in the red scarf. She followed a man into the Barcerra clan, but after bearing him one son, decided she had rather live with a man of the Cashitas, so she left him but took the son. But he followed her, wanting his son back, and so they agreed that at every Gathering they would exchange him, so he lives one year with his mother and one year with his father. . . . That's Attarah, she's just a girl, but her voice! Yovah swoons when he hears her. There was fever among the people at the last Gathering, but Attarah sang songs of healing, and everyone woke up well. . . . Hello there, Caleb, my boy! Why aren't you off helping your father gather wood for the bonfire? Now, we're going to Tamar's tent. You'll like her, I think—"

At first Rachel hung back, feeling strange and shy; her life had taken her so far from these simple rituals, from these continuous joyous interactions. She had spent so many years defensive, closed, sharing no thought and no emotion, that she had forgotten what it was like to be among people who shared everything. Then, too, she wanted neither pity nor awe from them, depending on whether they were most moved by her five years of slavery or her current position of glory.

But she need not have worried. The Edori offered her unquestioning welcome, instant affection. "Come in, come in!" Tamar cried as they stopped before her tent. "Taste the bread I have baked for tomorrow's feast. I have flavored it with hill flowers from the Heldoras and I think it tastes finer than the loaves from Luminaux."

"Tamar, this is Raheli, come to stay with me for the Gathering."

"Welcome, Raheli. Try some of the bread."

It was so easy to be among the Edori. That part she had remembered. The life itself was not easy—the inevitable wear of the constant travel; the vulnerability to the weather, to illness, to the marauding Jansai; the continual threat of starvation during a hard winter or a meager spring—and yet the life was so pure. Work, eat, love; obey the laws of Yovah and the seasons. No one interrogated her. Everyone greeted her with a ritual kiss upon the cheek. It was hard not to relax, to feel happy, to grow festive.

There were, among the strangers, old friends and clan relatives to the Manderras, and these greeted her even more effusively, drawing her into prolonged embraces or breaking into tears at the sight of her. But, like Naomi, all of these forbore to question her about her past nightmares or her present status. She was among them and she did not indicate she wished to talk about these topics, and so they squeezed her hand and offered her a taste of whatever they were brewing for the feast day.

Late in the afternoon, when Luke returned from his tours rounding up firewood and hunting for game, the women left him in charge of the children and the cooking fire, and headed off to the edge of camp to practice Naomi's song. First Rachel memorized the words, which were not particularly complex; then she listened three times while Naomi sang the part Rachel was to learn; then she hummed along with Naomi when she sang it through the fourth time.

"Now let me hear you sing it," Naomi commanded.

"No, I'll sing it against your part."

"But I'm not sure you've gotten it yet."

"Well, we'll find out, won't we?"

Naomi said. "Oh, very well. You're so stubborn. I sing one measure by myself first. You start on the same note I do."

So Naomi began her part of the ballad, and Rachel waited a full count until it was time to add her descant. She closed her eyes and began to sing, quietly at first, remembering what it was like to lay her music against someone else's. They were like two hands, pressing palm to palm; voice strained against voice with an actual pressure, pushing the notes upward and downward on the scale. Then it became a loom, Naomi's voice dark and Rachel's a bright gold thread weaving a pattern into the tight fabric. Then it became a race, Naomi's notes running, Rachel's chasing after. But they arrived in the same place simultaneously, Rachel two pitches above Naomi and the harmony absolutely perfect.

Rachel opened her eyes and smiled. Naomi was staring at her.

"That was fun," the angelica remarked. "Did I get all of it right?"

"Yes."

Rachel frowned. "What? Has my voice changed so much?"

"Where did you learn to sing like that?"

"I've been practicing a little the last few months."

"You always had a beautiful voice, but—Rachel!" The Edori woman shook her head in admiration. "Will you do a solo for us tomorrow night?"

Rachel turned away. "I must do a solo in less than a month before thousands of people. I think others should have the honor of performing at the Gathering."

"Yovah must have chosen you for your voice after all," Naomi murmured.

"Perhaps," Rachel agreed. "Certainly it was not because I suited the Archangel."

"They say he is very wise."

"Gabriel?"

"No, silly, Yovah. Maybe he chose you for Gabriel as well."

The next day dawned clear and beautiful. Here in southern Bethel, the air was more springlike than it had been in Velora, so perfect weather might have been expected—and the Edori had spent three days praying for just such a glorious day. The angels were not the only ones who could persuade Yovah to disperse the clouds and send forth radiant sunshine.

This was Feast Day, the most important event of the Gathering. All the work of preparation had been done; now there was nothing left to do but eat and sing. Early in the morning women hauled their stewpots and fresh-baked loaves and dressed venison to the tables laid out on one side of the double circle of fire at the center of the general camp. Thereafter, those who were hungry ate; the others performed, or watched the performers, or called out for musicians to delight them with another song.

Anyone who chose to could rise to his feet, move to the very center of the camp enclosed by the double ring of bonfires, and create music for the glory of the god. Most of the musicians were singers, but not all; some played reeds, some played pipes, some played fantastic stringed instruments carved from twisted, polished trunks of old trees. A few, like Naomi and Rachel, performed together. Some sang old favorite songs, others introduced new music they had worked on all during the long, dark winter months. From each clan, chroniclers stood and sang unadorned recitatives of the tribe's history for the past year, complete with births and deaths and changes, so that all the Edori could know who rejoiced and who grieved. No matter who sang, no matter what instrument was played, the drums accompanied them. From that unchanging, steady pulse, each performer got his rhythm; all Edori drew their heartbeats from the same unvarying source.

Rachel and Naomi were greeted with such extravagant applause when their song was ended that it was clear they would not be allowed to yield the stage without an encore. Rachel blushed but Naomi was triumphant. "What do you remember from the old days?" she shouted in Rachel's ear while the applause went on and on around them.

"That one song that we sang two years running," Rachel shouted back. "About the roses on the Gaza mountains."

"Oh, yes! I remember it. Give me the note—you start it."

So they sang a second piece and then, when the crowd still would not be quiet, a third. Rachel resolutely shook her head when voices called out demanding a solo, and she had to laughingly push her way through the throng to make her exit. She was flushed but exultant; it was no paltry thing, after all, to please the Edori at the Gathering. Hands touched her arm, voices cried out to her, gestures of approval, words of admiration. She smiled and nodded and made her thanks graciously, all the time edging for the far end of the camp to try for a moment of peace.

She finally broke through the second ring of fire and stood there a moment, relatively solitary, letting the fresh afternoon air cool her hot cheeks. Well, that had been a success. Yovah willing, her next performance would receive such acclaim.

"Ah, and that's the voice the angels think may shame them on the Plain of Sharon," said a burred murmur behind her. "Were any of them here today, you would have no more doubters among the divine ones."

She turned to smile a little self-consciously at Matthew, who had followed her through the double ring. "I wondered if you were listening," she said.

"You knew I would be."

"I am nervous about it still," she said seriously. "The Gloria. But I begin to think I can manage it."

"You've a voice to make even your husband's sound dull," he said.

But Rachel shook her head. "No," she said. "No one can sing like the angel Gabriel."

CHAPTER FIFTEEN

For practically the first time in his life, the angel Gabriel was experiencing remorse. He did not care much for the feeling. It was not often that he felt he had been in the wrong—indeed, he would not even now say that he had erred—but perhaps things could have been handled better. Rachel had behaved abominably, of course—but then she often did—and it had been unkind of him to let her leave for Jovah knew how many weeks without even a polite farewell.

Although there was no telling but that she had been glad to escape the Eyrie without being forced to lay eyes on him again. She could have come to his door the morning that she left; he was not the only one who had spoken hastily; she could have been the first to make apologies. No, not apologies—overtures. And she had chosen to leave without a word. Just as well he had not humbled himself to seek her out.

Josiah had promised him that his bride would humble him, but so far it had not happened. There was, after all, a bitter sort of satisfaction in that.

And yet, he should have said something. . . .

Between pride, regret, uncertainty, a nagging fear that she really might not come back and—well, there it was, may as well say it—a wholly unexpected sensation of missing her, Gabriel was not having a very comfortable time of it during Rachel's absence.

He was kept busy enough planning his conference and recruiting the Eyrie angels to make sure the powermongers of Samaria knew that he was in earnest. He sent teams of angels to Gaza, Breven and the river cities to create some serious havoc with the local weather patterns two weeks in advance of the scheduled meeting. This should make Malachi and Elijah and Jethro think twice about the existence of the god—and Gabriel's willingness to invoke his power.

He had sent Nathan to Jordana and Obadiah to Gaza—or so he thought. To Judith he owed the knowledge that the angels had switched assignments.

She had wasted no time, during Rachel's absence, in trying to insinuate herself into his daily routine. She synchronized her meal times with his; she made a point of bringing him new music or bits of news that she thought might interest him; she commented often on how tired he looked, offering to rub his neck or fetch soothing incense for him to burn. As always, he was torn between a wish she would go away and a desire to avoid hurting her. Then again, at times her soft, insistent concern did ease him a little. It was a nice thing, now and then, to be treated well by a solicitous woman.

This evening, she had brought him a glass of wine and a plate of cold food, since he had skipped dinner. He had been in Velora, discussing travel arrangements with merchants who offered transportation services between cities. At every Gloria there were mortals who needed to be conveyed from the Eyrie to the Plain of Sharon, and not all of them could be carried in an angel's arms. This year, Gabriel estimated that he would have twice the usual number of travelers to accommodate, and he wanted to make sure there would be room for them all. Rachel, of course, would need a carriage of some sort. Peter had informed him that all the urchins of her school had also expressed a desire to come to the festival, and there were any number of others for whom Gabriel would be responsible.

But the conversations had taken time, and he had missed dinner, and now here was Judith to make it up to him.

"Thank you," he said, smiling slightly as he allowed her into his room. "You always anticipate my needs."

"Well, I try," she said, giving him a smile and a sidelong look. "The beans are cold now, but they're delicious. And the cream sauce on the carrots—it's very good."

"Didn't you bring anything for yourself?"

"Oh, I ate hours ago. *I* wasn't down in the village, working hard."

"Oh, it wasn't hard work," he said, settling himself on a low stool and balancing the plate on his knees. "Just time-consuming. I'm so used to just taking off and going directly anywhere I want to go that I don't think much about the logistics of getting somewhere. The road conditions, the hours of travel time—for Rachel and the others to arrive on the Plain by the appointed day, they will need to leave at least four days in advance, maybe five. Five days! I can cover that distance in a few hours."

Judith had settled on the floor beside him like a docile puppy. "What would happen," she said, "if she was late?"

What would happen, indeed? "If Rachel was late to the Gloria?" he said a little sharply. "Why would she be?"

Judith gestured with her small hands. "Oh, suppose her carriage overturned or the horses grew lame and all the other carriages had gone on ahead and she started walking but she didn't get to the Plain until the day after she was supposed to—"

"Well," Gabriel said, "the Librera says that Jovah would show his displeasure in no uncertain terms."

Judith's guileless eyes grew quite big. "You mean—he would send down thunderbolts and destroy us all? If she was one day late?"

Gabriel toyed with a half-eaten chunk of bread. "She has a little more time than one day," he said. "The Librera says that if the Gloria is not sung on the scheduled morning, at sunset of that day Jovah will smite the Galo mountain from which the river springs. Three days later, if the Gloria still has not been sung, he will send lightning bolts to the middle of the River Galilee. Three days later—he will destroy the entire world." Gabriel smiled faintly. "Jovah works on the principle of threes, you see," he added. "Three chances, and three days between each chance. But after that—vengeance is absolute."

"But—" Judith leaned closer, her wide eyes fixed on his face. Her perfume was subtle and troubling; he could not help noting, as he always noted, the absolute perfection of her face. "But would he *really* destroy the world? The angels, the mortals—all of us? Would he really do it?"

Gabriel laid his plate aside and linked his hands around one knee. "Well, he hasn't done it yet," he admitted. "And the only

way to test the theory is to one day maliciously hold off the performance of the Gloria. Yet the fear of Jovah's power to annihi-
late us all is the only thing that enforces the tenuous harmonies
that exist in Samaria today."

She gave her girlish laugh. "Sometimes I don't think it's so
very harmonious even now," she said.

"No," he agreed. "I feel that we daily slip farther and farther
from the ideal of fraternity and interdependence that Jovah expects of us. There are factions among the Manadavvi, among the
Jansai—and yet, how much worse would it be, do you think, if
there were no fear of the god at all? What would keep the Jansai
from ravaging all of us? What would keep the Manadavvi from
raiding each other, stealing land and serfs and gold from their
neighbors? What would keep the angels from turning on each
other or from using their powers to selfish ends? If I did not believe in Jovah's wrath, could I not even now fly to Semorrah and
tell Lord Jethro that I wanted all his gold and all his bolts of silk
and linen, and the hand of his daughter in marriage, and that if
he did not do my bidding, I would cause the river to rise and
flood him and everyone who lived there? There will always be
powerful men who are tempted to misuse their power, and the
threat of a divinity with even greater strength is all that keeps
them in check."

Her fine brows had drawn together as she attempted to follow his argument. "But you already have a wife," she pointed
out. "You could not marry Lord Jethro's daughter. Although I
didn't know he had a daughter."

He couldn't help himself. He grinned. Metaphorical and eth-
ical speculation was wasted on the literal-minded Judith. "In any
case," he said, "I do believe in Jovah's power, and so I try not to
misdirect my own."

She smiled at him sweetly. "Oh, you," she said with great
affection. "You could never do anything bad."

He thought of the cadres of angels singing for rain, singing
for drought, over scattered locations in Samaria. "Could I not?"
he murmured. "I may be engaging in questionable practices even
as we speak."

She asked the rare insightful question. "Really? Something to
do with why you sent Obadiah to Breven?"

"To Gaza," he corrected. "Yes."

She shook her head. "No, Nathan went to Gaza," she said.

"Obadiah is in Jordana. I know because I asked him to bring me back a mother-of-pearl comb from Breven, and he said he would if he had time, but he didn't think he would."

Gabriel was frowning blackly. "So. That's why Nathan didn't bother telling me he was leaving— This has got to stop."

"What has to stop? Nathan going to Gaza? He was just there for a month and you didn't mind."

He shook his head impatiently. Impossible to believe she didn't know the situation, since everyone did, but he was not up to explaining it to her if she really didn't. "It doesn't matter. I'll deal with him later, when he's back. It's one more thing . . ." He let his voice trail off and stared somewhat morosely before him. One more damn thing to trouble him. First Rachel leaving without a farewell, then Nathan sneaking off to conduct his desperate, doomed romance. . . .

Judith had dropped to her knees and crept suddenly closer to the angel's stool. She laid one hand on his knee and with the other hesitantly smoothed back his hair. "I hate to see you so sad," she said in a low, anxious voice. "Don't they all know how much you have on your mind? Nathan, Rachel—all they do is make things harder for you, when you've got so much worrying you already."

"Judith—" he said, half-raising his hand to brush hers aside. But now she had lifted both hands to his temples and was rubbing the bones of his forehead and cheeks. He was too tired to fight her, and the massage felt so good. He shut his eyes and let her smooth away his tension, let her fingers work their way slowly back across the rounded planes of his skull. She had edged even nearer; he could feel the heat of her stomach where it rested against his outer thigh. The smell of her perfume was stronger now and even more disturbing.

When she kissed him, he was not entirely surprised. He even shut his eyes more tightly, knowing that the minute he opened them he would have to push her away, end all this. Her mouth was persuasive on his, incredibly soft; she nibbled his thin lips with her own full ones, brushing her mouth from side to side over his. Her fingers had traveled back to his face and now lay insistently against his cheekbones. He felt his clenched jaw muscles loosen, felt his mouth open under hers.

And he pulled away, suddenly and completely, snatching her hands in his before she could fall forward or back, before she could grab for his shoulders or his face. Her eyes were huge with desire; she stared at him with naked want.

"Gabriel," she whispered, and tried to free her hands.

"No," he said. He made his voice as decisive as he could, though he did not feel as if he could infuse it with any moral indignation. "Judith, this must stop here."

"I love you," she said, still whispering. "I always have."

"I feel great affection for you, Judith," he said, still in that firm tone, "but there can be nothing more than that between us. None of—this."

She didn't ask him why not. She knew. "But you don't love her," she said in that breathless voice. "She doesn't love you. It wouldn't be wrong for you to love me—"

"It would be," he said gently, "and we both know it."

Unexpectedly, she wrenched her hands free. She sat back on her heels and grew animated. "But I *love* you!" she cried. "I would do anything for you! I would not leave you when you asked me to stay—I would not shame you before your visitors—I would comfort you when you were hurt and feed you when you were hungry and love you every day— And what does *she* do for you? She flouts you, she laughs at you, she cares for nothing that you care about. Look at us, Gabriel!" She flung her arms wide, raised her chin so that he could better admire her sweet, even features. "I come from angel stock, I understand angel ways, I would be whatever you wanted me to be—and I love you. Think of her—half-slave, half-Edori, and all hateful. Which of us suits you best? Which would you rather come home to? Which of us could you truly love?"

True, it was all true; and yet, as she had bidden him do, he conjured up a picture of the rebellious, furious, unpredictable woman he had married at the direction of the god. Judith was willing to give him everything, and Rachel had never indicated that she wanted to give him anything, and yet—and yet— Since the day he had met her, ragged and shackled and defiant, he had been unable to put her out of his mind for more than a few minutes at a time.

"I don't know that it's a matter of love, Judith," he said soberly. "It is something as immutable as any of the god's laws. She belongs to me. Whether or not she chooses to accept me, I belong to her. There is no changing that. It simply is."

A moment more she stared at him, her face anguished and her whole attitude one of supplication, and then she jumped to her feet and went running from the room. Gabriel sat for a long time on the stool where she had left him, somberly watching the door as it swayed on its hinges, and thinking he must really rise to close it before someone else walked in. He was so tired that it was nearly an hour before he could make that much effort, and even then, after dropping the lock home, he rested a moment against the door frame until he had gathered enough strength to walk back across the room.

That had been bad enough, but there was worse to come: Three days before his meeting, he had an unannounced visit from the Archangel.

The two men had not met since the day of the wedding, and their last conversation, in Gabriel's mind at least, was perfectly fresh. So it was with some constraint that he greeted Raphael in one of the larger reception rooms on the middle level of the labyrinth.

"Angelo," Gabriel said, nodding as he entered the room. The great gold angel turned to him and smiled warmly. The effect was of sudden sunlight after days of grayness; but then, charm of manner had always been Raphael's strongest form of glamour.

"Gabriel," Raphael said, crossing the room to take his hand. Gabriel allowed it, but pulled away as soon as he could. "It is good to see you after so many weeks— But how is this? You look quite exhausted."

"Ill-considered use of my time," Gabriel answered briefly. "You're looking well, of course."

Raphael laughed. Indeed, as always, he looked superb. The luxurious golden locks, the deep golden tan, the tawny eyes, the huge flecked wings—everything about him glowed with its usual rich radiance. And yet—

"Preparing myself for a life of leisure," the Archangel replied lightly. "When you assume my duties and the center of the world shifts to Velora."

"Velora hardly seems like a place designed to be the center of the world," Gabriel said mildly.

Raphael laughed again. "Does it not? These days we hear many stories of the stirrings afoot in your small city."

"Do you? I can't imagine what."

"Your angelica," Raphael said. "It seems she is making her imprint upon the city—or upon the city's castouts."

Gabriel smiled slightly. Even less than he wanted to talk to Raphael did he want to talk to Raphael about Rachel. "Ah, yes," he said. "Her school. She has only made a small start on it so far, but I believe she has great ambitions. I confess it seems a worthy cause to me."

"But entirely worthy! We applaud her from every city and enclave. Will she be traveling to set up similar institutions across the land?"

"Once this one is stable, perhaps she will," Gabriel said somewhat stiffly. "I don't know all her plans."

"Could I ask her all the details? It is one of the reasons I stopped here today, to talk with her and learn what she could tell me."

Worse and worse. "I don't believe she'll be available for the rest of the day," Gabriel said.

"No? Is she in Velora, perhaps? I could go to the school and meet with her there."

"No, she's not in Velora."

Raphael's voice took on a note of concern. "Is she ill, then? I hope not. Is it a fever?"

"No, not a fever—I mean, she's not ill at all. She's just unavailable."

Raphael's face took on a quizzical expression. "She has not been locked in her room, has she? Really, Gabriel—"

Gabriel gave a short laugh. "Hardly," he said. "She's not here."

"Not here? Where can she be, with such a few short days remaining before the Gloria?"

"She's traveling."

"To?"

"Places she wished to visit."

Raphael laughed lightly. "Really, Gabriel, you needn't be so evasive. I am asking out of idle curiosity with absolutely no intended malice—"

True, maybe; true, probably, and yet Gabriel stubbornly refused to give him the information. "She's visiting friends," he said. "She'll be back in a few days. You can return then—or wait and address her at the Gloria, if you prefer, though I imagine all of us will be somewhat busy then."

"No doubt," Raphael said. "You and Rachel at least will become quite industrious then. I, of course, will be the one who suddenly has excess time on his hands."

"I am sure you can find useful employment for yourself," Gabriel said, aware that the words sounded unsympathetic but unable to come up with anything better.

"Oh, I am sure of it," Raphael said, looking at him in some amusement. "I look forward to the day you take on the duties of the office of Archangel."

"Then you have changed your mind considerably since the last time you were here," Gabriel said bluntly.

Raphael made a graceful *moue* which could, Gabriel supposed, be taken as apologetic. "We both spoke hotly and perhaps foolishly," Raphael said. "But I am convinced we both have only the interests of our world at heart. Let us cry 'friends' and forget all that."

Gabriel toyed with the idea of saying, *How could I possibly forget?* but decided to be more diplomatic. "Very well. I don't want to be warring with you—"

"Warring with me!" Raphael murmured. "Gabriel—"

"And I want the transition to go as smoothly as possible. I would appreciate your support."

"Of course you have it. If you would also care for my advice, I have a little of that."

"Certainly."

Raphael leaned forward, as if to whisper a secret. "Do not antagonize the powerful mortals," he said. "You may not respect them, but if they are unruly, they can make your life difficult."

Gabriel drew back, frowning slightly. "I have set out to antagonize no one," he said. "If anything, they have shown themselves far from willing to deal with me."

"And you have responded with threats and displays of temper! Gabriel, that is no way to ensure a smooth transition."

For a moment he was puzzled—and then, suddenly enlightened, he was reprehensibly amused. "Oho! So this is not just a chance social call you're making as you happen to be in the vicinity of the Eyrie? Let me guess— Were you called to Breven or possibly even the Manadavvi holdings, by angry tales of storm and flood?" He flung his arms out to indicate clouds, rainfall, inclement weather. "And let me hazard an even more indelicate guess. After soothing whichever angry leader you spoke to, did you spring aloft and try to reverse the elements? Turn back the snow, or coax forth the rain? But you had no luck, did you, Raphael? It has been some time now since you have been able to control the weather, has it not?"

Something ugly flashed across the Archangel's face, an expression so fleeting it was hard to decipher. Fury, fear, hatred; one of those, or all. "At least I don't waste my time and power playing stupid games with the clouds and raindrops," Raphael sneered.

"Then what is it you do waste your time on?" Gabriel said softly. "For I have it on good authority that you cannot call a thunderbolt from Jovah's hand, either."

Now the expression was clearer—absolute rage. "I was making a point to Malachi of Breven, and it suited me to summon no lightning," Raphael said icily. "You would be very foolish to extrapolate from that the idea that I could not call down the lightning if I wished."

Then do it, Gabriel wanted to say; but what he actually said was even worse. Still speaking in a soft, even voice, he said, "I find it difficult to understand why you are so reluctant to give up the trappings of power when no divine power actually courses through you. If you no longer communicate with the god, why do you continue to want to serve him?"

Since there was no possible answer to that question, it was perhaps fortunate that at this juncture the door opened and Judith stepped inside. Gabriel had not seen her since that disastrous interlude in his room several days before, and he was surprised to see her now; but she bore a small tray of food and drink in her hands, and kept her eyes on the floor before her.

"Hannah said the Archangel was here, and would need to be refreshed after a long flight," she said in a monotone. "She told me to bring this tray to you."

Of the two angry angels, Raphael made the quickest recovery. "Thank you, dear girl," he said, swinging round to face her and turn on some of the charm that had not worked on Gabriel. "I am quite thirsty indeed. Oh, it's you, Judith," he said, smiling at her as she came closer. "It's always such a pleasure to see your lovely face."

The face was lifted to his and fleetingly lightened with a smile. Ariel had told Gabriel years ago that Judith was an angel-seeker, but he had not quite believed it. And a few nights ago she had convinced him that her regard for him was genuine. Yet she had always liked Raphael, and Raphael had never been known to discourage the attentions of pretty girls.

"Do take your time refreshing yourself before you must leave," Gabriel said, faintly stressing the last three words as he headed for the door. "If there is anything else you need, I'm sure Judith or Hannah can get it for you. Excuse me, now, however—I have much to do."

"Certainly—I have no wish to keep you," Raphael replied. Judith did not even look up as Gabriel exited the room and closed the door behind him. He strode away as rapidly as possible, working off some of his tension and his own concealed anger. Only later did it occur to him that it might not have been a good idea to leave alone in one room the two people who, at the moment, had almost no incentive to wish him well.

It was only possible for Rachel to leave because Naomi had promised she would come to the Gloria. In fact, she told Rachel, a good number of Edori were planning to attend the Gloria for the first time in almost a decade, to see one of their own lead the masses.

"Have you ever been to a Gloria?" Rachel asked.

"No. I'm looking forward to it."

"But you do know where the Plain of Sharon is?" Rachel asked somewhat anxiously.

Naomi laughed at her. "I know where every plain and mountain in the whole of Samaria is!" she exclaimed. "As do you, as does any Edori child. Have faith, allali girl, I will be able to find you."

"It's just that—I hate to leave you—and I will be so busy at the Gloria. Will I have time to talk to you then?"

"All right. I'll come to you in Velora a few days before the singing. Will that satisfy you? And I'll ride with you to the Plain of Sharon, and dress you, and braid your hair. You can sleep in my tent the night before the great day dawns, if you choose not to sleep with your husband. Will that please you?"

Rachel hugged her. "Yes—it will satisfy me, it will please

me," she whispered into the dark hair. "But come soon. I am lonely already, and I have not even left you."

But eventually she was able to tear herself away. Matthew had already packed the black and the palomino—with lighter loads than the horses had carried from Luminaux, since Naomi and Luke had agreed to transport all their heavier and more awkward bundles for them. Rachel had wrapped the silver flute in five layers of silk and adjured Naomi numerous times to treat this bundle with special care, but the wooden demonstration pipe she had slipped in her own pocket to carry back personally. She thought she could while away some of the dreary miles of traveling if she learned to play it along the way.

"Yovah guard you," Naomi said, kissing her a final time, then holding her horse while she mounted. "Ride with the god's whisper in your ear."

The day was beautiful, but it was a good three or four hours before Rachel actually noticed that. Her mind was so completely focused back on the Edori camp that she had virtually no idea what kind of countryside they passed through, or whether they rode through sunlight or shadow. Matthew had to tug on her arm around noontime when he asked if she was hungry. Dumbly, she nodded.

"Ah, Raheli, it's not worth this great sorrowing," he said, half-laughing and half-serious as they sat on a spread blanket and munched on dried food. "You'll be seeing your Edori friends in just a few days. Naomi said she'd be in Velora before the week is out."

Rachel attempted a smile. "I know. It's just I—I don't suppose I even realized how much I missed her. It's as if she were the one who might have been dead instead of me, and now I've found her alive again I almost can't bear to leave her."

"Well, you don't have to be riding back with me," he said.

For a moment she misunderstood. "Well, of course I do! I have to sing at the Gloria! You know that."

"Of course you have to sing, girl. I didn't mean that you couldn't go back at all. But you could wait a day or two and travel with your Edori friends. They'll be in Velora in plenty of time."

Rachel lifted her eyes to his face, a suddenly arrested expression on her own. "That's true," she said slowly. "I could travel with them . . . But Gabriel didn't want me to leave at all, and if I don't come back with you—"

"I'll tell him where you are. A little delay, is all."

She chewed at the inside of her lip. "He won't like it," she said. "He'll think—you know he'll think that I'm not coming back."

"Well, but, if you are coming back, he'll have no reason to think that, now will he?" Matthew said reasonably.

She considered him, a small smile starting in her eyes. "Will you be able to convince him, do you think?"

"I've the gift of speech," he said loftily. "Why should he not believe me? Back you go, girl. Pack your horse and turn back to the campgrounds. I'll make your excuses in Velora, and you can have a few more precious days to spend with your Edori sister."

It was with much more animation that Rachel readied her horse this second time. "You have been such a good friend to me," she said, hugging Matthew quickly before swinging up on her horse's back. "Tell Gabriel—tell him I will hurry back to him. Tell him I *am* returning."

Matthew laughed up at her from his place on the ground. "He'll not doubt it," he promised. "Hurry now. Ride with care."

She rode quickly, but not quite as carefully as Matthew would have liked. Although she had just passed through this territory an hour or so ago, she had paid so little attention that it did not look at all familiar. It was not possible to get lost, of course; she knew exactly where the Edori camp lay, and she knew that she was headed in that direction. Nevertheless, as she drew farther away from Matthew, she began to feel unaccountably uneasy. Her uneasiness increased as the sunny day began, rather rapidly, to cloud over and grow cool.

She was perhaps two hours from the Edori camp when her palomino shied, pulling back so abruptly that Rachel almost lost her seat. She snatched at the bridle and held on while the horse danced in a complete circle, tossing its head and seeming unwilling to go a mile farther. Rachel peered forward down the trail, looking for something that might have spooked the horse, but nothing was immediately visible in the flat, wide prairie ahead.

"Well, there's obviously something up there that you don't like," she murmured, slipping from the saddle and letting the reins trail. "Something dead, maybe? Something we could go around? Let me take a look. Don't you stray, now."

She took a few cautious steps forward, but nothing leapt out at her, and nothing in the landscape ahead showed any sign of menace. So more boldly she began to trot forward, noting the unmistakable signs of spring here in the southern plains—the greening of the grass, the flowering of the flame-colored berry bushes that bloomed earliest and died quickest, the musical query and response of the shrub thrushes who swooped and glided overhead with such energy that she could hear the beat and whisper of their wings—

Their wings—

She barely had time to glance up before they were upon her, three great airborne bodies descending in a terrifying mass of arms and legs and feathers. She shrieked and ducked her head, scuttling sideways, trying to flatten herself to the earth and run forward at the same time. Hands grabbed for her and missed, the nails scraping along her cheek. Another hand tangled itself in her hair, but she wrenched free, feeling the hair nearly rip from her head. The air around her roiled with the wind of their wingbeats; their shadows blocked out the sun as they swooped and hovered over her. She beat at their reaching hands with her fists, and screamed again, more loudly, more despairingly. They were all around her; there was nowhere to run.

Someone gripped her wrists and someone else grabbed her once more by the hair. Then two arms went around her waist and the awful thing happened: She was lifted up, she was suspended, she was flying. The world below her careened crazily from side to side, then shrank, grew tiny, then began to stream by in a series of surreal, microscopic images. Trees, hills, the brown-and-green patchwork of fields, finger-sized rivers, palm-sized pools—they unfolded below her like small pictures of themselves taken from a strange, unnatural angle.

Nausea overtook her, and she shut her eyes. Still she could feel the wind whistling past her, much too fast, much too cool. She was freezing; except where her side and her shoulder were pressed against bare angel skin, her flesh was absolutely icy. She could feel panic crowding around her face and lungs with an actual physical pressure, but she did not have the strength to fight it off. She was afraid to open her eyes again, afraid to get another sickening glimpse of the countryside so far below her that she could not even guess how high above it she was, but she had to know. She knew, but she had to be sure—

Against her left shoulder, she could feel cold metal against her cold skin as the angel's arm cradled her to his chest. Cautiously, squinting against the possibility of any true vision, she opened one eye and took a quick look at the angel's nearest wrist.

It was clad in a gold bracelet studded with rubies.

She had, as she had thought, fallen into the hands of the Archangel's disciples.

CHAPTER SIXTEEN

It had been named Windy Point because the sound of the wind was unceasing. Night or day, through any room in the high, stony fortress, the wind whispered in, soughed in, moaned in, shrieked in, came sobbing in. It dusted behind servants as they walked down the long, rocky corridors. It toyed with curtains, tapestries, the hems of women's skirts. It sent the candles flickering, the fire to leaping, the glass balls of the chandeliers clinking together. And even in deepest summer it was prodigal with its diaphanous snow-cold kisses.

They had flown all night and arrived in mid-morning, though Rachel had only the most confused impression of time, voices and events. She had lain ill for most of that day in a room at the very top of the tall, narrow castle. They had left her on the bed, but she had, with a single burst of strength, managed to rise and stumble to the fire, where she had lain ever since on the chilled stone hearth. There had been bouts of retching, moments of delusionary terror, and she was still shaking as with a fatal ague, but slowly she felt her body and her mind recuperating. It was through sheer force of will now that she drew herself up to a sitting position, dizzy though it made her, and tried to beat some sense back into her yammering brain.

So. He had tried before, and this time he had succeeded. The man she hated above all others had taken her prisoner. Now it remained to be seen how he planned to kill her.

She lifted her head and made herself look around her room.

It had the feel of a garret, but perhaps, in this pile of rocks, it was the most elegant the fortress had to offer. The flaky gray stone of the walls was interlaid with seams of mortar—the castle had not been, as it seemed, hewn whole from the rocks of the mountain, but painstakingly built, brick by brick, high up in this most inhospitable of terrains. The place was hundreds of years old, and this room, at least, showed every day of its five centuries of use. The mortar was cracked and blackened; the cloudy pane of glass in the single window did not fit snugly in its splintered casement; and everywhere along the join of wall and wall, or wall and ceiling, little finger holes made passageways for the wind.

Rachel shivered and moved her eyes to the furnishings. The bed was wide enough, and covered with a thick quilt. Someone had attempted to brighten the dreary room with red rugs and a brightly patterned wall hanging. There appeared to be no separate water room, such as existed in the Eyrie, but there were eight or ten large jugs of water lined against one wall, and various pitchers and basins that could be used for washing. Certainly she was intended to make herself comfortable here.

The thought made her smile bitterly.

Mostly to see if she could do it, she rose to her feet and stood balancing herself for a few moments before the fire. From her standing vantage point, she continued her visual inspection of the decor. There was an armoire, a chest of drawers, a cheval mirror, a table and a chair; the one window, a single door. She circled the room to investigate each separate item.

The armoire was sparsely filled with a few old dresses, somewhat shapeless but thick enough to be warm. The shirt and trousers she was wearing were soiled and torn. She would almost certainly have to change into clothes that Raphael provided. The chest offered undergarments, a set of bed linens, soap and other personal items.

The mirror gave her back an image of wild hair, fanatic eyes and clenched hands, but she did not pause long enough to study the apparition closely.

The door, naturally, was locked.

For a long time she stood to one side and a little back from the window, unwilling to look out because she feared the view. She had never, to this day, had the courage to gaze from her one window in the Eyrie, terrified of the vertigo and nausea the height would evoke. She was not sure she could stand to peer out through this misty glass and see nothing but the gray tumble of rock down toward the blackness of some unimaginable ravine. And yet she had to look; she had to know what her chances of escape were.

So she crept closer to the glass, and, splaying her hands over her eyes to filter out the worst of the vision, she glanced quickly out and then back in.

But all she had seen was stone. Tall stone, slaty and streaked, rising instead of falling. She peered through the glass again, more fully.

Her window looked out on a view of the jagged mountain face as it clawed its way up to an uneven apex. Craning her neck, she could see the very top of the snarling mountain, stabbing three crooked fingers at the dour sky. Nowhere was there any evidence of greenery—hardy mountain shrubs, indomitable ivy, even a weed—just the bony fingertips of the mountain poking holes into heaven.

She, Raheli sia a Manderra, erstwhile Edori, erstwhile slave and future angelica, was imprisoned in her enemy's castle at the very top of the world.

Someone brought her food after what seemed like hours.

She had not been aware of hunger until she smelled the aroma sifting in from behind the locked door; then she was famished. A key turned in the lock, and two men entered, one bearing a tray and one merely guarding the exit. Neither of them looked at her directly.

"Who are you? Why am I here?" she demanded sharply, but was not surprised to receive no answer. The server bowed to her as he left, and the door was shut behind him. She heard the lock fall home. For a moment, she stared wrathfully at the closed door, but the lure of food was too strong. She crossed the room in a few quick strides and quickly consumed the meal.

Only after she had swallowed every bite did it occur to her that the dishes could have been seasoned with poison. She did not have much experience with toxins, except for the lethal powders that were periodically set down in Lord Jethro's cellars to keep the river rats from breeding, but she knew that a wide variety of them existed. Poisons that clouded the mind, poisons that caused hallucinations, poisons that could kill a man within minutes . . .

Well, if he had wanted to kill her outright, Raphael could

have simply had his angels drop her from the mountaintop, and she wasn't so sure he needed a prescription to drive her mad. The constant whine and wheedle of the wind would accomplish that, if terror didn't do the trick first. It seemed safe enough, all in all, to eat.

No one else came to the door for the rest of the day. Night came swiftly, judging by the light admitted by the imperfect window glass, or perhaps the shadows of the mountain brought night to this place sooner than to other parts of the world. Certainly it did not seem as though the sun could successfully reach past those accusing sentinels of rock and bring light or warmth anywhere near this bleak castle. At any rate, the chamber became dark, and Rachel felt exhaustion steal over her. She crossed to the bed, doubled the quilt over to provide additional warmth, and slept.

In the morning, as was her custom, she lay very still for a long time, not opening her eyes.

Cold; that was the first thing she became aware of. Her body was drawn up into a small knot, her arms folded across her chest to conserve whatever heat her flesh could generate, and yet she still felt sore and cramped with chill. Next, the eerie, discordant music of unarticulated wind intruded itself on her consciousness. She pressed her eyelids together, gathered her body tighter, but it was no use. She remembered exactly where she was and how she had gotten here.

But *why* was she here? What would happen to her next? Where was Raphael, and why had he not explained to her why he had taken her hostage?

She shivered under the quilt and refused to stir from the bed.

In an hour or so there was a commotion outside the door, and two servants entered again. One built up the fire, while the other laid down a breakfast tray. She waited until they left, locking the door behind them, before she threw off the covers and ran for the heat of the fire. They had brought extra fuel as well, so that she could stoke the flames when they died down. At least they did not plan for her to freeze to death—or starve.

No one came to speak to her; the day spread before her blank and gray and just a little menacing. To keep herself from thinking, she passed the hours doing voice warm-ups, running up and down the scale in half notes and then, as the tiresome day progressed, quarter tones. She practiced her intervals next, major, minor and dissonant, and then turned to breathing exercises.

Finally she remembered the learning pipes tucked in the trousers she had been wearing when she left Matthew, and she dug these out and taught herself how to play their thin, simple music. When she tired of this, she went back to the voice exercises. She did not have the heart to try real singing—somehow the notion of true music in this place was unthinkable, impossible. It was as if Jovah would not hear her in this fortress, even were she to offer his favorite masses. It was as if her voice evaporated into a vacuum, a room with no resonance, as if she did not sing at all.

And yet the wind provided a sinister and unceasing accompaniment, and its eerie melody lingered in the room even when she fell silent.

She was brought one more meal, another load of fuel, and received, again, no answers to her impatient questions. So the day passed, and it was nighttime again before she was quite ready for it.

She was not so tired this evening. She sat for a long time before the fire, wrapped in a blanket and moodily studying the flames. Earlier in the day it had astonished her to realize she did not feel as terrified as she knew she should; her predominant emotion, in fact, was anger. That he would take her, that he should dare, after all this time and once again . . . it was foolish, she knew, but if ever she was allowed to confront him, all her fury would blaze forth. She would tell him exactly how much she hated him. And then he would kill her, or do with her whatever he planned, and so anger was of no use to her whatsoever—but it had been her cloak, her weapon and her shield for so many years now that she could not lay it by.

Her meditations were abruptly interrupted by a furtive fumbling at the door handle. Her head whipped around. She narrowly studied the thick dark rectangle of wood while, on the other side, hands tried to force the wrong key into the lock. Her heart squeezed down. She glanced around wildly for a weapon, seeing none. The slight, secretive clinking continued for some minutes while her late-night visitor tried a series of keys, doggedly, one after the other. Rachel sat motionless on the hearth but her head felt close to bursting with the terrific pressure of her pounding blood.

For what purpose would a jailor visit a prisoner's cell by midnight, when all the rest of the world was sleeping?

The scraping of metal against metal ceased. Rachel strained

every nerve to hear a whispered curse or the sound of a renewed assault upon the door. There was a moment of silence so long that she almost believed her visitor had crept away, and yet . . . she could still sense a presence outside, ghostly and frustrated, speculatively eyeing the door. After a long, long moment of tension, she heard soft footsteps circle once, then retreat down the corridor. Surely she imagined it, but she also thought she heard the whispering, shushing sound of wing feathers brushing against the tattered bricks of the hall.

Three more days passed, identical to that first one. Three more nights, also identical, down to the midnight visitor. Each night, Rachel waited, breathless, soundless, before the door, hands curled into fists, heart pounding at a maddening pace, listening to the scratching and scraping at the lock. She never spoke, nor did the angel on the other side, but she was sure he knew she heard him, that he smiled to himself as he pictured her panicked face blanching on the other side of the door.

Every night, after he left, she gave in to her frantic terror. There was a stiff, rusted deadbolt lever on her side of the door, and every night when her visitor departed she struggled to twist it home. But it was soldered or bent into place; though she fought with it ten minutes or more, she could not get it to budge. She had no way to make her room secure—and she knew that sooner or later he would find the right key. The thought turned her colder than ever in her unwarmed prison.

The fourth morning, when the servants brought her breakfast, she was ready for them. Crouched to one side of the doorway, she waited till they had stepped just inside, arms laden with trays of food and wood for the fire. Then she dashed out into the hall and down the first turning the corridor took.

Instantly, there were shouts and footfalls behind her. She raced madly past doorways, through a crisscross of passageways, hopelessly lost within minutes in the gray tangle of arches and stairwells and doorways. The light along these halls was murky and erratic, filtering in through a few narrow windows irregularly appearing along the walls. The uneven surface of the flagged floor tripped her up several times as she made her incautious flight. Once she fell to her knees, scraping her hands as she broke her fall, but she was instantly up and running again.

She had nowhere to run. She had no hope of escaping. When more servants boiled up the stairwell from a lower level, running hard to cut her off, she surrendered with only token resistance. "I want to speak to Raphael," she said as they grabbed her arms and pinioned them tightly behind her. "Let me speak to the Archangel."

Obviously his staff had been instructed not to talk to her, for at first no one answered. She began to struggle then. She had pretended to flee merely to get attention. "I want to be taken to the Archangel!" she shouted, stiffening her legs and bracing her feet against the stony floor. "Take me to Raphael!"

Finally one of them answered, in a strange north country accent that she had rarely heard, even in her Edori days. "He iss not here," said the speaker, a drab but powerful man who looked as rugged and as flinty as the mountain itself. "He will b'back tomorree. See'm then."

So she allowed them to return her to her room. She half-expected her food or fire to be taken away from her as punishment, but there were no repercussions. The day passed as all the others had.

But this afternoon she spent some time working on the dead-bolt attached to her side of the door. Using some of the butter saved from her breakfast bread, she attempted to oil it into docility, but it stubbornly refused to move. Defeated finally, she tried to think of alternate methods of security or escape. Her eyes turned involuntarily to the window across the room. She had no wish to flee down the treacherous mountain, and she assumed Raphael had made sure she could not try it, but she had not even checked. Maybe the window lock would yield to her; maybe, driven to desperation, she would in a day or so be willing to risk the flight down the stony slope, into the black ravine. . . .

But she discovered, after twenty minutes of wrestling with the iron bolt holding the glass in place, that this lock too was immovable. She laid her opened palm against the cold, foggy pane and felt the glass shiver when the wind glided over it again. And again, sending in its inevitable plaintive call, part cry and part whisper; and again—

Turning away from the window, she nervously picked up her pipes, hoping with their sweet, childish music to drown out the mistuned oratorio of the wind. And indeed, she felt marginally better while she played, soothed and rehumanized, though she had not mastered the reeds well enough to play two notes simultaneously.

And then she realized why Windy Point seemed such a sinister place, so eerie and evil: There was no harmony here. Angels did not sing, voice against voice, as they did in the Eyrie on a constant basis; nothing, no one in Windy Point worked in concord. She had been right, a day—two days—years ago, when she instinctively felt that Yovah would not hear her from here. He had forsaken this corner of the world because it held no harmony.

She cradled the pipes against her chest and drew herself together in a small bundle. And she was lost in this soundless, soulless place, that even the god had deserted.

Depressed by the dirge of the wind and the bleakness of her own thoughts, Rachel had passed a difficult night; she fell asleep late and was still sleeping when Raphael's servants attempted to serve her breakfast. It was their pounding on the door that woke her, and she stumbled groggily across the cold floor to admit them. Well, it took some effort: She had pushed the heavy wooden armoire across the floor the night before, wedging it as tightly as it would go against the door frame. The idea had been to block the entrance of her midnight visitor, although she had not been sure the weight of the armoire would be enough to deter him should he be fortunate enough to find the key. It had stopped the servants, though, and that cheered her.

They threw her fulminating looks as they entered with their usual stock of food and fuel, and this time they watched her more closely to make sure she didn't make another break for freedom. One of them pointed an accusing finger at her as he prepared to leave.

"Too-night," he said, in that looping hill-country accent. "Yoh will hof dinner wif the angel."

"Raphael is back?" she demanded. "I will see him tonight?"

"Be ready," the servant said, and left, and locked her in.

Oh, she would be ready. She had been ready for five days now.

This day passed with even more excruciating slowness. Once she had washed and dried her hair, and decided which of the old woolen gowns was the warmest for the trek through the drafty castle to whichever dining hall Raphael considered suitable for entertainment, there was, as usual, nothing much to do. She practiced voice exercises again, played on her pipes, chipped at the two obdurate locks, and waited.

The light had begun to fail, the signal she interpreted as middle evening here, when the aging gray servant cum guard came to fetch her. She was on her feet before the door had completely opened.

"He iss here now," was the man's greeting. "You wanted so much to speak wif him."

Rachel swept haughtily before him out of the room, then waited for him to lead the way down the labyrinthine hallways. "Ordinarily, I wouldn't bother to spit on him," she said frigidly. "But today, I have a few things I'd like to say to him."

And that little spurt of defiance helped her gain confidence as she followed the guard down three flights of stairs and dozens of passageways till they gained the dining hall of the Archangel.

The smell of overcooked food told her that this was indeed a meal she had been summoned to. Otherwise, she would have thought she had stepped into a nightmare.

She had entered a huge room, so high-ceilinged that she could not tell if the roof was raftered or merely arched stone. Great doors led off the chamber in six directions, but there were no windows to let in light or air. The whole place was illuminated with clusters of candles, but still, it seemed gloomy and underlit. Unseen breezes teased at the insufficient flames and, in sudden swift gusts, extinguished whole candelabra at once. The flickering flames that remained revealed and then shadowed the activities below.

Everywhere, great angel wings were draped over chairs, tables, lounges and divans. There was something indolent, almost abandoned, in the outflung feathered limbs. Low voices were interrupted at sudden jarring moments by loud bursts of laughter; now and then a call rang out from one side of the room to the other. Glassware chimed against silver, pewter clinked against china, as diners poured wine and carved meat and passed plates, and yet the pace was so sluggish, the movements so slow—

Rachel had frozen in the doorway, seized with a curious, reluctant dread. The guard prodded her from behind but she remained where she was, looking more closely about her. Angels were intertwined with humans everywhere she looked. Those great white wings overlapped frail mortal shoulders and drew them into clumsy, inexact embraces. Nearly every angel in the room was male, and every human female. The women sat forward in the divine laps, wrapping their arms around the thick necks or running their fingers through the ruffled feathers. In a far corner of the room, three winged shapes gathered around one small human form; Rachel could vaguely hear a medley of seduction and supplication as the girl's voice rose higher and higher on a note of distracted panic. The silent servants who wound through the room brought pitchers of fresh wine to every table, and those who were not slumped forward on some shoulder or backward on some chair raised their glasses for more.

All the angels of Windy Point were drunken and stuporous; and this was the court over which the Archangel ruled.

"Rachel! My charming guest! Over here, my dear. We've saved you a place at our table."

The mellifluous voice jerked her head around. Even in this dim light, it was impossible to mistake Raphael. He had come to his feet and was waving her forward. From this distance, in this light, he appeared to be bathed in a topaz glow emanating from the sheen of his own body. Hair, feathers and skin shimmered with gold highlights. He stood in an aureole, motioning her toward his table.

She crossed the room and came to rest before him, simply staring.

"It is a bit much compared to the austerity of the Eyrie, isn't it?" he said sympathetically, pulling out a chair and gesturing for her to be seated. "It isn't always quite this relaxed, I assure you, but I've returned after a few days' absence, and my host is glad to see me. This is in the nature of a celebration, you understand. We are ordinarily much more decorous."

"I wonder why I doubt that," she said, finding her voice along with her habitual sarcasm.

"Because you are a sullen and suspicious girl by nature, of course," he replied smoothly. "I can't imagine what Gabriel sees in you."

Laughter erupted from a small circle gathered at Raphael's table; it was the first time she had consciously realized that Raphael was not at this post alone. She glanced quickly around to note three other angels at his table, two of whom she had never seen before—

and one of whom she instantly recognized. Saul. The fair-haired, rapacious angel she had first met in Lord Jethro's house—

He grinned at her. She felt an irrational wash of terror, and quickly looked away. Raphael was still smiling at her, extending his hand.

"But sit down, my girl, sit down," he said. "Eat with us. I understand you were so anxious to see me that you went scampering through my castle the other day. Unfortunately, as I said, I have been gone. But I'm here now, and you may converse with me to your heart's content."

"Gladly," she said, remaining on her feet. "But I wish to do so in private."

"Oho!" he said softly, smirking a little. "You wish to tell me secrets. I am flattered to be your confidant."

"I wish to hear the truth from you," she replied, "which, if I judge you correctly, you rarely speak before an audience. And I refuse to sit for even a minute in the presence of that—" She waved a hand at Saul. She would not acknowledge him either with name or epithet.

Saul laughed. One of the other angels said, in a slurred, uncertain voice, "Don't want to leave. Want to talk to the pretty lady."

Rachel waited. Raphael smiled. "Oh, very well, my dear. But remember, when the talk turns dangerous, that you asked for this little assignation, not I. Saul, take the others away. Leave the candles, that's a good boy. *And* the wine, please. You can get more at another table."

When the others had protestingly vacated the table, Rachel finally sat, perching on the very edge of her chair. Raphael lounged across from her, studying her through the amber candlelight.

"You know, I do think we must be related," he said musingly, as if it was a puzzle to which he had given a great deal of thought. "Surely you cannot be my daughter, though I admit my progeny must be scattered across half of Jordana. Or could I be wrong? Was your mother the type who would seek to ensnare an angel lover so she could boast of her conquests to her friends?"

"My mother died when I was a child, as you know," Rachel replied in a level voice. "But I think she was a virtuous woman."

"Your grandmother, then. Perhaps she dallied with my sire

or one of my uncles. It's no disgrace, really, none at all, to be an angel-seeker's offspring. It's one of the reasons, no doubt, Jovah has kept such good track of you through all your amazing changes of fortune."

"Yovah is not the only one who has tracked me," she said.

"True—very true. I have been interested in you for quite some time. And I have, as you may have guessed, authored one or two of your misfortunes. But you're such a resourceful girl. You survive everything. Truly you are an example to us all."

"And now you have brought me here," she said, still in that tight, controlled voice. "For no purpose that I can guess at. What do you want with me? Why do you want to kill me? What have I ever done to you?"

Raphael opened his tawny eyes very wide. "Rachel, my dear, my dear! Such ugly talk. Here you are in my house, for the very first time—can't we make some pleasant dinner conversation?"

"If you consider this social entertaining, then where's your wife? Shouldn't Leah be here?"

"My wife prefers to take dinner in her rooms on occasions such as this," Raphael said smoothly. "The excitement of my homecoming is sometimes too much for her." He smiled at Rachel engagingly. "You understand."

She watched him from narrowed eyes. "In her own rooms," she said softly, "by choice or by chain? Do you compel the angelica as you compel me?"

"No, indeed, she has free run of the place, though she rarely chooses to exercise her rights," he said. "She is a most indulgent wife, of course. She allows me whatever amusements I prefer, and in exchange I respect her wish for privacy. You see, we are much more well-suited than you and your so volatile spouse."

"I would not have said the god chose well when he matched you with Leah," she said, "but Yovah's ways have always been passing strange."

Raphael poured her a glass of wine and filled her plate with delicacies from the platters on the table. "Well, that's the interesting thing," he said softly. "Jovah did not exactly choose this wife for me."

"That's ridiculous," Rachel snapped. "He chooses every angelica."

Raphael nodded vigorously over his own glass of wine. "Oh yes, he chose mine! She was a Jansai girl, quite beautiful, with a great deal of courage and physical strength. Her parents were wealthy merchants and she despised them, and she had gone to live with her aunt and uncle some years before we were betrothed. I don't know how much you know about the Jansai," he added, "but strong-willed teenage girls are pretty much a rarity. Well, they are scarcely tolerated. She had had a rough time of it, poor girl, between one household and the next, but nothing had dimmed her really indomitable spirit. She had—it is hard to know how to describe it—an inner flame that was simply unquenchable. Or seemed unquenchable. The Jansai men, of course, are very good at quenching."

Rachel had begun to feel queasy. Without knowing the end of this story, she knew that she wouldn't like it. "What happened to her?" she asked slowly. "What was her name?"

He was smiling that warm, golden smile. "Her name," he said, "was Leah."

Rachel gave a small start. "Then," she said stiffly, "'they— and you—did a superlative job of quenching, because the woman who is your wife—"

"Oh, it's not the same woman," Raphael said almost gaily. "The Leah I was to have married is dead. Died, sadly, a few days before our wedding. My Leah—that was not her name originally, but you know, I find I cannot always call it to mind—my Leah was an angel-seeker who had spent a good deal of time convincing me that she would do anything she could to oblige me. You know how it is with angel-seekers, my dear—they're the worst kind of whores, but that often makes them the best kind of whores. So I switched them."

"You—" Rachel could not breathe. She was sure she had not comprehended. "You—what do you mean?"

"I switched them. The Jansai brought their Leah to Windy Point, all embarrassed apology because she was such a contrary handful, and I said, 'Jovah and I will tame her with love.' Indeed, those were my exact words. I said, 'Let her make a prenuptial visit with me for one month, and then we will have the wedding in Breven. She will be so docile you will not know her.' Well, they were only too glad to leave her on my doorstep, because, as you can imagine, she'd been no end of trouble to them for the twenty-some years of her existence. And when we arrived in Breven four weeks later"—he spread his hands so smoothly that no wine spilled from the goblet he held—"I brought my Leah instead of their Leah, and married her in front of Jovah and the angels and everybody."

"But didn't they—couldn't they— How could you fool them?" Rachel stammered. "Her parents, her family—"

"Well, you know how the Jansai women are," he said. "Very wrapped up in veils and cloths and so on. We had my Leah all wrapped up, and I never for a minute left her alone with her loving family. They were too delighted at the change in her to inquire too closely. Oh, perhaps they had their suspicions, but they didn't like to voice them. After all, what harm had I done them? Whether I'd married her or whether I'd disposed of her, I'd taken the rebellious girl off their hands. And I was Archangel and I had the ear of the god. They smiled and said they'd always known marriage would calm her down."

The distant roaring in Rachel's ears must be the physical manifestation of shock, but she felt no other symptoms. She had passed through horror to find herself sick and dull, sated with an awful knowledge. "You killed her," she said stupidly. "And you're going to kill me."

"Mmm, well, that was my original thought, I must admit," he said consideringly. "For so long, you did seem the one stumbling block to my plans. Because I know my Gabriel! He's not the man to try to fool the god with any plausible substitute. If Jovah told him, 'Marry Rachel, daughter of Seth and Elizabeth,' then no one but Rachel would do for him. And I thought, 'Ah. If I wish to prevent this man from becoming Archangel, what easier way than to dispose of his angelica?' But, as I say, you are a hard woman to kill. My compliments, of course, on your continued survival."

"So why am I still living—this time?"

He leaned forward, his beautiful face vivid with intensity. "For that very reason! Because Gabriel will not play the god false! The Gloria is scheduled for six short days from now—yes, you start, it is much closer than you realized!—and you and Gabriel are to lead it. If you are not there to sing at Gabriel's side, what will he do? Will he take Ariel or Judith or Hannah to the Plain and bid them to sing at his side? I think not. I think Gabriel is incapable of singing alongside any woman but the god's chosen bride—which is why you must be kept alive. Once you are dead, of course, Gabriel is free. The god may choose a new wife for him, or Gabriel may choose his own—but the original restrictions will be lifted. While you are alive, Gabriel is bound. Once you are dead, everything changes."

Now Rachel leaned forward, as intense as the Archangel. "But the Gloria must be sung," she said urgently. "Don't you realize that? If all the peoples of Samaria do not come together on the Plain of Sharon, the god will smite first the mountain, then the river, then the world. We will all die—you, me, Gabriel, every one of us. If Gabriel does not sing, will you sing? That is the power you are so desperate for—will you take it, and see to it that the world is saved?"

He flung back his head and laughed. Angels and mortals sitting across the room, too far away to overhear their conversation, caught the melody of that laughter and joined in. He straightened, started to speak, glimpsed her face, and started laughing again. It took him a good five minutes to regain control.

"Oh, I do apologize, but that is so funny," he said, shaking his head and pressing a hand theatrically to his heart. "Rachel, my dear, haven't you heard a word I've said? For the past *twenty years* I have led all the peoples of the world in a mockery of the Gloria! A false angelica by my side, and no love of the god in my heart! For twenty years! And no thunderbolts have fallen—no cities were destroyed—the world spins on as it always has. And as it always will! Rachel, it is such a monumental but such a liberating thought—*there is no god at all*! He does not guard us, he does not punish us, he does not know if we live or breathe or die—*he is not there*! I have contravened every law laid down in the Librera, and he has not struck me dead. *There is no god.* If Gabriel fails to lead the Gloria, and there is no Gloria, we will all survive. If I fail to lead it, if it is never sung again—nothing will happen at all. We have been enslaved, all these years, to the idea of a god, without any proof of his existence. And now it is time that the people of Samaria realize that what they have loved and feared and obeyed is a divine and comic hoax."

Rachel simply stared at him. She realized suddenly that he was mad—power-mad, certainly—but more than that. He was lunatic. If he had questioned the existence of the sunlight or the soil, she would have been less appalled. That anyone would doubt Yovah's existence was, to Rachel, absolutely incredible.

"You may not have believed," she said, her voice very low, "but the masses were sung. The harmonies were completed. The people of Samaria came together and satisfied Yovah's requirements. He did not strike you dead, though I can't guess why you were spared, but he withheld his wrath from the rest of the world because the rest of the world believed. Not a year of these twenty has gone by that angels did not hold hands with humans and sing of the glories of the god. The voice of Gabriel alone was sweet enough to gladden Yovah's heart—maybe it is Gabriel that the god listened for, and not for you. And Yovah heard that silver voice, and was pleased, and held back his wrath for another year."

"Well, maybe," Raphael said, unimpressed. "But he will not hear that silver voice this year if you are not at his side. And then we shall see what the god thinks of this whole world of gullible believers. And I can tell you what that is right now. He does not think of us at all."

"You're insane," she whispered.

He shook his head. "Oh, no," he said. "I am Lucifer. I am the man who will rip the mask off the face of the god himself."

Rachel rose to her feet. She had touched neither the food nor the wine, but she felt as disoriented as if she had been drugged or intoxicated. Dizzy, she brushed the table with her fingers to catch her balance; when a hand came out to steady her from behind, she was almost grateful.

"Ah, Saul," Raphael said, and she jerked away from the angel standing behind her. Saul grinned down at her. Fire seemed to flame around his head; his eyes were blacker than the ravine below the mountaintop. "Escort Rachel back to her room and make sure she is comfortable."

"Glad to," Saul said, reaching for her arm again. Rachel shoved him in the chest and stepped back, nearly tripping over her chair. Both the angels laughed.

"I don't want him near me," she said.

"I don't have the key to her room," Saul said. "I can't lock her in."

Raphael said, "Maxa will accompany you. He has a key."

"He could just give me the key," Saul suggested.

Raphael looked amused. "Maxa has the key," he repeated. "If you need it in the future, you will know where to find it." Saul laughed. Raphael came to his feet and made Rachel a lovely bow. "As always, I have greatly enjoyed your company, angela," he said. "I trust you will find things very pleasant during the remainder of your stay in my house."

And he allowed Saul and the gray-haired guard to lead her away.

For a long time, Rachel stood in the middle of her room and tried to make herself think. Raphael's offhand series of admissions—to murder, deceit, and heresy—were so complex, so unnerving, that any one of them could have struck her speechless. To have heard all of them so swiftly, one after the other, was almost more than she could comprehend. Slowly, the pieces began to fit together in her head.

He had been the source of her misfortunes all along. That much he had admitted in so many words, but now, for the first time, his actions made sense, at least as seen in the context of his warped ambition. It was Raphael who had destroyed her parents' village—Raphael who had ordered the destruction and enslavement of the Manderras—Raphael, no doubt, who had directed the Jansai to try to kidnap her on the very streets of Velora. How astonished Raphael must have been when Gabriel all unwittingly stumbled upon his bride in the slave cellars of Semorrah! How he must have schemed to get his hands on her even this late in the game, fretful that no opportunity presented itself until so close to the time of the Gloria itself. Or had he guessed, weeks before it crossed her mind, that she would be unable to resist the lure of the Gathering, and so bided his time until that great day dawned?

And now, after several attempts, he had secured her; and he would keep her at least until the Gloria was past; and then the god alone knew what would become of her.

And he was not the only one in this castle who wished her evil.

She shivered and shook herself free of her trance. If Maxa were persuaded to give Saul the key—and of this she had no doubt—the wanton angel presented her nearest and most immediate danger. The heavy armoire across the doorway had baffled the servants this morning, but would that stop Saul? She doubted it. But it was a starting point. She surveyed the room.

The bed was bolted to the wall, but there was the armoire, the chest of drawers, the cheval mirror, a table and a chair. She could employ them all. Working swiftly, she dragged every last scrap of furniture across the room, bracing each one against the last until, front to back, they formed a barricade that stretched from the doorway to within three feet of the opposite wall. She tried wedging pieces of firewood between the wall and the chair she had ended with, but there were no logs long enough or sturdy enough to bridge the gap.

Well, she was long enough. She could protect herself.

Accordingly, she wrapped the bed quilt around her for warmth and positioned herself on the floor, her back to the rungs of the chair and her feet laid against the unyielding wall. It was not a very comfortable position, but she felt a certain savage triumph lighten her mood as she tested the fit of her body in her line of defense. The angel had great strength; he might very well force the lock and push in the door so brutally that the wood splintered and her own bones snapped in two. But she would not be the first link in the chain to break.

She built up the fire again, then settled back in her place on the floor, a weapon in her hands. A thin, springy length of firewood, it ended in a raw point where it had been ripped from some dead tree. She rubbed it against the rough floor, methodically and incessantly, to sharpen its edge to a razor fineness that could pierce a man's chest if propelled with sufficient force. . . .

Driven by purpose and fortified by determination, she would have passed the night almost calmly had not the wind chosen this evening of all evenings to show off the full range of its bluster.

There was never silence in Windy Point, but Rachel had never heard anything like this. A storm must have moved in and settled, lashing the stolid mountain with rain and wind and hail. Every crack and joint in Rachel's room seethed and sobbed with air, rising first to a furious pitch of shrieking, then dropping to a low, desperate moan. The window clattered in its frame, but that jittering sound was lost beneath the almost human voice whispering through the chamber—screeching through, mewling, begging, chortling, bellowing—as its moods took it. Rachel clenched her jaw and resisted the primitive urge to wail in return.

So loud was the wind, so unremitting, that it covered the first telltale scrapings at the door. She did not realize that someone was trying to get in until she felt the shudder of the chair against her back; sudden pressure ran down the whole massed blockade of furniture and buckled her legs against the wall.

Choking back a cry, she stiffened her knees and shoved her shoulders against the rungs of the chair. She snatched up the pointed stick, holding it like a spear before her. Again she felt the scrape and shift of furniture inching forward. She braced her free hand on the floor and strained her whole body backward, making herself a wedge, a boulder, a bulwark, a thing of bone and rock and iron.

She did not know how long she remained there, inflexibly opposing a contrary pressure that had ceased to be exerted. It felt like hours that she kept her tense, arched pose. It was not her bones but her muscles that betrayed her, becoming shaky and loose and unreliable, unknitting from her elbows and her knees and causing her head to sag down from her numb spine. She collapsed forward, waiting for the whole room to rush inward as Saul triumphantly swept all her defenses before him, but nothing happened. He was gone; he had left sometime during the night. The lightening gray outside her window told her in the most dispirited terms that she had fought her way through to another morning.

She drew her knees up and rested her head upon them, still shaking in every muscle and joint. She had survived; she was not dead or ravished or even mad. Perhaps Yovah was watching out for her after all.

And then the wind started again.

By the time they brought her breakfast, two or three hours later, she really did think she was on the verge of delirium. It was Windy Point itself which had driven Raphael insane; the wonder was not that he had turned on the god but that he had not turned on himself as well. Sleeplessness, a sort of continuing, familiar terror, and the accumulated shocks of the past week were having their effect on her, but nothing like the maddening assault of the wind.

The knock on the door caused her to leap half a foot into the air, but she did not answer the first summons, nor the steadily more urgent calls that came in through the heavy wood. She did not have the strength to clear the furniture from the doorway, and she did not care if she never ate again. She would die here sooner or later. It might as well be of starvation, if the wind's demented music did not drive her first to fling herself into the fire—

The wind's music. She stood absolutely still, considering that. And then she ran across the room to the pile of clothing she had left on the floor the day before. Pawing through her dresses, linens and woolen stockings, she crowed victoriously when her hand fell on her learning pipes. Holding them up, she examined the instrument more closely to determine how it could be disassembled. She saw that the pipes were closely woven together with thin leather strips. If she had a knife, it would be easy, but—

She did have fire.

Crouching on the hearth, she held the bunched pipes against a half-dead ember. It took a long time for the leather binding to yield; her knees had given way and she had sunk to a cross-legged position long before the thin strap blackened and began to smoke. She brushed aside the coal and took up a rough piece of kindling, rubbing it along the weakened patch of leather till the last stubborn strands parted. The eight pipes rolled loose in her hand.

Sorting quickly through them, she picked three reeds—those that formed the major chord—and, after a moment's hesitation, the pipe that played the seventh. Then she crossed to the window, where the wind was most apt to blow in, and wedged the largest pipe into a narrow slit between the casement and the wall.

It was only a few seconds' wait before another gust surged in past the glass. And through the tube. And made a noise like a faun piping a love song to a beautiful unwary virgin.

She could make the wind play music.

Almost feverishly, she searched the casement for another convenient gap to hold the next largest pipe; nothing was quite right. But the reed that played the fifth interval against the big pipe's dominant note fit snugly into a crack right below the window.

And when the next blast of air shook the castle, she had harmony.

Her hands were shaking violently as she crossed and recrossed the room, looking for the right finger holes for her remaining two reeds. There was a place, finally, in the far wall for the middle pipe, the major third; when the wind rushed in and set all three pipes trumpeting at once, she thought she would fall to the floor and weep. She felt her shoulders unknotting, felt her mind growing light and peaceful. Such a simple thing, such a small thing, and yet she could feel the music healing her. One more reed to place—

It took her nearly half an hour but eventually she secured it, high above her bed in a tiny crack in a crumbling line of mortar. The outer counterpart of this wall, apparently, was half-protected from the elements, for the temperamental wind only reached it sporadically, sending faint, intermittent puffs of air through the throat of the smallest pipe. The three other reeds also sounded at random—sometimes the major third, sometimes the minor, every once in a while all three at once; when the seventh note sounded, by itself or in harmony, Rachel felt a shiver run from her shoulders to her fingertips. So must music have sounded to Yovah on the morning of the first Gloria of the world.

The longer the music played, the more lightheaded she grew. She was giddy; she began to dance around the cold prison which had suddenly become a place of grace and symphony. On a hunch, pirouetting past the blocked doorway, she paused; snaking her fingers behind the armoire, one more time she tried the stubborn, immovable deadbolt. As if oiled by a smith, it fell smoothly into place. She laughed aloud. Music had restored her, and harmony had made her safe.

The euphoria on top of her strenuous night left her exhausted and drained. She collapsed onto the bed, still smiling foolishly as the erratic lullaby played from the walls around her. She was so relaxed now that the minute she closed her eyes she was asleep, and she slept through another mealtime and repeated poundings at the door.

It was the last hour of the afternoon when she opened her eyes, as she could tell by the faint gold light limning the irregular pane of her window. She had slept deeply if not as long as she needed to; she woke clearheaded and sober, though not completely rested. Her fire had gone out and the room was freezing. She had forgotten to retrieve her quilt before she slept, and now she shivered with a deep and ineradicable chill. Her pipes still chirped sweetly at odd moments, which caused her to smile faintly, though she did not feel in the least cheerful. But she did not need to be cheerful; what she needed was to be serene, and that the harmony had accomplished.

She had awakened knowing exactly what she must do.

She had decided, the instant she had secured the door, that she would not open it again. Clearly, there was no way out for her but death, although Raphael intended to prolong her life as long as it suited his purposes. If she must die, she could at least make the sacrifice a meaningful one—and the only way her death would not be a total waste would be if it freed Gabriel of his bond to her before the Gloria.

Which meant that she must kill herself, and instantly.

And there was only one sure way.

She was numb with cold, but that was a good thing, she thought. She rose, shaky with chill but not with nerves, and glanced around the room for anything that might still need doing here. No; nothing. Slowly enough, because she was not eager, but firmly enough, because she was not afraid, she crossed the room to the single rattling window, and tried the lock that had so intractably stayed in place.

And it, too, yielded under her hand. And the window swung open, and all the icy wet mountain air poured in, swirled around her, and laid its hungry kisses on her hair.

She had to fetch the wooden chair to gain enough height to climb out, and she had to wriggle her shoulders to force them through the narrow casement, but all in all, it was not hard to escape. The fortress was built into the pitched terrain of the mountain, so that the angled, rocky ground was only a few feet below her. She jumped, landed awkwardly and fell to her shoulder, bruising her hip, thigh and elbow. This high up, outdoors at the onset of night, it was colder than she had believed possible. But none of this mattered. None of these discomforts would she have to endure for long.

Fighting the wind, which lashed at her hair and the loose ends of her skirt, she struggled uphill toward the highest point of the mountain. Twice more she fell, once knocked over by a blast of air so strong that it forced her to her knees and once twisting her ankle on a buried rock. By now, her toes, fingers and cheeks had lost all feeling. Her brain was nearly numb as well—or perhaps she was just trying not to think. Frozen foot before frozen foot, up the dark mountain she went, into the teeth of the wind.

She reached the very top of the mountain without once looking ahead or to either side for the terrible view laid out around her. She had kept her eyes doggedly on her shoes and the mealy ground through which she found her insecure footing. Now at the mountaintop it became even more important that she not look outward, not until it was too late, not until she wanted to be made so dizzy that she fell.

Here at the very peak there was a promontory that overlooked the vast ravine down which the mountain itself retreated. Slowly, with infinite determination, Rachel inched forward to the very edge of the outthrust ledge. The wind whipped around her, spinning her first to one side and then to the other, but miraculously, she kept her balance. Her unbound hair streamed wildly about her face and shoulders; her skirt flattened against her thighs, then belled around her knees. She was so cold now that she felt, oddly enough, fevered. If she put her fingers against a frozen puddle, she thought, she would cause the ice to sizzle into steam and water.

When her feet shuffled clumsily to the rim of the outcrop, loose stones rolled away from her shoes and clattered over the edge. She heard their hollow clicks and echoes as they bounced down the mountain. It did not sound so far. Carefully, she lifted her eyes from their fixed attention on her toes and took in the scene below her.

Black emptiness at the base of a huge, angular well. The mountain she stood upon curved forward from either side to form a rough, precipitous canyon whose wicked slopes were almost vertical. Jagged boulders and spikes of wind-whittled rock offered their brittle spines to the fading light of the sun. The ravine was so immense that no sunlight fell all the way to its depths. It could easily have plunged straight through to the core of the earth itself.

Rachel drew a long, ragged breath and did not look away. She had feared this her whole life, and yet, at this moment, she embraced it—the wild tumble of rock, the vertiginous height, the pummeling wind. Overhead, she heard the harsh call and flapping wings of mountain birds—vultures, perhaps, suspecting a death in the offing, or eagles, furious at this invasion of their domain. It was all so bitter and yet so beautiful. It would bring her the release she must have; it would set her free. It had been designed for her.

She took one last, lingering look around, at the gray face of the sheer mountain, at the luminescent horizon lit by the milky sunset, at the silhouette of the giant mountain hawk winging swiftly her way, and then she closed her eyes.

"Into thy great hands, Yovah," she murmured, and stepped off the cliff.

CHAPTER SEVENTEEN

Up to a point, Gabriel's conference with the Samarian powermongers had been a success. They had all come, at any rate, and they had all been furious. Behind the fury he had sensed a *frisson* of fear, and that was exactly what he'd intended.

He had refused to see any of them until they were all assembled, another ploy designed to irritate. Hannah had shown them all to a small meeting room and offered them food, and then faithfully reported to Gabriel their various condemnations of his intelligence, his character and his methods. But they had all come, and none of them left during the two hours he made them await his pleasure.

"My lords," he said to them all impartially upon entering the room. It was another deliberate slight, proof that he grouped them all together and did not care how they jockeyed for power or prestige in each other's eyes. There were ten men in the room—Manadavvi, Jansai, river merchants and a lone Luminauzi official—and none of them looked pleased to see him.

The first one to speak, not surprisingly, was the patrician Elijah Harth, who seemed the most affronted. "How can you possibly defend your actions?" the Manadavvi demanded coldly. "You come to us to preach unity, and at the first chance, you try to sow discord. It's an ill beginning for all of us, Gabriel."

The angel nodded acknowledgment. None of the others was intelligent enough to attack first; they were still muttering phrases like "total outrage" and "how dare he." Elijah had gone straight to the point.

"I have acted precisely because you have proved to me that you have no interest in unity," Gabriel responded.

Lord Jethro slammed his open hand on a wood table, causing the glasses and trays of teacakes to rattle. "Ha!" he cried. "Myself I have done what I could to please you—fed you, entertained you, listened to your everlasting lectures—and what do you do in return? Send the river rising up over the breakwater! Don't deny you did it—it's been raining up in the Galo mountain for weeks now, and I know you and your angel tricks—"

"Rain over the river, drought in Breven, wind in Gaza," counted off Malachi, the Jansai leader. In his round fat face, his narrow eyes almost looked amused. "What's the point, Gabe? What's the problem? We didn't bow down low enough to you?"

"You didn't listen," Gabriel said softly. They all had to stop their muttering in order to catch his voice, because he refused to raise it. "You told me—each of you—that you had no intention of changing your ways to suit the teachings of the god. Malachi of Breven as good as told me there was no god at all." There were muffled gasps and a few sidelong looks which Malachi ignored with no trouble at all. "Elijah—Jethro—Samuel—Abel—all of you swore to me that you could not alter a single item in your trade agreements, could not give up one of your privileges, could not free your slaves or enfranchise your workers or redistribute your wealth. And I said these things must be done to ensure harmony. And you said you did not care."

"But Gabriel, the things you ask for are preposterous!"

"The *trade* agreements! It took me twenty years—"

"And these things have been in place for two decades now," Elijah cut in over the various indignant exclamations. "You say we have lived in disharmony with our god—but if that is so, why has he not made his displeasure known? Why has he not struck down a merchant or a slaver? Why have we all prospered and grown rich? Because Jovah favors us, that's why."

Satisfied voices rumbled their endorsement of that argument. Gabriel spoke calmly.

"And perhaps Jovah is readying himself to strike you. Perhaps he endured the reign of Raphael because he knew, as a god reckons time, that the tenure would be brief—and that all things would be made right again when a new Archangel ascended. Perhaps—"

"Gabe, is this all about the goddamned Edori?" Malachi broke in. "Is this about you and that allali slave girl—"

He had steeled himself for this. There was no chance they would not try to taunt him with Rachel; and so he remained cold. "This is not about my wife," he said with glacier calm. "And it is only in part about the Edori."

"Because, Jovah give me salvation! if you don't stop going on and on about the damned slaves—"

"It is also about the Manadavvi bondservants, who are virtual prisoners to the feudal land system, and the non-status river workers who will not be given citizenship in any city—"

"You're crazy!" Jethro roared. "You want to rip apart the whole world so a few miserable laborers can cast a vote in a city election—"

"He's not crazy, he's a fanatic," Elijah said in a voice as icy as Gabriel's own. "And fanatics think their vision supersedes the reality of everyone about them."

"You can call it fanaticism," Gabriel said. "I prefer to think of it merely as justice."

"Gabriel, see, they're not really people," Malachi said with a confiding, earnest air. "Those Manadavvi peasants, the river rats, even those damned Edori—they aren't *people*, not like us."

"They are people," Gabriel said. "And to Jovah, their well-being is as important as yours. And if he is displeased at their treatment—"

"Well, now, that is the sticking point, isn't it?" Malachi said pleasantly. "What Jovah might do to us if you tell him we've been bad."

"Which is why," Gabriel said, nodding at Elijah again, "I brought the rain and the drought and the wind to bear on you before you came. To remind you that Jovah has power—and that I can funnel it."

"I have to tell you," Malachi said, "I'm not so impressed with a few weeks of hot weather. I've lived through worse, and always survived. Drought comes every few years to Breven, and we get through it and don't even bother to tell stories about it."

"Well, the river doesn't rise every year over Semorrah, and I say flat out that I won't stand for it!" Jethro declared.

"I'm sure our host will tell us we'll stand for it as long as he has a point to make," Elijah said. "But I have to ask myself if that's true."

Gabriel watched him. "Meaning?"

Elijah made an elegant motion with one well-kept hand. "Oh, we all know the tricks angels can play with weather—or say they can play with weather. And I grant you that I have seen thunderstorms move in and out on command. I have seen rivers rise, snows abate, clouds lift, and it was all very impressive. But how much of that, I ask myself, is really because the angel desired that it be so? It rains. It snows. The clouds move away. Eventually these things happen whether or not an angel flies aloft and puts in his prayer to Jovah.

"And when you examine it," Elijah continued, his voice more intense, "is that such an awesome power for a man to have? The ability to bring rain? If that is all he can do, should we be so impressed with an Archangel—with any angel at all? We have been taught since we lay in our cradles that angels could ask the god to bring down thunderbolts to punish evil men—but have any of you ever seen that done? Do you in fact believe it is a feat an angel is capable of? If the god will not smite us, and the angels cannot cause the god to smite us, why do we honor the angels? Or has the time come when we can dispense with the angels and worship the god in our own way?"

There was a shocked but speculative silence in the small room as everyone present began to consider the vast implications of the Manadavvi's speech. Gabriel, who had foreseen no other conclusion, waited imperturbably. Malachi, as he had expected, was the next to speak.

"How about it, Gabe?" he said. "You want to prove him wrong—here and now? We can all go out to the top of your mountain and watch you call down a thunderbolt. I'd believe you then. We probably all would."

"I have too much respect for Jovah's powers to do anything so foolhardy," Gabriel replied. "Were I to call down a thunderbolt, its force would be so great it might destroy the entire hold. It could kill a hundred men where they stood. I am not so desperate to make my case."

"Well, then," Malachi said equably, "I'm afraid you don't have a pig's chance on feast day of making us see things your way."

Gabriel nodded again and came to his feet. "Very well," he said. "If that's the case, so be it."

The others eyed him uneasily, rising uncertainly. He had gone to some trouble to summon them here; it seemed odd that he would so tamely accept their open defiance.

"Very well what?" Malachi asked. "You mean, you're just letting everything go on as it has done?"

"Exactly," Gabriel said smoothly. "The rains, the droughts, the storms in Manadavvi. All will continue unabated."

Now there was another angry murmur as they began to perceive his game. "You can't allow that," Jethro blustered. "If the river keeps rising like this, Semorrah will be under water in a month."

"And Castelana," someone added.

"Wait," someone else said. "If the winds don't stop, the whole summer harvest will be ruined."

"That's exactly his plan," Elijah said stonily. He faced Gabriel across the room, a proud, angry man who was not used to being outmaneuvered. "If weather is his only weapon, he will use it to the death. Is that not correct? You think to starve us out, flood us out—"

"If necessary," Gabriel said pleasantly. "I can continue the present patterns until the whole face of Samaria changes, until Gaza becomes a desert and all the cities are swept away. You are lords over your lands, but your lands may not be rich for long. All the wealth of Samaria can be redistributed when the earth itself changes. And believe me, I have the power—and the willpower—to change it."

They were staring at him. They did not entirely believe him, but they were not certain that he was not speaking the truth.

"Impossible!" Abel cried finally, his voice faint and his face chalky. "Even if you had such power, the other angels would not allow it—"

"Would they not?" Gabriel asked softly. "Ariel has agreed to my conditions. She does not like them, but she will not countermand me."

"The Archangel—" someone gasped.

"Raphael?" Gabriel said. "Raphael has never been able to control the elements as I have. He will be of very little use to you, I'm afraid. In fact—"

Exquisite pain suddenly lanced through his arm so sharply

that he thought he had been stabbed. He clutched his arm, staggering a little to one side, glancing down quickly to gauge the severity of the wound, astonished that someone would dare attack him here in his own hold in front of all these witnesses. But there was no blood. There was no blade in his flesh. Only the cool amber glass of the god's Kiss set into his very bone.

"In fact, we'll see what Raphael says about that," someone was saying, and Gabriel forced himself to look up, to ignore the fiery arrows shooting up his arm. Elijah and Malachi were watching him curiously, but no one else seemed to have noticed his sudden inattention. "He's due to come by the river cities in a day or two—we'll ask him to take a hand in this. There's no way he'll let you destroy the whole lot of us."

Gabriel let his hand fall, though his whole arm now burned with a peculiar ragged flame. "I would advise you to do so," he said, as steadily as he could. "Ask him to intervene on your behalf with the god. I would like to know how he answers you."

The river merchants had begun filing out the door. Malachi was right behind Jethro, murmuring the details of what seemed to be a business deal. Elijah hung back a moment, regarding Gabriel with serious, somber eyes.

"This is a wretched day's work you have done, angelo," said the Manadavvi leader when the rest of the room had emptied. "You are dragging us all into a morass from which there is no easy climb out. You speak of harmony, but you are throwing us all into discord."

"If you believed in the laws of Jovah, you would believe in my cause as well," Gabriel said. "You would see that you and these others are the ones who have been led astray."

"Have you no doubts? Do you not question whether one man with power should have the right to overturn the lives of hundreds who see the world from a different view?"

"I am not one man. I am the heir of hundreds of other men and women who shaped the world according to Jovah's plan. What you have made of Samaria is not what they intended."

"But the world changes."

"And it will change again."

"Jethro was right," Elijah said, very low. "You are crazy." And he too left the room.

*　　*　　*

Gabriel spent the rest of the day fighting the urge to fly down toward Luminaux and see what was happening at the Edori camp. By his reckoning, the Gathering had ended the day before, but there were undoubtedly a few of the nomads still left, cleaning up the site, or visiting between clans. He was not interested in the Edori, of course; he was irrationally and helplessly worried about Rachel.

The sharp pain in his arm had slowly abated. Now it was a dull throb, no worse than a day-old bruise—and yet he couldn't quite forget it. Until he had met Rachel, he had never had any sensation in his Kiss at all. It had led him to her, it had charted for him her unwilling reactions to his presence. He could not help but think any flash in its depths now was in response to something she had done or experienced.

But she had not even spoken to him before she left. She had hated him since they met. She would not appreciate his flying down to Luminaux to spy on her when she was with her Edori friends.

And she would be home in two or three days. He could wait that long to ask her what had disturbed her so much that hundreds of miles away with his mind wholly focused on something else, she could reach out to him with such unexpected force.

The next three days were very long. He kept himself as busy as he could. In fact, he spent a good portion of that time out on the Plain itself, overseeing the building of temporary shelters and food tents for the thousands of people who would gather here to sing the Gloria or merely observe it. He had no idea of just how many people would arrive. In Raphael's prime, once, four thousand people had attended the Gloria, but that figure had dropped off in recent years—particularly as the Edori stopped coming. For his own inaugural performance . . . well. There were a lot of people who didn't like him. But there were a lot of southern Jordana farmers and Gaza sheepherders and small-town dwellers who did; and the Edori, of course, could be expected to show their support for his wife. It was hard to say. He thought he might draw quite a crowd.

He returned to the Eyrie late the day before he calculated that Rachel would be back, and spent the next morning trying to curb his restlessness. The ache in his arm had completely disappeared, but now the Kiss flickered at odd moments with foreign lights, colors that he had never seen in its crystal heart before. He did not want anyone noticing the phenomenon and asking what it might mean, so he wore one of his fine long-sleeved shirts around the Eyrie all morning, and hoped no one asked him if he was cold.

He was singing the harmonics with Eva in the hour past noon when he spotted Matthew crossing the open plateau, talking with Hannah. His heart lurched against his breastbone; he actually missed a note of the song, causing Eva to turn wide, wondering eyes his way. He caught the beat again instantly, but his mind was no longer on music. He was scanning the faces of the other people who were strolling, sitting or standing outside in the arena, enjoying the gorgeous weather. Rachel did not appear to be among them. How long had Matthew been back?

He could not, as he wished, break off in the middle of his song and go rushing down to look for her, but never in his life had he found it so hard to sing. When two of the other angels arrived a few minutes early, ready to take their turn in the duet, Gabriel motioned them in and allowed the younger one to finish his own part. "Sorry," he mouthed at Eva, and quickly left.

Thank the god she was back. He had been more worried than he realized.

She was not, however, in her room. Well, then, in the dining hall, or visiting with Hannah. He would try the dining hall first.

She was not there—but Matthew was, hungrily consuming a late lunch and telling Hannah amusing stories. The Edori waved when the angel came in, and Gabriel came over, forcing a smile.

"So you're back," Gabriel said. "How was the journey?"

"It was fine from start to finish," Matthew said. "We spent a day with the oracle and a few days in the Blue City and many days with the people, and every day was a feast for the soul."

"Matthew says Rachel sang at the Gathering," Hannah said.

Gabriel looked sharply at the Edori. She had been singing? Had that been the source of the pain in his arm? "And was she nervous?" he asked. "I know she is not used to performing—"

"Ah, the girl sings like honey bubbling up through rock," Matthew said. "I had heard her sing years before, mind you, and I knew, or thought I knew, what to expect, but the voice of her—! You would not believe it. It stopped even my strong old heart."

"I hope she didn't overdo it," Hannah said somewhat anxiously.

"No, no, just a couple of songs. She was that embarrassed at the applause and the praises, but all of it rightfully hers! You've picked yourself a fine one, Gabriel."

The angel smiled again. "And where is she?" he wanted to know. "I went to her room, but—"

Matthew opened his dark eyes very wide. "But she's not here! She decided to travel back with her Edori friends."

Gabriel felt a sudden nauseous clutch in his stomach. "She's not here?" he repeated stupidly. "But—I thought she'd come back with you."

"Aye, and she meant to. But you should have seen the girl, so sad and drooping as the two of us were riding back alone. So I told her, 'Lass, you go back to camp, and ride in with the people. I'll tell your fierce husband that you'll be here as soon as their horses bring you.' So she went back."

"But—when will they be arriving?" Hannah asked, more visibly distraught than Gabriel. "There is so much left to do—"

"Two days from now, it should be," Matthew said. "They planned to leave two days after I did, and the Edori travel fast."

"Is she safe?" Hannah said, again putting into words Gabriel's exact concern. "I mean—"

"Safe? With the Edori? Dear lady, they travel their whole lives long. How could she not be safe with them?"

"But you're sure she is coming," Gabriel said, and for the life of him he could not keep the urgency from his voice. "These Edori *are* coming to the Eyrie—they do plan to go to the Gloria."

"Oh, aye. Most of the Edori do. Don't be troubling yourself, Gabriel. She's with friends. She's happy. She'll come back to you calmer for a few days spent with her people."

"They're not her people," Gabriel said sharply, before he could stop himself. Matthew's dark eyes fixed on him, but the Edori said nothing. Gabriel took a step backward. "All right. If she's not here, she's not. Two days, you said? I'll be looking for her then."

And he stalked out, not even bothering to wonder what the stolid Edori and the cool-mannered Hannah might make of his unmistakable perturbation.

So that was bad enough; and the intervening two days were

nothing, as far as he was concerned, but a test of endurance; but there was worse to come. For when the first Edori bands arrived in Velora, he flew down to look for his wife—and she was not there.

He had had the foresight to ask Matthew which clan Rachel had traveled with, so he was able to ask the first Edori he saw for the location of the Chieven campsite. This he discovered with no trouble, and he found himself smiling at the pretty young woman who crouched over her fire, cutting up meat for a stew.

"Naomi of the Chievens?" he asked as she came to her feet, wiping her hands on a wet rag.

"You must be Gabriel," she said, and again her mischievous smile woke a like response in him. "I've heard you described."

"I can't tell if I should be pleased or alarmed that you recognize me from that description," he said, "since it cannot have been a flattering one."

She laughed aloud. "You'd be surprised," she said. "Did Rachel send you for her things? I packed them most carefully, since she was so adamant—"

Instantly, his good humor vanished. "Send me?" he repeated quickly. "But she— Matthew said she was with you."

Her own smile abruptly faded. "With me? No, they left the campsite two days before we set out—"

"Yes, and Matthew said she was so lonely for you that she turned back that same afternoon. That she decided your clan would be here in time . . ." His voice trailed off. The dark eyes looking up at him were huge with fright.

"But she never came back," Naomi whispered. "We were there two more days, she knew right where we were. She could not have gotten lost—"

He felt physically, violently ill; for a moment, he thought he might actually faint. He put his left hand over the Kiss in his right arm. "Something happened to her," he said, as calmly as he could. "I knew it at the time, but I didn't believe— What could have happened after she left Matthew? They could only have covered a short distance before she turned back. Were there Jansai in the area?"

Naomi shook her head. She was still staring at him, but now her hands had come up to cover her mouth. She had strong, roughened hands, used to labor, quick and deft, but they looked helpless and shaky now. "The Jansai rarely bother the Edori in Bethel," she said, her voice thready and faint. "And they would not take a lone girl who looks as she does—she does not appear to be Edori—"

"They tried to take her one day in Velora," he said grimly. "Or—it was very strange that they attacked her here—perhaps . . ."

"Raphael," Naomi breathed.

He felt his blood quite literally reverse itself in his veins. As soon as she said it, he knew she was right. But— "Why Raphael? Why would he have any reason to take her?" Gabriel demanded. "It makes no sense."

"I know," Naomi said, her voice still so low he could hardly hear her. "I never truly believed her before. But—"

"Before? Before when?"

"When her parents died. When her village was destroyed. She said it was destroyed by angels."

The earth rocked explosively under Gabriel's feet. Unconsciously he put out a hand to steady himself, and was surprised when the Edori woman took hold of it. Her chilly, spasmodic grip was actually a comfort. "She told you that Raphael destroyed her home?" he said. "She named him?"

"Not then. She was very little, you know, when we found her. She just wept and wept and spoke of the angels flying in like giant hawks, ripping houses from their foundations, throwing fire into the gardens— But it was years before she mentioned Raphael. And then, once we saw him. We were in Luminaux the summer she was fourteen, and he was there. He was in a parade going down the blue streets, and Rachel saw him, and she said to me, 'That's him. That's the one who led the angels that killed my family.' And I looked, and I saw that it was Raphael—and I told her never to say such a thing again."

"And she never did?"

"Not to me. I doubt if she said anything to anyone else. I was—I thought she was hallucinating. I thought she must be wrong. The Archangel—" Suddenly her voice changed, became a cry. "Oh, Gabriel! What have I done? What's happened to her?"

Now he was the one to squeeze her hand for comfort. "You have done nothing. None of this is your fault. If Raphael has indeed taken her—"

"But why? What does he want with her?"

Gabriel shook his head. "I don't understand. It has something to do with power, but I don't know exactly what he hopes to gain—tying my hands, perhaps. But if that were so, why has he not told me he has her? It makes no sense."

"What will you do?" Naomi asked.

He disentangled his hand. A cold, pure rage was coursing through his body, replacing the shock, the fear, even the anxiety. That he would *dare*. That he would *dare*. "I know where she is—where she must be," he said. "I leave for Windy Point on the instant."

"How will you rescue her?"

"Perhaps I will merely kill Raphael with my own hands."

"You can't do that," Naomi said, genuinely horrified. "To take a man's life—"

He smiled grimly. "I have never done it," he said. "I don't know that I am capable of it. But I will retrieve her, never fear."

"Wait—you must take food with you—blankets," she said, turning back toward her tent. "Let me get you—"

"Naomi, I have no time. And I cannot carry—"

"You can carry this much," she said from the tent. "Be still a moment. You can't travel all that way with no provisions."

Within minutes, she was back, and he had to admit her packing was efficient. She had filled a leather pouch with dried meat and fruit, a flask of water and a flask of wine. The pouch was attached to a thick leather strap that she swiftly buckled over his shoulder, being careful not to touch his wings. Across his other shoulder she slung a soft, closely knit wool blanket that was so thin and light he could scarcely feel its weight. This she looped once around his waist and tied at his hip.

"There. That won't get in your way any, will it?" she asked breathlessly.

He shrugged slightly and arced his wings once, back and forth. "No," he said, unexpectedly smiling at her. "Thank you. You've been magnificent."

She came closer. She wanted to take his hand again, he could sense, but she didn't quite have the nerve. "Bring her back," she said. "She is— I lost her once, and she is so precious to me. Bring her back."

"I will," he said, and moved away.

"Gabriel!" she called after him. Impatiently he turned. The

Edori woman stood watching him, her face puckered with worry, her whole stance forlorn.

"What?" he asked.

"Be good to her," she said, so softly he almost could not hear her from a few yards away. "She loves you."

He was working his great wings; he was aloft; he was angling up over and past the Eyrie and continuously gaining altitude; and still those words sang in his mind. *She loves you. She loves you.* What had Rachel told her friend that she would never tell him, or had the bright-eyed Edori drawn this conclusion with no hard evidence from Rachel herself? Was it possible it could be true?

He shook the questions from his mind and concentrated on the task at hand. It was a good eighteen- or twenty-hour flight between Velora and Windy Point. It was unlikely he could go all that way without stopping. He should have paused at the Eyrie, perhaps, to tell someone where he was going. If he did not return within a day or two, there would be pandemonium. So close to the Gloria for him to be gone, without a word to a soul . . .

Well, if he did not find Rachel before the day of the Gloria, his presence would be worthless anyway. Archangel and angelica singing in harmony, that was what the Librera specified. Without Rachel's voice, his own meant nothing.

Without Rachel, his whole life meant nothing.

She loves you.

It could not possibly be true.

Night gradually superseded day as Gabriel flew steadily, tirelessly, across the world. He followed an unswerving northeast course for the Caitana Mountains, cruising at a dangerously high altitude. None of the other angels, he knew, liked to travel so far above the earth, complaining of the bitter cold and the buffeting winds, but he had always liked it—the higher the better. The higher he flew, the nearer he felt to Jovah, the more convinced he was that the god laid a warm hand across his back and guided him between the stars. A fanciful thought, of course; there were no stars this close to the world. And even if he broke through the barrier of Samaria's heavy atmosphere, winged his way out into the dense black night of space, he would not be any nearer to his god. Jovah was everywhere, above the clouds and below them; he resided in the peaks above the Plain of Sharon, he slept in the empty rooms at Mount Sinai. He was in the Eyrie—he was even,

Gabriel had to believe, in the porous, brittle stones of Windy
Point. For surely Jovah had not allowed Rachel to go there all
alone, without protection.

There were no prayers specifically designed to guard a dear
friend who had fallen into the hands of the enemy. On Samaria,
among all its people, no one was supposed to have any enemies.
But there were prayers of benediction, of defense and preserva-
tion, and these had been sung in the past over a traveler leaving
on a quest or an adventurer attempting some perilous feat. Surely
Jovah would hear these supplications and understand. Surely, he
would wrap his hands around the angelica's frail body and protect her from harm.

On and on Gabriel flew, so high above the terrain that he
could barely make out its whorls and features in the light of the
three-quarter moon. Now and then he caught the distant sparkle
of firelight from some traveler's camp or the widely scattered
lights of homesteads. It was long past midnight before he was
aware of his first fatigue, but it was not severe. He dropped a few
hundred feet to take advantage of the warmer air closer to the
surface, but he did not slacken his pace. A sense of inexplicable
urgency drove his wings in their unfaltering cadence, a nameless
fear kept his eyes open and his mind alert, even as the texture of
the night began to fray slowly into dawn. He had wasted too
much time already; he should have set out on his search the day
he felt the Kiss burn in his flesh. He could not delay an hour
longer, even a minute, or he would be too late.

He did not know what would happen if he was too late. He
did not know what doom he sensed, or even how logical his panic
was. He only knew that the certainty of it kept him in the air
another hour, and another, until sunrise gave way to mid-morning
which gave way in a slumbrous, heated fashion to noon.

He was in Jordana now, no more than two hours from
Windy Point. But the fast, sustained flight had wearied him almost
to the point of idiocy. He felt his wingbeat slow and his vision
begin to blur. It would do him no good to arrive at Windy Point
dazed with exhaustion, unable to do battle with Raphael or succor his wife. He angled in for a landing, feeling dizzy and motion-
sick as his feet finally touched the unmoving earth.

It was perhaps an hour past noon. He would let himself rest
four or five hours, and then be on his way again. Undoing Naomi's careful knots and buckles, he removed the blanket and the

leather pouch from his shoulders and made a hasty camp. A few mouthfuls of food, two swallows of water, and he stretched out on the half unfolded blanket. Within minutes he was asleep.

His dreams were dark and violent, and prominently featured Rachel and Raphael. His wife was crying; the Archangel was laughing. Blending in with Raphael's voice was a higher, sweeter laugh that he could not place, though he knew he recognized it. His dream-vision shifted and he was staring at the perfect heart-shaped face of Judith. She continued to laugh. He reached out huge hands to slap her across the cheek—once, twice, a third time. She backed away from him, smiling still.

With a supreme effort of will, Gabriel forced himself awake, disturbed by his dream and no longer interested in sleeping. It took him a moment to get his bearings. He was lying in a patch of sunlight, covered with a light sweat, and his hand was tangled tightly in the hem of the blanket. He had not been hitting anyone after all.

But perhaps the unconscious anger at Judith was not so misplaced, for hadn't he left her alone with Raphael upon the occasion of the Archangel's last, ill-fated visit to the Eyrie? It had been the last time he had seen Judith as well; Hannah had told him that she had left the mountaintop to reside, for the time being, in Velora, and he had not had it in him to feel even the smallest regret. But she might have done him a grave mischief before she left—she might have told Raphael, who had wanted to know, just exactly where Rachel was—

He sat up, shaking his head and stretching his cramped arms. A little tired still, but fine; ready to travel. He stood, flexing his great wings and feeling their smooth, oiled response. He could fly another whole day, and a day after that, if he had to, to get to Rachel in time. . . .

In time for what?

He glanced up, gauging time by the position of the sun. Two hours or a little less until sunset. Already the sun was gliding on down toward the horizon, which, in this part of the country, meant the jagged range of mountains just past the Caitanas. He needed to get to Windy Point before the sun went down. There was no way to explain his conviction, but he was absolutely sure. At sundown, the whole world would falter or disintegrate on its own. . . .

Shaking his head again (where were these absurd fantasies

coming from?), he took three running steps and flung himself aloft. Instantly, the wind took him. Northern Jordana was a tricky place to fly through at any time, and today, it seemed, the country was suffering from the tail end of a storm. Gabriel fought the errant currents, gained altitude and settled into a fast, mile-eating pace.

The sun flirted with him, dropping behind a mountain peak, then reappearing at some lower pass, molten and golden-red. The troublesome wind suddenly swirled once around him, then settled under his wings like a dog making itself into a footrest for his master. It was almost as if the breeze had been shaped by unseen hands, leashed, and brought to serve him. In any case, it made his flight easier and faster. He was over the stony terrain around Windy Point just as the sun dipped completely below the horizon.

He was so high that he had to drop sharply to get on a level with the fortress. Until this moment, he had not given a single thought to how to breach the hold—whether to fly to Raphael's public landing space and announce his arrival, or try to land on one of the spiky turrets and make his entry in secret. Now, with the castle in view only a few hundred yards away, he decided to circle once or twice and see if any good ideas presented themselves.

It was then that he noticed the hard pressure building in his right arm. Merciful Jovah, what was happening to Rachel now?

He circled once, as slowly as he dared, eyeing each narrow window and grilled doorway with mounting frustration. Even if he set down on the roof of the highest corner tower, there seemed to be no easy way into the castle; and even if he was able to creep in with no one seeing him, how would he find Rachel?

On his second circuit, he saw a sight that stopped his heart. A lone figure stood on the very last inch of a narrow, un-promising promontory that jutted over the ravine on the western face of Raphael's mountain. Wind whipped at her hair, and her skirts flew wildly about her legs; by those features he knew the figure was a woman. By the way the faded light of the sun clung lovingly to the golden hair, he knew just which woman this was. . . .

"Rachel!" he shouted, but the wind was against him; it carried his voice away from her. He dove forward madly through the turbulent air, fanning his wings as furiously as they would go.

She stood there, on one of the highest peaks in Jordana, immobile, looking down at a sight guaranteed to make her ill. And then, as he watched, as he strained every feather and muscle to reach her, she closed her eyes and stepped off.

CHAPTER EIGHTEEN

The plummet, the swoop, the shock of being snatched from the air. Crazed, tangled moments of falling and rising simultaneously, as great white wings lashed desperately to fight the hungry pull of gravity. Rachel had no breath to scream or speak. She was crushed to a wide bare chest, she felt the effort of every labored wingbeat, she felt the angel's will overcome the earth's. Slowly the angel's strength lifted them back toward the mountaintop, back to safety and sure ground.

And they cleared the mountaintop without pausing and flew on, into the red heart of sunset; and flew on, and flew on.

Rachel did not know how long it was that she lay mindlessly in the angel's arms, her eyes closed, her hands curled inward, aware of nothing except the speed of his movement and the heat of his body. It took her some time to sort out the fact that she was not dead, that she was no longer a prisoner, that she had been rescued. It was even longer before she realized that she was actually flying, at a great height over the earth, and that she did not care—she felt neither nausea nor terror. In fact, she felt almost nothing at all.

But she knew—had known, without even seeing his face, without hearing a word (for he spoke none)—who held her in his arms. Gabriel. Wherever they were going, however long the flight lasted, she was safe. Gabriel had come for her.

Hours passed; she knew by the changing colors against her closed eyelids. First gold, then scarlet, then indigo, and finally no color at all. She felt the snowy play of starlight across her face, down the whole length of her body. Except where the angel's arms passed around her shoulders and under her knees, except where she was pressed against his chest, she was frozen, she was no warmer than the stars. If he released her, dropped her to the earth, she would shatter into so many fragments of ice.

But he would not drop her. That was the only thing she was sure of.

It occurred to her more than once that she had been mistaken—she had not been rescued; she had plunged the whole distance to the stony ground, and now she was dreaming the strange, wistful dreams of the dead. For surely nothing could be less real than this, traveling changelessly, ceaselessly, on a windy plane between the moonlight and the earth, without fear, without thought, without feeling.

And then the steady forward motion altered; they slanted downward, slowing, almost seeming to reverse. Rachel shook her head and tried to focus. She opened her eyes and gazed below her at the dark patterns of the unlit ground, coming closer, growing larger with alarming speed. She watched almost idly as shadows resolved themselves into hillsides, trees and boulders, as perspective shortened and grew more familiar. Still, she was unprepared for the abruptness of the landing, the sudden cessation of motion, the dull heaviness of the stubborn earth.

Gabriel caught his balance first, and then he set her on her feet. His hands still gripped her shoulders or she would have fallen, pitched forward straight into him or backward onto the hard ground. She tried to collect her thoughts. Surely she must say something.

He spoke first—in a strange hoarse voice, accentuating each word by giving her a quick shake.

"What in the god's name were you doing there?" he cried. "How could you be at Windy Point—how could you be so careless—and how could you, how could you, throw yourself off the mountain—"

She jerked her head from side to side, trying to force some sense into her mind, trying to remember, trying to think. "Gabriel—stop it—Gabriel—"

He visibly calmed himself, fighting for control. "Tell me what happened," he commanded. "I know you left with Matthew and turned back for the Edori camp. What happened then?"

She took a deep breath. Even under the imperfect illumination of moonlight and starlight, she was afraid to look directly at him. He was too furious. He was too beautiful. "I was a few miles from where I'd left Matthew," she said, speaking carefully, remembering as she said them how words were formed in a person's mouth. "I heard—wingbeats. I looked up." She shrugged against his grip. "There was nowhere to run to escape them. They carried me to Windy Point."

His hands tightened on her shoulders; he knew how gruesome that flight had been for her. "And then?"

She felt some of her own strength coming back to her, or maybe it was feeding into her directly from his body, poured into her veins from his palms and fingertips. "And then they put me in a room where the wind blew all day. All night. You never heard anything like that wind."

"I've been there. I've heard it. So—what happened? What did Raphael say? Why did he take you?"

"I didn't see him for days. And then he—there was this dinner he had me come to. It was—" She glanced at him, fleetingly, sideways. Even in this nonexistent light, his eyes were so blue they astonished her. She looked away. "He's crazy," she said, in a voice only slightly above a whisper. "Gabriel—that whole place. It was a scene of madness. Drunken and drugged and—and—terrible—"

"What? What do you mean?"

"The angels lay around, sleeping in their wine. There were women—angel-seekers, maybe, but some of them didn't seem to want to be there—and it smelled like the incense the Jansai use when they're trying for hallucinations—"

"Sweet Jovah," Gabriel murmured. "I know he's—but I hadn't thought— So what did he say to you?"

"He says there is no god," she whispered. "But Gabriel, that's not true, is it?"

"No," was the instant response. "It's not true. But he's said it to enough other people that some of them are beginning to wonder. He's trying to—I don't know what he's trying to do! Destroy Samaria, I think. He does not want me to become Archangel, and he has done what he can to stop me. But taking you—it makes no sense to me. Why does he want you? What good could it do him to kill you?"

"He didn't want to kill me," she said in a low voice. "At least, not right away. Not this time."

"This time?"

"He tried. When I was little. Raphael and his angels destroyed my parents' village." She glanced at Gabriel again, to see what expression of disbelief or outrage crossed his face, but he was merely watching her, grim and unsurprised. "There was so much fire. There was so much noise. And in the air—hundreds of bodies, wings, arms, hands, flinging things, grabbing at people. We ran, those who hadn't been killed already—we tried to run. I saw angels swoop down on fleeing men and lift them and hurl them back down to the earth. I saw them toss children into the river, I saw them throw stones at women screaming on the ground . . . My father had grabbed me. He was a huge man and he could carry me, I was not so big. He had grabbed me and he was running, and I could see the shadow of angel wings form around us on the ground . . . I don't know what weapon they killed my father with. He fell forward, and I was hidden under his body. I heard the screaming and the killing go on for hours and hours after that, but nobody came for us again. When it was quiet, I . . . pushed my father's arms aside. I crawled out into the night. Everyone around me was dead. I ran away, and ran and ran until I came upon the Edori—"

"It was Raphael?" Gabriel asked quietly. "You're sure of that? He led the angels who attacked you?"

"I saw him. All gold and beautiful. The sun fell on his face and on his wings, and I thought I had never seen anything so terrifying in my life. He knows I saw him. He looked straight at me and laughed. But my father grabbed me and ran before Raphael could even stretch out his arms and take me—"

"The god protect us," Gabriel whispered. "Why didn't you tell me this before?"

"Who would believe such a story? Not even Naomi believed me. But it's true. And he has tried to take me, or kill me, ever since."

"But you said, this time he didn't want to kill you. This time—"

"Yes. This time he just wanted to keep me prisoner in Windy Point."

"Then why, Rachel?" he demanded, and his voice was suddenly harsh. He shook her again, once, hard. "Why would you try to jump off the mountain? Didn't you know I would come for you? You know what you mean to us—to all of Samaria! How could you try to kill yourself, throw your life away, when so much depends on you? What were you thinking?"

She wrenched herself free of him, at once blazingly furious. "I thought to kill myself to save all of you!" she cried. "He said he would keep me till the Gloria passed—so the Gloria could not be sung! I knew that as long as I was alive, no other angelica could sing beside you. But if I was dead, you could choose whomever you pleased and carry her to the Plain of Sharon—"

"Sweet god of mercy," he breathed. He reached out a hand to her but she struck it aside.

"And you must have realized it, too!" she shouted at him, backing away. "You must have realized it, when you saw me leaping from the cliff! You could have let me fall, you could have been free of me— All the trouble and all the turmoil could have died with me at the foot of the mountain—"

Too quickly for her, he moved forward; he disregarded her flailing arms and gathered her into a smothering embrace. She struggled futilely against his tight hold, unwilling to be comforted, unwilling to be soothed, but her muffled cries and her beating fists had no impact on him. He merely pressed her closer, murmuring soft words into her tangled hair, warming her with his own body, supporting her with his own strength. She was so tired. She was so cold. She could not speak, or fight, or stand. She began crying helplessly and bitterly against his chest. His arms were the only thing in the world that were real.

His arms, his voice. "Hush," he whispered, over and over again. "Hush, now, Rachel, precious Rachel, don't cry. How could I let you fall? Hush, Rachel. Who would I have beside me but you? No one. No one. I would let the world be rent in half before I would sing with any woman but you. . . ."

She was only half-aware of it when he scooped her up in his arms again and then knelt, bringing both of them to the ground. He wrapped her in something soft and warm, then laid her with amazing tenderness on the thick grass.

"I have to build a fire," he said, still in that sweet, murmurous voice. "Stay here. I won't go far from you."

"Gabriel," she said, but she said it so softly she was not sure he heard her. She heard his footsteps move away, but she was not afraid. She knew he would come back. She closed her eyes and, even before he returned, she slept.

Upon waking, Rachel lay for a long time with her eyes shut, luxuriating in a sense of well-being. It was late morning; she could tell by the thickness of the light across her closed lids. She had never felt so rested, so warm, so secure, so content.

She squeezed her eyes shut even tighter, willing the sensations to last. No thought, no memory; no truth. She knew better than to open her eyes, look about her, and discover the perils of reality.

If only she could live in this moment forever.

She lay motionless, afraid that any abrupt movement might shatter the illusion, bring her sharply into some dark, cold present. Yet her arms felt loose and relaxed, her long legs stretched out instead of curling inward as they usually were when she woke. So often she slept cramped with cold, huddled under some insufficient blanket, but now she was suffused with a glorious heat. She was enveloped in softness, a silken texture against her face, her throat, the flesh of her arms and legs. She turned her head cautiously from side to side, risking the destruction of the illusion, just to feel the play of that downy weight against her cheeks, her chin, the tip of her ear. She had never felt anything so incredibly soft, velvet-rich, feather-light, blood-warm—

Feather-light—

Very, very slowly she opened one eye. The world was fiercely bright; half-blinded, she clenched her eye shut again. Too bright; as if full sunlight filtered down through something immaculately white . . . She opened both eyes this time.

She was in a tent of white feathers, covered from head to toe by their snowy expanse. Below her was a white blanket, offering what padding it could against the hard ground. Outside, mid-morning sun beat down, adding its own iridescence. But she was inside, in a cocoon of mist and feathers—

She was sleeping under the quilt of Gabriel's wing.

Which must mean that Gabriel was sleeping beside her.

Even more slowly, with infinite care, she reversed her position, inch by inch, until she was facing inward. Gabriel's wing was draped so completely over her, touching the ground on either side of her body, that it was hard to orient herself in relation to him. But surely that was his back, solid against the feathered white wall, and the shadow so near her head his own mane of tousled black hair.

Sweet Jovah singing, he had slept beside her all night, and kept her warm with his wings; and perhaps he did not hate her after all.

She did not move again, fearful of waking him up. She lay there and considered the events of the night before.

Well, he had saved her life. Surely he had been under some compulsion to do that, even if he hated her. She was, after all, a woman marked by the god, and as such, valuable by divine decree. He had been angry, actually furious—had spoken harshly to her, as he had more than once in the past—but she knew all about using anger to camouflage other emotions. And it was the reason for his anger that was intriguing—he had been afraid for her, distraught that she planned to take her own life.

Had he really said he would sing with no angelica but her? Had she dreamed that? And if he had really said it, had he meant it—?

Dearest Jovah, he would be flying her back to the Eyrie today, carrying her in his arms. He was so strong; he would not falter once, would not think of setting her down so that he could rest. Her face burned. Her whole body clamped together in one wave of embarrassment. How could she let him carry her all that way for all those hours—

Her unwary movement had caused her wrists to brush against the sensitive feathers. There was a quick, seemingly involuntary tightening of his wing upon her, and she felt his whole body shift. She froze, but the feathers twitched and lifted. Gabriel had rolled over and was peering in at her. Instantly the white light under the feathered tent took on a sapphire cast.

"You're awake," he said gravely. "How do you feel?"

"Lucid," she said, surprising herself by being able to talk quite normally. "Better than last night."

A quick smile passed across his face. "You were lucid last night," he said. "Are you hungry? Naomi sent a few provisions with me, but there's not much to choose from."

"Naomi?" she repeated, sitting up. Instantly his wing fell away from her. The sun-warmed air suddenly seemed cool against her bare skin. "When did you speak to Naomi?"

"Yesterday—no, the day before. I went looking for you when Matthew said you were returning with the Edori. She helped me figure out where you were."

"Then she's at Velora?"

"Everyone is. Waiting for us." He laughed softly. "At least, I imagine they're waiting for us. Since I told no one—except Naomi—where I was going, everyone may be frantically searching for my body along the roads and mountains of Bethel."

"So nobody knows where you are?"

"Or where you are. I'm glad I'm not one of the poor bewildered fools left behind to wonder what's happened." He had risen and gone to fetch the leather pouch that held their meager supplies. "We had best make haste back."

She was ravenous. He gave her first choice of the food, and she ate more than her fair share, but he did not seem to begrudge her. He watched her with shadowed eyes. "Sometime you'll have to tell me everything that happened to you at Windy Point."

She thought of the long night barricading the door with her own body, the sessions of near-madness brought on by the ceaseless wind. "Maybe," she said. "But one thing I do need to tell you. Leah—"

"She was there?"

"I didn't see her. Raphael told me—" Rachel took a deep breath. "She's not really the woman he was supposed to marry. Some Jansai princess. He killed that woman and put an angel-seeker in her place."

Gabriel opened his mouth to refute the possibility, then slowly compressed his lips again. "It could be true," he admitted after a moment's stunned thought. "Jansai women are kept closely under wraps—none of us had met her before the wedding. But Rachel, that means—"

"I know," she said. "It's worse than we thought."

"I keep thinking," he murmured, "the Gloria is in just a few days. Then everything will be all right again. But then I think, he's gone to so much trouble already to prevent the Gloria. Surely he won't stop now."

Rachel finished her food quickly and got to her feet. Gabriel stood beside her. "Then let's get back as soon as we can," she said.

He reached for her; the shock of his touch made her tremble involuntarily. He dropped his hand.

"I'm sorry," he said quietly. "I know you're afraid. But there's no other way to get back in time. You'll be safe."

She smiled weakly. "I know," she said, and stepped forward to put her arms around his neck. "I'm not afraid."

At the Eyrie, all was mayhem. Someone had spotted them from a distance, so when they arrived, touching down on the central plateau, nearly a hundred people were awaiting them. Rachel was so weary that she actually clung to Gabriel as he set her on her feet, and he kept an arm around her when he felt her stagger. Voices, faces, questions, demands—images and words all ran together into a blur. Rachel knew that Gabriel had to be at least as tired as she was, yet she heard him field inquiries and rap out quick questions of his own. All she could do was stand there mute and exhausted.

"Here—Hannah—take her to her room. Give her something to make her sleep," Gabriel was saying. He transferred custody of her dead weight to other hands, and someone began leading her away.

"No—" she protested faintly, but in truth it was all she could do to put one foot before the other to navigate the hall. Never before had her own room here felt so welcome.

"Would you like me to help you bathe before you sleep?" Hannah was asking. "You might feel better if you got cleaned up—"

So she looked a fright; what a comfort. "After I sleep," Rachel muttered. "Thank you. I just want—I'm so tired—"

She was asleep before Hannah left the room.

It was late afternoon when she lay down, and night fell and was far advanced before she woke again, wondering where she was. It was not the arrangement of shapes and shadows that reassured her, but the blended voices of the angel singers, sprinkling their lullabies across the Eyrie.

It occurred to her to wonder if she would ever again sleep as soundly, as trustfully, as she had under the shelter of Gabriel's wing, but then she was furious with herself for even thinking about it. She squinched her eyes tightly together to make herself go back to sleep.

It was relatively early when she woke again—an hour or two past dawn. She did not bother with her usual game; the instant she was awake, she opened her eyes and sat up.

"I'm not even going to look in the mirror first," she murmured, standing up and finding all her muscles shaky. "I'm just going to take a bath."

She showered and rinsed, showered and rinsed, in the warm falling stream of the water room. She was combing out her tangled wet hair when she stepped back into her bedroom to find she had company.

"Maga!" she exclaimed.

The angel turned at the sound of her name, then flung herself across the room with her arms outstretched. "Rachel, Rachel, we've been so worried about you! It's so terrible! Raphael—and then you were kidnapped—and I still can't believe what they've been saying."

Rachel laughed. "Calm down. Let me get dressed. Tell me what you've heard and I'll tell you what I know."

Thus it was to Magdalena that Rachel owed her knowledge of what had happened at the landholders' meeting. "Gabriel really threatened to change the face of Samaria with the weather patterns?" she said slowly. "And Ariel has agreed to it?"

Maga nodded, her face troubled. "She doesn't like it—well, she *didn't* like it, but now that we're hearing all these awful stories about Raphael—well, it looks like Gabriel was right all along."

"He is," Rachel said absently. "But have Elijah and Malachi and all the others been told about—me, and Leah, and everything else?"

"I don't know. But I heard—"

"What?"

"They say that people are already starting to gather on the Plain," the angel said in a rush. "Merchants from the river cities, and Jansai clansmen, and Manadavvi . . . And Obadiah came back from the Plain late last night and said Raphael and Saul and some of his angels were already there."

"Raphael's coming to the Gloria?" Rachel said sharply. "But he doesn't even believe in Jovah."

Maga nodded. "Gabriel says he's there for some kind of mischief."

"Oh, no question."

"So he left this morning to see what he could find out."

Rachel had been standing at the mirror, still working out the knots in her hair. Now she turned and stared at the angel. "Ga-

briel's *gone*? But he—I thought he would take me with him—"
Abruptly she closed her mouth.

"He asked if I would bring you as soon as I could. Or Obadiah."

Rachel turned back to the mirror. She was so angry she could scarcely focus on her reflection. Angry with him, angrier with herself. Of course he would leave her without a word; he had done it over and over again. Stupid to think that everything had changed just because of a night spent camping out in the cold. He would have kept anyone warm with a fold of his wing; it was merely a measure of courtesy. "I'd prefer to travel with the Edori," she said. "They'll be leaving for the Plain today, I'm sure. We'll arrive in plenty of time."

"But Rachel. Gabriel said—"

"Gabriel," said Rachel incontrovertibly, "is not here."

There was a flurry of attention to endure when she did finally emerge from her room, a troubled Magdalena at her heels, but Rachel bore that well enough. She did not mind so much when it was Hannah and Matthew and Obadiah inquiring after her adventures, but even so she did not have much patience for the constant retelling. She wanted to get to Velora quickly, back to Naomi's tent, back to the Edori who cared for her.

She even allowed Obadiah to ferry her down to the city, and found a moment to wonder why she had ever been afraid to be carried up and down that insignificant mountain.

"You've changed," Obadiah said quizzically, cradling her perhaps a bit closer than necessary against his chest. "Time was you'd have been faint or furious by the time we landed."

"I've flown so much lately, I'm beginning to feel like an angel myself," she responded in the same light tone. "Heights do not frighten me at all anymore."

"Truly? Then let me take you for a little ride—" He dipped and spun crazily in the air, causing her to shriek and clutch his neck.

"Stop it! Stop it!" she cried, pretending to strangle him. But she was laughing; he was not alarmed. He did, however, resume normal flying after a breathless moment or two.

"If you aren't afraid, why won't you let me fly you to the Plain?" he asked. "Or Maga. Although I'm stronger than Maga. I should really be your first choice."

"I want to travel with the Edori," she said.

He touched down, a somewhat more graceful landing than the two she had experienced in Gabriel's arms. Then again, Obadiah probably had had more practice taking women on pleasure jaunts through the Samarian skies.

"You just want to make Gabriel mad," he said calmly. "As usual."

She was about to deny it, and then she smiled. "And do you think I'll succeed?" she asked.

"Oh, yes," he said. "As usual."

He had brought her directly to the Edori camp, and he waited long enough for Rachel to introduce him to Naomi, Luke and their brood. Naomi, Rachel could see, was surprised to learn that she would be responsible for bringing the angelica to the Plain of Sharon, but she covered her surprise quite nicely until the angel had left. And then she waited till she had heard every last word of Rachel's escapades before she took up the matter of travel arrangements.

"A frightening, evil man," was her grave pronouncement on the Archangel's machinations. "It terrifies me to think he has for so long acted as the link between the god and men."

"Jovah is gracious," Rachel murmured, "to care for us still."

"Gabriel came here—did he tell you?—looking for you," Naomi said. "I told him what you'd said about Raphael destroying your village. And he believed me. And that's when I got really scared."

"He believed me, too," Rachel said. "But I had stopped being scared by then, because at that point I was with Gabriel."

"Which brings us to the most interesting question of all," Naomi said. "Why aren't you with Gabriel now?"

"Because he left this morning while I was still sleeping," said Rachel coolly. "Leaving orders that I was to get to the Plain as fast as I could."

"So why didn't you go with that nice blond boy who brought you here? Or I'm sure one of the other angels would have taken you—"

"I'd rather go with you."

Naomi leaned forward to try and read secrets in Rachel's closed face. "Arguing with him again?" she said softly. "Or is it still? You can't miss the Gloria, you know. You really can't."

"I don't want to miss it. We'll get there in plenty of time. If we start right away."

"I liked him, Rachel," Naomi continued. "He really is beautiful."

"Very," Rachel said dryly.

"He was so frightened for you. He seemed—when we realized where you were—he looked as if he had been stricken blind. He took my hand to help him keep his balance."

"He *what*? He did not."

"It's true as Yovah's mercy."

Rachel shook her head impatiently. "What do you have left that needs packing? I'll help you. We do have to leave within the hour."

And she turned away to survey the neat tent. She pretended not to hear Naomi's whispered words. "So you do love him. I thought you did."

The Chievens made excellent time traveling to the Plain of Sharon. They were a small clan with few elders, able to cover ground quickly. It was a trip that normally took about four days, but they made it in three and a half, arriving the afternoon before the morning that the Gloria was scheduled to be sung. Rachel felt a certain amount of guilt for cutting it quite so close, but she had not missed the nearly omnipresent shadow of angel wings overhead during their entire journey. Gabriel had sent someone to watch over her, and if she had dawdled too long on the road, he would have had that someone carry her willy-nilly to the Plain. She couldn't decide if the knowledge pleased or enraged her.

At any rate, early that afternoon, they crossed the low peaks that formed the southwest boundary of the Plain, and descended into the huge, bowl-shaped arena. There were already at least five thousand people camped in the wide, grassy valley, and their tents and standards made gay, colorful patterns against the luxuriant grass. The sun, canting just a little to the west, picked out the blue, violet and rose-quartz colors of the stubby mountains that formed a ring around the whole Plain. Only one peak possessed any claim to height, and that was the Galo mountain, tallest in Samaria, which hid the icy source of the Galilee River. The rest were easy grades, little more than foothills, slaty and amiable in the spring sun.

"Well, we're here," Naomi said as they picked their way through the thick grass. "Now everyone can stop worrying."

But, as they shortly learned, even Rachel's arrival could not alleviate the worries that had accumulated at the Plain of Sharon in the past few days.

CHAPTER NINETEEN

Gabriel had been sound asleep when Obadiah and Nathan burst in upon him, Nathan clearly just startled from his own bed and Obadiah showing the unmistakable signs of a long hard flight. He knew there was trouble before either of them spoke.

"Gabriel, Raphael's at the Plain of Sharon," Nathan exclaimed before Obadiah could open his mouth.

"*And* most of his angels," Obadiah said.

Gabriel swung himself out of bed, by sheer willpower overcoming his lingering exhaustion. "Did you speak to him? What did he say?"

"I saw him making the rounds of the Manadavvi camps. You know how he likes to spread his golden presence over all the landholders at events like this. Only, this time—"

"It's not his event," Gabriel finished.

"And we didn't expect him there at all," Nathan added.

"Oh, I expected him," Gabriel said wearily. "I just couldn't get there any quicker. He must have left Windy Point almost as soon as we did. Sooner, maybe. Maybe he doesn't even know Rachel got free . . . Did you speak to him at all, Obadiah? Hear what he had to say?"

The blond angel shook his head. "I just took off for here. I didn't want him to—well, I thought he might try to stop me. Not that I'm afraid of him."

"Well, you should be afraid of him. We all should be," Gabriel said. "All right. Nathan, come with me. We leave for the Plain in thirty minutes."

"I'm coming back with you," Obadiah said.

"No. You stay here, sleep, follow us as quickly as you can."

"Bring Rachel," Nathan said.

Obadiah nodded. "Of course."

Gabriel looked for a moment at the worn familiar floor. Rachel . . . If he did not wake her to tell her this news, she would never forgive him. And how could he leave her? During that long flight back he had marveled at how quietly she lay in his arms, as if she trusted him, as if she felt safe with him. He had thought of the hundreds of things he would tell her as soon as they returned to the solid ground and peaceful setting of the Eyrie. How fearful he had been for her safety, how greatly he regretted his angry words the week before she left, how she had come to mean more to him than he had expected, than he had thought possible . . . And then they had landed in the midst of a crowd and she had left with Hannah, and now he would be disappearing on a mission that he could not delay. But he knew Rachel. She would expect him to have delayed long enough to say goodbye.

"Bring Rachel," he said softly, "if she'll come."

There were more than a few people already gathered on the Plain of Sharon. There were hundreds. Arriving around the noon hour, from the air Gabriel identified most Manadavvi clan standards, as well as banners from Jansai towns, the river cities and Luminaux. Edori camps with their distinctive dark tents were clustered on the northwest edge of the Plain; independent farmers and homesteaders banded together for companionship in small groups among the larger ones. More horses and caravans and wayfarers on foot breached the mountain passes from all directions even as he circled down for a landing.

"Now what?" Nathan said, touching down a few yards away. "Are you going to confront him? And say what? Anyone can come to a Gloria, you know. Everyone is welcome."

"Ariel's here," was Gabriel's brief reply. "First I'm going to ask her if she's heard anything."

They found the Monteverde pavilion easily enough, its gold and emerald flags snapping smartly in the light wind. Angels and mortals milled together in hopeless confusion, but one of the younger angels quickly located Ariel for them.

"Good, you're here," was Ariel's greeting. "Did you bring Maga? Or is she still at the Eyrie?"

"I left her with Rachel," Gabriel replied. "What's going on here? Have you talked to Raphael?"

Ariel shook her head. "He won't talk to me—and none of the Manadavvi will tell me what tales he's been spreading among them, either. I know there's something going on, because they're all looking ruffled and secretive. But—what can he do, really? He can't stop the Gloria, can he?"

"Is Josiah here?"

"Yes, and Jezebel and Ezekiel as well," she said, naming the oracles who served Gaza and Jordana. "Why? Do you think they know something?"

"They know a lot of things," Gabriel said with a faint smile. "Take me to them, please."

The oracles and perhaps a combined dozen of their acolytes had set up camp in white tents directly in the shadow of the Galo mountain. Josiah, the eldest of the three, had the largest tent with the most lavish furnishings. Jezebel and Ezekiel, the angels found, were already with him.

"Gabriel. I'm glad you're here," was Josiah's welcome. Gabriel nodded to him, then made a quick, formal greeting to the white-haired half-blind Ezekiel. He was a good five years younger than Josiah but far less able; he should have been replaced ten years ago, Gabriel thought. And then he grimaced. Clearly Raphael had not cared what sage served him, since he did not believe the seer had any useful function at all. Next, Gabriel shook hands with Jezebel, a solemn, dark-haired woman nearly his own age. Ariel had more than once called Jezebel the smartest person she knew.

"I couldn't get here any sooner," Gabriel said. The angels all settled as comfortably as possible on stools set out by the silent acolytes. "What have any of you heard? Why is Raphael here?"

"He does not believe in the god," Ezekiel said in his thin, quavering voice. "He does not believe the god can punish him."

"Yes, I've learned that," Gabriel said. "But—"

"He does not believe the god can punish any of us," Josiah said quietly. "And he wants to put his theories to the test."

"In what possible manner?"

"He wants to suspend the Gloria," Jezebel said. "To prove

to you—and us—and everyone, that the god does not listen, does not strike and does not even exist."

Gabriel could only stare at her.

"How do you know this?" Ariel demanded.

"He summoned us to the mountain this morning," Jezebel began.

"The mountain?"

"He and his host have made camp on the top of Galo mountain, the very place where the thunderbolt will fall if the Gloria is not sung—if indeed the god exists, and listens, and is willing to punish us for disobedience," the Gaza oracle continued.

"And his plan—no, his offer, is this," Josiah said, taking up the tale. "He and his angels will wait on the mountain until nightfall tomorrow. If the thunderbolt does not fall at sundown as promised, we—you, I, all of us—will admit there is no god, and we will cede to Raphael such power as he is able to take and keep over all the landholders of Samaria. The angels will disperse, the oracles will leave their mountaintops, we will give up all claims to divine connection. And all will know there is no god."

"Sweet Jovah singing," Ariel whispered.

"And if we don't agree to this?" Gabriel demanded. "If we say, 'This is a risk we are not willing to take' and we sing? How can he stop us? We are hundreds of voices and he is but a few."

"He has fashioned—weapons of some sort," Jezebel said. "He demonstrated their power to us on the mountaintop. They look like long, hollow wooden tubes, except they are not of wood, and they throw fire a hundred yards away."

"Fire!"

"And whatever that fire touches, burns. I saw Saul throw fire at a bush, at a rock and at a flying bird, and each thing flamed and disintegrated into ashes. It was frightening."

"If we do not agree to his terms, he says he will turn the fire tubes onto the people gathered on the Plain for the Gloria," Josiah said quietly. "He says if we are afraid of conflagration, we shall have it one way or another, if we do not do as he says."

Gabriel sat staring at the canvas flooring beneath his feet. There seemed to be no way out—there was death and disharmony down any of these limited paths, and it was Raphael who had shepherded them to this bloody crossroad. How could he allow Raphael to turn strange weapons against helpless, trusting people? Yet how could he stand by, and let the god's deadline pass, and open the whole world to destruction? For when that thunderbolt struck the mountain, who could tell how severe its power would be, where the reverberations of its force might echo?

And if the thunderbolt did not fall—?

He looked up to find everyone else in the tent anxiously watching him. Even Ezekiel had his milky blue eyes turned his way. There was to be no debate, apparently. They waited for him to decide.

"We have no choice," he said quietly. "We have to let the deadline pass. We will watch in silence as the sun goes down, and see if the god does indeed destroy the mountain—and Raphael and every last angel standing beside him."

"Gabriel," Nathan said in an urgent voice. "We could—you and I, a dozen of us—could fly to some other point. Hagar's retreat, perhaps, where Jovah's ear is sensitively attuned. Raphael would not hear us there. We could sing a small Gloria, loud enough to avert disaster—Jovah would understand—"

Gabriel shook his head. "It is the worst thing we could do," he said gently. "For if Jovah heard, and spared us, he would be sparing Raphael as well. And the Archangel would believe for certain there was no god, and the people gathered on the Plain would believe Raphael, and all Samaria would fall into chaos and dissonance anyway."

Jezebel was watching him with her calm dark eyes. "And if we wait on the Plain in silence, and the sun goes down, and no thunderbolt falls on Raphael? What happens to all of us then?"

"Then we will know," Gabriel said simply. "And if it is true there is no god, and for five centuries we have worshipped nothing but a myth, then it is time we learned that."

"If no thunderbolt falls, and Raphael declares himself ruler of the world, we have some grave problems," the Gaza oracle continued. "For he is not the man to lay aside a weapon once he has discovered how to use it."

Gabriel nodded. "Yes. I realize that. Even if we learn that there is no god, we will have to find some way to contain Raphael. At the moment I have no ideas."

"But, Gabriel, the lightning will strike, won't it?" Ariel asked, her voice very troubled. He thought it strange that she directed the question at him, and not at one of the oracles. "When we disobey the god, he will punish us—he will smite the mountaintop, he will cause the rivers to rage. He watches over us and hears us and responds to our actions. I have believed that my whole life. Surely it is true?"

He looked over at her, his favorite friend, the angel to whom he felt closer than any other except his brother. "Are you asking me if there is a god?" he said, still in that soft voice. "All I can say is, I believe there is. I feel him when I sing. He has responded to my prayers countless times. He guides my actions and he dwells in my heart. I know he is there."

He paused a moment. "But will he smite the mountaintop?" he continued. "Will he indeed turn wrathful at our disobedience and strike us down for our loss of harmony? I don't know. Perhaps his power is not as great as we have always believed. Perhaps he loves us too much to punish us by fire and death even when we have disobeyed him. Perhaps, for some reason, he wants our faith to fail and a false Archangel to rule Samaria for twenty more years, or fifty. His ways are inscrutable to me. I do not know that the thunderbolt will fall."

He took a deep breath and looked around the tent. They were all still watching him, their faces tense, worried, speculating on potential horror. But they were all listening to him, as if only he of all the angels on Samaria could have the answers, speak the truth.

"But I believe it will," he said, "and then we shall know the wrath and might of Jovah."

Rachel did not return with Obadiah, of course, so he sent the angel back to watch over her journey.

"Shall I fly above her at a discreet distance?" Obadiah inquired.

"Don't bother," Gabriel said. "Even if she doesn't see you, she'll know I sent you."

"At what point do I swoop down and carry her back to the Plain?"

"If they have no chance of arriving here by tomorrow night." Gabriel hesitated, then added, "If that becomes necessary, try not to frighten her."

Obadiah laughed incredulously. "Frighten Rachel?" he said. "It can't be done."

Only one small part of him was free to fret over Rachel, however. Another small corner of his mind noted that Maga had returned with Obadiah and been welcomed by Nathan with a gesture that would definitely be classified as an embrace. He wanted to express his severe displeasure, but he did not have the time, or the heart.

If the world is to end in a day or two anyway, he thought, *they may as well have their kisses now.* The thought was unutterably depressing.

He had no time to think of Nathan or even Rachel, because the situation, which had been as bad as he thought possible, overnight had gotten worse.

He had gone to the Manadavvi camp to seek out Elijah and Abel, to try to make some kind of peace with them now that Raphael had so obviously lost his mind. He found them preparing to depart.

For Mount Galo.

Elijah greeted him with cool aplomb. "I am sure you have come to debate theology with me again, Gabriel," he said. "And of course I enjoyed it so much last time. But, as you can see, I am in a hurry."

It had been a moment before Gabriel realized where the landowner was heading. "You're going to the mountain," he said flatly. "To stand beside Raphael and defy the thunderbolts."

Elijah nodded. "Exactly," he said. "Raphael has made it very clear that those who stand with him will reap tremendous rewards. Those who doubt him will be overlooked. I have spent a lifetime accumulating my wealth. I am not ready to lose it over such a simple test."

"A simple test—! Elijah, don't you know, don't you fear—?"

"I know that you cannot prove to me there is a god, and Raphael can prove there is not," the Manadavvi cut in. "I am tired of being governed by sanctimonious angels who flap their wings at me and murmur of Jovah's might. Well, I too am mighty, and I am not afraid. And you will find I am not the only one who welcomes this chance to defy you and laugh in the face of the god."

And that proved to be true. Gabriel spent the next two days among the powermongers, the Manadavvi, the Jansai, the rivermen, and was dismayed to find how many of them had defected. Oh, Malachi and Jethro and the others were no surprise, but there were more—small, petty landowners who saw a chance to increase their holdings by joining the renegade Archangel. Even a few independent farmers and herders had decided to make the hard climb to the top of Mount Galo, to prove their allegiance to Raphael and their defiance of Jovah.

Those who stayed behind were fearful, accusatory and close to panic, as Gabriel also quickly found. They bombarded him with questions and demands—"Is there a god? Can you save us? How can you let Raphael imperil us all? Call down the lightning now, prove to us that Jovah is strong"—and he soothed them as best he could, which was not very well. He set the other angels to the same task, so that the wide wings hovered over every campfire, brushed every small tent, spreading calm, spreading hope, what little there was of either.

He had been surprised to find young Lord Daniel of Semorrah still in his father's tent near the other rivermen. Gabriel had never had a high opinion of Daniel, thinking him just his father's shadow, and he said as much in his greeting.

"So your father hedged his bets, did he?" he asked. "He stands beside the Archangel and you wait on the Plain with me. Either way, one of you survives and safeguards the family coffers."

Daniel turned a pale, strained face to the angel. "That was my father's thought when I refused to accompany him," he admitted. "But I—I do not wish to die in a blaze of white light when the god shows his anger. I had rather live, even without the wealth and glory."

"So you believe, then?"

Daniel clenched his hand. "Unwillingly. I would rather not believe. But I am afraid to go to the mountain and wait for the sun to go down. I am afraid of what will happen to my wife and baby when the world is destroyed."

Gabriel glanced around the plush tent, trying to remember who Daniel's wife was. Ah yes, the colorless Lady Mary, at whose wedding he had discovered his own bride . . . Then the child must still be in the womb, and the mother had not had the strength to make this arduous journey. "How many of your father's people have gone with him to the mountain?"

"Enough," said Daniel bitterly. "Enough so that if Raphael does speak truth and the god does not act, I am disgraced and ridiculed forever. But I—" He shook his head. "I cannot go."

"I cannot go, either," Gabriel said softly. "And I would not if I could. Those of us who remain behind will have a greatly changed world to attend to after the thunderbolt does its damage."

The young man raised his eyes to the angel's. "It will fall, then?"

"It will fall."

Rachel had arrived with her escort several hours before Gabriel was free to seek her out. He had met again with the oracles and the other angels, discussing what else they could do that they had left undone. They could think of nothing. All of them were obsessed with thoughts of the morrow, the day of the Gloria, the day which this year would pass in silence.

The day which would end, one way or another, in disaster.

It was sunset before Gabriel made his way to the Chieven campsite on the outskirts of the big Edori conglomeration. Rachel was adding wood to the fire. Naomi was cutting up food for a cauldron, and Luke was working behind the tent canvas, rearranging spikes and guys.

Naomi saw him first and smiled. "Have you come to have dinner with us, angelo?" she asked gaily. But her eyes warned him. He nodded at her briefly.

"I came to inquire after your journey," he said. "You made good time."

The Edori woman laughed. Rachel had straightened quickly at Naomi's hail, and now she stood uncertainly, listening to the light tone of their talk. Plainly she did not like it. "We did not dare to be late," Naomi said. "Not with the angelica in our charge."

"I thank you for bringing her safely to me," Gabriel said quietly.

"And you will eat with us? Luke used to say I was the worst cook of the Chievens, but I have greatly improved, I assure you. And Rachel has made two dishes that are delicious. There is no end to her talents."

"As I constantly learn," he said. "Yes, thank you. I'll be glad to join you for the evening meal."

Rachel could stand it no longer. "Gabriel, we've heard strange things since we arrived," she said. "They say that Raphael has taken shelter on the Galo mountain and that there will be no Gloria sung tomorrow—"

"All true," he said. He could not resist adding maliciously, "So you need not have hurried quite so fast to get here."

She shook her head impatiently. Her hair was gold in the firelight. He remembered the silken feel of it against his arms, against his chest. "Gabriel! So what happens tomorrow?"

If you had been here, you would have heard this whole discussion as it occurred, he wanted to say. "Tomorrow we wait," he said gravely. "At sundown, the god strikes or does not strike, as he chooses. And then we either acknowledge Raphael as our leader—or we try to pin the world back in place. Tonight there is nothing I can do about any of it."

Luke came around the tent corner hauling a carved stump of wood. "Don't see how you can sit on the ground with those wings," he said doubtfully. "So you might try this—but it won't hold you much higher. One way or the other, you won't be so comfortable."

"Nonsense, I can sit on the ground and spread my wings behind me," Gabriel said pleasantly. "I have done it before. Where would you like me to sit?"

"We're not quite ready yet," Naomi said. "In a minute."

The girls came giggling out of the tent just then, half shy and half flirtatious, and made quick curtseys to him upon their mother's command. Naomi handed him a plate and a fork, Luke explained to him the construction of the tent, the girls joined in the conversation at intervals. One of them actually tugged at his hand once to get his attention when their father had talked too long. He smiled down at her, grinned at Naomi, listened courteously to Luke.

All this time, Rachel did not say a word. She was furious, he knew, that he would come to this place, invade her haven, charm her friends, leaving her no place to run that he could not follow. It was as much Naomi's doing as his own, and Rachel would realize that, too. Well, let her rage. He was here, he would stay, he would make it very clear that there *was* no place on Samaria she could run where he could not retrieve her. He had found her in Semorrah, he had found her at Windy Point, he had found her with the Edori. When would she learn? He was behind her at every turn.

"Dinner," Naomi said, and they sat down in a haphazard circle a few feet from the fire. Gabriel waited until Rachel had taken her place and then settled down beside her. He swept his great wings carefully behind him, yet there was no way to keep them completely out of the way. One of them settled lightly over Rachel's shoulders; he felt her involuntary start, though she did not, as he half expected, leap to her feet and move elsewhere. Naomi's youngest daughter sat on his other side, glancing behind her at the white feathered wall so close to her shoulder. He smiled down at her. She smiled happily back.

"Will you sing, angelo?" Luke asked.

Gabriel shook his head. "I am a guest here. Please, you pray."

He intercepted Naomi's glance at Rachel, but Rachel shook her head. So, none of the famed duets, not tonight, not for him. Naomi sang instead, a quick sweet Edori prayer of thanksgiving. He listened appreciatively.

"I hope yours will be one of the voices raised to Jovah when the Gloria is finally sung," he said, when the prayer was over and they had begun to pass the food.

"She not only sings, she writes songs," Luke said.

"Really? I would like to hear some."

"You just heard one."

Naomi appeared to be blushing. "Oh, hush, Luke," she said. "I will sing, gladly, but when will the Gloria be held? If not tomorrow—"

"According to the Librera, we have three days," Gabriel said. "And then the bolt falls again."

"So—the day after tomorrow—"

"Or the day after that. If the mountain really is destroyed, I foresee at least a day of turmoil and mayhem. That will take some calming before people are ready to lift their voices in prayer."

"What will you sing?"

Gabriel indicated his wife with a slight motion of his head. "That is up to the angelica."

Naomi addressed her friend directly. "Raheli? Have you decided?"

Rachel's voice was so low it was almost inaudible. "No."

Naomi was laughing. "Well, have you *practiced*? Do you have any ideas?"

"I've practiced," Rachel said, still in that quiet voice. "I will know what to sing when the time comes."

It was not the most relaxed meal Gabriel had ever had in his life, and yet he was strangely comfortable and loath to leave when it was over. As soon as the last child laid her fork down, Rachel was on her feet, gathering plates and taking them to the water bucket for washing.

"You girls help Raheli with the dishes," Naomi directed. "Luke, could you add more wood to the fire? It will be a cool night."

When the others had left them, Gabriel and Naomi sat face to face in the dark. The others were close enough to overhear, so they talked very softly. "She says she is staying in our tent till it is time for the singing," Naomi said. "I know she should be with you—"

"There is a place set up for her in my pavilion," he replied. "Perhaps she will choose to use it in a day or so." He smiled briefly. "It's a little crowded here."

Naomi laughed. "The Edori like it crowded."

"Tomorrow as the sun begins to set, we will gather and watch the top of the mountain. Bring her with you and wait with us. We should all be together when the god makes his will known."

Naomi rose to her feet with her usual sturdy grace. "I'm glad you came to us tonight," she said. "She would have been so hurt if you had not."

"Yes," he said, also rising. "I think I am at last beginning to understand her."

"It's not very hard," Naomi said. "She's afraid to want anything because everything she's ever loved has been taken away."

"And she would rather show anger than fear."

"Yes," said Naomi. "And those are the keys to Rachel."

He left Naomi and crossed to where Rachel stood, drying dishes with the girls. "Walk with me a few steps," he said. "I must go back."

She was startled to be asked; she had no easy refusal ready. Handing her drying cloth to the youngest girl, she followed Gabriel onto the unlit Plain until he came to a halt.

"The Eyrie pavilion is that way, under the blue awning," he said, pointing. "I wish you would come stay with us. You have your own place already set up. You could bring Naomi if you like."

"I'm happy where I am," she said instantly.

"You know I had no choice but to come here," he said somberly, studying what little of her face he could see by the scattered starlight. "I did not abandon you in the Eyrie. But I had no choice. I had to come."

She took a step backward but he caught her wrist, holding her there. "It shall be as you choose," he said. "You stay with me, or you stay with them—now, and once the Gloria is sung. But don't think you can hide from me, wherever you go. There is not a place in Samaria—not in the mountains or the valleys, not in the rivers or the plains—not in Ysral, should you be able to sail to it—where you could go and leave me behind. And if I leave you, for any reason," he added, tightening his grip as she struggled to free her hand, "I will return to you. That is as certain as the sun rising tomorrow morning and the thunderbolt falling tomorrow night. That is as sure as the god's existence. I will come back to you, or I will find you—over and over again, as often as we are parted, until the end of the world itself."

If she had an answer to that, she was not allowed to speak it. He drew her so swiftly into his arms that she did not have time to pull free. His wings wrapped around them both; they stood in a shell of white feathers, warm, protected. He bent his head and kissed her, feeling a savage excitement kick through him, feeling the sharp heat flare in his arm, feeling his whole body dissolve. The starlight changed over them while he laid his kiss upon her mouth; the constellations moved before he lifted his head.

When he finally dropped his arms, she stumbled back a little, to be caught by the net of his wings, still folded around them. She stared up at him with an expression so intense he could not read it, but still she did not speak.

"Remember," he said, and gradually folded his wings back. "You were chosen for me, and you are mine."

He was not surprised when she turned and ran back for the Edori camp without uttering a word. He watched till she was safely within the perimeter of firelight and Naomi had come over with her hands outstretched. Then he took two running steps and flung himself into the air.

He would fly the icy currents until he was too weary to think. And he wanted to be as close to his god as possible while he reordered his troubled, giddy mind.

CHAPTER TWENTY

It was a truly awful day.

Since she had scarcely slept for the entire night, Rachel could not indulge in her usual game of holding back conscious thought during the first moments she was awake. She had been thinking all night, haunted by an endless cycle of worry and speculation. *What if the thunderbolt falls? Will it bring the whole mountain crashing down? What if it doesn't fall? Raphael becomes lord over all Samaria for as long as he lives. It has to fall. But what if it doesn't fall?* Every scene of her life in which Raphael had figured replayed itself repeatedly in her head. The destruction of her parents' village, the sharp conversation on her wedding day, the terrible dinner at Windy Point—always, gold and laughing, he stood before her, catching her in his filmy wings and then flinging her off some unimaginable height. . . .

At moments like these it was almost a relief to have thoughts of Gabriel intrude, though these memories were almost as unsettling. She squirmed on the hard bed and tried not to make too much noise as she attempted to get more comfortable. But there was no getting comfortable.

Well, he had kissed her. Had wrapped those ivory wings around her and held her so closely that she was smothered in white. At any rate, something had made it impossible to breathe. And he had kissed her . . .

She turned again, wholly tangled up now in her thin blanket. She thought perhaps she had just bumped someone's head but no one uttered a sleepy accusation. She tried to lie still, tried to empty her mind. Perhaps sleep would yet come.

But it was the words before the kiss that had really undone her. *You were chosen for me, and you are mine.* As if he no longer regretted Jovah's selection, as if he had never really hated her, as if he had come to love her.

Sweet god singing, if she ever allowed herself to love Gabriel, she would die of it. She would expire in a sapphire and alabaster haze. He would make her over, or she would give herself over to him; she would be a flute that responded to a single voice, a harp shaped to a possessive hand.

She would have liked to get up in the middle of the night and steal from the campground, running to some far finger of land where even Gabriel (should he choose to look) could not find her—but tomorrow would very possibly be the end of the world, and she was pledged to stay and watch it.

So she fought with her blanket a little more, then gave up and watched dawn filter through the dark roof of the tent, and remembered.

The day itself was the longest, slowest, most nerve-racking stretch of time she had ever endured. Her only comfort was that it was just as bad for everyone else.

She was the first one up, and had the little Chieven campsite to herself for a while, but every other Edori who emerged in the next couple of hours followed her actions exactly. They stepped from their tents, looked up at the mountain for a long time, glanced away, and then, as if they could not help themselves, looked back. There was nothing to be seen on that high, hazy peak, but it drew all eyes. There, the renegade angels and mortals waited; there, the god would strike—or would not. There, the fate of the world rested.

"I'll go mad before sunset," Naomi said only a few minutes after they had breakfasted.

"Before noon," Rachel said. "We must find distractions."

Luke elected to stay behind and see to the camp, but Rachel, Naomi and the girls walked two miles across the Plain to the place where most of Velora was bivouacked. Peter and all of the students were there, having arrived an hour or two behind Rachel the day before. Spotting her from a distance, Katie and Nate and ten of the others came running up, forming a milling, vociferous circle around her.

"Angela, angela! You was took by the bad angels! Angela, will the fire rain down today? Will the god blow them all off the mountaintop—?"

It had been weeks since she had seen any of them; they looked half-wild and very young. Laughing, she hugged as many as she could get her arms around.

"I don't know what will happen today— Yes, they took me to Windy Point, but I escaped. It was very exciting. Have you all been studying? Have you been practicing your songs?"

Peter approached and eyed her ruefully over the tops of the bobbing heads. "This will be a hard day for them to get through," he remarked.

"Hard for all of us," Rachel said. "But I thought it might be easier here than just standing and watching the mountain."

She introduced Naomi and the girls, who were instant favorites; the street children were fascinated by all things Edori. Matthew had also come to spend the day with the schoolchildren, so he and Naomi and Rachel spent several hours teaching them Edori games and songs. The lunch hour arrived, and it took a while to cook and distribute the meal, and so that passed some time; and then Rachel and Peter insisted on holding a few regular classes, which the children protested but eventually agreed to. And then they played games again and the children practiced their new Edori songs, and then it was dinnertime, and most of the day had been gotten through.

There had been, meanwhile, a fair amount of activity on the Galo mountain. Rachel knew this—everybody knew this—because no one had been able to keep from watching the gray peak more or less constantly. Mostly the activity was of the mortal variety, as bodies could be seen toiling up the slope in ones and twos. Defectors, opportunists, atheists, power-seekers, angel-seekers—a motley, villainous assortment Raphael was drawing to his cause, Rachel thought. Still, it was frightening to think there were that many people who believed him when he said there was no god—who were willing to chance death to make a fortune.

Now and then one of the rogue angels made an appearance, lifting gracefully off the mountain and gliding over the Plain in slow, lazy circles. Although she knew Raphael could no longer have any interest in taking her—he was playing an entirely different game now—Rachel could not help feeling a little thrill of terror every time those sinister, soundless wings made a shadow across her face. She would never feel safe while Raphael was alive.

However long that might be.

It occurred to her to wonder if, bad as it was this day on the Plain, it was not even worse on the mountaintop. Surely it was no easy thing to sit on the site of proposed destruction and while away the hours. She remembered the nightmarish scene of revelry she had witnessed that one night at Windy Point. Perhaps they had all passed the day drinking wine and merrymaking, sure that the sunset would bring them limitless power—and not caring if it brought them death.

As the interminable day at last began lengthening into a sultry, golden twilight, the angels camped on the Plain also began circulating, visiting each individual campsite. Obadiah and Nathan swirled down before Peter's camp, to the delight of the cheering schoolchildren.

"Gabriel wants everyone to move as far north as possible," Nathan said without preamble. "He's afraid the mountain will crumble after the thunderbolt falls, and anyone near it will be crushed."

"Do you need help packing and moving your things?" Obadiah asked.

Peter glanced around. The children had already raced away to begin rolling up their clothes and sleeping bags. "No . . . Actually, the move will be a welcome diversion. It has been a long day."

"It has indeed," Nathan said solemnly. Obadiah caught Rachel's eye and winked. Somehow, she felt heartened.

"Us, too," Naomi said, calling her daughters over. "It looks like we should move our things."

Rachel trudged back with her, helped pack up the bags, strike the tent, scatter the fire and load the ponies. But over and over again her eyes turned upward—not to the mountain, where the renegades gathered, but to the cobalt sky where a single angel flew in measured, sweeping turns over and over again around the perimeter of the Plain.

He had been aloft since shortly after lunchtime, and since he had taken flight, none of Raphael's angels had swept mockingly across the bowl of the meadow. Which was why, no doubt, he had taken wing, establishing his possession over the Plain, declaring himself the leader, the symbol of the faithful followers of

Jovah camped out below. Although she could not hear him, Rachel knew he had spent these last few hours in quiet, uninterrupted prayer. The Kiss in her arm burned with a faint, steady fire. She always knew when Gabriel was singing.

What did he pray for now? she wondered. For the god to strike, or for the god to withhold his might? She could not imagine Gabriel invoking Jovah's wrath, begging for death and destruction, even to confound his enemies. No, that was more in her line, she who had so much anger in her heart. Gabriel might ask the god, even now, even a short hour before sunset, to light Raphael's way, to pour balm and grace and beauty into his heart, to open his eyes, to make him believe. Either that, or he was praying for the safety of all those others in his charge, asking that the mountain not fall on them, that they be rewarded for their piety.

Whatever he sang, whatever he prayed for, he was a magnificent sight, and Rachel could not keep her eyes off him.

It was a huge, disorganized, muddled group that eventually rearranged itself on the north side of the Plain of Sharon only thirty minutes or so before the sun would go down. It was not so strange that Rachel, finding herself between Manadavvi and rivermen, should turn away from them, take a few steps in another direction, and discover herself somehow with the group she had avoided since her arrival on the Plain: the angels of Monteverde and the Eyrie.

It was as if they didn't notice her return, or as if she had never left, for those who saw her or accidentally brushed against her nodded casually or made some offhand comment. "At least the weather was fine all day," one of Ariel's angels said to her in an idle way. Eva asked her if she wanted something to eat. Someone else told her she should put on heavier shoes because "it gets cold when the sun goes down."

Obadiah stopped, and frowned down at her, but not as if he were mulling over any of her recent sins. "Have you seen Judith today?" he asked abruptly.

Rachel hadn't even thought of Judith in weeks. "No. Was she here?"

He nodded. "She came in with Magdalena, I'm sure of it. And she was here yesterday. But no one remembers seeing her today."

Rachel gave one quick, perfunctory glance around the angel

pavilion. "Well, I suppose she could be taking a nap or something—"

Obadiah gave her an ironic look. "Twenty minutes before the world ends? I don't think so."

Rachel patted her mouth, simulating a yawn. "I'm a little tired myself."

But he was genuinely worried. "I don't know where she could be," he said.

"Do you care so much?" she asked curiously.

He was defensive. "I know she's difficult and spiteful. But she— You are not so happy with your own life, and hers has not been much easier. There are reasons she is as she is."

"No doubt," Rachel said dryly, then added, "I haven't seen her, but she must be here somewhere. Judith is never far from the angels."

He stared down at her a moment, a strange, stricken expression on his face. As one, they turned their eyes to the high gray mountain.

"Surely not," Rachel said softly.

"She always liked Raphael," Obadiah murmured. "He always flirted with her, which Gabriel never did. She's not really an angel-seeker, you know, but she does like to be around the angels—"

Rachel laid a hand on his arm. "If she's there now, you can't do anything for her," she said. "If she went there, she chose to go."

"Maybe not," he said. "Maybe she was merely walking alone across the Plain, and Saul or Raphael swept down—"

"Gabriel has been patrolling the Plain all afternoon," Rachel told him gently. "And Raphael has gathered enough nonbelievers to his cause. He has no need to take prisoners."

"But she'll die," Obadiah whispered.

"All of us may die, when the mountain comes down," Rachel said. "We have all made our choices."

He still looked so miserable that she put her arms around him, carefully sliding her hands under the silken wings. She pressed him to her, patting him on the back. He dropped his blond head to rest it on top of hers, and hugged her in return. She had rarely tried to give anyone comfort before. It amazed her that it was such an easy thing to do.

But when, still wrapped in that friendly embrace, she lifted her eyes a fraction, she saw that Gabriel had landed and was standing not five feet away from her, watching her with close attention. Slowly she turned her gaze away from him and pulled herself from Obadiah's arms.

"How much time now?" she asked, looking up into his sad face.

"Fifteen minutes, maybe," he said.

She ran her hands for warmth swiftly up and down her bare arms. "It seems to be getting cooler. And—it's harder to breathe. It feels the way it feels before a storm."

He nodded. "The clouds are gathering high above the Plain. See? Black clouds. Storm clouds."

"So high," Rachel murmured. "Even if they held lightning, it couldn't strike the earth from there."

"Maybe. Maybe—"

Rachel glanced once more around the camp. Gabriel had moved away; now he was deep in conversation with Ariel. Nathan and Magdalena stood on the edge of the angel encampment, totally enfolded together. She stood with her back against his chest, and they were wrapped in an inner layer of her wings and an outer layer of his. Through the translucent feathers a double glow of light played faintly—his Kiss alight, and hers. As Rachel watched, he bent his head and pressed his mouth to her hair. The lights flamed briefly higher.

The edge of sunset made a faint scarlet streak across the sky.

"Rachel—has anyone seen Rachel?" The frantic voice was Naomi's, coming from somewhere behind her. Before Rachel could turn and call out, she saw Gabriel spin around and point. Angel and Edori both joined her where she stood with Obadiah.

Naomi hugged her tightly. The Edori looked shaken and fretful, she who was usually so serene. "I looked around and you were gone and I didn't know where you were—and with Raphael so close—"

"I'm sorry, I'm sorry. I just wandered over here—"

"People like to keep track of you," Gabriel murmured. Those were the first words he had spoken to her all day. "You shouldn't make it so difficult."

Naomi took her hand. "Let me wait with you."

"Where are Luke and the girls?"

"In camp. It's you I'm worried about."

Gabriel took Rachel's other hand, and smiled down at both

startled women. "Between us, we'll keep her safe," he said. Rachel could not pull away from one of them without pulling away from both. She felt her color rising, and said nothing.

"Look," Obadiah said suddenly, sharply.

Everyone on the Plain was staring upward.

Setting at last, the sun spilled a rich carnelian color across the darkening sky. Wisps of peach, violet and saffron deepened as they watched, changed to tangerine, indigo and gold. The silent black clouds that had roiled in lower and lower now began to smooth out, to melt into the blackness of oncoming night. The air was thick and sluggish, stirred by occasional heavy currents; it was as if the mountains themselves breathed in and out, slowly, laboriously.

Nothing and no one else moved. The rich colors of the sunset thinned and grayed. A faint white light showed around the ringed perimeter of the dark mountain, separating it by the slimmest margin from the blackness of the sky. As if it were being sucked downward into the soil of the earth, that light too began to fade.

"Look," Obadiah whispered again.

As the sky turned black, the mountaintop turned golden. Raphael's followers had taken their fire tubes and set the peak ablaze. In the brilliant orange light, one great shadowy shape leapt upward, a black silhouette of huge wings beating and long arms extended before him.

The perfect acoustics of the Plain carried his words to all the shocked listeners in the field below.

"I am Jovah and I am Lucifer," he cried. "I am your leader and your king. Look at me and know that Raphael is your god."

And he flung back the shadow of his head and stretched his hands to heaven and dared anyone to contradict him.

And the seam of the heavens ripped open, and a white light sizzled across the sky. The mountaintop exploded in a jagged blaze of fire. Thunder ricocheted from one stone peak to another in waves of crashing sound. Light flashed a second time, a great white sheet of it, suspended like a writhing wall between heaven and earth. Everything was visible in that single frozen frame of merciless light—screaming faces, tumbling rock, falling bodies. The third bolt fell before the thunder could sound again, and all that could be seen by that brilliant blaze was a gaping cavity of black.

Then a deep-throated boom rolled across the Plain, gaining

volume and momentum as it traveled. The earth heaved underfoot, buckled by the weight of that sound; the mountains themselves rocked forward and back. The tumultuous roar went on and on, so loud it absorbed all other noise and created a sort of silence.

Then abruptly, there was no air. There was no light. There was no sound.

Rachel staggered sideways as the earth stopped shivering. All that held her up was Gabriel's hold on her wrist—Naomi's hand had been ripped from hers, but Gabriel's fingers had never relaxed their grip. Disoriented and terrified, she cried out, and he swung her into his arms, cradling her head against his chest, covering her blinded eyes.

The winds came then, rushing across the dark Plain. Rachel felt Gabriel brace himself against one fierce gust, and then another. His wings wrapped themselves around her, and his back took most of the force, but still she felt the shudder and whine of the gale whipping around his head, razoring through his feathers, shaking the very foundations of the world.

And the rain followed, sudden and soaking, a rain that would last forever. It lashed down with the force and fury of a river in full spate, driving them backward, turning the ground beneath them to swampland. Hail fell briefly but brutally, beating upon their heads and upraised arms. It hit the soggy earth with a sound like a hand slapping across a face.

Then it slackened, and died away, and only the rain was left washing through the cool air like the tears of Jovah falling.

Still cocooned within Gabriel's embrace, Rachel heard sounds and voices begin to form again in the soggy dark. "Take shelter! Everyone, to your tents and your awnings!" "Build a fire if you can." "Where's Eva? Where's Ariel? Has anyone seen Josiah?" The words, the very sounds themselves, seemed remote and tinny to Rachel, as if they were shouted from a great distance, or as if her ears had been permanently damaged, scarred by the impact of the god's wrath.

For he had struck the mountain and Raphael was dead. Yet they had lived, and Gabriel himself had kept her safe. Rachel did not even try, but she knew she could not break free of his hold. She did not want to.

And then she heard her name again in that high, frantic voice. "Rachel? Rachel? Has anyone seen Rachel?"

Gabriel's arms loosened with a seeming reluctance, and his wings folded back. "She's here. She's safe," he said, and Naomi ran over to take her in a tearful embrace. At the sound of his voice, all attention turned Gabriel's way. Angels and mortals cohered around him, restless and stunned and hopeful.

"Gabriel, what now? What next?"

"The thunderbolt came, Gabriel. The mountain is down, it's on fire. What do we do? When will the rain stop?"

"Gabriel, do you think—"

"Gabriel, do you know—"

"Gabriel—"

From the shelter of Naomi's arms, Rachel turned her attention to him, too. They were all there, instantly materialized, Ariel and Nathan and the oracles. There was almost no light to see by, for the rain had extinguished even the stars, but someone had brought over a feeble torch and by that, and the white glow of Gabriel's wings, they could see his face. It was the only thing to believe in.

"The thunderbolt fell, as the god prophesied," Jezebel was saying gravely. "Raphael and all his followers are dead."

"What next?" Nathan interrupted.

"We sing in the morning," Ariel said.

Gabriel dragged a hand across his face. He looked unutterably weary. "The day after tomorrow, perhaps," he said, and his beautiful voice was strained. "I heard the mountain come crashing down. Who knows what else it brought down with it? We must investigate the damage tomorrow. We can sing the next day."

"But Gabriel! The god is already roused to wrath—"

"He will allow us three days," the angel reminded them. "He gave us those three days for a reason. I think we will need one or two of them."

"And then? In three days? If we do not sing—"

"The thunderbolt falls again," Josiah said quietly. "So says the Librera."

"Falls where?" someone asked.

"Does it matter? We will sing."

"But where?" the insistent voice repeated. "Where would the next bolt fall?"

And suddenly Rachel remembered. She drew away from Naomi's shoulder, where she had rested her head, and felt energy and power flow back into her muscles. The fitful torchlight gave off an uneven, half-lunatic illumination. Angel shapes and even mortal figures were weirdly distorted and surreal. Yet she saw distinctly now; her head was remarkably clear.

Josiah was speaking. "The Librera says that Jovah will first smite the mountain, and then the rocks of the Galilee River, and then the whole world."

"The rocks of the Galilee River?" Ariel repeated. "What does that mean? Where is that?"

But Rachel knew. And Gabriel knew, for he was staring across at her with eyes so blue they tinted the air between them. "Rachel," he said, or maybe he just shaped the word with his lips, for no one heard him speak.

"Semorrah," she said in a voice that carried to the whole circle. "He will strike first the mountain, and then Semorrah." And clenching her hands at her sides, she shocked everyone by laughing.

CHAPTER TWENTY-ONE

Impossible as it seemed, the next day was worse.

The night had been bad enough, for the angel pavilion had been swamped with terrified visitors begging for help or reassurance. Rocks from the falling mountain had shot into the far encampment, wounding twenty or more people, some seriously; the relentless rain was turning the whole place into a dangerous mud slick; and panic and desperation had done the rest. Gabriel had spent most of the night moving from campsite to campsite, offering comfort, bandaging up cuts that anyone else could have dressed with more efficiency, promising that the god's wrath would be averted before the lightning fell again. He had seriously considered flying aloft and praying that the rain dissipate before they all drowned, but was stopped by the thought that it might be sacrilege.

Rachel, of course, had disappeared.

He went by the Chieven camp once during his rounds, thinking to talk to her, if only briefly, but neither she nor Naomi was there. Naomi's two daughters were wide-eyed and silent, but, like most of the Edori children he had seen this night, relatively composed. Luke told him that the women were out on errands of mercy.

"They both know a little of the healing art," he said. "They've gone to the other camps to do what they can."

Which reassured Gabriel a little, but not entirely. For he

knew, if no one else did, what Rachel's strange, hysterical laugh had meant. It was not just a nervous reaction, as everyone else supposed, oh no. It was delight. It was exultation. It was the dizzy expression of the triumph one felt when the god answered one's most heartfelt prayers.

Gabriel worked until he was too exhausted to take another step or stretch his wings one more time; and still he worked, moving among his people, until there were no more pleading hands outstretched to him. It was far past midnight by this time—closer to dawn. He returned to his tent and slept dreamlessly for perhaps five hours. He might have slept forever if Nathan had not awakened him.

"What?" he said, rolling instantly to his feet, knowing there was fresh trouble. "What's happened?"

"The mountain's down."

"Yes, we knew that—"

"And the river has flooded, pouring out of the hole in the mountain, like—like nothing I've ever seen. And the rain won't stop—"

"Yes?"

"And they're evacuating Castelana and the other river cities, but—"

"Semorrah," Gabriel whispered.

Nathan nodded. His own face was pale with fatigue. No telling how long he'd been awake or when he'd gone to bed. "The bridge washed out last night—or collapsed when the mountain fell," he said. Gabriel momentarily envisioned that thin, spidery bridge. Yes, the dancing earth would have quickly sent that structure splintering down. "And the river is so rough they can hardly get a boat to the docks to take on passengers. Well, a few ships have loaded and made it safely to shore, but another one—went down. . . ."

"Dearest Jovah. Sweet god of mercy," Gabriel whispered. He closed his eyes. A vision of Rachel laughing rose before him. He opened his eyes again. "The angels," he said. "We can carry them all to safety—"

"Gabriel, there are thousands of people in Semorrah! There are perhaps a hundred angels left. We could not clear that city in less than a week, and even then—"

"Maybe I can stop the flooding," Gabriel said, his voice suddenly brisk. "I will ask the god. But there must be a way to get them all safely out of the city—"

Nathan was staring at him. "Why? If the water goes down, they are safe enough there."

"That is where the next thunderbolt is to fall," Gabriel reminded him.

"Yes, but only if we do not perform the Gloria! You said yourself we have three days. We will sing tomorrow—"

Whatever Nathan saw on his brother's face stopped his voice. "Gabriel?" he said tentatively. "You do think . . . we can avert the god's wrath, do you not? You do believe we can save Semorrah and ourselves?"

God above, he was so tired. Every muscle, every bone, ached with its individual protest, but his heart was sorer than anything else. "If we sing, yes, I believe we can," he said quietly. "But I am not sure that Rachel—I am not sure that, given a chance to see Semorrah destroyed, she would not take it. She hates that place with a passion you cannot even conceive of."

"But—why? And surely, even if she hates it—"

Gabriel shook his head. "It would take too long to explain. You would have to understand Rachel. You would have to *be* Rachel. I think—I think she would let the city go."

Nathan's face was a study in disbelief.

"I'll do what I can about the river," Gabriel said. "You find Josiah, and tell him what I have just told you. And then find Rachel. She will probably be with the Chievens or with the schoolchildren of Velora. Bring her to our pavilion. Have Josiah talk to her. Perhaps he can convince her to sing tomorrow and spare the city. If not—" Gabriel spread his hands in a hopeless gesture. "We must do what we can to evacuate Semorrah."

And so he went aloft, his wings feeling heavy and sluggish as he beat them against the humid air. Within minutes, his black hair was plastered to his head; his skin and even his flying leathers were soaked through. It was a cold, steady, eternal rain. It could flood the whole earth in a matter of days. He lifted his face to it, closing his eyes, submitting himself to the god's will. As Jovah chose, so be it.

He flew higher and higher, aiming for the icy, dry air above the cloud line, but he realized after a while that there was no such place. The rain fell from the top of the heavens themselves; there was no getting above the storm. So he circled at this high, cold altitude, shrouded on all sides by the falling rain, and he meditated a moment. Then he began to pray.

The falling water seemed to muffle his words, wash them down to earth, instead of letting them float upward to the god. He banked and altered his position till his body lay on an almost vertical plane, and he tilted his head back. Now his music rose from his mouth in a direct line up toward the god. His wings made rhythmic stroking passes through the sodden air. The sibilant hissing of the constant rain made a net of sound around his head.

There were songs to disperse the rain clouds, even such clouds as these; songs to shift aside the laden air, dissipate the collected water. But he did not sing these. Who was he to try, with his frail voice, to countermand the will of the god? Instead, he lifted his voice in songs of entreaty and obeisance, prayers of faith and supplication. *Deliver us, Jovah, from the outward symbols of your wrath. We have doubted you, we have turned away from you. But you are mighty, and you are merciful. God, do not destroy us now. Let us live to learn again to love you. . . .*

He sang for an hour, maybe two, his voice oddly deadened against the damp air, the swish of his wingbeats sounding as loud to his ears as the muted strains of song. Never had he worked so hard and felt so little response from the god. The rain still fell. The clouds still loured all about him, pressing in with an actual weight. He who was never cold began to feel a chill creep from his fingertips backward to his heart.

Well, he had asked for forgiveness. He had prayed for mercy. He would be more specific, though it bordered on heresy: He would beg the god to stop the rain.

Accordingly, when he sang again, he turned to the prayers that would shred the clouds and call forth the high, gusty winds. These were the prayers he knew best, the lyrics he could sing almost without conscious thought. These were the melodies that, from long familiarity, he loved the most. The god had always heard him when he sang these prayers. Surely the god would hear him now.

Almost instantly, he felt a change in the saturated currents around him, though at first he was not sure what the shift portended. A sudden swift blast pushed him from his stable position.

The rain was no longer falling straight down on his head; now it blew diagonally against his face. He banked sharply and regained altitude, feeling the icy hand of the wind butt into him again.

And he saw the black fist of the cloud open its fingers and let the light of heaven seep through.

He stayed aloft another half hour, singing the same words over again, but by then it was clear that his prayers had been answered. The rain thinned and petered out. The clouds shook themselves and fell to pieces. The sun was hazily glorious through the lifting mist.

Jovah was still there, and Jovah still listened. The worst of Gabriel's fears could be put aside. But he was haunted by terrors almost as bad.

It was early afternoon before he landed, circling once over the whole Plain to assess the extent of damage. Big dark Galo was simply gone. A raw, blackened pass now broke the ring of the mountains. From the throat of this opening poured the glittering waters of the Galilee River, welling up from some underground source that had heretofore been partially stoppered by stone. Even now, from the air, Gabriel spotted a cadre of men throwing boulders into the great open mouth of the river, trying to dam its flow back to normal levels. It looked impossible.

He landed a few feet from the blue awning that marked the Eyrie pavilion and looked for someone he could trust with a single, urgent question. Hannah was the first one who appeared.

"Is she here?" he asked without preamble.

"Rachel?" she said. "Yes, in her tent."

"Has Josiah been to see her?"

"He's there now. He's been there a while."

Gabriel's heart squeezed painfully down. If Rachel had been feeling rational on the subject, it would not have taken long to persuade her. "Thank you," he said distractedly, and made his way as quickly as he could to the small tent he had had erected for her.

Before he could get close enough to listen for voices, the flaps parted and Josiah stepped out. The old man looked tired and drained; the night had been as hard on him as it had been on the angels. He saw Gabriel and nodded, unsmiling, and crossed to the angel's side.

"Well? You've talked with her?" Gabriel demanded.

Josiah nodded again. He looked weary enough, or disappointed enough, to weep. "I've talked with her. She has made up her mind, and there is nothing you can say to her that I did not. Go get some sleep, Gabriel. The world will not turn tomorrow without you."

Josiah gripped the angel's arm, then left, stepping carefully and unsteadily through the camp debris. Gabriel stared after him, then turned around and stared at the tent. After a moment, he forced his feet to take him forward, and he pushed aside the canvas flap and went in.

When, over her protests, Nathan had carried Rachel to the angel pavilion, she discovered that she had never been so angry in her entire life. Considering that she had spent a great deal of the past five years in a constant simmer of fury, that was saying a lot; but it was true. She would not speak to him after he deposited her inside the small tent that had been set up for her. She almost could not focus her eyes and take in her surroundings once Nathan left. So when Josiah arrived a scant five minutes later, he was unfortunate enough to find her on her worst behavior.

"Good, you are here," he said, ducking his head to enter and rubbing his hands to ward off the damp chill. "Nathan didn't know how long it would take him to find you."

She swung round on him, and the wrath in her eyes caused his mild face to open up with a wary surprise. "I should have known," she said tightly. "Gabriel expects the worst from me but does not have time to deal with me himself. Have you come to make me see reason?"

"And I've come to hear reason, if you'll speak it," the oracle said quietly. "Perhaps you'll tell me why Gabriel asked me to talk to you about the fate of Semorrah."

She laughed harshly and a little wildly. Josiah waited patiently, and she began to pace around him. "Merely because I have longed to see Semorrah destroyed my whole life. I have called down Yovah's curses upon it. And now, without any further prompting from me, the god is poised to wipe out the city and everyone who lives there. Gabriel thinks," she said, "that this will please me."

"And will it?" he asked.

She whirled to face him. "To see the white city smashed by

Yovah's hand? Yes! I would stand on the riverbanks and dance! I would fall to my knees and sing the god's praises! I would invoke the curses again, if I thought the thunderbolts were falling too slowly. Yovah," she said, her voice falling to an intense whisper, "shower your wrath upon this thrice-damned city. Strike it with fire, with thunderbolts—cover it with storm and flood—"

She stopped abruptly and waited for his shocked reprimand, but he merely watched her out of sober, puzzled eyes.

"And what Gabriel wants," she said, in a more normal tone, "is to have me stand beside him tomorrow and sing the prayer that will turn aside this disaster. He wants me to lift my voice, and soothe the god and save Semorrah."

"Yes," said Josiah. "And that is what I want as well."

She laughed again, more faintly, pressing her hand to her mouth and shaking her head with slight, disbelieving motions. "I have been docile till now—"

"Hardly," Josiah murmured.

"I have. I have done what they asked of me—learned their songs, lived in their high, stone prison, left my Edori friends. I have been— Every part of my life has been shaped by angel intervention, don't you see? It was Raphael who cast me from my parents' home and drove me into slavery—it was Gabriel who swept me from Semorrah to the Eyrie— Over and over again, the course of my life has been violently changed, by outside forces, by angels. Nothing—at no point in my life—never have I had a moment's free will. And now—"

"Now is not the time to exercise that will," Josiah interrupted her. "Yes, the angels were the instruments of your changes, but the plot was laid out by a divine hand. It is part of the mosaic of our life on Samaria. You were chosen by the god to play your part. The path that brought you here was twisted, yet it has brought you here, to this place on this day—and this is the time for you to play your part, to speak your lines, to fulfill your destiny."

"I have been given no choice!" she cried. "The god's hand marked me, and my life has never been my own! I never asked to be angelica, never asked for the hazards it would bring me, and it is not a role that I want! Surely at some point in my life there must be a choice offered to me—and I must be able to choose as I desire!"

"And why should your life be different from that of any other man or woman?" he asked her sharply. "Who among us is given choices such as you talk about?"

She stared at him.

He swept his arm out to indicate the pavilion beyond, the whole of the Plain, all Samaria. "A child is born—angel or mortal, male or female—to a wealthy family or to a poor farmer. The child has no choice in that matter. The fever takes his parents when he is young, so he is abandoned on the streets of Semorrah. Or Luminaux. Maybe a stranger is kind to him—maybe he is caught by Jansai and sold into slavery. Where is the choice in that? Maybe he grows to adulthood fine and healthy, and a run-away horse-cart knocks him into the ground and slices his arm off, or his leg. Did he choose this tragedy? All of us are victims, at some point, of a malicious fate or a scheming god. What makes you think you are different than any of the rest of us to find your life shaped by events you cannot control?"

She raised both hands, palms out toward him, in a warning gesture. "Yes, very well, into each life some chance misery or good fortune falls," she said. "But even the meanest man, the most miserable child, has moments now and then where his will decides his destiny. He can choose to steal, or he can choose to starve—he can invest his money in farmland or gold mines—he can pick the woman he will marry or the slave he will abuse. Many factors may be out of his reach but he makes personal decisions—every day!—which will influence the course of his life."

"Yes, and so do you. So do we all," Josiah said. "And because we do not have control over those larger issues it becomes doubly, triply important that the choices we *are* allowed to make are the right ones—that we are not guided by hate, or spite, or fear, or revenge, or anger. If your life has brought you, struggling and screaming, to this one day in your life, Rachel—think! Is this how you make your choice? Is this how you display your heart? By standing aside, silent, so that death can sweep down? So that thousands of innocent people can die? Is this how you choose when it is allowed you to choose?"

She had turned from him as he flung his stern words at her, but now she swung back. Her face was ravaged with grief; she was actually crying, but she was still so angry that she did not appear to be aware of the tears.

"No!" she cried. "Of course it is not! I would, if I could, level the city with my own hands. I would see every last river merchant die, every overfed, rich slave owner swept into the rising river." Her voice quieted, if only slightly. "But I know better than you, Josiah, who the innocent of Semorrah are—the abandoned children who live in the alleyways, the slaves driven in from Jordana, the timid daughters of the wealthy merchantmen, sold and bartered like so much property—do you really think I would condemn them all to death?"

"But then—you said—"

"*Gabriel* thinks I would," she said, and her voice was so bitter and so hopeless that Josiah reached out to her. She backed away from him, swinging her head. "*Gabriel* thinks I am that lawless. I am that vengeful. I am that cruel."

"You have given him reason to think so," Josiah said very gently.

She nodded. She was so weary she wanted to sink to the floor, sift into the earth, dissolve into particles of dirt. "Every reason," she said tiredly. "But he still should not think it."

"That is not a fair test for Gabriel," the oracle said seriously. "It is not reasonable to expect him to pass it."

"Nobody ever said I was reasonable."

"Let me explain to him—"

"I can make my own explanations," she interrupted sharply. "If he bothers to ask me, then I will tell him."

He shook his head; there was no soothing the troubled waters that lay between these two lovers. "Then you will sing tomorrow?"

She made a *moue* of resignation. "How can I not?"

He came forward, took her into a light embrace. She endured it for a moment and then pulled away. "Do not hate him forever," Josiah said. "He loves you. But he has no choices either. In his hands lies the fate of the world."

"And mine."

"And yours. Do not blame him for gripping your hands rather too tightly. He is only trying to keep us all safe."

She was still standing in the middle of the tent, feeling the contrasting pulls of physical exhaustion and spiritual turmoil, when Gabriel bent his black head and stepped hesitantly inside.

* * *

"Rachel—" he began.

She did not turn to look at him. "I know," she said in an ironic voice. "You came as quickly as you could."

"Well, I did," he said cautiously. "It has been a difficult day."

"In every respect."

He came closer. "I wanted to ask you—"

She whirled on him. "I know what you wanted to ask me! Josiah has already asked me. Your brother has already asked me. Save Semorrah! Pray that the god intercede to spare the city." She flung her hands out. "So? Go ahead. Ask me."

He studied her with a close, troubled attention. When he spoke, his voice was soft, persuasive. "I understand," he said slowly, "why you would want to see the city leveled into the water. I do understand. It is not just that you have suffered there—and that countless Edori have suffered there—it symbolizes every kind of suffering to you, everything terrible. Greed, and hatred, and abuse. I understand that it is not revenge that motivates you, but justice. And you have a passionate sense of justice. I understand all this, but, Rachel—it will not do."

He put out a hand, palm up, in a curious and vulnerable gesture. "The city cannot be cleared, you know," he went on. "The river has stopped rising, but the harbors are flooded, the bridge has fallen, and there is no way for angels to ferry thousands of people to safety. You remember your friend Lady Mary? She is in the city, carrying her unborn child. How many Edori slaves are there, watching the river rise and looking in fear toward the heavens? These are the people you would condemn to death if you refuse to sing tomorrow. You cannot believe in a justice as fierce as that."

He left her deeply shaken. The gentle, almost kindly words unsettled her and dissipated much of her anger—but she had begun with a great deal of anger, and she still had plenty left. She gave him a shrug of feigned indifference.

"Innocent people have died before this, and will die again," she said. "If I choose to stand silent beside you tomorrow, there is nothing you can do to change my mind."

"Is there not?" he asked, very low. "Is there not some personal penance you would impose on me? You have complained before about my arrogance, my self-righteousness. I will become humble. I will beg you for their lives, if that is what you want. Ask me."

She looked over at him, marveling. "How can it mean so much to you?" she asked. "You have no friends in Semorrah. The wealthy merchants hate you, and the others you don't even know. If they died, you would not see their faces in your dreams."

He gave a small shake of his head. "How can I explain to you?" he asked. "You will call it arrogance if I claim that the weight of all those lives lies heavy on me. You have always believed that Jovah hears every voice raised to him in prayer—well, I am not Jovah, but I hear the voices, too. Each voice. I am the safeguard of every soul on Semorrah, whether or not I know the faces. I have never in my life asked Jovah to throw down a thunderbolt to destroy another man—not because I didn't believe that he would not answer me with lightning, but because I believed that every man's life was sacred. Invested with a purpose and a divinity of its own. If I had been Jovah—" He stopped, troubled by the sacrilege of that, but went on. "If I had been Jovah, I would not have been able to smite the mountain yesterday. I would have let all of them live."

"I would have struck them all down," Rachel said swiftly.

He nodded. "I know. But surely you cannot extend the same fate to Semorrah."

She turned away from him again. "And if I refuse to sing?" she asked over her shoulder. "Will you bring Ariel or some other woman to sing in my place?"

"You are angelica," he answered. "It must be you."

"While I live, I am angelica," she agreed. "But if something were to cause me to die, suddenly, in the middle of the night—"

He made no answer. She swiveled back to face him. His blue eyes were locked on her so fixedly that she was momentarily dizzied. "But I forget," she said softly, "how much you value human life."

"Even to save Semorrah, I could not harm you," he whispered. "To save the whole world. If you refuse to sing—tomorrow, or ever—so be it. The world will perish, and we will all perish. But I cannot raise my hand against you."

It was impossible to draw a breath. She managed to speak with the sparse air somehow left in her lungs. "Very well, then, I have my terms ready," she said. "I will sing tomorrow—and walk away from this Plain. You will return to the Eyrie without me, and you will not follow me, and you will not seek to bring me back. You will not set angels to scouring the countryside looking for me. I will return for your next Gloria, and your next and your next. And you can expect no more of me than that for the rest of your days."

It was as if he had not heard her. His gaze was so vivid, so intense, that it trapped her in an azure prison. Almost, he reached his hand out to her; she had the definite impression of an impulsive movement forcibly checked. She envisioned him laying his cool fingers against her face and peeling back her skin, peering inside her head, reading the coded text of the brain inside her skull.

"So," he said, and again his voice was so low it was nearly inaudible. It was almost as if he were speaking to himself. "You were going to sing anyway, and all this anger is for me, for not believing in you."

"Oh, no," she said, with an attempt at carelessness. "I don't care if you believe in me or not."

He nodded, but not as if he were responding to her words—rather, as if he were acknowledging some unvoiced protest spoken soul to soul. "Very well, then, hate me for it," he said, "but it is something I am glad to know."

She jerked herself violently to one side, to escape the spell of his stare. "Very well, then, we understand each other," she said curtly. "We sing tomorrow. At what time are the festivities supposed to begin?"

"The hour past dawn," he said. "I will come for you. Will you be in Naomi's tent?"

She would have been if he had not assumed so. "I will be here," she said instantly. "I will be ready."

"Sleep as well as you can," he advised. "It will be a long day."

As if she would be able to sleep this night. As if she would ever be able to sleep again. "Till tomorrow, then," she said. He nodded at her and left.

He had not been gone three minutes when she began to cry. She was still weeping—silently, ceaselessly, in utter black despair—when Naomi came to her two hours later. She could not even tell Naomi the two things that made the tears run so bitterly down her cheeks: that he would not give her up even to save the world, and that tomorrow she was pledged to leave him forever.

*   *   *

Gabriel had not expected to sleep, but he did—dreamlessly, peacefully. The world held very few terrors for him now. The god had proved his existence; storm and flood had subsided at his prayers; and the angelica had agreed to lead the multitudes in the mass that would save them all.

True, Rachel would hate him for the rest of her life. But that was something he would wrestle with later, after the Gloria was sung, after the world was secured for one more year. For tonight, he would fall exhausted upon his cot just one more servant of the god. On the morrow he would awaken as Archangel.

He woke early, but he was not the first one up. He smelled cooking fires and cauldrons heating up even in the predawn dark. He rose, washed himself thoroughly and dressed with care. Black silk trousers were tucked into his black boots; a fine lawn shirt was fitted carefully over his shoulders and his massive wings. He wore a silver belt and his silver wristlets, and his eyes looked like jewels set deliberately in his face.

Leaving his tent, he went directly to Rachel's and was not surprised to hear soft voices within. Naomi was the one who invited him to enter when he called out a greeting, but he had eyes only for Rachel once he stepped inside.

She was a statue of gold from her hair to her dress to her thin sandals. She wore a gold sash around her waist, thickly embroidered with sapphire-blue flowers in the pattern of her husband's family, and sapphire earrings dangled from each ear. Her hair had been arranged in some impossibly complex fashion. Perhaps ten braids had been started halfway down her back, and tied, and the individual plaits had been linked together by a blue satin ribbon, creating in effect a shawl of her own bright hair. She had her back to him when he came in, but as he just stood there, staring at her, she turned to face him.

"Will I do?" she asked him coolly.

He nodded wordlessly. Naomi began chattering before he had marshaled his thoughts. "I have told the angelica she should wear the wristbands of the angels, but she says she left hers in the Eyrie. Could she borrow some? I know it is traditional to wear them."

Rachel looked annoyed. "What do you know about traditions among the angels?" she asked.

"I know enough," Naomi said firmly. "The angelica stands

on the Plain and raises her hands, and the sun catches the jewels in her bracelets. Isn't it true, Gabriel? So you need bracelets."

"I have brought her something she can wear instead," he replied, crossing the tent. He had wrapped the slim package in a blue silk scarf. Rachel took it reluctantly from his hand.

"Is it a tradition to exchange gifts on the morning of the Gloria?" she asked.

"On the first Gloria, it often is. It is not required."

She motioned backward, at her cot, and Naomi retrieved a long leather case. "I got this for you in Luminaux," she said.

He could not believe it. She had bought him a present, and she still intended to give it to him. "I'm honored," he said gravely. "Open yours."

She unfolded the scarf and looked down a moment without speaking. "Let me see," Naomi said, taking the package from her. "Aaah," the Edori woman sighed. "These are so beautiful—"

"Put them on," he said.

Rachel extended first her right hand, then her left, and Naomi helped her with the gloves. They were made of a gold net so fine that the latticed threads were almost invisible. Around each wrist were sewn circlets of sapphires, clustered together so densely that they looked like bracelets of solid blue. She turned her hands palm-up, palm-down, and the jewels glowed in the torchlight of the tent.

"Thank you," she said with no inflection. "I will be happy to wear them."

Naomi was smiling at him. "I know what she got you," she said. "I'm the one who brought it back from Luminaux."

He examined the supple case for a moment just to prolong the anticipation. He still couldn't believe it. "From Luminaux, is it?" he said. "I thought perhaps I was getting a gift from an Edori craftsman."

"This is better," Naomi promised.

When he pulled back the flap and slid out the silver instrument, he was delighted and astonished. "A flute!" he exclaimed. "I've always wanted— This is so beautiful!" He held it to his lips, but pulled it away before blowing into it. "It is meant to be played, isn't it?" he asked. "Or is it just ornamental?"

"It's not a flute, it's a recorder," Rachel said. "And yes, you can play it. It's supposed to be relatively simple to learn."

He put his lips to the thin silver mouthpiece and breathed.

The sound that filled the tent was sweet, eerie and wistful. Tentatively he moved his hands, breathed again; the new note was just as pure, as otherworldly, as true. He pulled it from his mouth and gazed down at it in happy disbelief.

"This is—Rachel, it's wonderful. Did I ever tell you how much I wanted to play a flute—or recorder, whatever? I'll have to learn this right away."

She was smiling faintly. "You mentioned it once or twice," she said.

He shook his head. "I'm thrilled." Then he realized that the silver chain should be slipped over his head so he could carry the recorder with him always, and he adjusted it around his neck and smiled even more broadly. "I wish I could play it now," he said. "I'd play it for the god."

"Next year, perhaps," Rachel murmured. And he looked over at her, wondering what would have happened—between them and to the whole world—by next year's Gloria. Some of his happiness faded.

There was a brief and awkward silence, but it was broken by voices outside. "Rachel?" a woman asked. "Gabriel?" a man called out.

"Maga," Rachel said.

"And Nathan," Gabriel added. "Time for us all to go."

Naomi threw her arms around Rachel's shoulders. "Sing with your whole heart," she murmured into her friend's ear. "I will be with the Edori, singing with you. Pray for all of us."

She left the tent, the other two right behind her. "Don't you look wonderful!" Maga exclaimed, pulling Rachel aside to admire her dress and her jewels. In the first faint light of dawn, Gabriel nodded over at his brother.

"Is everyone ready?"

"All gathered. Time to begin."

They stood in the middle of the Plain, more than six thousand of them, and watched the sun come up over the low eastern mountains. Rachel took her place in the center of the great, quiet crowd. Semicircles formed around her, first the angels with their massed white wings, then the Edori, then the townspeople and farmers and wayfarers gathered here to listen to her prayers and offer their own to the god.

Gabriel stood beside her and took her hand, which she per-

mitted, though she did not look his way. As the sun lifted over
the edge of the mountain, she raised her face. Her eyes were closed
but she seemed incredibly calm, completely focused, listening to
some inner clock chiming the hours and minutes. In the infant
light, her bright blues and golds faded, grew translucent; she
seemed made of sun-colored mist just breaking apart over a
freshly washed sky.

When she began singing, the whole world fell silent to listen.
Her voice ran before them like river water between wide, ancient
banks, smooth and dark enough to seem both silent and motionless. Gradually the notes brightened, grew crystalline, as the song
took her higher, into her truer range. Gabriel felt his blood pause
in its accustomed race. His breath grew shallow, soundless. Her
voice wrapped around him like arms twining about his neck; it
dazzled the air with bursts of light; it flung him bodiless into the
great empty sky and filled his head with music.

He was so transfixed by her singing that at first he did not
recognize the song. When he did, he was left dizzied by a succession of shocks, each more momentous than the last.

It was the Lochevsky *Magnificat* immortalized by Hagar, a
piece so demanding that most singers were forced to split its octaves between three voices. Yet she sang it as effortlessly, as beautifully, as the great angelica soprano.

She had pitched it precisely in his key. Consciously or not—
willingly or not—she knew his voice so well, she knew exactly
what range he required, how to best show off his skill.

She trusted him. Difficult as the female solo was, the tenor
role was not much simpler. The parts were so interdependent that
she could not have hoped to sing the mass unless she had utter
faith in his ability.

She had chosen the song for him.

She loved him.

He tightened his grip on her hand as her first solo came to
its sublime conclusion. His voice slipped in alongside hers, mellow
and rich; the voices fell together like diving sea birds, then spiraled
up again, arrowing skyward. Her voice steadied, held on one,
sustained high note while his danced beneath hers, changing colors, changing keys. Then she faded away, dropped back, while
his voice dominated in the first male aria.

The words; it seemed he had never listened to the words before. "Though the whole world shun you, yea, I believe. Though

you turn your face away, yea, I believe . . . What do I have if not my love for you? Though everything perish, still there will be my love. . . ."

He sang for her; there was no way she could not know he sang for her. He saw the flame-colored light flaring through the sleeve on her right arm. His own Kiss burned with a painful heat. Although by now his hand was crushing hers, she still made no move to pull away.

"For the world slows and the stars falter, and all that remains is you . . ."

He was almost startled when the silent crowd suddenly sang its first choral response. "Yes, there is love . . . Yes, there is beauty . . . Yes, we believe in the wisdom of our god . . ." The voices rolled over him, like rain, like ocean water, vast and eternal. He sang out his cry of belief again; and again the voices answered. "All that remains is you . . ."

Now Rachel's voice soared above the rest, and the other singers fell silent. Again, he was reminded of a bird, this time something wild and colorful, adorning the skies with its brilliance. This recitative was supposed to be an entreaty, a supplication, but Rachel's voice was exultant, ecstatic. "And where shall we turn if not to you, our shield, our defender, our beloved and our god . . . ?"

Jovah would never fail to answer such a prayer. Truly the god had chosen well when he laid his hand upon this woman's head.

The mass lasted a full two hours. The sun was fat and yellow, the whole sky a rich, hard turquoise, before the formal music came to an end. Everything appeared more solid by this time; even Rachel had lost her ethereal look of the early morning. The piece ended on a series of dramatic "amens" performed by the whole crowd of six thousand, and then there was a moment of profound silence. Rachel hesitated, then slowly raised both her hands toward the blazing heavens. Gabriel's hands, one still locked with hers, rose up simultaneously. Azure fire shot from about their wrists and made a jeweled tent over their heads.

Rachel sang the last, long, sweet amen in a clear, exuberant croon. The crowd nearly drowned her out with shouts and cheers, and suddenly they were engulfed in bodies—angels, mortals, Edori, children—all pushing between them, tearing their hands apart, sweeping them into fierce embraces and laughing with delight. Gabriel let her slip away from him, returned the enthusiastic hugs, the playful, triumphant slaps across the arms and back. The cries sounded all around them: "Archangel!" "Angelica!" "Magnificent, angela!" "Marvelous, simply breathtaking!" "Rachel, what a voice!" "Straight to the god's ear, Gabriel, straight to his heart!"

His own heart was full. Surely the god had heeded this prayer. If no other voice on Samaria moved him, this one would have. While this woman lived to sing to the god, the world would survive forever.

The mass was not the end of it, of course. The singing went on for the rest of the day. Angel choirs from Monteverde and the Eyrie had prepared their own pieces; soloists and orchestras from Luminaux, from Velora, from Castelana, even from among the Manadavvi, had requested permission to perform; and this year, for the first time in nearly two decades, several of the Edori clans had offered their own joyful, primitive music.

But the mass was the only piece in which they all participated. Now the great crowd broke up, and the Plain began to resemble a fairground. Cooking tents sprang up magically. Some ate while others sang and others listened. The sun tilted past the invisible line of noon and began its leisurely, contemplative descent. And still harpists strummed, trumpeters rejoiced, flautists called, drummers pulsed. And singers lifted their voices to the god.

Nathan and Magdalena stood hand-in-hand and sang a duet so sweetly that Gabriel laid aside his evening meal (some Edori concoction of cornbread and onions) and pushed through the crowd to get closer. Like Rachel, Maga stood with her hand enfolded in her partner's; her eyes were closed, her face was peaceful. The Kiss on her arm was a living opal, multicolored and unfathomable. On Nathan's arm, his Kiss glowed with a muted, milky light.

"And who shall we believe if not the god?" asked Rachel next to Gabriel, this time speaking, not singing, the words. The effect on his heart was much the same, however. "He knows and tells us, if we would but have faith."

He smiled down at her, though the expression on her face was somewhat severe. "I believe in him," he said mildly. "Why would you think otherwise?"

She nodded over at his brother and Magdalena. "It is the god who brought them together," she said. "Josiah says Yovah does nothing without a purpose. I think it's time to lift the ban on the intermarrying of angels."

He drew a deep, swift breath. "I know," she hurried on before he could speak. "These unions before have resulted in monster children—terrible, pathetic things. But this time—I'm sure that this time it will be different. Yovah wants those two to be joined together. He could not say so any more clearly."

"Whether Jovah approves or not, there does not seem to be any way I can keep them apart," he said softly. "And so, with grave misgivings, I am forced to agree with you. Besides, I need them. And I need them together."

Her eyes searched his face. "Need them for what?" she asked.

"Someone must go tend Windy Point," he said. "I don't know if any angels are left there, or if they all perished on the mountaintop—but in any case, there must be angels in Jordana, and soon. That whole province has been desperately neglected too long. Nathan and Maga are the best we have to spare."

She studied him. It was nearly full dark now, and it was hard to make out her face. "So," she said, "your first decision as Archangel meets with my approval. Will you be as thoughtful and wise for all your days as leader?"

"Probably not," he said. "I will look to you for guidance."

She turned away, not that he could read anything in her face, anyway. "I'm not very good at advising others."

"Well, I will listen," he said, "when you have something to say."

She seemed to nod, then she seemed to shrug. It was too dark to really tell. "Wish them luck for me," she said.

So she had meant it last night. Of course, she had meant it. She always did what she said she would. "You're leaving now?" he said as calmly as he could.

She gave him one quick look. Again, he could not read her expression. "In the morning. Early."

"Do you need anything?"

She shook her head. "No."

"Rachel—" he said softly.

She took a step backward. "We made a bargain," she said. The beautiful voice was edged with panic. "I'll be here for the next Gloria."

He had to clench his hands in the silky folds of his black trousers to keep himself from reaching out to her. "Don't make me wait a whole year," he said, his voice very gentle. "Not that long."

"This is too hard," she breathed. "Everything between us is too difficult. We are like noon and midnight, chasing each other from one side of the world to the next. Let it go—let the world spin on between us."

"If you want me, call for me," he whispered. "I will hear you, though you call from the other side of the world. Yours is the only voice I hear. If you leave now, you leave me in silence."

"Listen to the silence," she said. "Ask yourself if this is not peace."

"I don't have to listen," he said. "That silence is empty."

"No silence is empty," she said. "Goodbye, Gabriel. Yovah guard you."

"Jovah keep you in his heart," he replied.

And he watched her walk away.

Within seconds, she was lost in the crowd. Even her gold gown, her bright hair, turned to shadows in the darkness. His hands, unknotted now, half-rose of their own volition. *Don't leave me*, he wanted to say. *Stay with me. You love me. You left your heart behind; stay with me as well.*

But he knew better; he had learned. She could not be coerced, persuaded, convinced or changed, and to set his will against hers was to turn her more stubborn than stone. Still, it was all he could do to keep from running after her.

Stay with me. Don't leave. I love you.

CHAPTER TWENTY-TWO

Gaza in spring was a glorious sight. They kept away from the northeastern reaches, where the lush Manadavvi farmlands would even now be unfurling their emerald banners under the watchful eyes of Yovah. Manadavvi had never been especially gracious to the Edori. Instead they wandered through the garden miles of the southwestern coastline, exchanging a few days' work for food, selling their own trinkets and items they had picked up in Luminaux and elsewhere, living like the gypsies they were.

Within the first two days of the journey, Rachel had moved into her own tent, a spare that the Chievens had acquired when two small families merged into one. Naomi had protested, and the other Chievens had looked on in surprise, for the Edori liked to live cluttered and crowded together. It was virtually unheard of for a single woman to sleep alone, with no friend or family alongside her.

"I have slept in your tent too long. You need to have privacy within your own family," Rachel told Naomi.

"You are my family."

"I will be your family in the tent pitched right beside yours. See? The canvases will touch."

"I don't like to think of you lying awake, all alone."

Rachel laughed. "All right. Let your girls sleep with me a few nights. Will that make you happier? I will have company, and you will have your husband to yourself."

Naomi grinned. "I am always able to find time alone with my husband, thank you for your concern."

"I'll take the girls anyway. For a few days."

But that was a concession to Naomi only. In truth, Rachel was dying to be alone, and she was glad when, several nights later, she was able to send the laughing children back to their parents' tent. True, she lay awake a long time that night, in silence and in solitude, but hearing other sleepers breathing in the dark had not made the night hours pass any more swiftly. Nor did solitude give her the clarity she had desired. She curled herself as tightly as she could on the narrow woven mat, and willed herself to sleep.

More than that, she willed herself to stop thinking. She could hardly have been less successful. Images rose to her mind in a constant, surreal montage, arriving and fading in no particular order, all carrying equal weight. Thus visions of Raphael flaming above the mountain were succeeded by a picture of Obadiah laughing at her in a Velora cafe. She remembered a day in Lord Jethro's kitchen when she had spent three hours scraping at the verdigris on a hammered copper kettle. She lay in Simon's arms, whispering, running her fingers around and around the smooth, lightless node of crystal in his arm.

She stood wrapped in Gabriel's wings on the Plain of Sharon, and he kissed her.

It was as if every strand of her life lay scattered before her like so many threads awaiting the weaver's skill, but she could not lift her hands and work them into a design. She had complained to Josiah that she had been given no choices, that she had been thrust violently from one hazard to the next—but here she was, free at last to follow her own inclinations, and all she could do was study her past and wonder what her life had prepared her to choose.

She had thought once, in Velora, that she could make the abandoned children of the cities her life work—but now she had left them behind, under kind supervision, it was true, but still she had left them. Well, she had thought she would make loving Simon her life work, and that dream had dissolved as well. Perhaps there were no dreams substantial enough to live for; perhaps nothing could be trusted to last, not faith in the god, not commitment to a cause, not hope, not love.

She stirred on her mat and turned over. But look at Raphael:

He had schemed with a single-minded ferocity to retain his rank as Archangel, not caring who or what was destroyed in pursuit of his dream. He had slaughtered, lied, preached heresy and brought down the wrath of the god. It had killed him in the end—it had killed hundreds—but he had never lost his unshakable conviction, had never faltered or turned aside.

And yet that was wrong as well. Surely any dream that heedlessly sacrificed the lives, the hopes, the beliefs of others was an evil one; to pursue it was to court damnation.

Very well, then Josiah. Now, his life was pure, serene and intensely focused. He passed his days in study and contemplation; he communed with the god; he believed absolutely in his work and in his master. No doubts, no moments of indecision. And yet he was kind, thoughtful, a beacon of wisdom and hope.

Well, it sounded attractive, but she would go mad. She knew herself well enough to laugh at the thought of herself as an oracle. She needed more action, more interaction, voices around her and a way down off any mountain.

She threw aside her blanket and attempted once more to arrange her bones in a comfortable position. The Edori lived what she had always considered the ideal life. Like Josiah, they believed in a personal connection with the god, and this belief made them gentle, welcoming and peaceful. Yet they were not locked in any stone prison. They wandered from the Gaza gardens to the blue granite streets of Luminaux to the Breven deserts. They were free.

But it was just such formless freedom that left her fearful now. Where was the structure, where was the purpose, what was the function of a life that expended itself aimlessly over the sands and hills of a whole world? Should a man or a woman live and die having accomplished nothing, leaving behind no record, no deed, nothing but the daily acknowledgment in the joy of living? She had thought that would be enough—should be enough—but now, three weeks past the exodus from the Plain of Sharon, it seemed like an empty reason for waking in the morning. Perhaps, she thought, her joy was insufficient. She did not know how to be glad enough.

If she had her life, her whole life, to spend as she would, she wanted to make it matter. She wanted to build something, create something, endow something, leave something behind. She wanted to be a healer, like the wise woman in her parents' village. She wanted to be a great artisan, like the flautist in Luminaux.

She wanted to be a farmer, who tended the soil and brought forth food and oversaw the continuous, complex cycle of life.

What was she fitted to do?

She retrieved the covers she had thrown aside moments ago, turned once more on her pallet, and tried to find ways to shut her mind off from thinking.

They traveled slowly southward, following the coastline into Bethel, making by easy stages for Luminaux. When they stopped at the small shipping towns along the way, Rachel had learned, she was wise to cover her bright hair and never to volunteer to sing at any public functions. Everyone knew the name of the gold-haired woman who traveled with the dark Edori. And anyone who had heard her debut performance was unlikely to forget her voice.

These factors aside, it was amazing to find how popular the Edori were in the Bethel cities these days—indeed, although to a lesser extent, in Gaza as well. They were used to being tolerated in most of the larger cities, and often welcomed in some of the smaller trade-based communities, but they had for years encountered some hostility and disrespect anywhere they went. Suddenly, now, Edori were in vogue. Children crept up to their cook-fires at night, wanting to watch the tents going up and smell the strange aromas of the food. Merchants, craftsmen, goodwives, even politicians, found reasons to come to their camps, offer hospitality and inquire about the state of the roads.

Rachel had feared, at first, that such friendliness had been mandated by the Archangel—that he had sent a call through the whole province asking everyone to be on the lookout for the absent angelica. But none of the townspeople asked after her. None of them even appeared to scrutinize the Edori faces too closely, to ask significant questions, to remark that the Archangel's wife had disappeared and did they think she had gone back to her Edori brethren? No, the cordiality was indeed for her sake, and all the Edori knew it, but it was not cordiality with an ulterior motive. These citizens were merely thankful that the Edori had sheltered the angelica in the days when she needed shelter, and they were trying to dismantle walls of animosity which had stood for generations.

So it was a good life, and everyone (except Rachel) slept trustfully in the parks outside each town and seaport. And they continued to move southward, and the questions continued to circle in her head.

She was not alone nearly so much as Naomi had feared. The Chievens were a small clan, fifty strong, and among their numbers were three young men who still lived with their families. One of them was wooing a girl who was capricious and willful; the other two, Isaac and Adam, had turned their attention to Rachel.

She had forgotten what it was like to be courted by an Edori lover.

Isaac reminded her just a little of Obadiah, though of course they looked nothing at all alike. Isaac was tall and a little slimmer than most Edori. He wore his black hair very short, though braided with gold and silver threads, and he liked to dress in colorful shirts and trousers. When he sang at night around the campfires, he performed humorous original compositions that made everyone laugh.

"He's a fine boy," Naomi whispered to her one night as they listened to Isaac's comic song. "His mother was a Carallel."

"Ah, that's where he gets his voice."

"Yes, but his aunt had the raising of him. His mother died of the black fever when he was little. He was better to his aunt than her own daughters."

"I like him," Rachel said.

Naomi watched her in the dark. "Do you?" she asked, and nothing else.

But she liked Adam better. He was a quiet, serious man a year or two her junior, and he lived with his parents and three younger siblings. His father had injured his leg in a hunt some years back, and Adam had assumed the headman's responsibility for his family's tent. He made sure they had plenty of meat, that the canvas was in good repair, that his mother's handwoven baskets were on display when barterers came to camp, and that his teenaged sisters dressed properly instead of showing off their fresh new bodies to the visiting burghers.

His face was set in stern lines, and his eyes were uncommonly dark, but when he smiled he possessed such a sweetness of expression that he was utterly transformed. He smiled rarely. He seldom sang, and then in a fogged, rusty tenor that Rachel found infinitely attractive. His little brother followed him around the camp from sunup till bedtime.

When he had spare moments, he came to Rachel's tent and

offered to help. "I noticed a rip in your canvas," he would say, as he arrived with his hands full of tools. He cut her a new tent pole when her own began to splinter. He brought her extra meat on the days his hunting had gone well. He was a man who provided for those around him.

It was impossible for Rachel to tell if he helped her out and came by to visit simply because she was a woman living alone and he was a man who took care of people, or if he was expressing some deeper affection, initiating the first steps in the circuitous dance of courtship. About Isaac she had no doubts. He had begged her to sing with him at the campfire, had bought her ribbons and scarves in the border towns; he had admired her hair, her face, her laugh. Adam had made none of these overtures.

Yet he reminded her of Simon. Sweet Yovah, he reminded her of Gabriel. At night, she watched him, tickling his brother before sending him off to bed, and wondered if it would be a sin in the eyes of her god, her Edori or her husband if she seduced him.

The Edori were not usually so strict about conjugal vows. Well, of course, they did not believe in marriage, anyway. But she—there was no use pretending otherwise—she was different. Set apart by her race and her role. And the fact that she had a very prominent spouse. What they might tolerate, even encourage among other young women, they might view unfavorably in her.

Yet she watched him. And thought about how long it had been since she had lain with a man.

They camped for nearly a week outside of Luminaux. During the days, they went, singly and in groups, into the Blue City. Luminaux had always been a lure for the Edori. Here they were most welcome, here their goods brought the best prices or the highest-quality merchandise in barter. Well, Luminauzi welcomed everyone, but the Edori had always felt that they were especially liked here.

One day, Rachel took a load of weavings to the market and was extraordinarily pleased with the payment she was offered. She spent half the money on gifts for Naomi and the girls, and held back the rest of it, in case she ever needed it. She was annoyed with herself for doing so; that was an allali way of living, to save money against the future. Edori never saved, or worried about the days to come. Yet she could not bring herself to squander it all.

After she had made her purchases, she wandered around the city just for the sheer delight of admiring its beauty. She stopped by a huge, simple fountain, a slab of blue marble set almost perpendicularly into a pool, with water racing nearly imperceptibly down its smooth face. So silken was the water, so free of ripple or break, that she had to reach her hand out and touch the stone to be sure it was not just glistening in the sun. She flattened her palm against the worn, cool marble. The water frothed white at her wrist, then untangled into clarity again. She pulled her hand back.

"I do that every time I come to Luminaux," said a sober voice behind her, and she turned to smile at Adam. "This is my favorite place in the city."

"I never saw it before," she said, drying her fingers on her shirt. "I like it."

He took her bundles from her without asking. "You've been busy," he said.

"Presents. I couldn't resist. Naomi has done so much for me—I wanted to do something in return."

He did not tell her that Naomi was glad to perform favors for her friends, lived for such opportunities. He merely nodded. "Have you eaten?" he asked. "It's nearly time for dinner."

"I'm starving."

They went to an outdoor cafe, Adam carefully balancing Rachel's bundles on one of the extra chairs at their table. They ordered wine and delicacies with names that neither of them could pronounce. Sunset drifted down, rose-quartz and aquamarine. Rachel continually glanced from her surroundings to her companion's face. He did not seem to belong here. He was perfectly at ease, even smiling from time to time, but it was an incongruous picture, the somber Edori in the most sophisticated city in Samaria.

"Do you like Luminaux?" she asked finally.

He looked up from his plate, where he was carefully cutting a piece of meat. "As cities go. Yes," he said. "I'd rather be on the open plain, or even in the desert. But there's a—a wildness in Luminaux. A freedom. It's not so confining."

She could not help laughing. When he looked inquiring, she

shook her head. "I have been in places so much more confining than a city," she said by way of explanation. "This one feels very open to me."

"You're a half-child now," he said.

Her hands stilled on her wineglass. "Half-child?" she repeated.

"Or maybe you always were." He caught her expression. "You don't know the word? A person who lives in two worlds, whose heart is split in two. It's usually applied to Edori who have gone to live in a city or a town—who have fallen in love with some farm girl, maybe, or who become crippled in an accident and cannot travel with the others. They stay behind when the Edori move on—but they always miss the Edori."

"But I'm back with the Edori now," she whispered.

"Half of you," he said.

She wanted to say, *All of me*, but she could not.

It was dark by the time they finished their dinner. Adam tied all her packages together with a piece of twine he got from a shopkeeper, then slung the whole together over his shoulder. They wandered aimlessly through the glittering streets, stopping first at one street corner, then another, to listen to musicians entertain. Adam bought each of them iced chocolate-flavored drinks, and they sipped these as they walked. The streets were filled with color, light and motion. Globes of gaslight illuminated every blue cobblestoned roadway, and hundreds of couples were out, walking and laughing and dancing, just as they were. Even the breeze seemed eager and excited, scampering from place to place.

A big crowd and a lifted voice lured them down one wide boulevard. There was a small, brightly lit stage and a barker bawling out invitations. "Sing for gold, citizens! Sing for gold! Who among you can pray like the angels? Just three coppers and you can try your voice against your friends'. Who'll sing for me? Who'll come show us how it's done?"

There were already eight or nine takers standing on stage with him, jesting with each other and humming their warm-up notes. It was nearly irresistible. "Two more," the hustler was pleading. "Another lady, another gentleman. Who'll show us how good they are? You, sir—I'm sure you've got a fine baritone, now."

"He sounds like a frog in midsummer," a woman called out, and everyone laughed.

Adam nudged Rachel. "You should sing."

"I can't do that. It's not fair."

"It's only three coppers. You're the best singer in the crowd."

"You can't be sure of that."

He actually laughed. "Well, then, if you're not, someone else deserves to win."

"Adam, I—"

The sharp-eyed barker had noticed their arguing. "You, lady," he cried, pointing to Rachel. "Your young man is begging you to try. I can always tell. Come up here and show us how it's done."

Adam pushed her forward, and while she turned to scold him, other hands tugged at her arms, pushed her toward the stage. Oh, why not, after all? She was angelica—the god stayed thunderbolts for her—but there had been no stipulations that only amateurs could enter this competition. And no one would lose more than three coppers. She laughed, let herself be thrust toward the stage, and dropped her pennies in the barker's hand.

"Now we've got our ten!" the man called out. "Here are the rules. Each of you is to sing one verse of 'River Cara,' and the crowd will applaud as it sees fit. Whoever receives the most applause will win all the coppers. Does everyone agree to this?" Everyone assented. "Then you, sir! You shall sing first."

The first two men and the first woman all had fine voices, nothing spectacular, but good to listen to on a warm night under the stars and the flaring lamplight. It was impossible to sing "River Cara" badly. The crowd responded favorably, laughing and clapping, calling out for encores.

The second woman had a thin, sweet soprano that gave a wistful turn to the lovesick lyrics, and her performance was greeted with even greater acclaim. The next three singers also received enthusiastic endorsements, but by the time the eighth and ninth singers stepped up to do their verses, the audience was starting to get a little bored. They sang well enough, but everyone had already heard these stanzas; the applause was polite but perfunctory. A few people on the fringes began to edge away.

Rachel was last. The barker pointed at her. "Come forward, lady," he called. "You'll have to sing your guts out to win over these tin-ears."

A few laughs greeted this comment. Rachel stepped to the edge of the stage, found Adam with her eyes and smiled. She'd covered her hair with her scarf, and she checked to make sure the cloth was still in place before she opened her mouth to sing.

> *"We stood at the River Cara's edge,*
> *And vowed we would love forever.*
> *I have been true to my lover's pledge,*
> *But you fled with the rushing river."*

The lyrics were so simple, they were banal; it was the music that made the song such a universal favorite. Rachel put her heart into it. No reason not to sing with feeling if you were going to sing at all. She extended her hands, palms cupped, as if river water dripped between her fingers. When she finished, she flicked her fingers at the crowd as if to shake the water from her hands. People in the first two rows actually stepped backward.

There was a moment's complete silence before the crowd broke into wild, mad cheering. Even the contestants behind her were applauding noisily. Rachel smiled, a little embarrassed (surely she was above this, but actually she was enjoying herself tremendously), and shook hands all around with the others on the stage. She accepted the thirty coppers from the showman and bent forward to hear his voice over the still-cheering crowd.

"You sing like an angel!" he shouted into her ear.

She could not help laughing. "So I've been told," she said, and climbed down the rickety stairs into the enfolding throng. It was a moment before she could locate Adam, pushing through the crowd to her side. He took her arm and looked down at her. He was laughing. She stretched up and kissed him on the mouth.

But something went awry after that. They rode back to the camp in near silence, Adam leaning over from time to time to touch Rachel's arm or guide her horse around some obstruction. They had no trouble seeing, for the full moon lavished them with light. Now and then they smiled at each other, still saying nothing.

But something was wrong. They dismounted before Rachel's tent, letting their reins trail to the ground. Adam stood close to Rachel, waiting; it was clear he was waiting. She was the married woman, it was up to her to give the signal. She lifted her hands to his shoulders and tilted her head back, surveying his face in the bleached, ghostly light. He looked so serious. He looked as if it would take no more than a kiss to make him fall in love with her.

She could not draw his head down. She could not put her mouth against his.

"I'm sorry," she whispered, and dropped her hands.

"Sorry for what?" he asked, his voice almost as soft as hers.

"For—" She could not explain. She shrugged.

"Rachel," he said.

She smiled briefly. "I never make it easy on anyone," she said, though he could not possibly understand what that meant. "Adam, you're so sweet. I want to fall in love with you."

"Then do," he said.

She shook her head. "I've made a lot of mistakes," she said. "I don't want to make this one."

"Rachel," he said again, this time with a note of protest in his voice. She shook her head once more, pressed her fingers fleetingly to his lips and stepped away from him. The tent flap closed soundlessly between them. It was five or ten minutes before she heard him move away, his footsteps accompanied by the heavy shuffle of the horses' hooves. She sat on her pallet the whole time, unmoving, waiting while he waited. Even after he left, she stayed motionless for some time, scarcely breathing, not allowing herself to think.

She was still sleeping the next morning when Naomi came in and woke her up. "Breakfast," the Edori woman said cheerfully. "Time to get up and get moving."

Rachel rolled over so her back was to the visitor. "Why?"

"Because we're leaving this afternoon. You've got to pack your things and strike your tent."

Rachel sat up. "When was this decided?"

"Last night. While you were out flirting in the city."

Rachel gave her friend a hostile look, but accepted the tray of food that was handed to her. "What makes you think I was flirting?"

"Well, you came back with Adam."

"And how do you know *that*?"

"I heard you return."

"And what else did you hear?"

Naomi looked innocent. "Nothing. What should I have heard? Did you have an argument?"

Rachel said nothing. She concentrated on eating. Naomi finally relented.

"Well, I'm glad you sent him away," she said. "I've been worried, you know. I didn't like to say anything, but—"

Rachel took a swallow of juice from a heavy ceramic mug. "And why should you be worried? Why *shouldn't* I have allowed him to stay the night with me, if that's what I wanted—what he wanted?"

"Because you love Gabriel," Naomi said quietly. "And you shouldn't be here in the first place."

Rachel laughed shortly. "Where should I be? Back at the Eyrie?"

"Yes."

"Well, I won't go back there, till—till forever, maybe."

"You're breaking your heart over him. So you were angry and you told him you were never coming back. That's not the kind of vow you have to keep—to anyone."

"He doesn't care if I come back or not."

"You know that's not true."

"He didn't even ask me to stay! Not once—not a word—"

"You had already told him you were leaving! What did you expect him to do, beg you? He's a proud man—"

"Well, so am I proud!"

"What you are is stubborn! And—"

"And anyway," Rachel interrupted, "*yes*, I did want him to beg me! He did beg me, you know that? He pleaded with me to save Semorrah. He would have gotten on his knees and groveled so I would save the lives of total strangers—and yet he couldn't say a word to ask me to stay. If he had cared, don't you think he could have pushed aside his pride for once? *Asked* me? The angelica is supposed to humble the Archangel, that's what they told me. But nobody makes that man humble."

"He would have let the world go up in flames before he brought himself to harm you," Naomi said soberly. "You told me that yourself. You know he loves you. You're just afraid of how much you love him."

Rachel laughed shortly. "Nobody's afraid of love."

"Everybody's afraid of love, because love is what hurts the most. I look at you and Gabriel, and I see a man who has made himself over because he loves a woman. And I see a woman who has shunned the man at every turn. Did you ever tell him you love him? Did you risk your life for him? Did you push aside your pride for him? Did you change for him? What have you done to prove your love? All you did was leave."

"I can't go back," Rachel whispered. "I can't—I don't know what to say to say to him—"

"Then bring him to you. Send him a message. He will know how to read whatever you write."

But it was not as easy as that. She could not think of what to put in a letter to Gabriel. So she packed her clothes and rolled up her tent and moved on with the Edori another day, and another.

They had traveled by slow stages on a northwesterly route away from Luminaux, and the third day, they crossed into the shadows of a narrow mountain range. These rounded green hills shaded upward into small, pointed beige peaks, incongruously situated in the middle of the vast southern plains.

"The Corinni Mountains," Isaac told Rachel when they made camp in the shelter of the foothills. Adam had kept his distance the past few days, though when he saw her, he always gave her that sweet, wistful smile. Isaac, however, had been around more than usual. "Though I've heard one of them called Hagar's Tooth."

"Hagar's Tooth?" Rachel repeated sharply. "Why?"

He shrugged. "That's what the Luminauzi call it. I don't know why. I do know that the only way up the biggest mountain—that one, see?—is on a hard, steep road that's lined with iron stakes." She stared at him and he laughed. "No, really. I've been up it partway. Iron stakes, as big around as my fist, on each side of the trail. They went all the way up, as far as I could see."

"Hagar's Tooth," Rachel repeated. "Yes. I remember now."

She spent the night in camp, but in the morning, when the rest of the Edori prepared to move on, she made her farewells.

"Here?" Naomi asked blankly, looking up from the bedroll she was securing. "In the middle of nowhere? It's not safe to leave you here alone."

"It is. Trust me. I want to stay here. Leave me enough food for a few weeks, and I'll be fine."

Naomi protested, as did Luke and Isaac and a few others who were apprised of her decision, but in the end Rachel convinced them. They gave her enough food to last a month, left her the tent and various tools, and took turns bidding her solemn goodbyes. The girls cried. Isaac kissed her on the mouth, Adam kissed her on the cheek.

"Get word to me," Naomi whispered, hugging her goodbye. "If no sooner, come to the Gathering next year."

"I will," Rachel promised.

Finally, they were gone, a small dark caravan disappearing into the flat gold horizon. Rachel did not watch them till they were out of sight. She had her own journey to make by nightfall.

They had been camped about an hour from the foot of the mountain Isaac had called Hagar's Tooth. It was a little past noon when Rachel made it that far, found a broad, dusty trail and began to climb.

At first, she saw nothing of the iron stakes Isaac had mentioned, and she wondered if she had chosen the wrong peak, or the wrong path. But a few hundred yards up the mountain, the wide roadway narrowed suddenly, becoming rocky and overgrown. The trees which had been cleared away at the base of the mountain now clustered more closely together, brooding over the trail with a sort of watchful mistrust. They grew so thickly on either side that their upper branches intertwined, making a dense ropy canopy above the path.

And then she saw the iron stakes. As Isaac said, they lined the trail from this point to the highest level she could see. They were as tall as a man, about four inches in diameter, and topped with sharp spikes. Some of them were rusted over, and a few of them had toppled to the ground, but there were still hundreds and hundreds left—stiff, silent guards whose only purpose was to keep any great winged creature from landing along this slope.

Hagar had built her retreat to be angel-proof. Rachel did not need to see the house to know that it, too, would have iron sentinels around it, atop it, ringing it in all conceivable directions. Hagar did not want idle guests coasting in for a quick visit, toying with her affections and destroying her peace of mind. Any angel who wanted to see her must come like a penitent, trudging up the long, steep hill and trailing bright feathers in the dust behind him.

It was a slow, wearisome climb, and the way became more difficult as she ascended, though it was never impassable. The entire afternoon had disappeared before Rachel made it to the top of the mountain and stumbled, almost accidentally, into the little clearing that held Hagar's retreat. But then she forgot her tired

legs and dry throat and her eternal, circling memories, and
laughed out loud.

Despite the hundreds of very tall stakes driven around the
clearing and at random through the gardens and grounds, Hagar's
home was a place of instant charm. It was haphazardly built of
warm red stone and roofed with green ceramic tile, and it sported
four chimneys at odd corners. A small stream ran so close to the
house that it paralleled the northern wall and curled around an
ornamental fountain which it had once, apparently, played
through. At one time, some tenant had been a lover of flowers,
for there were three distinct gardens blooming even now, half-
choked with weeds and wildflowers, but still retaining some of
their formal patterns and cultivated dignity.

Oh, she could love it here. She could live here her whole life.

It took her a week to make the house habitable. Gabriel had
not been able to remember when the last angelica had had any
use for Hagar's retreat. Given the state of the interior, Rachel
would have guessed it had been more than a hundred years since
anyone had set foot in it. Dust, dirt, bird droppings, mice nests,
dried leaves, living weeds, a family of rabbits and a hundred families of spiders had taken the place over. The furnishings were
sparse but some of them, surprisingly, were still usable, particularly the fine old wood tables, chairs and chests of drawers. It was
harder to find something comfortable to sleep on, and for three
nights, Rachel made a quilt of her cloak and lay on that.

But on the fourth day, she made several agreeable discoveries.
The first was a locked cedar closet whose key hung on a hook
right beside its door. Inside were feather pillows, woven pallets,
wool blankets, embroidered quilts and all manner of linens, fresh
and unspoiled. Inside were also twenty or thirty dresses hung
along one long rod, dresses of every color and cloth imaginable.
Rachel pulled them out one by one, holding them up to her chest
and noting that they fell exactly to her ankles. Gowns of blue silk,
green cotton, white linen; dresses with embroidered cuffs, jeweled
collars, lace sleeves, plain bodices. A queen's wardrobe here.
No—an angelica's.

So that solved the problem of what to wear and what to sleep
on. Later in the day, she solved the mystery of the long, narrow,
windowless room on the northern side of the house. It had two
small doors built into one wall and a deep channel carved into

the floor, lined with green ceramic tile. There was no fireplace in this room, but the small stove in the corner heated up quickly— and caused the ceramic channel to grow hot to the touch as well, as though heat from the stove was being funneled under the floor-boards, under the tile. Initially, Rachel had been puzzled and decided to leave the room alone.

But that afternoon while she was outside drawing water for dinner, she noticed an overgrown ditch running from the stream toward the house. And when she cleaned out the leaves, branches and other debris, she found the ditch lined with the same green tile. And then she realized: Hagar had wanted a water room like the one she had gotten used to at the Eyrie. She'd had part of the stream diverted to run through her house, and added on the stove to heat up the water when she wanted to bathe. The water must go in one door and out the other . . . and surely there must be meshes of wire or cloth to keep out fish and small animals and floating insects. . . .

It took her most of the next day to clean out the exterior ditch and rig up sluices and screens, but by nightfall, Rachel had water running through Hagar's house again. She celebrated by taking a long hot bath. Oh, this was sublime, this was pure ecstasy. The water bubbled over her, warm and soothing, constantly renewed, and flavored with the fresh scents of moss and forest. Wild and safe at the same time. She was never leaving this place.

During the next two weeks, she worked in the gardens. It was impossible, of course, to obliterate a century of neglect in a few days, but she made a tremendous improvement. She even made another pleasant discovery: There was a fourth garden, a vegetable plot, and even now it was growing heavy with tangled tomatoes, corn, squash and beans. With the vegetables, the fruit she had found, the fish in the river, and the dried meat she had brought from the Edori camp, she could live a long time.

Maybe forever.

Rachel was so happy here that she sang all the time. Sometimes she was not even aware of the fact that she was singing until she caught sight of herself in one of the long, narrow mirrors in almost every room (Hagar, or someone, had certainly liked to look at herself). Then she would see herself—hair in mad disarray, old gown covered with dirt and grass, arms laden with flowers or dust rags or tools—mouth wide open and singing so vigorously she could almost see the notes glittering in the air. She would laugh, and stop, and keep it down to a hum for an hour or two. But then she would notice the music again, and realize it was coming from her.

She paid no attention to what she was singing. It could be anything—Edori ballads, the childhood lullabies she had learned so long ago, snatches of Luminaux street songs, even some of the masses she had studied back at the Eyrie. Now and then she heard herself wordlessly caroling the melody to one of the prayers she had heard Gabriel or Obadiah sing, prayers for rain or sun or wind or protection, she was not sure. She did not know the lyrics to these songs, and perhaps it was just as well. She did not know what she would pray for if she were to lift her voice right now to the god.

And then she began to wonder. Gabriel had told her once that there were places in Samaria where Yovah's ear seemed most attuned, and Hagar's retreat was one of those places. If she were to stand here now, at the front door of this little cottage, and fling her arms out and raise her voice in song, what would she ask for? The god had listened to her once, down on the Plain of Sharon. Rachel no longer doubted that her voice had the power to move him. But what would she pray for? What did she want?

Bring Gabriel to me, she heard a voice in her head say; and it was her voice; and it was the only thing she wanted. But she did not know how to ask that of the god. There must be something else she could request. She would like, a second time, to feel as if she could call on her god and have him listen.

It was three more weeks before she found the key to the silver box in the bedroom that must have been Hagar's.

She had unearthed the box before she had been in the house four days. It had been in the back of a closet, covered with rotting silk and a handful of loose dirt and a nest that might have belonged to mice ten years ago. Black with tarnish, it was still beautiful—a wide, flat, shallow case of chased silver. The top was studded with sapphires set in a fleur-de-lis pattern, and by that Rachel had known it as Hagar's. The lock, which was also made of silver, was too stubborn to yield to prying, and Rachel had been reluctant to break into anything so cool and beautiful.

But then she found the key, on a ring of keys hanging just inside the doorway of the small stone shed situated about two hundred yards upstream. She had not yet determined the purpose of the shed—a smokehouse? a dairy? a storage room?—nor had she found any of the locks that the other keys fit. But she knew as soon as she saw it that the tiny silver key would turn in the ornamental silver lock, and she hurried back to the house to retrieve the crusted box.

When she pried off the lid and stared inside, she could not have been more surprised or more excited had she found a cache of unset jewels. Carefully, reverently, she lifted out the brittle, browned sheets of paper, afraid they might shiver into dust at her touch. The notes and staffs could have been drawn by anyone, but the verses and the sparse comments in the margins could only have been written by one hand. Hagar's personality fairly leapt from the page; each word seemed to have jumped from her pen to the paper in quick, impatient downstrokes. She had scrawled titles across the tops of a few pages, but more often than not, the music began with a treble clef, a key signature and the opening words of the song.

Slowly, Rachel glanced through sheet after sheet of music, skimming the lyrics and reading the author's remarks in the margins. "Too boring. Change to minor key?" Hagar had written once. On another page: "Needs an additional stanza." On another: "Uriel will like this." On another: "For Daniel, not that he'll ever get to hear it." On another: "My favorite."

But the composition that Rachel paused over was the one she had looked for since she first realized what was in the box. Like the others, it had no title, and it carried a brief comment from the musician: "The music of desire." Rachel hummed the opening measures softly, just to get a sense of the melody. Even inside the house, even without whispering the words, she felt the power of this music. She heard the rustling trees fall silent to listen, she caught the startled inquiry of the passing birds. She felt the god hold his breath and wait to hear more.

This, then, could be her letter to Gabriel, her invitation, her apology. He would understand this message. When she decided she was ready to see him again, she would step outside her cottage and lure him to her side with this song. He would come then; she would wait until she was certain.

She rose to her feet, brushed the dirt from her knees and walked straight out the front door. Holding the music before her, learning it as she went along, she sang the ballad with her whole heart. Only the god could hear, and the wild creatures that made their homes on this mountaintop, and the trees and the river and the mountain itself; but it seemed as if the whole world listened. Rachel closed her eyes, pressed the music to her chest and sang the song over a second time.

Only the god could hear her, but Gabriel would come.

CHAPTER TWENTY-THREE

In the first chaotic days that followed the Gloria, it was easy for Gabriel to gloss over the answer every time someone asked him where Rachel was. It was hard to keep track of anyone in all that confusion. He left Ariel and the Monteverde angels to oversee the emptying of the Plain, while he and Nathan and Obadiah flew to Semorrah to do what they could for that beleaguered city. The water was indeed very high, lapping over the wharf streets and sending warehouse mice and cats seeking higher ground. Yet the bulk of the city was safe—filled with terrified people who greeted the angels with heartfelt cries, but still above water.

They worked there for two days, mostly calming the residents by their sheer presence, but also helping put to rights fallen buildings and crumbling power alliances. They were really there to prove that the god would not strike the city, that the music on the Plain had been effective, that they had averted disaster with their prayers. When the danger passed—three days after Jovah had struck down the mountain—they were free to go.

They returned to the Eyrie, but only briefly. There were still so many trips to make, so many oaths to receive, and this was the psychological moment to exact fealty from the Jansai and the Manadavvi. Gabriel thought of the miles he had to cross, the pleas he would have to make, and he felt exhausted. What he wanted was to sleep a hundred years, and then fly off to find Rachel.

Speaking of Rachel. "I thought she was with you the last few days," Hannah said to him the morning after his return. He had risen late, but Obadiah and Nathan were still lingering over their breakfasts, and he had joined them. Hannah had found them within minutes.

"Who, Rachel?" Nathan had answered his mother. "No, she came on back to the Eyrie."

Gabriel watched his fork make patterns in the food on his plate. "Gabriel," Obadiah said. "Where's Rachel?"

"You mean you didn't send her back here?" Nathan asked in surprise.

"She hasn't been here at all," Hannah said quietly.

Gabriel looked up. "She's with the Edori," he said.

"She just spent *months* with the Edori!" Obadiah exclaimed.

"Well, now she's spending some more months with them."

"Did you quarrel?" Nathan wanted to know.

"When did we not?"

"How long will she be gone?" Hannah asked.

"I don't know. As long as she wants. She says she'll be back in time for the next Gloria."

"The next—but that's a year away!"

"I know."

"Do you want me to find her?" Obadiah asked quietly.

Gabriel gave him one quick, fierce look. "No." The younger angel raised his eyebrows and sat back in his chair as far as his wings would allow.

"Do you know where she is?" Hannah asked.

"No. She's safe. I would know if she wasn't. Let it go. This is between the angelica and me."

No one said anything for a few moments. Gabriel concentrated on his food until a servant brought fresh biscuits, and they all had another helping.

"So," Obadiah said finally. "What next?"

"I have to go to Breven," Gabriel said, "to Semorrah again, to Castelana, to the Manadavvi holdings—make the whole circuit. See what kind of cooperation I can get now that everyone knows I'm not bluffing. And now that most of the malcontents"—he paused—"are dead."

"Do you want us to come with you?"

Gabriel rubbed his hand over his face. "I need someone to stay behind and see to whatever crises arise in Bethel while I'm gone. That should be you, Obadiah. Nathan—I want you to come with me as far as Jordana."

Three pairs of eyes were instantly fixed on his face. "Jordana," Nathan repeated. "You mean Windy Point."

The Archangel nodded. "Not all his angels joined Raphael on the mountain. Some of them must still be there, or perhaps they're in hiding elsewhere. And Leah. I didn't see her at the Plain, although she could have been there. We must find out what the situation is."

"When do we leave?"

"Tomorrow."

The flight to Windy Point was uneventful, though Gabriel found himself continually watching the ground below him when they were near enough to make out shapes and figures. From the air, it would be easy enough to spot a small caravan of Edori, though it would be difficult to tell which clan they were and who rode with them. . . . But he did not see any Edori at all.

They arrived at Windy Point early in the day under a beaming sun. The fortress, always uninviting, seemed particularly dour this day, and they circled it once from the air. Gabriel was trying not to remember the last time he had arrived at this castle, seeking a way in, and the sight that had greeted him on a promontory a few hundred yards above the towers. . . .

"I don't see any signs of life at all," Nathan called to him. "Perhaps it's been abandoned."

"We've got to go in," Gabriel called back. They banked and dropped slowly, aiming for the public landing ledge on the lower level of the fortress.

The wide portcullis was standing open, and no one stopped them as they entered. Neither did anyone answer their shouts of greeting or their hammering on the metal gong in the entry hall.

"I don't think anyone is here," Nathan murmured.

"You may be right."

"But it feels—creepy in here."

"I know."

They chose a corridor at random and began exploring. They did not even encounter servants in any of the halls or kitchens or anterooms they first checked. The passageways echoed emptily with their two sets of footfalls and their infrequent, low-voiced words.

"No one in here."

"Nothing in this room."

"I don't like this."

They went through the entire lower level of the fortress without coming across a soul. As they climbed up to the second level, both of them paused a moment, washed with a faint sense of dread, but they said nothing and continued up the stairs.

The first room they came to was the great dining hall, haphazardly lit by sun through the filthy leaded windows. Here they found nearly everyone who had not accompanied Raphael to the Gloria.

They lay together at tables and on wide chaises, and now and then, embraced upon the floor—lovers and good friends with their arms around each other, more solitary fellows with their heads pillowed upon their hands. Angels lay intertwined with mortals, spreading their great soft feathers over their supine companions. Platters of meat and plates of bread and pitchers of wine still sat upon the tables. The only sounds were the small patter of fleeing mice and the droning buzz of hungry insects.

"It does not smell like death," Nathan said, his voice very faint, wondering. "Could they all be merely drugged? Sleeping?"

"A powerful potion, to keep men sleeping for a week," Gabriel replied. He stepped forward, carefully descending the stone steps into the room. "Let us see."

But they were dead. Between them, the brothers checked for breath at every mouth, felt for every absent heartbeat. There were perhaps fifty bodies in the room, half of them angel, half mortal. Not one was living.

"I feel sick," Nathan said when they met each other in the center of the mausoleum.

"And well you should."

"Raphael did this? To everyone who did not believe him, who would not go with him to the mountain?"

"So it would appear."

"But he—they were his friends, his disciples—"

"Raphael had no trouble dealing death. He had done it for twenty years, though we didn't know it. It was life he could not sustain." Gabriel glanced around the room one more time. He was feeling remarkably detached from all this, but he was not deceived. It was merely the flip side of Nathan's undisguised horror. It was too large for him to comprehend, so his mind dealt with it coolly. He could not stand to examine the reality too closely. "Did you see Leah among the corpses?"

"No. You didn't either?"

"No. She must be somewhere in the fortress."

They found her, three levels up, in an ornate bedroom decorated in swaths of pink silk. She appeared to be sleeping; the three maids who attended her seemed to doze as well in their overstuffed rose-colored chairs. Gabriel was taking nothing for granted, however. He examined each woman, touched his fingers to each slack mouth.

"All dead," he said to Nathan, and motioned him out the door.

They went through the fortress from top to bottom, efficiently, methodically, opening every room and closet to see if they could find any living refugees. There were none. They had one moment of strange excitement when, at the very top of the castle, they happened upon a narrow corridor down which they could hear patchy music playing.

"Someone's alive," Nathan whispered, grabbing his arm. "Gabriel, do you hear it? Someone's playing a flute or something."

Gabriel nodded, and they crept slowly down the hallway. It was a novice, perhaps a child, blowing fitfully on a reed pipe. They could hear first a single note, then a broken chord, then a single sustained note again. The doorway into the small room was open; this musician was making no attempt to hide.

But when they edged cautiously into the chamber, it was empty. They looked quickly at each other and then searched the room again with their eyes. There was no place to hide. No one was in here. For the moment, the music had stopped.

"Haunted?" Nathan breathed.

Gabriel was examining the door. It had been broken open with some kind of heavy weight, and the lock had been smashed. He showed Nathan, who shrugged.

They both jumped when the music started again, two notes, then one, then a minor seventh chord, all blown in concert with the rattling of the window casement as the wind shook the glass. Gabriel's eyes went quickly around the room, following the pull of the music.

"Look," he said, pointing first to one reed stuck in the wall, then another, as he spotted them. "The wind is the musician."

Nathan's eyes were wide. "Who would do this?"

"Anyone who lived in this castle and loved harmony. There was no other music in Windy Point."

"Who, though? And where is he now?"

Gabriel spread his hands. "Dead, now, no doubt. Raphael seems to have left no one behind."

"This has become an evil place," Nathan said softly. Gabriel nodded.

They left shortly after that, making their way as quickly as possible down the winding hallways and out through the port-cullis, into fresh air and sunshine again. Gabriel felt a tremor from shoulders to heels as he stepped outside the fortress. It was as if he shook off a malevolent spirit trying to curl between his wings and wrap icy fingers around his throat.

"Aloft," he said to his brother, and they sprang in tandem into the air, rhythmically stroking their wings against the heavy, capricious wind. Gabriel angled himself upward, over the mountain, through the low-lying clouds, into the frigid layer of atmosphere where breathing was just barely possible. Nathan asked no questions, but followed closely. Gabriel slowed to a hover, his great wings sweeping the air with a steady motion, and raised both arms above his head.

When he began singing, he felt Nathan's shock even in this cold, still place. He clenched his hands, keeping his arms upraised, and continued to sing. The air was so clear that his voice rang against it like a hammer against a chime. His breath was so warm, so heavy, that his words seemed to take bodily form and fill the empty skies around them with birdlike shapes. He forced his fingers apart, stretched his hands to Jovah and sang the prayer again. Behind him, Nathan added his baritone in harmony. Their voices climbed through the snowy atmosphere and reached the god's ear.

Lightning shot between them, nearly singeing Gabriel's wing. The Archangel fell back, lost altitude, and beat the air madly to regain balance. Seconds later, sound arrowed down after the burst of light, a rolling boom that sounded like glass crashing all the way down the stairwell that linked the sky to the earth. Then a huge explosion threw the sound back up to heaven, wave after wave of rumble and collapse.

Gabriel folded his wings back and began to drift downward, Nathan behind him. They landed somewhere in the Caitana foothills, far enough away that they did not have to see how the thunderbolt had sheared the fortress from the mountains, destroying every stone and stick of the castle in the process.

"Even so," Nathan said over their campfire that night, "none of the problems that are Jordana have been solved."

"I know," Gabriel said. "First, we have to pick a site and build another hold. Perhaps in the southern part of the province this time. Near the Heldoras, I think."

"A fortress can wait," Nathan said impatiently. "Who will watch over Jordana? Which angels? Who shall lead them? Someone who can deal with the Jansai, not to mention the river merchants—"

"I've already decided all this," Gabriel said. "Didn't I tell you?"

"No, who?"

"You, of course."

Nathan stared at him. Gabriel smiled, for the first time in this long, dreary day. "Well, who else?" the Archangel asked reasonably. "You're the one I trust most."

"But Gabriel—"

"I know. You'll need help. We'll send a third of the Eyrie angels, a third of the Monteverde angels. We will all be spread too thin, but we will do the best we can."

"But Gabriel, I—"

"Of course you can do it. I know it will be difficult. Ariel and I will help as much as we can."

"But—"

"And I certainly don't expect you to do it without friends," Gabriel said. "Ariel has already agreed to donate Magdalena. Permanently, of course. You do realize that this is a lifetime assignment. That you and your children and your children's children will henceforth be citizens of Jordana—"

"*Magdalena*?" Nathan cried. "You and Ariel agreed—"

Gabriel smiled again. "This time, we are heeding the wisdom of Jovah," he said gently. "The two of you seem to have been called together for a purpose. This is the only purpose I can think of. Will you do this for me? I can think of no harder task in all of Samaria and no man I would rather ask to assume such a heavy burden."

"Yes," Nathan said, his voice low and strangled. "Yes. But Gabriel, you knew I would."

*   *   *

The next few weeks passed in motion. Gabriel flew between Breven, Semorrah, Monteverde, Luminaux, Mount Sinai and the Heldoras so often that he began cursing the slowness of his wings, wishing for a faster mode of transport. He could not imagine how anyone endured the tedious hours of travel on foot or even by horse.

Yet everything was coming together. He found the merchants, the Jansai, even the haughty Manadavvi, cowed and eager to come to terms. The liberation of the Edori was the first step, and next were the sworn oaths to leave all peoples in peace and in freedom. It would take him months or years to sort out some of the other injustices, particularly among the wealthy Gaza landholders and their tenants. But he had made a start.

He spent time with Nathan and Maga in the Heldora Mountains, watching the construction of the new hold. This was to be modeled more after Monteverde than the Eyrie, an open, accessible community in which mortals mingled with angels. So be it; angels had been aloof too long. Maybe it was time to find new ways into and out of the Eyrie, so that anyone could come there who wished . . . and any who were there could leave. . . .

But anyone who had wanted to leave the Eyrie had already done so, and showed no disposition to return.

It was late summer, and Gabriel had seen no sign of Rachel, heard no word. He had not really expected to, and yet he had hoped. He could not keep himself, still, from scouting out the campsites he saw below him during his long, wearisome travels, looking for Edori, for certain Edori, for one woman traveling among Edori. But he never saw her. He never got close enough to the ground to identify gold hair shining incongruously bright among all the dark heads clustered in the camps. He kept his word.

Two months gone by, nearly three. Nine more months, at the longest, before he would see her again. He willed the world to begin spinning faster, the days to shorten, the nights to whirl by. That next time, he would swear no vows, he would accede to no impossible terms. He would make no mistakes. The next time she left him, he would be right behind her.

Gabriel was in Velora when the strange rain began falling. He had stopped to check on Peter and the orphanage so that the next time he saw Rachel, if he ever saw Rachel again, he could tell her how well all the children were doing. The Archangel and the schoolmaster had just stepped outside to complete their farewells when the rain began to patter down around them. Only it wasn't rain.

"You'd think you were in Breven," Peter remarked, holding a palm before his mouth to screen out the dry, drifting particles. "Sandstorm like this."

"I don't think it's sand," Gabriel said. All around him was the oddest, softest hissing sound as the tiny grains whispered through the air and sprinkled to the ground. He could feel the mealy buildup in his hair, in his wings. He fluttered his feathers impatiently to clear them.

"No, I believe you're right. It's—well, rice or something. Seeds, I think. Great Jovah, where is this coming from?"

"I have no idea." Gabriel squinted up at the overcast sky and could see nothing but the swirling mist endlessly forming and falling. "I can't even guess what it *is*."

People were sticking their heads out of doorways and windows, cupping their hands to catch the strange bounty. The children had, by some primal telepathy, instantly realized something unusual was afoot and broken free of their teachers and their classrooms. They were already running through the streets, catching the falling seeds in their open mouths, dancing under the dry, slick rain.

"Oh dear. I'm sure they shouldn't be eating this, whatever this is—" Peter began.

Gabriel laughed. "It's falling from heaven," he said. "Surely Jovah is sending it. It must be safe."

"But what *is* it?"

"I don't know."

No one in Velora, in fact, seemed to know, but like Gabriel, many citizens seemed to have deduced that Jovah was sending them some kind of rare gift. Already, buckets and pans and cook pots had been set outside in front of doors and on top of flat roofs. Women walked through the streets with their skirts spread wide to catch the grains as they fell. Gabriel stopped a dozen or so as he passed them, asking, "Do you know what this is?" All of them smiled and shook their heads.

He flew back to the Eyrie to find a similar scene in the arena in the center of the hold. Every imaginable container had been laid out on the open stone; the plateau was so crowded with trays and cauldrons and vases that he scarcely had room to land. He ducked quickly inside the first open door and shook the seeds from his hair.

"What *is* this stuff?" he demanded of the first person he saw, who happened to be Hannah.

She was smiling. "Don't you know? It's manna."

"Manna?" He glanced back toward the plateau, still snowy with descending seed. "But it hasn't fallen on Samaria in generations—"

"I know."

"And why has Jovah chosen to send it to us again after all this time?"

"Someone must have asked him for it," she said, meeting his eyes squarely. "It is said that Hagar herself first wrote the prayer that the god responded to with this gift."

And then he knew where Rachel was, and that she wanted to see him.

Two days later, he left in the morning and arrived at the foot of the Corinni Mountains in the early afternoon. He had brought gifts with him, and he carried as well his silver recorder on its chain around his neck. In his free time (what little there had been of it in the past weeks), he had practiced. He now had a repertoire of six fairly creditable, albeit simple, songs.

As befitted a penitent, he made no attempts to ease or shorten his journey. He began on foot at the base of the mountain and toiled upward uncomplainingly. He was not used to this particular kind of physical exertion, but he was in good shape, and the climb did not tire him or curb his building excitement. Nonetheless, he paused to rest about halfway up the mountain, dropped his bundles and freed his flute from its case.

He played his six selections twice apiece, serenading the birds, the wild foxes, the trees, the god and anyone else who might be listening. The pipe sounded just right here on this steep slope made half of stone and half of forest; it could have been birdsong or rainfall or dawn wind. He was sure that his idle melodies floated upward, skipping over the cruel iron spikes and skirling into the small house at the top of the mountain.

Retrieving his packages, he continued the climb. The pathway narrowed till he felt his shoulders and his wings squeezing together to avoid scraping against the metal railings. The tips of his feathers trailed behind him in the dirt. No glorious entrance for him. He would arrive humble and disheveled as any mortal man.

But when he crested the final hill and gazed down into the clearing around the cottage, he could not help smiling. Flowers rioted in three gardens, smoke curled from two chimneys, and the smell of baking bread drifted back to him like an invitation. Rachel was nowhere in sight. He picked his way down the small hill, crossed the yard and knocked hopefully at the door. Then he held his breath until she opened it.

She was dressed all in blue, and her gold hair lay unbound across her shoulders. She looked like a peasant girl minding her mother's house, or a wise woman enmeshed in her own spells, eternally beautiful, eternally young. She was not smiling. But she did not look angry or surprised to see him at her door.

"Angela," he said.

"Gabriel," she replied, inclining her head regally. "I see you undertook the long hard walk to my house."

"It did not seem so steep or so tiring."

"This is not a place made to welcome angels."

"No, it was a place built to shelter angelicas. Have you found it comfortable?"

"I like it better than any place I have ever been, I think."

He smiled. "May I come in?"

She moved aside. "Please do."

He had to duck his head and draw his wings tight about him to step under the low lintel. Inside, the smell of flour and yeast was extremely strong. What he could see of the cottage was very spare, very clean, enlivened here and there with bright splashes of intense color. How much of this was Hagar, how much Rachel?

"I brought you a gift for your new home," he said, and handed her a rolled bundle that was a hearth rug. He had gotten the rug in Luminaux, for no reason except that its aqueous blue and green colors reminded him of things he had seen in Rachel's room. He had not then considered under what circumstances he might be giving it to her.

She took it from him, shook it out and laid it in front of the cold fireplace on the far wall. Instantly it looked as if it had been purchased for just that spot. From across the room, she turned to face him.

"And did you come all the way from the Eyrie just to bring me something for my house?" she asked.

"No," he said, smiling. "But I would have flown that whole distance just to bring you presents, and then flown home again."

"What have you been doing with yourself these past few months?" she asked.

She still stood apart from him, so he moved closer, slowly, so as not to alarm her. "I have traveled between every town and hillock of Samaria, meeting with people and plotting out the next twenty years," he said. "I have installed Nathan and Maga in Jordana, and they are building a new hold in the Heldora Mountains."

"What happened to Windy Point?"

"Gone," he said. "Sliced from the mountain by the hand of the god."

She lifted her chin and considered him, but she did not ask what role he had played in the destruction of the fortress. "Good," she said.

He smiled again and stepped nearer. "And," he said, "I have learned to play a song or two on the instrument you gave me as we waited to sing the Gloria."

"I heard you. Or at least I heard someone piping a little while before you came to my door."

"That was me."

"Have you come all the way from the Eyrie just to play me songs on your recorder?"

"No," he said. "But I would have flown all that distance just to play for you, if it would have pleased you, and then flown home again."

Now, faintly, as if she could not help herself, she allowed a smile to show around the edges of her mouth. "But I could not let you fly all that way and fly home again, without at least offering you a meal," she said. "Are you hungry? I could feed you."

"Yes," he said, and let it go at that.

She turned and led him to the kitchen. Here, the aroma of baking bread was mixed with heavier, more seductive smells. Forcefully the image came back to him, of a witch-woman brewing up philters in her isolated cabin. The small table was set for two.

"Sit down," she said. "Would you like water? Or wine?"

"Wine," he said. It was a night for intoxication. "Your food smells good."

"I like to cook," she said. "I haven't had many chances lately."

"In Bethel," he said, "everyone is cooking these days."

"Why is that?"

"There's a strange new spice that the women have discovered. They use it to flavor everything—bread, meat, wine, cake."

She was again standing across the width of the room, but now she was definitely smiling. "And have you eaten many of the delicacies these women have been cooking?"

"Not a one," he said carefully. "I've touched nothing except the dishes prepared by my own hand."

"No wonder you are hungry, then."

"I know."

"Do you dislike this new seasoning?"

"Not at all. I'm sure I would love it if I ate it from the proper plate."

"I've used it in all the loaves and casseroles I made for you tonight."

"I'll have large portions of them all."

She drifted closer, half against her will, it seemed, but driven by her own excitement. Gabriel came to his feet, slowly, not wanting to startle her away.

"What a risk you run," she said softly. "Don't you know that the spice is desire, and that it will flavor whatever nourishment you take from this day forward?"

She was close enough. He grabbed her hands and held them though she tried for a moment to pull them away. "I told you," he murmured, "I have not eaten such a food for so long I cannot remember how it tastes."

She stopped struggling, and he swept her, none too gently, into his arms. She flung her head back, pushing him away a little with her hands against his shoulders.

"Desire changes nothing," she said a little breathlessly. "Passion erases none of the troubles that lie between you and me."

"None of them?" he said and drew her closer. When he kissed her, he felt her change to silk in his arms. She had been caged and restless; now she preened and became content. Her arms slipped around his back, lay warm and flat between his feathers and his skin. He kissed her again and again, until he lost count, until he had had enough kisses to make up for having had only one up to this point in his life.

When he finally freed her, though not completely, she was laughing. "It must be a stronger drug than I knew," she said. "For it is effective when you have done no more than smell the baking bread."

"You seem to have succumbed to it yourself," he noted.

"Well, but I have been cooking for days."

"Oh? And who were you expecting to feed with all your stews and casseroles?"

She pushed him away, pressed him into his chair and crossed the room to fuss with items on her iron stove. Her face had colored with the heat of the fire or some thought that left her blushing.

"Well?" he said, because, after all, it was time she said it. She turned to face him, finally, still just a little aloof but not shy at all.

"You," she said at last. "I would have waited forever for you."